# ARKANSAS WEDDINGS

# ARKANSAS WEDDINGS

## THREE-IN-ONE COLLECTION

### SHANNON TAYLOR VANNATTER

BARBOUR
PUBLISHING

Dear Readers,

I hope you enjoy getting a glimpse of my home state of Arkansas. I enjoyed sharing the local flavor of Romance, Arkansas, where romantics go to get married and send their wedding invitations and Valentine cards to be re-mailed with the Love Station postmark. I don't live there, but it is about twenty-five miles from my rural home. The waterfall is real and best found by going to the Romance Post Office for directions. Rose Bud, Arkansas, is seven miles away, and the stately Darden-Gifford house stands watch over the small town.

The towns seemed like the perfect place to weave tales of couples who must turn their hearts over to God before they can find their true loves. While Adrea and Grayson fought to overcome guilt and fear, Laken and Hayden struggled with bitterness and trust, and Shell and Ryler wrestled with low self-esteem and forgiveness—my prayer is that my fictional characters' trials might strike a cord with a reader.

As a writer, my dreams come true through readers, and I'd love to hear from you.

May God richly bless you,

Shannon Taylor Vannatter
www.shannonvannatter.com

# WHITE ROSES

# Dedication

To my very own Pastor in Shining Armor for all your love and support.

I'd like to thank my mother, Veta Taylor; my critique partner, Lorna Seilstad; and longtime friends Ruby and Stephanie Garner for sharing their knowledge of flowers and florists.

# Chapter 1

"Whoa!" Adrea Welch teetered on top of the rickety three-step utility ladder. With both arms flung out, surfing style, she regained her balance and pressed a hand to her pounding heart.

"Let me hold that for you," a deep voice echoed from the back of the sanctuary.

The man hurried toward her. Emerald green eyes, windswept sable hair, and an irresistible cleft in his chin. Late-twenties, maybe thirty. Probably the groom. All the impossibly handsome men, especially the nice, mannerly ones who hung out in church, were taken.

Especially in tiny Romance, Arkansas.

But looks weren't everything and he might never have been in a church before, just here for the wedding. Underneath that heart-tilting smile, he might be a jerk.

"Thanks." She glanced down, making sure he wasn't helping as an excuse to check her out. He wasn't. Instead, he studied her work.

"I'm almost done." Adrea looped yellow roses through the white lattice-work archway.

"The church should invest in a better ladder."

"Actually, it's mine." She weaved ivy through the roses and climbed down. He was tall, at least six foot three. The top of her head came just about nose level on him.

"Are you in the wedding party?" He slung his jacket over one shoulder. Shirtsleeves, rolled up almost to the elbow, revealed muscled forearms.

"I'm the florist." Always the florist; never the bride. "Adrea Welch."

"A-dree-uh."

She nodded at the correct pronunciation. "Very good, but I've been known to answer to Adrian and Andrea."

"It's nice to meet you, Adrea." He offered his hand. "I'm the pastor at Palisade over in Rose Bud. Grayson Sterling. Most folks call me Pastor Grayson."

She suppressed a gasp and shook his hand. Warmth spread over her at his firm, yet gentle grip.

"I'm sorry, have we met?"

"Um, I usually do the white roses."

The light in his eyes snuffed out.

Six years of standing orders for his wife's birthday, their son's birthday,

9

and their anniversary. For the last two, he hand-delivered the flowers to the cemetery. And added Valentine's Day to mark the date of her death.

"Sara always treasured them and thought it so romantic to get flowers from Romance." His voice sounded forced. "Even though mine is always the same order, you make each one unique."

"I actually enjoy the challenge of making each array distinctive." *How lame. Might as well tell him I take pleasure in arranging flowers for his dead wife.* "She must have been a very special lady."

"Yes." He stuffed his hands into his pockets. "How long have you been at Floral Designs?"

"Seven years."

"I've been a patron and pastored the church almost that long." He frowned. "Odd that we've never met before."

"I hardly ever go out to the showroom, and only started decorating wedding sites in the last few months." She fluffed the swirl of tulle at the base of each brass candelabra to catch the rainbow of light reflecting through the lone stained-glass window.

"This is the first wedding I've agreed to officiate since Sara. . . So, you attend here at Mountain Grove?"

"From the time I can remember, and my sister's husband is the preacher." She cocked her head to the side, surveying the archway. Yellow roses were her favorite. Once upon a time, she'd planned to use them for her own special day.

She checked her watch. Almost time for the round of afternoon weddings to start. "I better get out of your way."

"Nice meeting you. I'll pick up Sara's arrangement later."

"It'll be ready." She hurried out of the church, slipping on her jacket. *Preachers really shouldn't look so good. How could any self-respecting Christian female concentrate on the sermon?* He definitely lived up to the romantic hero her employees mooned over every time he came to pick up the roses. No wonder the salesclerks called him Prince Sterling.

Adrea stashed empty boxes and transport forms in the back of the van.

Three down, three to go. And none of the nuptials were hers.

Her hometown thrived on weddings. Half her livelihood came from weddings. She was so sick of weddings.

A Valentine balloon bouquet tried to escape from the van. She punched a heart-shaped, pink foil number bobbing beside her head.

"Roses are red, my love," a tinny tune played. "Violets are blue-ooh. Sugar is sweet my love, but not as sweet as you."

She slammed the door shut.

Okay, time to count blessings. She started the engine.

Number one: She and her older sister had recently bought the floral shop. Number two: Since couples came year-round to get married in if-you-blinked-you-missed-it Romance, the town's notoriety made for a busy floral shop. Number three: It was Valentine's Day, their biggest day for weddings and roses.

Twenty-five and the co-owner of a successful business. Yet a sigh welled within her.

Just two years ago, she'd been the soon-to-be bride blissfully planning her own ceremony. Until three weeks before the big event, when Wade crushed her illusions with his curvy blond floozy, clad only in a towel.

She shook the thoughts away as she rounded the curve and turned into the lot at the post office. Adrea managed to get Mom's roses out of the van without any trouble from the balloons.

Samantha—just Sam—Welch stood at the counter with piles of wedding invitations threatening to topple.

"Hi, Mom." Adrea set a crystal vase on the counter.

"Hey, baby." Mom's smile brightened and she stopped stamping long enough to inhale the fragrance of the dozen long-stemmed roses. "Your father."

"Is a very sweet man."

"Are you okay?" Mom's brow furrowed.

"I'm fine."

"Haylee thought you might need her to spend the night and said something about eating Yarnell's Death-By-Chocolate ice cream straight out of the carton."

Adrea's eyes misted at the thoughtfulness of her seven-year-old niece. "I'll have her over soon, but we won't need sinful treats. I'm fine. Really."

Mom chewed on the inside of her jaw and surveyed Adrea with her intense sapphire gaze. Unconvinced, she went back to hand-stamping the invitations with a practiced, speedy precision. The rhythm of *clunk, clunk, clunk* echoed through the small office, toiling out the results of Romance's other claim to fame. The remailing program.

Valentine's cards arrived in droves for the unique *Love Station* postmark only in use each February 1–15. Year-round, brides from all over the country mailed their invitations in overstuffed manila envelopes, just to have them remailed from Romance, Arkansas.

Mom had stamped Adrea's invitations and taken care of them when the plans deflated like a balloon detached from the air hose. She didn't know how Mom had handled it. Sent don't-come-to-my-wedding-it's-not-going-to-happen cards? Somehow, Mom had let everyone know the engagement was off and no one asked questions.

"I met the pastor at Palisade just now." Adrea grabbed a stack of finished invitations as they began a slow landslide and scooped them into two piles.

"That poor man. It doesn't seem possible two years have passed since his wife died."

Adrea nodded. "I heard he's thinking of resigning. Maybe Mark could

11

apply for that church. Wouldn't that be perfect?"

"To us." Mom raised an eyebrow. "Your brother feels very strongly called to be an associate pastor."

"I'm so afraid he'll end up somewhere else." Adrea hugged herself. "I mean, he just came home, and there aren't any churches around here that have associates."

"Searcy has several." Mom's stamping never lost rhythm. "Don't worry, God will work it out and put Mark right where He wants him."

"You're right. I better scoot; it's our busiest day."

"Tell me about it." Mom stopped stamping long enough to massage her wrist.

—∞—

Adrea wiped away a tear, then turned to sweep the smattering of fallen leaves and trimmed stems from the workroom floor.

As always, the pale flowers made her grieve for a woman she'd never met. Especially since she'd met the man left behind. She buried her nose in the cool satin of a fragrant blossom then added a few more fern fronds to the plastic container.

From births to proms and graduations, running the floral shop thrust her into the middle of the lives of countless strangers. She delighted in her work. Except for Valentine's Day, funerals, and white rose days.

What must it feel like to be the object of such devotion? It was hard to fathom how a man could love a woman so much he placed a standing order to mark each special occasion then continued the tradition even after her death. She swiped at another tear.

Maybe she felt a kinship with Sara because she'd arranged the white roses for so long. *Or because Sara died on what should have been my wedding day.* She squeezed her eyes shut.

Their happily-ever-afters had vanished like vividly colored Valentine's balloons caught in a vicious wind and swallowed up by angry clouds.

She filled the holes between the roses with snapdragons and Queen Anne's lace. Turning the arrangement slowly around, she checked each side for balance.

The showroom door opened and her sister, Rachel, entered jostling two large balloon bouquets, looking as if she might float away like Mary Poppins. "These are for Mrs. Carlisle. Maybe I can get them delivered before she gets the chance to add something else to her order."

"Actually, she already called."

"Let me guess." Rachel tapped her chin with a forefinger. "She's invited four more people and needs us to whip up another centerpiece for her Valentine's dinner."

"*Six* more guests."

Rachel smoothed a hand over her hairdresser-enhanced auburn hair.

"Guess I better get busy with the extra flowers."

"Already did it, before she ever called." Adrea picked up the fluted crystal vase filled with red roses and pink carnations from behind the counter and set it on the worktable.

The sisters high-fived.

Rachel tied a heart-shaped weight on both clusters of balloon ribbons. "Mom said you stopped by."

Adrea propped both hands on her hips. "Do y'all call each other as soon as I leave?"

"We're just worried about you. How many almost brides spend their time fulfilling the dreams of other brides?"

"I'm fine." *How many times have I said that today?*

Rachel handed her a tissue and picked up Mrs. Carlisle's centerpiece. "You're entirely too empathetic for this place."

Adrea glanced at the clock. The lavender butterfly on the second hand made slow progress visiting each silk blossom–surrounded number. Almost two o'clock. Anywhere else the gaudy business-warming gift from their brother would be too busy. Especially set against pastel wallpaper bursting with an astounding assortment of flowers. But for the workroom, perfect.

"Before you go, can you take the white roses out front?"

"Sorry, I'm fixing to make deliveries. Besides, the customers love it when the hermit comes out to visit." Rachel threaded the balloons through her fingers. "Can you give me a hand?"

Adrea helped load the van, then waved her sister off. Alone in the back parking lot, the hair along the nape of her neck stood on end. Someone was watching. She scurried back inside and locked the door.

*Just my imagination.*

Silly. Rachel only had two nearby deliveries and would be back soon.

Adrea undid the bolt, and with jittery insides, picked up the white roses. She hated working with customers in the bustle of the showroom. It never failed, whenever she went out front, a client always cornered her with compliments. Nice, just not her style. She much preferred a thank-you card.

The back door flew open behind her. She spun around to see a man. His shaggy, dishwater blond hair hung almost to his shoulders in greasy clumps, hiding his eyes. She sucked in a breath to scream, but his hand clamped over her mouth.

"I didn't think I'd quite get that reaction." Wade's words slurred together.

If he hadn't spoken, she wouldn't have recognized him. Her gut twisted at a whiff of alcohol. She pushed his hand away, put some distance between them, and gulped deep breaths of blossom-perfumed air.

He'd lost weight. Gone was the handsome, well-groomed, charming man she'd once fallen in love with. Gone was the layered hairstyle, casually gelled back from his face. Gone was the self-confident golf instructor who'd put an engagement ring on her finger and promised to love only her. Wasted.

"What are you doing here? You're not driving like this?"

"I hitched a ride and waited until Rachel left, so we could talk."

"You were watching the shop?" She shivered. Someone spying on her, even someone she thought she knew, gave her the creeps.

"I knew she'd never let us talk in peace. Do you remember what day it is?"

*How could I forget?* Adrea closed her eyes, clutching the roses. "I'd like you to go now."

He steepled his hands, as if in prayer. "Please, Adrea. Our second anniversary. Or it should have been anyway."

"Wade, just go. We're over. You're engaged to—someone else." She couldn't bring herself to say the name. "I have to take these roses out front."

"They can wait." He grabbed the white roses, and they crashed to the floor, flinging water and twisted flowers.

"Look what you've done!" Fresh tears stung her eyes.

"Hey, don't cry." He moved toward her, ready to provide comfort.

She sidestepped him.

He tried to pull her into his arms.

"Don't." She jerked away and slapped him so hard her fingers stung.

The connecting door to the showroom opened.

—∞—

Grayson hesitated, his gaze taking in the pretty florist he'd met at the church, the red handprint appearing on the man's cheek, and finally the ruins of a flower arrangement on the floor.

He shut the door behind him. "Excuse me, but we heard a noise—the clerks were busy so I offered to check. Is there a problem?"

"Who are you?" The man looked from Grayson to a jittery Adrea, suspicion clouding his eyes. He took a menacing step toward Grayson.

Drunk, disorderly, disheveled. The shop's back door stood open. Had this guy just wandered in off the street or did he know Adrea? Though Grayson barely knew her, she didn't seem like the type to hang out with drunks. Yet, the man seemed possessive toward her.

"Just a customer." Grayson offered his hand. "Grayson Sterling."

The man's jaw dropped. He stepped back. Without another word, he spun around and ran out the back door, slamming it behind him. Vase-laden shelves rattled in his wake, but nothing fell.

*Odd reaction.* Grayson turned back to Adrea.

With shaking hands, she pushed dark bangs out of her too shiny, midnight blue eyes.

"Are you all right?"

"Fine." Her voice quivered.

*Anything but fine.* "I realize it's none of my business, but should that guy be loose on the streets?"

"He's drunk, but he said he's not driving, and he'd never intentionally harm anyone." She stooped to retrieve the container from the heap in the floor. "I'm afraid I dropped your flowers."

He winced at the sight of the damaged roses, their heads forlornly nodding.

"I'm sorry. I'll make a new arrangement." A tear trickled down her cheek. She wiped it away. "It won't take a minute."

His gut twisted. "There's no rush. My son's begging to go to the park anyway." He knelt to retrieve errant leaves and petals. "Let me help you clean up this mess."

"That's not necessary." She grabbed several paper towels and sopped up the spill then took the refuse from him and threw it all in the trash. "I'll take care of it."

With trembling fingers, she plucked the flowers, ruined or not, from a block of foam and tossed them into a compost bin. She grabbed a contraption and began stripping the thorns from a few fresh roses on the counter.

He should go. But his feet wouldn't move. The handprint on the drunk's face proved she could take care of herself, yet she looked so shaken. So vulnerable.

She winced and blood dripped onto the translucent petals of a white rose. "You're bleeding."

"It's nothing." Calmly, she removed the embedded thorn and popped the fleshy part of her right thumb into her mouth, only to gag. She crumpled the crimson-stained rose in her fingers and tossed it in the bin.

"Are you sure you're okay?"

"I'm fine. Really. And I'm sorry about the delay." She washed the puncture. With no paper towels left, she rubbed her palms down slender, jean-clad thighs and dug out a fresh roll from under the sink.

"It's not a problem."

The back door opened, and the clerk he usually saw in the showroom entered. She frowned when she saw him.

"Pastor Grayson? Is everything all right, Adrea?"

A blush crept up Adrea's neck. "I'll fill you in later."

"Good to see you, Rachel." He offered his hand. "I wondered where you were today."

"Just had a couple of deliveries."

"Well, I better get back to Dayne." What if the drunk came back? He ran his hand over his jaw and turned back to Adrea. "You really should consider locking the back door in the future."

Rachel's eyes widened.

"I'll come back in about forty-five minutes. No rush." With one more glance toward Adrea, he strolled back to the showroom.

The door shut behind him, and Adrea darted to the floral refrigerator.

The perfect romantic hero. A knight in shining sterling.

But a deep sadness lurked in the emerald depths of his sparkling eyes. The knight had lost his lady.

Arms laden, she chose another container.

"What happened?" Rachel crossed her arms and leaned against the counter.

Adrea unloaded on the worktable and touched a tender blossom to her nose. "Nothing happened, other than some broken flowers."

"Okay, I'll bite." A storm brewed in Rachel's brown eyes. "How did the flowers get broken, and why did Pastor Grayson think you needed to lock the back door?"

"Wade stopped by," she squeaked.

Rachel propped her hands on slim hips. "Isn't he supposed to be in Missouri?"

"Probably just here to visit his mother." Though Helen hadn't mentioned it. "He was drunk."

Adrea's gaze locked on her sister's.

The phone rang. Adrea reached for it, but the red light already glowed. One of the salesclerks had nabbed the call.

"I just don't want you falling for his 'poor me' routine." Rachel rolled her eyes. "I still can't believe you almost married him."

"Yes, but I didn't." She picked up the rose-stripper.

"Thank You, God." Rachel looked heavenward.

"Listen, I know you have this thing about trying to protect me, but I can take care of myself. I can handle Wade."

"You sure about that? You seem kind of shaky to me."

"I'd never seen him drunk before. He'd been sober for two years when we met." Adrea hugged herself. "He's like a different person." *And it's my fault he started drinking again.*

"The nerve of the jerk. Today of all days."

"Can we drop it?" Finished with the roses, she inspected her thumb. Another split nail, just from arranging flowers. Flimsy and paper-thin, they'd never recovered from her childhood nervous habit of biting. And Wade's visit made her want to do more than nibble.

"Are you sure you're okay?"

"It was just a thorn." Adrea held her hand out for her sister to see. "It's not even bleeding anymore."

"I didn't mean your thumb." Rachel touched her arm.

"I'm fine. Really." She took several cleansing breaths and slowly rotated the flowers to inspect them from every angle. Satisfied, she turned her back to the counter and leaned against it, begging her heart to slow. "Can you take the roses out front? And let's not charge him since he had to wait."

"Sure." Rachel picked up the arrangement and turned toward the showroom.

Adrea grabbed a heart-shaped crystal vase off the shelf. She filled it with red rosebuds, fern fronds, and baby's breath, then turned to the final bridal bouquet of the day.

She started with a cluster of fuchsia stargazer lilies in the center and worked them into a V shape. She loved the traditional cascading type rather than the popular rounded, hand-tied variety. It was what she'd planned to use for her wedding.

As the bouquet took shape, she imagined it in the trembling fingers of a blushing bride. She clasped it in front of her and stutter-stepped across the floor. "Dun, dun, duh-duh. Dun, dun, duh-duh."

The showroom door opened and Adrea's measured stride faltered.

Helen's blue-tinged updo blended with her periwinkle suit. Southern Belle to the bone. She looked a good eight years younger than sixty-five.

With a wistful sigh, Adrea went back to the worktable to add more baby's breath. "I was just wondering why anyone would come halfway across the country to get married in Romance. We even have a couple coming from New York this year. Do they think the name of our town will guarantee their happily-ever-afters?"

"Someday"—Helen hugged her—"you'll make a lovely bride, with all that dark hair and creamy complexion. I'm sorry this is such a difficult day for you, dear. And I'm sorry about Wade. I told him to leave you alone."

"It was no big deal." She'd hoped Helen wouldn't learn of his visit to the shop.

"I so wanted you to be my daughter."

Adrea's chin trembled. "I so wanted to be your daughter."

Helen handed her several fuchsia ribbons. "Good news; I think Pastor Grayson has decided not to resign."

"Actually, I met him this morning."

"He's such a wonderful pastor." Helen clasped her hands together. "It's just been really hard for him since Sara died."

"Maybe God gave him a gentle nudge to stay in the ministry." Adrea threaded the satiny strands through the blossoms and snipped off the ends, leaving several trailing wisps shimmering along the stems. After final inspection, she wrapped the creation in white tissue paper and gently packed it in a large carton with the bridesmaids' bouquets.

She kneaded the tendons in her cramping hands and turned to the numerous corsages and boutonnieres lining the worktable. With sore, raw fingers, she stuck long, pearl-studded pins into the stems of each one.

Helen tucked the finished product into clear cellophane bags.

Weddings. With vehemence, Adrea jabbed the pin into the groom's rosebud.

"Careful." Helen took the boutonniere from her. "You need a break."

"I do." Her stomach knotted at the irony of her words. "Two more weddings to deliver, then we're out of here."

—⁓—

With Dayne tucked in bed, Grayson stood on the back porch, stroking Cocoa's velvety ears. The heavy dog leaned against his leg.

When he'd returned for the arrangement, everything seemed calm at the floral shop. The salesclerk had tried not to charge him, but he'd paid anyway.

Was Adrea okay? He couldn't get her trembling hands and voice off his mind.

He looked up at the stars and drained his coffee cup. Caffeine couldn't hurt him. He never slept anyway.

Stepping inside, he took off his coat and sniffed the air. Apple and cinnamon. Something baking, as usual, in the freshly painted pale peach kitchen. Sara's favorite color. But it wasn't the same.

He sat at the pedestal table and lay his face against the cool oak surface.

"Gray, you okay?" Grace's voice quivered.

"I miss the old house." He pushed up from the table. "I miss her."

Grace's slender arms came around his shoulders, and she rested her chin on top of his head.

His twin had given up her life to help with Dayne. She'd cut back her thriving catering business in Searcy and moved to Rose Bud with them. All for him. For his future. A future without Sara.

Only to hear him grumble about the new house because the air didn't smell of Sara's soft, sweet perfume.

"It's just a bad day." He ran his hands over the smooth wood. Sara had ordered the table from a catalog and waited three weeks for it to arrive. She'd made an adventure out of it by sewing a red and white checked blanket and serving picnics on the floor.

"I took her clothes to the Red Cross for hurricane victims this morning. But not the curtains she made. Even though they don't fit any of the windows here. . ." Grayson closed his eyes. "I just couldn't."

"I know it was hard, but you did good." She hugged him tighter. "Sara would be glad her things went to people who needed them."

He concentrated on not letting her feel the sobs welling within his chest.

Grace patted his shoulder. Grabbing his empty coffee cup, she walked over to the counter. "How was the wedding?"

"I pasted a smile on my face, joined the happy couple in holy matrimony, and took Dayne to the cemetery." Poor Dayne. A five-year-old shouldn't think it was normal to go to the cemetery on Valentine's Day.

He stared out the window at the inky sky. "I never imagined this day would be anything other than a joyous occasion for Sara and I to share a special, romantic dinner. Instead of celebrating with my wife, I left the church where we were married to place flowers at a cold, marble stone."

She poured a cup of coffee and added one teaspoon each of creamer and sugar. When she turned to face him again, her shiny eyes swam in unshed tears.

Lifelong friends with Sara, she hurt almost as bad as he did.

"I'm sorry. Maybe the move was a bad idea." She set the cup in front of him.

"It's not that." He took her hand. "I shouldn't have let the deacons talk me into staying at the church. I should have resigned back when Sara died."

"They don't expect miracles." She stepped behind him again and massaged the tense muscles in his shoulders. "They know what you've been through."

"I need to seclude myself in the office and not come out until I have a sermon for Sunday. I need to go see Mrs. Jones. I haven't checked on her since the funeral." *How can I comfort the grieving, when I still grieve?*

"Why don't you take them up on hiring an associate pastor?" Grace pulled a chair beside him and sat.

"Palisade has never had an associate."

"I know, but the church has grown, and I think it's high time you got some assistance."

*An associate could hold the church together so I can fall apart in peace.* Tempting. He could call his old professor for recommendations. See if there might be someone local. . .

"It's just the day. I'll be better tomorrow."

"We both will be." She kissed his cheek.

—∞—

The February morning air burned Adrea's lungs. Each breath formed a visible cloud as she jogged around the walking trail.

Another Valentine's Day behind her and she hadn't handled any weddings for two days. She silently thanked God for the much-needed reprieve.

With the park to herself, memories stirred of the many times she'd set up flowers for countless happy couples there. Maybe a jog wasn't such a good idea after all.

A cream-colored sedan pulled into the parking lot. A small boy in a marshmallow-puffed coat bounced from the car, followed by a chocolate Labrador retriever. A hooded man, probably his father, braved the frigid air. She looked away from yet another reminder of what she didn't have.

"No, Cocoa! Come back!" The boy's voice cut through the stillness.

"Dayne! Stop!" the man yelled.

As she turned toward the commotion, she saw the small boy, his little face awash in tears, chasing the Lab. Tongue lolling, the dog gained a huge lead, leash dancing behind.

Adrea gasped as the pair veered straight for the highway. Darting from the path, she cut in front of the dog and stomped one foot solidly on the leash. She grabbed it before he could jerk it away and send her tumbling. Momentum threatened to propel her after the large animal, but she pulled with her entire body weight until he stopped.

The boy caught up, sniffling. As he buried his face in the dog's coat, the man joined them.

An incredibly handsome man. Grayson Sterling.

His breathing came in raspy wheezes. Young and in good shape, it didn't make sense for him to be so short of breath.

"Are you all right?"

He clutched his chest and opened his mouth. Only a gasp came out.

*Why didn't I ever take CPR?* She tried to remember what she'd heard about injuries he'd sustained in the wreck. Nothing to do with his lungs. Just his knee.

The boy stared wide-eyed, tears again coursing down his cheeks.

# Chapter 2

"Sit down here." Adrea motioned to a bench. Heart ricocheting, she grabbed her cell phone from her pocket. "I'll call an ambulance."

"No, don't." Grayson sucked in a ragged breath between each word. "I'm feeling better."

"You sure?"

"I tried to run and hurt my knee."

That didn't explain his shortness of breath.

His eyes darted to the little boy.

Taking his cue, she knelt to the child's level and tried to sound calmer than she felt. "He'll be just fine."

After several breaths, the gasping gradually eased. "With my bad knee, I can't keep up with these two. I could just see Cocoa running into traffic, with Dayne right on his tail."

Tires locked up and squealed nearby, as if for emphasis.

With a wince, he closed his eyes.

Adrea cringed, waiting for the crash. Thankfully, none came.

Grayson cleared his throat. "Dayne, did you say thank you?"

The boy turned his tear-streaked face toward her. "Thank you."

"No problem. I love dogs."

Several chocolate-colored hairs stuck to the boy's wet cheeks.

"Maybe you should take this." Adrea handed the leash to Grayson and fished a fresh tissue from her pocket to wipe away the fur and tears.

"We really appreciate your help." With his breathing returning to normal, he placed a firm hand on his son's shoulder. "Don't ever run off like that again, Dayne."

"Sorry, Daddy." The boy looked at the ground.

"If Cocoa ever gets away again, just call him. Once the squirrel climbed the tree, he would have come back if you had simply called him."

"But I don't want him to go to heaven, too." The boy's chin puckered.

A hard lump formed in Adrea's throat.

Grayson hugged his son. "He probably wouldn't have run into the street. He's smart. Full of life, but smart. From now on, I'll hold his leash."

"Okay."

Adrea watched in silence, until Grayson turned back to her.

"Sorry to drag you into our little melodrama." Grayson's voice fell flat. No life left. "Dayne, this is Adrea. She does Mommy's flowers."

The boy shook her hand. *Adorable.*

"At Miss Helen's store? She goes to our church."

"Actually, my sister and I just bought the shop, but Miss Helen still works a few days a week." She tweaked the child's cold-reddened nose. Though he was blond, he had his father's striking green eyes, paired with numerous dimples.

"Again, we appreciate your assistance today." Grayson clicked his tongue at Cocoa. "We better go; I need to get to the church and it's colder than I realized."

She watched him leave. *Going through the motions for his son's sake.*

—— ⁓ ——

Alone at the shop at the end of a long day, Adrea couldn't get her mind off the encounter with what was left of the Sterling family, though two days had passed. For six years, she'd created white rose arrangements for Sara and never met them. Now, she'd bumped into Grayson three times within a week. Weird.

She reached up to the top shelf to retrieve the silver-filigree keepsake box. Inside the red velvet lining, she dug until she found the card.

*Thank you for your gesture of kindness.*
*My family and I will never forget your thoughtfulness.*
*May God bless you,*
*Grayson Sterling*

Tracing her fingers over the handwritten, masculine script, she remembered the white rose casket spray she and Helen had lovingly put together. With no bill. She placed the card on top, closed the lid, and put the box away.

She checked the doors one more time and hurried to her car. The fuel gauge demanded her attention. Though she loved her hometown, it would be nice not to have to drive seven miles just to get gas.

As she entered Rose Bud, the cemetery beckoned. Not a living soul stirred. She pulled into the gravel parking lot.

The heavy iron gate groaned as she stepped through. With no clue where Grayson Sterling's wife was buried, Adrea strolled across the hardened earth covered with dormant yellowed grass. Indented graves interspersed with more recent, rounded mounds. Row upon row of aged, weather-beaten, and faded tombstones mingled with dust-spattered glossy newcomers.

A bird burst from a spindly bush. She pressed a hand to her heart. With a panicked beat of wings, the sparrow flew away.

Just as she was about to give up, she caught a glimpse of the white roses. They stood out among the other vibrant flowers and led her to a grave marked by a large, polished headstone.

Adrea remembered Sara's youthful beauty well, from the newspaper articles about the senseless hit-and-run accident that took her life. After running into the family left behind, seeing the cold marble monument brought the tragedy into sharp focus once again.

With a shiver, she read the epitaph: BELOVED DAUGHTER, WIFE, MOTHER: GONE TO MEET JESUS.

At least Grayson Sterling knew where to seek comfort for his grief. With a heavy heart, for someone besides herself for a change, she trudged back to her car.

A profound thought wrenched her gut.

"God, are You shoving him in my face to show me something? That's it. You're showing me that he's lost more than I ever thought about losing and he's going on, preaching Your sermons and raising his son—while I wrap myself in self-pity and bitterness, coveting other people's weddings. I lost a man I didn't need. A man who couldn't be faithful and couldn't be strong enough to beat the bottle."

She dropped to her knees on the cold ground.

"Oh Lord, forgive me for my selfishness and be with Wade. He needs You to help him get sober again. He knows You, Lord. Help him to let You reintroduce Yourself." As she prayed for the man who'd broken her heart, the bitterness melted away. Forgiveness settled in her soul. A forgiveness she hadn't realized she needed to give. "Thank You, Lord. Thank You."

Before standing she added, "And, Lord, please be with Grayson and his little boy. Their world shattered two years ago, and I know they're still suffering. Give them comfort and strength, as only You can. Amen."

—⁂—

Grayson turned into the driveway of a rambling, old, two-story house on the outskirts of Romance. He rechecked the address. It had to be the right place, but it certainly didn't look like apartments. Yet, there were several cars parked out front.

A large enclosed balcony gracing one entire side of the house erupted with flowers, despite the chilly winds of late February, while only a few potted plants or lawn chairs dotted the wraparound porch. Must be divided into separate living quarters. A shame. He loved aged, spacious homes and hated seeing them cut up into apartments or converted into businesses.

A siren moaned in the distance. He took several deep breaths.

*Stop being absurd. Every ambulance doesn't carry someone I love inside.*

The siren drew close. Pressure welled in his chest, threatening to burst through. The ambulance wailed past. He prayed. Relax. . .inhale. . .exhale.

*Think. Sis is in the middle of catering a wedding. Dayne is at Mom and Dad's house. None of them would be on the road right now.* The pressure eased.

Regaining control, he sat a few minutes longer, then stepped from the car.

Inside, he saw a long hallway with a door on each side and a staircase in the middle. He climbed the steps, located the right number, and rang the bell.

When the door barely opened, it wasn't a young seminary graduate who greeted him. Instead, he peered through the crack at a child.

"May I help you?" the little girl asked.

"Does Mark Welch live here?"

"Yes, but he's in the shower. You can wait if you want." She started to close the door. "Sorry, but you're a stranger."

"That's true. I'm fine out here."

If only he could have gotten in touch with Mark. Moving the meeting up, with someone he'd never met before, might make Mark feel uncomfortable.

Within minutes, Grayson heard a male voice. The chain released and the door opened. A man, his dark hair still damp, beckoned him inside with a frown.

"She's out in the greenhouse." The man waved toward glass doors. "I'd like to give you the third degree, but I have to leave soon for an appointment. Count on it next time, if there is a next time. For now, you're welcome to go on out. Just watch yourself."

The man, presumably Mark, darted down the hall, leaving Grayson no chance to explain his presence. Moments later, the whir of a blow-dryer sounded from somewhere.

Unsure of what to do, he walked around the island, separating the floral-themed living room from the sunny yellow kitchen, toward patio doors. A woman knelt inside the glassed-in balcony, surrounded by an explosion of colorful blossoms.

She worked with the various plants, unaware of him. Potting soil streaked her red T-shirt and blue jean shorts, smudged her face, legs, and feet. With her long brunette hair pulled into a high ponytail and dirt everywhere, she was beautiful.

The splendor of the small, carefully tended garden came nowhere near the beauty of the woman in its midst. He studied her profile, the slight upward tilt of her small nose, the soft curve of her lips. Red polish adorned all twenty nails. Despite the grime, she exuded elegance.

Something familiar about her tugged at him. Adrea Welch. Of course, Mark and Adrea Welch. *Adrea Welch is beautiful—and married.* Grayson backed away from the door.

He didn't remember the deacons saying Mark was married with a child. He'd slogged through so many résumés they'd all begun to run together. And he'd never been detail oriented.

One detail stood out. Adrea was not available.

He shoved his hands into his pockets. *Great. I'm betraying my wife by finding this woman attractive and on top of that, she's married.*

The pressure started to build in his chest once more.

*Why should I care if this woman is available? She's simply the florist. End of story.*

His left temple throbbed.

*Sara.*

He'd never considered whether a woman was single or not—had never cared, even since his wife's death.

Bewildered and a bit frightened at such foreign thoughts, he considered leaving.

Adrea looked up and saw him.

Acting quickly, so she wouldn't realize he'd been watching her, Grayson opened the door. The moist potting soil mixed with the perfume emitted by dozens of different sweet-smelling flowers in the surprisingly warm room.

"Hello." Surprise reverberated in her tone. Her arched brows drew together. With the sun still peeking over the roof, she shielded her eyes to look up at him.

He forced words from his constricted throat. "Mark has an appointment at the church with one of my deacons, who can't make it. I tried to call but didn't get an answer."

"You're here to interview him?"

"I decided to come and invite him to a casual lunch instead. I tried to let Mark know about the change in plans."

Adrea retrieved the cordless phone from a soil-strewn bench. "I guess the battery is low—or filled with grit."

Grayson concentrated on the flowers surrounding them. Greenhouse lights warmed pink orchids, white lilies, purple irises, and a whole host of others he couldn't identify.

The young girl, maybe a few years older than Dayne, sat on a redwood bench with a terra-cotta pot between her bare feet. Bent almost double, she planted bulbs. If only he'd noticed her before. She'd probably seen him watching Adrea.

"This is Haylee, my—"

"We already met." Haylee blushed. "I answered when I went in to get a drink." The little girl wagged a finger. "But I didn't undo the chain. I thought he was a stranger."

"And you acted appropriately." He smiled at the child, hoping to relieve her anxiety. "Mark told me I could wait out here." *In a roundabout way.*

"Why didn't you tell me someone was at the door, Haylee?"

The girl shrugged. "He didn't ask for you."

Adrea patted the child's knee. "Next time, let me—"

The door slid open, and Mark popped his head out. "Yo, Adrea, I need help with my tie."

"Sure, I'm coming." She clapped her dirt-coated hands together and wiped them down the sides of her shorts. "Let's go inside, Haylee. We'll finish up here after Mark leaves."

Grayson stepped aside to allow Adrea and Haylee access.

Mark waited in the kitchen, dressed in a tan suit, his hair now dry.

"Don't come near me, Adrea. You're covered in grime."

"Don't worry, I'll be washed up in a minute."

"No time to wait." Mark paced the living room.

"Take deep breaths and I'll be right with you." She dashed to the sink.

In the adjoining living room, a Road Runner cartoon transfixed Haylee.

"So, Mark, you graduated in December?" Grayson leaned against the dividing island.

"Yes." Mark frowned.

"I'm sorry, I tried to call—"

"Okay, let's see about that tie." Adrea returned, wiping her hands on a dish towel.

The smudges had disappeared from her face.

"Hurry, Adrea." Mark fidgeted.

She put her hands on his shoulders. "If you'd be still, I could tie it faster."

Grayson's insides squirmed as the intimate scene served up a painful reminder of him and Sara on a busy Sunday morning.

"You're not making a very good impression on Pastor Grayson." Adrea whispered in Mark's ear.

"Pastor Grayson?"

"Sorry, I never got around to introducing myself. I'm Grayson Sterling."

"You're the pastor?" Mark disentangled his tie from Adrea and turned around wide-eyed.

"Nice to meet you." Grayson offered his hand. "My deacon, Dr. Tom Deavers, got called to emergency surgery, so I decided to meet with you instead. I studied under Professor Cummings at seminary and he highly recommended you."

With a stiff handshake, Mark hung his head. "I'm so sorry, Pastor; I had no idea. I thought you were here to see Adrea."

Odd. What kind of man encourages his wife to have male visitors? She must meet with vendors for the floral shop at their home often, hence the comment about the third degree.

"No need to apologize." Despite his own discomfort, Grayson tried to put Mark at ease. "A simple misunderstanding."

"Let me finish." She moved in for another attempt with the tie.

"No need for the tie, either. I'm not wearing one. Relax. We're just two men of God, having a casual lunch together."

"It's nice of you to suggest Mark doesn't wear it, but if he takes off my hard work, I'll hurt him." She laughed, a melodious sound, and patted the tie. "There, all done."

Grayson shifted his weight from one foot to the other.

"Sorry I have to leave, Haylee, but we'll do something fun when I get back." Mark tousled the child's hair.

—∞—

At the Rambler Café in Rose Bud, the waitress, with eyes full of sympathy, seated them at the corner table. She took their order and scurried to the kitchen. Grayson understood. Everyone felt sorry for him, whether they knew him or not. Sometimes he wished he could escape from the cloying compassion. He'd love to get away. Far away. To somewhere people didn't know what had happened. Away from the crushing weight of his grief.

Grayson surveyed the plank walls, the shelves above each window lined with plants, antique books, and plates. His gaze strayed to the table by the window. Nothing unique about it, just melamine with black chairs. His and Sara's table.

He took a sip of coffee. "All of the other applicants are from other states. I was hoping for someone local, so when I saw you studied under Dr. Cummings, then read his letter, I wanted to meet you."

Mark fiddled with his paper napkin. "Listen, back at the apartment. I'm sorry I thought you were there to see Adrea. She's had a rough time lately."

"No harm done." *What happened to her? Anything to do with the drunk?* "I need someone fast."

Mark's hands stilled, and his eyes met Grayson's.

Grayson shifted on the squeaky vinyl seat. "I'm having a hard time. Now."

"I'd really like to help you." Sincerity shone in Mark's gaze.

"For the past two years, I've gone through the motions." Grayson cleared his throat. "My pastoring skills have slipped. I'm running on empty, and I have a hard time focusing enough to study. My son needs me. I'm all he's got, and I'm afraid the church takes too much of me away from him. To be honest, I'm rethinking my decision to stay at Palisade."

Mark's jaw clenched. "I don't feel a call to pastor."

"That's not what I'm asking."

The waitress brought their drinks.

"I tried to convince the congregation they could get someone else. Someone who wouldn't need an associate." Grayson sipped his sweet tea. "But they still want me to stay. If you take the position, you'll handle most of the evening services for a while, at least."

"I can do that." Mark squeezed a lemon slice into his ice water, ripped a blue packet open, and stirred its contents into his glass.

"Members of the congregation aren't telling me their problems, health issues, nothing." He looked out the window. A tractor putted along with a large, round hay bale on the fork. A convoy of vehicles followed. "Right now, I need to focus on Sunday morning and the pastoring part."

"I'm your man." Mark ran his finger around the rim of his glass. "A lot of associate pastors go into the field with the intention of moving up to senior pastor. Not me. I feel God called me to be a helpmate. To take the load off, in whatever area needed."

"Every time I tell God I'm quitting, He gives me a good kick in the backside. Maybe He's answering both our needs." Grayson swallowed hard. "Let's talk doctrine."

The waitress approached, her tray laden with food.

—⁓—

While Adrea cleaned the already clean kitchen, Haylee finished watching the vintage cartoon DVD.

"Beep, beep." The Road Runner outsmarted Wile E. Coyote once again.

Palisade had never had an associate and even when Mark told her they were looking into it, she didn't really think it would happen. Adrea had never expected Grayson's path to intersect with Mark's, much less have him appear on her balcony. All manners had flown from her head. She hadn't even asked if he wanted something to drink.

*Why did Mark think he came to see me?*

After the cartoon ended, they ate lunch and finished potting, then washed up. Adrea glanced at the clock.

Two hours had passed since Mark's departure. A nice jog in the park would be good about now. Jogging always burned nervous energy and made the time pass faster.

Mark's key clicked in the lock. He stepped inside, pulling his tie loose with a preoccupied look, revealing nothing.

"How did it go?" *Sound optimistic.*

"I don't know. We got off to such a bad start with my assuming he was here to see you. I should have known. I guess I was hoping you'd met someone."

"He stared at Adrea," Haylee said.

"He did? When?" Mark frowned.

"Before she saw him, when we were out on the balcony. I watched him, standing inside the door, staring at her."

With heart and mind racing, Adrea searched for an explanation. "I'm sure he was surprised to find me here. He's bought flowers from the shop for several years." She touched Mark's arm. "It wasn't a bad start. A little misunderstanding. No big deal."

The furnace clicked, then kicked on with a steady hum. "Yeah, but since I didn't realize who he was, I promised to give him the third degree in the future and sent him in your direction."

Adrea felt the warmth of a blush. "You weren't expecting your interviewer to show up here. I'm sure Grayson understood and thought the whole thing funny."

"It was kind of funny." Haylee giggled. "You should have seen the look on your face when you realized who he was."

"See?" Adrea poked Mark in the ribs. "Tell me about lunch."

"He just asked me doctrinal questions. At least we're on the same wavelength there."

"That's good. Listen, God will put you where He wants you, no matter how your interviews go. And this is probably only the first of many."

"In the meantime, let's go to Searcy. Maybe the roller rink." Mark raised an eyebrow. "Any takers?"

"Yay!" Haylee clapped her hands.

Grayson stood at the kitchen sink, ever-present coffee cup to his lips. In the backyard, Dayne cavorted with Cocoa. Giggling and barks echoed. The dog had been a blessing and kept Dayne company.

The aged panes of glass needed the cracked caulking scraped away and reapplied. Maybe storm windows, too. The old house supplied endless projects. A good thing. Kept his mind busy.

The doorbell rang. "I'll get it." Grace laid the cone of white icing beside a cookie sheet lined with pastries.

Ginger and vanilla. Still warm. His hand hovered over a delicate cream puff. She'd know. She always knew.

"Ahem."

He turned to see Helen Fenwick in the doorway, holding a casserole dish with both hands.

"You didn't have to do this." A whiff of lasagna made his mouth water. "But I'm glad you did." He took the pan and set it on a hot pad on the counter.

"I heard Grace mention she had a wedding and a birthday today, so I knew she wouldn't have time to feed you and Dayne."

Her smile seemed forced.

"That's so thoughtful of you." Grace returned to her pastry decorating.

He pulled out a chair for Helen. "Sit down."

"I didn't come to stay. You eat your lunch while it's still hot."

"Only if you'll share it with me."

"Very well then." She sat. "Where's Dayne?"

"In the back with his dog." Grayson unwrapped the foil pouch on top of the lasagna dish to reveal garlic and butter steaming from the thick toast fresh from the oven.

"Okay, I'm done." Grace balanced several flat boxes on her hip. "Since you were so good at not stealing anything, I left you a few treats. Be back later."

"Bye, dear." Helen's eyelids looked puffy.

Grayson waited until they were alone. "Is everything all right, Helen?"

Moisture pooled in her blue eyes. "You have enough of your own problems."

"I'm your pastor." He handed her a tissue. "Please tell me what's wrong."

"It's Wade." She dabbed her eyes. "He's back in town."

"Is he drinking?" Helen had often asked for prayers on her alcoholic son's behalf.

"Yes. Off and on since his broken engagement a couple of years back."

"Why haven't you told me this?"

"I didn't want to burden you with anything else." Her hand trembled. "I shouldn't have told you now."

*I have to pull myself together. The congregation—my congregation needs me.*

"I was headed for the church after lunch. I'll wrap up a few things there and we can go talk with him, if you like."

She shook her head. "One of the deacons can help me with Wade."

"I've wanted to meet him anyway. Is he staying with you?"

"No. He's at some horrible motel-turned-apartments in Searcy, a good forty-five-minute drive."

An ominous chill crept down Grayson's spine. "I know where that is." *Basically, a drug house.*

—◊◊◊—

Adrea climbed the staircase two steps at a time, glad to be home after a long week at work. She loved the greenhouse with its private entry and her garden there. Yet, she longed for a real home instead of an old house with all its character slashed into four tiny apartments. A real yard, instead of a lot shared by all the tenants. . . A real place of her own.

She stepped around Mark's shoes in the middle of the floor. The apartment definitely felt more like a home with him there, even if he couldn't manage to pick up after himself.

"I'm home." No response. She checked the oven and announced louder, "I'm home."

"Yo, Adrea. It's about time." Mark's voice came from his room. "I'm starving."

His running joke, ever since they'd rented the first *Rocky* movie, always made her smile. "Is food all you ever think about?"

"When I'm hungry, it is."

Minutes later, Mark stepped up behind her in the kitchen. Adrea turned to tousle his hair.

"So did you hear anything from any churches?"

"Not yet." Mark plopped on the couch. "So you'd met Grayson Sterling before?"

Just the sound of his name made her pulse flutter.

"At the shop a few weeks ago and then we sort of ran into each other at the park." Adrea chose her favorite paring knife and sliced a tomato. The sharp blade cut clean lines through the soft pulp. "He's had a standing order for his wife for six years."

Until a hit-and-run driver carved his heart apart, just like the tender fruit in her hands.

"He still buys the flowers even though she died?"

A knot formed in her throat. "He takes them to the cemetery."

"Sad." Mark looked at the floor.

"He always comes to sign the card personally." She arranged the slices on a saucer. "The salesclerks call him Prince Sterling, and his four annual appearances are the highlights of every year."

"So, with all those visits to the shop, you never met him until a few weeks ago?"

Adrea shrugged. "I never work out front. So, what did you think of him?"

"Knowledgeable, compassionate. . . I could work with him."

"Maybe you will." *It's so nice to have him home, Lord.* In the few months since he'd graduated, he'd become so ensconced in her routine, it almost felt like he'd never left. *Please keep him close.* "God will work it out and put you exactly where He wants you."

"I forgot until I put this shirt on today." He pulled a small jewelry box from his shirt pocket. "I bought you something before I left Memphis."

"You didn't have to do that. How sweet." Finished with her task, she washed her hands and sat down beside him. She opened the gift to find a tiny ring with a pale yellow stone. "Oh, how pretty."

"It's a toe ring."

"I've never had one." Adrea stooped to her bare foot and slipped the ring on. "Is that the right place to wear it?"

"Beats me. Rachel will probably know. I got her and Haylee matching bracelets, but this made me think of you. Those toes need all the help they can get."

"Thank you. I love it, despite your tasteless remark." She threw the empty box at him.

He ducked. The phone rang and Mark grabbed it.

"Hello? Yes. It's good to hear from you. Really? When do you need an answer? Yes, I'll get back with you; and thank you."

"A church?"

"Palisade."

Her breath caught. Grayson's church. "Well, of course they want you. Why wouldn't they?" Palisade would keep him in Romance. She should be thrilled.

"It's a trial period. Interim type thing."

"When do you have to answer?"

"Couple of days. I better go do some praying."

She hugged him. "I'm so proud of you. First interview and you ace it."

—◊—

Adrea turned into her parents' drive. Sam and Theo Welch sat in the porch swing, swaying slowly in the March breeze, both still trim and athletic. Mom's dark auburn hair remained without a trace of gray, with no help from her hairdresser. Daddy's thick mane had long ago turned silver; his rich brown eyes surrounded by laugh lines.

"Mark hasn't shown up for his own celebration dinner?" Adrea rolled her eyes.

"No and dinner's ready." Mom propped a hand on one hip.

A three-legged calico cat sat on the step.

"Hey, Tripod." At the sound of his name, he curled around Adrea's ankles. "Hey, boy, I missed you, too."

She picked Tripod up to scratch his special place along the side of his throat. He purred his appreciation. The long-ago abandoned cat had been her last rescued stray before she left home.

Only a kitten then, it seemed he was so grateful, he'd never put on "cat-titude" airs. When Adrea called, he came, just like a dog. Now around seven years old, she longed to take him with her each time she left, but her landlord didn't allow pets.

Mark turned in and parked next to her car. She set Tripod down.

"Yo, Adrea. I'm starving."

"Imagine that." Mom swatted at him, then followed with a warm embrace. "Dinner's ready. Just waiting for you. The others are inside."

Adrea lagged behind to walk in with him. "You look tired."

"I've prayed over this decision more than I've slept lately."

"So since you have a job, do you think we could get a house one of these days?"

"A house, huh?" Mark laughed. "Palisade can't pay an associate that much. I'll probably have to do some counseling on the side. And besides, it's just an interim."

"Yes, but they'll love you."

"You always have such faith in me. Someday, you'll have a husband to buy a house with. All in God's timing."

A sigh escaped. "I'm fine, but not fine enough to go there."

Mark stopped on the porch and gently gripped her forearms. "I just want you to know, you're young, beautiful, and precious. Just because you fell for a jerk in disguise, your life isn't over. I know how much you want a family and I'm praying for your future."

She blinked away the sting of tears.

He kissed her forehead.

Rachel, her husband, Curt, and Haylee joined the procession to the kitchen.

The aroma of pork loin permeated the air. A dish Adrea hadn't mastered. While Mom's turned out moist and fork-tender, Adrea's attempts came out dry and the consistency of cardboard.

"Will you ask the blessing, Curt?" Daddy asked.

As the family bowed their heads, a symphony began to play on Adrea's cell phone. She grabbed it. An unfamiliar number appeared and she turned it off. All eyes were upon her.

"Sorry about that." Adrea turned the ringer off.

The doorbell rang.

"Who could that be?" Mom frowned.

"Y'all go ahead. I'll get it." Adrea jumped up, intent on ridding her family of interruptions.

As she swung the heavy oak door open, every nerve ending reverberated.

How could he have the nerve to come here, especially with Mark around? By the looks of him, Wade really didn't know what he was doing.

# Chapter 3

S tepping outside, Adrea quietly closed the door behind her. "Why are you here?"

"We really didn't get to talk the other day."

"No, I mean here." She pointed to the house.

"I wanted to see you. Mark said Mom—I mean." He shook his head, as if to clear it. "Mom said Mark was celebrating something, so I figured you'd be here."

He'd gotten his hair cut into his usual casually layered style, but dark, sunken circles still shadowed his ice-blue eyes. She'd once dreamed of their children with those eyes.

Without the bloodshot effect.

"Look." Her voice shook. "We're over. We have been for a long time."

The door opened and a glaring Mark stepped out. The veins in his neck looked ready to erupt. "What are you doing here?"

"I need to speak with Adrea." Wade's watery eyes pleaded with her.

"Well, she doesn't want to see you. Ever again. Do you understand?" Mark barked a derisive laugh. "I doubt it, you're so drunk you can't even slur straight."

"This doesn't concern you." With effort, Wade enunciated each word slowly and clearly. "This is between her and me."

Mark launched a fist.

"Mark! No!" Adrea grabbed for her brother's arm—too late.

Wade stumbled back, cupping his mouth. Blood dripped from between his fingers.

"Just go. Please." She squeezed her eyes shut. "We don't have anything left to say."

"What's going on?" Daddy stood in the doorway. "Wade?"

"Hello, sir." Wade tried to sound sober but failed. His voice wobbled and so did his stance. "I'd just like to talk to Adrea. Alone."

"You want more?" Mark raised his clenched fist again, white knuckled.

Daddy stepped between the younger men. "It's time for you to leave, Wade. Now."

Wade wiped his bleeding lower lip with the back of his hand. With one more pleading look at Adrea, he slunk to his black Escalade.

She could see another man in the driver's seat. Thankfully, Wade wasn't driving.

Mark flexed his blood-speckled knuckles.

Adrea couldn't tell if it was his or Wade's.

"Go clean up, without alerting your mother." Daddy pointed at Mark, using his best shame-on-you tone. "We'll talk about that temper of yours later. You could lose the interim job we're supposed to be celebrating over a stunt like that."

Her brother hung his head and went inside.

"Listen, Daddy, I know you're worried." Adrea hugged herself. "But I'm not stupid."

"Sweetheart, we don't think you're stupid." He put his arm around her, and they settled on the porch swing. "But, you're very sweet and softhearted. I just don't want you to get reeled into his web again."

"And I won't. I can't help Wade. The only one who can help him is God."

The door opened and Mom stuck her head out. "Hey, what's going on out here? The food's getting cold and I can't even seem to interest Mark in eating."

—⁜—

Sunday morning dawned bright and beautiful, but Adrea's stomach flipped and flopped.

Mark drove past their church, in the middle of Romance, with its plain white block facade. Not known for its splendor, with out-of-date gold carpet and pews with no cushions, the church's charm dwelled in the warmth of its congregation.

From the time she could remember, her family had attended the small church of fifty or so faithful. When Pastor Frank retired, fiery young Curt came to town and promptly married their sister.

"Look, you really like Mountain Grove." Mark covered her hand with his. "Since I've been away, I got out of the habit of going to church with the folks. But you haven't. You don't have to do this."

"I want to. You know Mom and Dad would come, too, if they didn't teach classes." Adrea flipped down the mirror on the back of the visor and dabbed on mauve lipstick.

Palisade was in Rose Bud, eight miles farther from the apartment and quite large. Helen said the congregation numbered 150. Approximately, 148 strangers. And one all-too-familiar pastor.

With Mark at Palisade, she'd be more deeply drawn into the lives of the equally irresistible pastor and his son. *Maybe Mark won't get the position permanently.* She mentally kicked herself. *Palisade will keep Mark close. And keep me from being so lonely.*

As he pulled into the lot, the redbrick exterior looked big and imposing.

"It means a lot that you're willing to support me."

She managed a brave smile. "Let's go."

They entered the church. Adrea surveyed the high wood ceiling. Deep burgundy carpet cushioned each footstep. The pews shone, freshly polished, with padded seats in an exact shade to match the plush floor. Every window boasted stained glass.

Just as pretty as she remembered from the last wedding she'd done there. Prettier than Mountain Grove.

Until recently, she'd never thought of where Mark's calling might lead— or realized she'd feel compelled to support him. And on top of everything else, there was her attraction to Grayson Sterling.

At the back of the sanctuary, Mark introduced Adrea to several people, with an impressive grasp of names and positions. With his powerful sermons and charming, boyish personality the congregation would love him.

As she met several welcoming members, Adrea began to feel comfortable. Until she saw Grayson and Dayne. Her breath hitched.

With them, she saw a fresh-faced woman who looked as if she could go horseback riding at a moment's notice. *Strong resemblance. Must be Grayson's sister.*

Dayne ran to greet them. The adults followed.

"Hi, Adrea, I'm so glad you came to church." The boy grabbed her hand.

"Me, too. I hoped to see you this morning."

"Are you gonna come here all the time?"

"We'll just have to see."

A deacon pulled Mark aside as the adults caught up with the excited child.

Grayson began making introductions. "This is Grace, my twin. This is Adrea, the florist over in Romance."

"I've seen your lovely work at numerous weddings."

"You have?"

"I'm a caterer. Delectable Entrees. Is this your first visit to Palisade?"

"It is. I've always attended Mountain Grove, but as long as Mark is here, so am I."

As Mark rejoined the group, Grace turned to him. "Ah, the prospective associate pastor. My brother works entirely too hard. I hope you'll permanently take the position, along with some of his load." She extended her elegant hand.

"We'll have to see what everyone else thinks of me and how well I fit in."

"My sister, Grace," Grayson said. "This is Mark Welch, Adrea's husband."

At Adrea's sharp intake of breath, Mark tried to cover his laughter with a cough.

—⁓—

Grayson cleared his throat.

"Well, I assumed you're married, since the two of you live together." He knew of other churches lowering their standards to go along with the ways of the world, but not his church. He didn't know what else to say.

Surely, he hadn't contacted a young seminary graduate living with a woman out of wedlock. Surely, Dr. Cummings wouldn't have recommended such a candidate as a potential assistant pastor.

"Mark is my brother." Adrea blushed a pretty shade of pink.

"I apologize." A sigh escaped Grayson. *At least, I wasn't attracted to another man's wife.* "That day at the apartment, I just assumed. . . Who is Haylee?"

"Our niece."

"Well, I had a whole little family set up."

"What class do you plan to attend?"

*Grace to the rescue.* She tucked her hand in his elbow.

"What are the choices?" Mark asked.

"We have an adult, men only, women only, and a new singles class. I go to the adult. We're studying the writings of the apostle Paul."

"Sounds good to me." Mark grinned, looking ready to follow Grace anywhere.

"What about you, Adrea?" *Don't sound so anxious.*

"The adult is fine."

Her words made his heart beat faster. Though he tried not to look at her, she was even prettier in her yellow dress with high-heeled sandals and a matching ring just above the knuckle of the second toe of her left foot. Her nails were peach today.

The harpist began to trill a hymn.

Ready to flee Adrea's suddenly available presence, Grayson turned toward the stage. "I better get up there."

—∞—

After the closing prayer at the end of the service, Mark whispered, "Will you come stand with me as people leave? I'm kind of nervous."

Adrea's mouth went dry. One hundred forty-eight strangers.

She linked her arm through his. "People will think we're married."

"That was weird, huh?" Mark escorted her toward the back of the sanctuary. "So is Grace attached?"

"We're about to greet people and you're worried about getting a girlfriend."

He shot her a crooked grin.

The congregation began to scatter, and several people came to shake their hands as Pastor Grayson made introductions. While trying in vain to memorize names and faces, Adrea watched for Helen, hoping to get the chance to speak with her friend.

Ah, someone she knew. Jack Phillips. The mechanic/deacon wore permanent grease under his nails and taught the adult lesson this morning. Though Jack was a great teacher, Grayson's presence in the class distracted her. Jack introduced his family and the first group moved on. A break in the crowd lengthened.

"So is she?" Mark interrupted her thoughts.

Adrea had been too engrossed in memorizing to remember their discussion. "Is who what?"

"Is Grace attached?"

"I don't think so. Seems like Helen told me awhile back that Grace moved in with Grayson and Dayne after Sara's death." *I mean, Pastor Grayson.*

"If Grace will agree to lunch, will you come with us?"

"Yes, now perform your duties before you get dismissed on your first day."

Soon Mark was in his element and Adrea knew he didn't need her hovering over him. She strolled outside to stand in the warm sunshine.

A few minutes later, Grace joined her. "So you plan to join us for lunch?"

"Yes, where are we going?"

"The guys said it's up to you and Mark."

"The guys?" The tiny butterflies in her stomach turned into luna moths.

"Dayne and Grayson are coming along."

Before Adrea could respond, Dayne stood at her elbow, bubbling with excitement. "We're going to Dexter's!"

Mark joined them. "The new pizza place in Searcy?"

"No, Dayne." Grayson shook his head. "We agreed that Mark and Adrea could pick."

"Why not Dexter's?" Mark asked. "I love that place."

Grace shielded her eyes from the sun. "They always have a dozen birthday parties happening all at once."

"It's loud." Grayson grimaced. "And not a good place for adult conversation."

"Who needs adult conversation?" At a kid-centered place, she could avoid Pastor Grayson. "I love their pizza."

"Pizza is my favorite." Mark's childlike glee melted Adrea's uneasiness into a smile.

Grace raised elegant fingertips to her temple. "It's the noisiest place on earth and gets on most adults' nerves."

Despite her no-frills look, with minimal makeup and straight, long hair, Grace's nails modeled a flawless French manicure.

"Who said we're adults?" Mark grinned at Grace.

Adrea could tell he was smitten from his dopey gaze.

"Can they ride with us?" Dayne asked.

"Let's take my car, so we can all fit." Grace motioned toward a white sedan. "That is if you don't mind Dayne's booster seat."

"Adrea, hello."

She turned to see Helen, with red-rimmed eyes and perfectly coiffed hair to match her slate dress. "I looked for you all morning."

"I'm so glad you and Mark will be here." Always free with hugs, she embraced Adrea.

"Me, too."

"Pastor, could I speak with you and the new associate?" a young man asked.

Grayson and Mark stepped away.

"Come on, Dayne." Grace took the boy's hand. "We'll wait in the car."

Adrea touched the older woman's arm. "Are you okay?"

"The usual. Half the time Wade doesn't answer when I call." Helen's chin trembled. "He should have stayed in Missouri. Away from that girl."

Adrea patted her hand. "Maybe we can check on him this week."

"You're such a dear. So, you're going to lunch with Pastor Grayson?"

"He and Grace invited both Mark and me."

"You and Mark will fit in perfectly here." She glanced over Adrea's shoulder. "I think the pastor's ready."

The two women hugged again, and Adrea turned to see Grayson waiting a few yards away. He matched his stride to hers as everyone else headed for their cars.

"Adrea, sit in the back with me." Dayne patted the seat.

Mark was already up front with Grace, while Grayson, Dayne, and Adrea sat in the back. Just like a family.

The usual commotion of Dexter's dispelled Adrea's niggling discomfort. She counted eight birthday parties in progress. Laughter, excited voices, and numerous festive horns echoed around them.

Dayne dragged Adrea from one video game to the next, soundly beating her at each until their order arrived, served by a clown on Rollerblades.

Mark blessed the food.

Though the gleeful squeals of delight surrounding the group forced them to speak loudly, the adults managed to carry on a conversation. Pastor Grayson and Mark discussed the month trial period and then a membership vote.

"It's really my decision, but I like the congregation to have their say in such an important step." Grayson served Dayne a second piece of pizza. "After all, Palisade has never had an associate before."

"I can't hear half of what you're saying." Grace leaned closer. "This really isn't a good place for discussion."

"Why don't you all join us for lunch next Sunday?" Mark sipped his water-turned-lemonade. "At our place. After Adrea graduated high school and we got the apartment together, she was a horrible cook. That's partly why I decided to go to seminary."

Adrea's breath caught. Not another lunch with Pastor Grayson. She elbowed her brother in the ribs.

"Ow! You didn't let me finish. Much to my relief, her culinary skills have greatly improved."

"That's nice of you to ask." Grayson shot a well-mannered look toward Adrea. "But maybe you should check with your sister on this. She may not want to cook for five people."

"I don't mind at all." *Didn't sound very convincing.* She pasted a smile on her face. "I just didn't like Mark advertising my once dismal cooking. Please come."

Grace folded her napkin. "Can I bring something?"

"Just yourself. Oh my. One of my invited lunch guests is the best caterer in town. Now, I'm nervous."

"Don't be ridiculous. Anything you fix will be great."

"You know"—Mark grinned—"I was just kidding about the decision to go to seminary."

Adrea jabbed him again.

"Ow!"

After the meal, the men disagreed over who would pay the ticket. The restaurant had cleared of the after-church crowd and only the birthday partiers remained, with children on a giddy sugar high. Seeking peacefulness, Adrea stepped outside to wait.

"Yo, Adrea." Mark slung his arm around her shoulders. "I guess I should have asked you first, but I got caught up in the moment. Want me to cancel?"

"Of course not. It's fine."

"We could have it catered. Hey! We could get Grace to cater our lunch."

"That would be great. 'Would you join us for lunch and can you bring the food, too?' " Adrea laughed. "Don't worry, I really don't mind. It'll be fun."

*Fun? An afternoon spent trying not to eyeball the great-looking preacher with even more emotional baggage than me.*

—m—

Since Helen's visit, Grayson had tried to catch up with Wade, but Adrea's distress call surprised him.

He pulled into the lot of the run-down motel-turned-apartment-complex. Mildewed concrete blocks with peeling white paint trimmed in a neon lime color. Adrea's silver G5 sat next to Wade's Escalade.

How much longer could Wade afford his fancy ride? Helen said he hadn't worked since he'd come to town.

Grayson's deacon, Jack Phillips, parked beside him, and they headed toward the building.

"Nice place," Jack deadpanned.

"Yeah. Look, I'm not sure what we'll find here. Wade is an alcoholic. Adrea brought Helen to check on him. He's drunk and she's upset."

"I'm prepared. My uncle was a drunk."

They climbed the rusty iron steps to the second level and Grayson knocked on the door. "Wade."

The door opened.

Adrea greeted them with worry-filled eyes, holding a trash bag. "I shouldn't have brought her here. I didn't know who else to call." She gestured to a doorway.

Dreading what he might find, he crossed the living room, followed by Jack. The smell of garbage greeted them. Grayson's stomach turned.

Helen sat by the bed. Splayed across the sheetless mattress, in a grungy T-shirt and shorts, Wade looked dead. His oily hair matted to his head, and dark circles under his eyes told the tale—along with the whiskey bottle on the floor. He looked familiar. The drunk from the florist shop. This was Wade Fenwick?

Empty fast-food containers lined every available surface, and flies buzzed from one rotting morsel to the next. Wadded clothes, remote controls, and beer cans strewn across the floor created an obstacle course. Grayson traversed the refuse.

"Helen?"

The older woman whirled around. "Oh, Pastor Grayson. Jack." Her face crumpled. "What do we do now?"

Grayson put a comforting hand on her shoulder. "We could try to convince him to go back into rehab."

"He's been too many times to count." Her watery voice wobbled.

"What about Mission 3:16?"

"You know, I don't think he's ever been in a Christian facility." Helen wrung her hands.

Wade stirred and slowly opened his eyes. "Adrea? Don't leave me," he muttered.

# Chapter 4

Grayson frowned. "Hello, Wade. I'm your mother's pastor, Grayson Sterling."

Unfocused eyes widened. "No. It can't be. I'm dreaming again? How did you find out?"

"Just calm down, Wade," Grayson spoke slowly, as if to a simpleton. "Your mom is here, and this is Deacon Jack Phillips."

"I'm sorry. I didn't mean to hurt anyone."

The distraught man lost consciousness again.

"What's he talking about?" Jack whispered.

"He must be hallucinating. I'll call the mission and see if they can help." He turned toward Adrea, who was still picking up trash in the living room. "Take Helen home. Jack and I will handle things from here."

Adrea nodded. The haunted look in her eyes reflected the depths of her soul.

She'd worked for Helen and he could see the two women were close, but why would Wade call out for Adrea in his drunken stupor?

That morning at the shop, he'd hoped Wade was just a drunk wandering the streets, harassing anyone who left their doors open. Could Adrea be in a relationship with Wade?

—*∾*—

Feeling shaky, Adrea climbed the stairs to the private balcony of her apartment.

What would Grayson think of her if he knew she'd caused Wade, an alcoholic, to go back to drinking? Had Wade said anything incriminating today?

Mark sat with his feet propped on the coffee table, reading his Bible. So serene. Nothing like the day she'd had.

She unlocked the sliding glass door, threw her keys on the cheap melamine counter, and walked around to plop beside him, striving for casual.

He frowned. "Yo, Adrea. You okay?"

"Just peachy." Her stomach knotted tighter.

"How's Helen?"

"Worried about Wade."

"You're not getting involved, are you?"

"I'm just trying to support her. She called before I left the shop. She put Wade in a Christian rehab center today."

"Grayson told me about it. He said you took Helen to Wade's apartment."

42

"I didn't want her to go alone. I'm involved for Helen's sake. Not Wade's."

"Poor Helen." Mark shook his head, satisfied with her explanation. "I get the feeling you're uncomfortable around Grayson."

"Why would I be?"

"You tell me."

Mark knew her so well.

Adrea took a deep breath, debating on how much to tell him. No matter how hard she tried to relegate Grayson to the back of her mind, he remained at the forefront. She replayed each conversation they had, each time she saw him, again and again in her mind. Like a teenager.

"You'll think I'm silly."

"Just tell me, Adrea. I've never thought you were silly a day in your life, even when you were probably really silly. You've got a crush on him."

She shrugged. "Guess so. Now you think I'm silly, don't you?"

"Absolutely not, because I have a crush on his sister. Apparently the Sterlings are irresistible to the Welches."

"The thing is, Grace is available and she seems to like you, too."

"So Grayson likes you. What's the problem?"

"He's still in love with his wife." She propped her feet next to his. "It's only been two years."

"Two years is a long time. Maybe he's ready to move on."

"Trust me, he's not. Whenever he mentions her, fresh pain snuffs out the sparkle in his eyes."

"Ooh." Mark winced. "You've got it bad. I hadn't noticed a sparkle in his eyes."

Adrea's face warmed. She elbowed him. "Two years is a long time, but not when a couple shared a love like he and Sara apparently did. Just trust me, Grayson Sterling is not available. And the last thing I need is another troubled man on my hands."

"He does have his share of baggage." Mark frowned. "Should my interim become permanent, we'll have to socialize with him. Would you rather I back out of this church and try somewhere else?"

"Don't you dare! You let God make the call. So, the church may make Grayson an indelible fixture in our lives. I'll just have to get used to his presence."

―⁓―

Saturday afternoon, Adrea borrowed Haylee for a walk in the park. Daffodils nodded in the gentle breeze. A few families dotted the landscape with children and various-sized dogs scurrying about.

Haylee ran ahead, with ginger pigtails flying and long, coltish legs flailing. So similar to her mother at that age. Bright sunshine made it warmer than she'd expected, and Adrea wished she'd packed a lunch.

"So you're not coming to Mountain Grove again tomorrow?" Haylee asked as Adrea caught up.

"Mark really needs me to support him." Adrea tugged a pigtail. "It's like when you have to read a book report in front of the class; it helps to see a friendly face or two in the crowd."

"So he's preaching the morning service, but couldn't you come to night-time church with us?"

"It would seem weird if I only went when he preaches."

As they walked across the crisp grass, something large crashed into the back of Adrea's legs, knocking her off kilter. She screamed.

Strong hands on each shoulder helped to restore her balance.

"Sorry about that," a familiar voice apologized. "I guess Cocoa remembers you."

She turned to see Grayson and Dayne, with Cocoa straining at his leash. What did Wade say in his sometime conscious state? *Does he know about Wade and me?*

"With my bum knee, I can't hold him back when he goes full throttle."

Grayson didn't act any differently toward her.

Adrea stroked Cocoa's chocolate fur and turned to Haylee. "This is Cocoa and Pastor Grayson's son, Dayne."

The calmness of her own voice surprised her. For some reason her heart was about to beat out of her chest. *Must be adrenaline.*

"Hey." Dayne waved.

"Hello." Haylee responded with a shy grin.

"It's nice to see you again, Haylee." Grayson winked.

"Daddy, I'm hungry." Dayne kicked a pebble off the sidewalk. "Can Haylee and Adrea come on our picnic?"

"It's nice of you to invite us, but your father probably only packed for two." Adrea wrapped her arms around Cocoa's neck. "You go and we'll keep Cocoa company, if you don't mind. I promise not to let go of his leash."

"I can't let him drag you across the park." Grayson smiled, devastatingly unaware of his own attractiveness. "Grace packed enough for an army. Unless you have plans?"

Lunch with the drop-dead gorgeous preacher. *Might as well get to know my brother's earthly boss. Maybe put in a good word for Mark.*

"Actually, we're on our own today. I left Mark at home to do his Bible study in peace."

"I knew I liked him. He's studying while I hang out in the park."

Bingo. "Mark was so worried when his interview got off to such a confusing start."

Grayson laughed. "As I told Mark, our initial meeting convinced me he was the perfect candidate for associate pastor. I wanted a human being, not some stuffed shirt. His down-to-earth personality, much prayer, and the recommendation from Dr. Cummings made the decision for me. I'm anxious to hear his sermon."

"Me, too." A dog barked, followed by the excited shout of a child. Cocoa's ears perked up.

"In the meantime, you ladies can help us pick a spot for our meal, since Dayne and I can never agree."

"On the way here, I wished we'd packed a lunch." Adrea looked across the park. "How about that big sycamore over there by the swings?"

"That's where I picked." Dayne jumped up and down. "Two against one, let's go!"

She expected the excited boy to run ahead, but he remained close by his father's side. Apparently, Grayson's warnings, after Cocoa chased the squirrel, had worked.

As Adrea helped spread the blanket, Haylee stayed close by and Dayne dug through the wicker basket.

"I don't believe I've ever seen a real red-and-white-checkered picnic blanket." Adrea sat with her ankles crisscrossed and ran her hands over the soft fabric. "It's beautiful."

"Sara made it." His eyes dimmed.

"My favorite." Dayne removed a container from the basket and repeated the statement with each subsequent find.

With the contents emptied, Grayson blessed the food.

The chicken salad sandwiches beat Adrea's favorite deli.

Dayne carefully tore the crust of his sandwich away and fed it to Cocoa. The large dog waited patiently for an offering, then took each bite delicately between his teeth, careful not to nip his beloved owner.

"This is delicious." Unsnapped jeans would feel good about now.

"I'll tell Grace. She's the most sought-after caterer in town." Pride echoed in his voice.

"So she's working today, while we enjoy her mouthwatering food."

"Trust me. She wouldn't have it any other way."

Dayne and Haylee hurriedly finished their meals and ran to swing nearby. The young girl had finally warmed to the little boy.

"I'm glad the kids are having fun." Grayson watched Haylee push Dayne higher and higher.

"She's painfully shy. As a kid, I was the same way."

"Really? You don't seem shy now."

"I'm better than I used to be." Warmth crept up her cheeks. "For my first three months at the shop, Helen put me in the showroom. It was torture. Eventually, I realized I was more uncomfortable *not* talking to the customers than I was while attempting to make conversation. I still tend to clam up when I'm out of my element." *Or get nervous and prattle. Like now.*

"So, that's why I never met you. You hole up in the back and play with flowers." Several birds landed in the tree above. Grayson flinched.

"Is something wrong?" Adrea asked.

"On one of our first dates, I took Sara on a picnic and a bird decided to relieve itself—on my head."

Adrea tried to stifle her laughter but failed. "What did you do?"

"Sara always had a very weak stomach, so she threw up, cleaned me up, and we ate. That's when I knew she was the girl for me." He looked off in the distance, lost in memories. "I try to avoid trees."

The deep timbre of Grayson's voice cast a spell on her. He smiled, which deepened the crinkles at the corners of his eyes. Her fingers tingled to smooth away the lines of worry and grief. The sable lock of hair playing across his forehead in the mid-March breeze gave her the urge to brush it back from his brow.

*Concentrate on something else. Anything but him.* She noticed an ant, threading its way through the grass, struggling to carry a bread crumb Cocoa had missed.

"Daddy, I don't feel so good."

She looked up in time to see Dayne throw up.

Adrea's heart tumbled for the sobbing boy.

Sympathetic with her new friend's plight, Haylee patted his back.

Ineffectively, Grayson tried to clean the boy's face with a dry paper towel.

"I'll get wipes." Adrea jogged toward her nearby car.

Grabbing the towelettes, she ran back to the still sobbing boy and began washing his face and neck.

Grayson pressed his hand against Dayne's forehead. "You don't feel warm. You probably ate too fast and then played too hard. I should have made you wait and digest longer."

"We'll get you cleaned up in no time." She tried to assure the child while working on his shirt, then turned to his father. "Does he have extra clothes?"

"Actually, we picked up some fresh laundry from Mom's this morning." He flashed a sheepish grin. "She does our ironing."

"Do we have to go home, Daddy?"

"I'll get you another shirt. We'll stay for a while, but if you feel sick again, we'll have to leave." Grayson went to his car.

Adrea had the boy cleaned up by the time his father returned. Always the first to hurl at the sight of anyone tossing their cookies, it amazed her that the incident didn't sicken her. Instead, she simply dealt with the problem.

"Since Dayne seems fine now, I think we'll go." She threw their trash away.

"I doubt it's anything contagious. He got his weak stomach from Sara."

"If it's a virus, we've probably already been exposed. It's not that. Mark will wonder about us. And speaking of ironing, I do his shirts."

A dog yapped. Cocoa raised his ears and stared off in the distance. Following his gaze, Adrea saw a golden retriever lunge into the air to catch a neon orange Frisbee.

"Thanks for helping with Dayne. Seems like every time we're distressed in the park, you show up to save the day."

"No problem." Adrea smiled. "Thanks for letting us crash your lunch. Please tell Grace how much we enjoyed her delicious meal."

"Don't go." Dayne grabbed Adrea's hand.

"We have to go home, but I liked having a picnic with you."

"Even though I threw up?"

"Well, I wish that hadn't happened, for your sake, but it didn't bother me."

"One time my Sunday school teacher threw up because a boy in class did."

Grayson scrunched his nose. "We don't need the details. Tell Adrea and Haylee good-bye."

"Bye, Adrea, bye, Haylee. I'm glad you came today."

"We are, too." Just how glad, Adrea didn't want to think about. She patted Cocoa on the head, then regretfully steered Haylee to the car.

"See you tomorrow," Grayson called.

—⁂—

Grayson paced the kitchen floor. Grace should have been home by now. Numerous times, he'd called her cell and gotten no answer. His heart thudded in his chest. He couldn't get enough air in his lungs. Not again. It couldn't happen again.

He closed his eyes and the memories swirled. Sara looked so peaceful by the glow of the dash light. With her seat tilted back a bit, she fell asleep. The slightly wilted white rose lay in her lap.

In his rearview mirror, he could see Dayne curled to the side in his car seat, with one arm flung over his face.

Grayson stopped at the four-way, looked both ways, and continued. A flash of light to his right. The impact hurled the car sideways. A white explosion hit him in the face, the car spun, metal tore, glass crunched. The car slammed into something solid and came to an abrupt halt. His right knee jammed into the steering column. His scream mixed with cries from the backseat.

Sara was silent.

He shook the images away and took several deep breaths.

Willing his fumbling fingers to work, he dialed the hospital. Just as it rang, the back door opened. Grace. Marvelous, healthy, all in one piece, Grace. He hung up.

"Where have you been?" He rushed toward her with a hug.

"Can't breathe," Grace whispered.

He eased up but couldn't bring himself to let go. "You're late." His voice broke on a sob.

"Oh Grayson." She rubbed her palms over his back in soothing circles. "I told you I had a big luncheon today. It went longer than I planned."

"I tried to call." *At least twenty times.*

"My cell needs charged. I'm so sorry I worried you."

Steeling his resolve, he pulled himself together and let her go. He sank to a chair.

She touched his cheek, her eyes bright with tears. "You can't go on like this."

"I'm okay. Really." He wiped his face with a paper napkin. The wooden legs of his chair scraped against the tile floor as he scooted closer to the table. He leaned his elbows on the surface, his face in his hands.

"Maybe a counselor would help. Mark does counseling on the side."

"I have the best counselor in all of heaven. I'm fine. Just call me next time."

"I promise. And I'll make sure my cell is charged, so I can leave it on vibrate."

"How did your luncheon go?"

"Great. Several people asked for my card." She opened the cabinet and got a glass. "So, what did you do today, other than almost have a coronary over nothing?"

"Dayne and I had a picnic in the park."

"Oh good." Ice clinked into the glass she held under the dispenser. "Quality time."

"That, too, but we actually ran into Adrea and her niece, so Dayne invited them to join us."

"Where was Mark?"

"Home studying. They loved your sandwiches."

"Good thing I sent extra." Grace filled her glass with ice water and took a sip. "So, Adrea's very pretty and seems really sweet."

Grayson cleared his throat.

"I'll take it you agree."

Something in his chest boiled. "It wasn't like a date or anything."

"I didn't say it was."

"We had a picnic in a very public place with two kids." He stormed out of the kitchen.

She followed. "Grayson, you know Sara would want you to move on. To be happy."

He took the stairs two at a time.

—⁜—

Saturday evening, Mom and Dad stopped by the apartment.

Adrea tried not to fidget as Mom surveyed her from hair to toenail.

"You're too thin." Mom tapped her chin with a forefinger.

"I weigh the same as the last time you saw me." Adrea hugged her mother, who weighed only slightly more. Somehow, Mom always wanted to fatten her up.

"You're taller than I am. You need some meat on your bones. Men don't like beanpoles. Isn't that right, dear?"

"Yes, dear," Daddy said.

"Daddy, you're supposed to be on my side."

"Sorry, sweetness, after thirty years, I've learned to just agree with your mother. It keeps the peace."

Mom playfully swatted at her husband. "I thought you might need help with tomorrow's lunch."

Adrea lifted the lid off the slow-cooker. The brisket bubbled with floating potatoes and carrots.

"Smells like everything's under control." Mom settled on the floral sofa beside Daddy. "So, Adrea, are there any candidates on the horizon? Surely a big ole church like Palisade has plenty of eligible bachelors."

"There are no candidates." Adrea straightened the magazines on the coffee table. "Besides, candidates are in politics. Why don't you bother Mark about women? He has a thing for Grace Sterling."

"I already told her." Mark flashed a beat-you-to-it grin.

"Tell me about him?" Mom prompted.

"There's no him." Adrea fluffed a throw pillow and sat beside their dad.

Unsatisfied, Mom turned to her son. "Mark?"

"There are a few sparks flying between Adrea and my potential new pastor."

"There are not." Adrea hurled the pillow at her brother.

He caught it.

"Grayson Sterling?" Mom smiled at the possibilities.

Mark nodded. "Adrea calls him Prince Sterling."

"I do not!" Adrea jumped up.

"I always knew you'd make a perfect preacher's wife." Their mother clasped her hands together as if in prayer.

"Mother!" Adrea propped both hands on her hips. "Mark, I'm never speaking to you again. There are no sparks."

"You're protesting too much, dear. Ooh, and a twin. I might just get twin grandbabies."

"Mother!"

"Tell me more, Mark." Mom patted the seat beside her.

"When I first met Grayson, he assumed Adrea and I were married." Mark chuckled. "He even thought Haylee was our daughter. When he learned different, I've never seen such relief on a man's face."

Incapable of stopping the conjecture, Adrea rolled her eyes heavenward and left them to it. "I'll go iron Mark's shirt."

A few minutes later, as Adrea and the iron steamed, Mom entered the room.

She perched on the edge of Adrea's yellow satin and lace comforter. "So Grayson sounds wonderful."

"He is, but he's still in love with his wife. She's only been gone two years."

"Well, he can't go it alone forever. He's a young man. His son needs a mother."

"You may be right." Adrea sighed. "But I don't feel up to the challenge of getting a man to move forward from his past. I tried that with Wade."

"Sorry I brought it up. You know I just want you to be happy." Mom touched her hand. "We're leaving. Turn the slow-cooker down soon, or the meat won't be tender."

―⁓―

After class, Adrea waited on the steps of the church until their parents caught up.

Mark stood with Grayson at the entrance to the sanctuary. "Mom, Dad, I'd like you to meet Pastor Grayson Sterling. This is his son, Dayne, and his sister, Grace. Everyone, our parents, Theodore and Samantha Welch."

"Call me Sam." Mom surveyed the stained-glass windows lining the sanctuary with a rainbow of color bursting on the white walls.

"And I'm just Theo."

"It's a pleasure to meet both of you," Grayson said as Daddy pumped his arm. "I'm glad you could join us for the service."

"We wouldn't miss Mark's first official sermon at Palisade." Mom hugged Grace a little too eagerly.

Mark winced.

Adrea stifled laughter.

"Go ahead; put the pressure on, Mom. It's not like I wasn't nervous already."

"You'll be fine." Mom kissed his cheek, imprinting him with her trademark fuchsia shade. "I've been praying for you."

Branded many times before, Mark wiped the smear away with his handkerchief as Rachel and Haylee arrived.

"I didn't know y'all were coming!" Mark hugged them.

"I wanted to surprise you. I couldn't miss my brother's first official sermon."

The harpist began a hymn.

"Thanks, sis. It means a lot to me. I better get up there."

Everyone found seats.

The congregation sang; then Mark took the pulpit, obviously ready to launch into his sermon.

"Ephesians 3:17–19 says, 'That Christ may dwell in your hearts by faith; that ye, being rooted and grounded in love, may be able to comprehend with all saints what is the breadth, and length, and depth, and height; and to know the love of Christ, which passeth knowledge, that ye might be filled with all the fulness of God.' "

Several amens echoed.

Mark flipped back toward the Old Testament, Bible pages rustling. "Now turn to Isaiah 53:5, 'But he was wounded for our transgressions, he was bruised for our iniquities: the chastisement of our peace was upon him; and with his stripes we are healed.'"

Adrea's eyes welled with tears several times during the service. Mark's sermon demonstrated how deeply Jesus loves us. Enough to leave His heavenly home and come to live among us, knowing He would be savagely beaten and killed.

When the altar call came, she went to thank God for sending His Son to save her soul and Jesus for enduring the punishment for her sins. It made her dilemmas seem so trivial.

She memorized a few more members of the large congregation. Red hair, nosy, Sylvie Kroft. No husband, at least no one mentioned him. Gray hair, slightly stooped over, Mrs. Jones, kind, forced smiles. Tom Deavers, the deacon/doctor with a handshake so firm, her fingers ached afterward. His wife, Patty; sons Tommy, Timmy, and Terry. She only saw Helen in passing. The older woman seemed a bit more at peace. Maybe Wade's treatment was going well.

—⁂—

When she and Mark arrived at the apartment, a mix of smells permeated the kitchen. Succulent beef brisket and the perfume of flowers, from her garden and the shop, filled the air creating a captivating aroma. Their parents arrived in time for Daddy to help Mark put both leaves in the table and round up every seat they owned, even a couple of lawn chairs.

Just as Adrea took their dessert from the oven, the Sterlings arrived, followed by Curt, Rachel, and Haylee.

"I'd like to offer my help." Grayson leaned against the counter. "But I'm useless in the kitchen."

"I'll help." Grace stepped around the dividing island.

"There's not much left to do other than put ice in the glasses." With trembling hands, Adrea set the final plate on the wall-to-wall table. "And, Grace, you do this sort of thing all the time. You are taking this day off."

"I can handle ice." Grayson grabbed a glass and Adrea heard clinking.

With the table ready, Mark said the prayer and they all took their seats.

"So, how's the church?" Curt passed the rolls.

"I love Palisade. The people are wonderful. I only wish. . ."

Adrea watched Grayson mentally leave, though he sat at their table with his glass of sweet tea halfway to his lips. Conversation stalled as everyone waited for his return and he snapped out of the memory.

"Sara always loved this area. In fact, we were married at Mountain Grove. My typical bride wanted her wedding in Romance."

"She'd be proud of you." Mom patted his arm.

"Mrs. Fenwick is definitely proud." Daddy passed the brisket. "She was

51

singing your praises to everyone she saw."

"Dear Helen. I'm afraid I haven't always been there for her." A shadow passed over his face. He glanced at Dayne. "Adrea, this is one of the best meals I've had that my sister didn't cook."

Her face warmed. She gestured toward her mother. "Mom helped."

"I didn't do a thing." Mom, a firm believer that the way to a man's heart was through his stomach, grasped the opportunity to plug Adrea's cooking. "Adrea had it all prepared before our arrival."

"But Mom taught me how."

"A bit belatedly," Mark said. "Ow! Adrea, you have the boniest elbows." Laughter followed the exchange.

After the meal, the children ran to play outside. Mark and Grace insisted on helping Adrea clean up, but Grayson managed to shoo them away to supervise the kids. Traitors, her parents, Rachel, and Curt disappeared also.

Alone with the man of her dreams. A man who still loved his deceased wife.

"How does Mark like the church?" Grayson gathered the plates while Adrea loaded them.

She turned on the dishwasher. "He loves it."

"What about you? What do you think of Palisade?"

"At first, the size intimidated me, but I'm getting used to it. However, it'll take me quite some time to learn everyone's name." She set the yellow quilted place mats back on the table.

Grayson wiped the countertops. "Don't worry, you'll get to know them all. They'll make sure of it. If anything can be said of the people at Palisade, they're very friendly. Once they get to know you, you'll get hugs instead of handshakes."

"I'm already getting a few."

Finished with the counters, Grayson leaned against the refrigerator.

She could feel him watching her.

"Mark did a great job on the sermon this morning."

"Did you really think so?" Her voice quivered.

"Of course, didn't you?"

The steady hum of the dishwasher, followed with a gurgle, and the clunk of two plates together filled the pause.

"I thought he was awesome. I just wondered if you really thought so or if you were simply being nice."

"If I didn't truly enjoy the sermon, I wouldn't say anything."

"I'm so proud of him."

Grayson pulled out a chair and sat.

Though she'd hoped to escape his presence, Adrea followed suit and claimed the seat across from him.

"He's got my vote and the congregation seems to like him, as well. With

Mark to rely on, I can focus better on what I need to do."

"It was only one sermon. Let's not get ahead of ourselves." Adrea decided to broach the issue on her mind. "I'm thinking about trying the women's class for a few weeks. And if Mark were to stay at Palisade, I heard the kindergarten/first grade class needs a teacher. I used to teach children at Mountain Grove and really enjoyed it, but I stepped aside to let a newer member have a chance."

The dishwasher stopped between cycles. *Drip, drip, drip.* The steady beat on the stainless-steel sink punctuated the silence.

His jaw twitched. "You'll do anything to get away from me." His teasing tone sounded forced.

Adrea felt the blush creep across her cheeks. She hoped he was unaware of how close he was to the truth. She stood and turned the faucet handle until the drip stopped then reclaimed her seat.

"No, really, you should attend whichever class you feel you'll get the most from. So, you've given me another reason to vote Mark in." Grayson fiddled with the lace edging on a place mat. "Sara used to teach that class."

"I'm sorry. I didn't mean—"

He held up a hand. "It's okay. We have to move on. Since Mrs. Roberts's illness, Mrs. Jones has filled in. She's good with the kids, but since her husband passed, she's been distracted. The kids need some consistency."

"I'll pray about it."

"It's nice to have people willing to volunteer." He cupped his chin between forefinger and thumb, then propped his elbow on the table. "You and Mark fit in well. That's one of my favorite things about Palisade. Everyone pitches in to help. I've seen churches where the same five people do all the work while the rest of the congregation sits and warms their pews or, even worse, complains about the way things are done."

"I like to do my part." Adrea straightened the salt and pepper shakers in a nice line. "Though my time seems to become more and more limited. I thought owning the florist shop would allow me to set my hours, maybe work only three days a week. Instead, I work five and most weekends." *And I'll probably spend them running into you at weddings.*

"It seems your shop is doing quite well; you could hire more help. If there's one thing I've learned in this life, time is short. Take time for the important things." Sadness washed over Grayson's face.

She ached to ease his pain. Her heart twisted. She covered his hand with hers.

# Chapter 5

Their eyes met.

Grayson's heart hammered.

Slowly, she moved her hand away from his and clasped both of hers in her lap, as if she feared they might betray her again. "I doubt very seriously that you ever neglected your wife."

He cleared his throat. "No, but I could've made more time. Now, it's too late to make up those precious hours."

"I'm sorry."

"At first, I was in shock and had to hold myself together for Dayne's sake. Then things calmed down and everyone else went on with their lives. For a while, it seemed the more time passed, the worse I missed her. Now, it depends on the day, the memories." He noticed tears building in her eyes. "I didn't mean to depress you."

"It's just very sad." She looked down at the table.

"It's actually nice to talk to someone." His fingers traced the intricate quilt line of the place mat. He struggled with the longing to reclaim the warmth of her hand. "Even after two years, people don't know what to say or fear the subject will upset me."

"They mean well."

"They do. I just wish everyone wouldn't treat me as if I might crack at the mere mention of Sara's name."

Grayson's cell vibrated and he jumped. "Excuse me." He stood to dig it from his pocket. "Hello?"

"Pastor Grayson?" Helen's voice quivered. "I'm sorry to interrupt your afternoon."

"Don't be. Tell me what's wrong."

"Wade's trying to check himself out of the treatment center."

"I'm glad you called. I'll be right over." He hung up.

"Let me get your coat." Adrea retrieved his suit jacket from the closet by the front door.

He slung the jacket over one shoulder and hurried out, sorry for Helen's distress, but relieved to have the excuse to get away from Adrea. Talking to her was simply too easy.

～ɯ～

Three weddings and two funerals would keep the shop busy for the week. A wedding on Tuesday. Who would want to get married on a Tuesday?

Rachel worked tirelessly, right at Adrea's elbow. Normally, the sisters' affiliation worked well. While Adrea preferred immersing herself in flowers and rarely entered the glass-shelved, mirrored showroom, Rachel loved the customers and the sales end of the business. Though she often helped with arrangements, she found the solitude of the windowless work area stifling. Unless orders swamped them, she spent most of her time out front with the customers.

Yet this morning, Adrea couldn't shake Rachel. Each trip from the work-table to the floral refrigerator, Rachel tagged along. Initially, the subject had been Mark's sermon. However, Rachel soon got around to the topic of her interest.

"So, you seem to have spent some time with your new pastor." Rachel raised an eyebrow. "Haylee said something about a picnic in the park."

*Casual. Keep it casual.* "Haylee enjoyed it." She added more baby's breath to the bridesmaid bouquet. Maybe Rachel couldn't hear her heart beating double time.

"He's positively dreamy." Rachel packed the boutonnieres and corsages. "The stuff Christian romance novels are made of. I always thought the Prince Sterling nickname fit."

"If you like that type." From the corner of her eye, Adrea saw her sister taking in every expression and cracked under the pressure. "Okay, okay, he's really handsome and very nice. In fact, there should be a law against preachers being so easy on the eyes."

With a wistful expression, Rachel looked toward the ceiling. "I can just imagine him sweeping you into his arms."

"People don't get swept into each other's arms. They hug."

"Well, Curt and I never hug. He always sweeps me into his arms."

Adrea rolled her eyes. "Besides, Grayson Sterling is still mourning his wife."

"Maybe so. But you're alive." Rachel pointed an orange tiger lily at her.

"Just drop it. Please. For right now, he's my pastor. End of story." Adrea packed the cellophane bags containing boutonnieres and corsages into a cardboard box.

"Okay, if he's still in love with his wife, who has been gone for twoooo loooong yeeeears, why did he invite you on a picnic? And why did you take Haylee and Dayne with you?"

"It wasn't like that." Adrea propped her hands on her hips. "He didn't invite me. Haylee and I ran into him and Dayne at the park. It was totally unexpected, just like the first time I ran into him there."

"So, you seem to hang out in the park an awful lot lately."

"You know very well, the park is one of my favorite places." She scooted the full box across the tile floor with her foot with a *shwoosh*. "I jog three times a week, and it's where I go to unwind and relax."

"Maybe he's hanging out there in hopes of running into you."

*Why is he there every time I turn around and never before? Maybe he's always been there and I just didn't know who he was. No, he's not the kind of man a woman overlooks.*

"He has a young child. Kids like parks." *No way is he coming to the park in hopes of running into me.* "It's just coincidence. Besides, the church is bound to entangle our social lives. And on top of that, Mark is interested in his sister, Grace."

A big smile lit Rachel's eyes. "Well, Grayson Sterling has grieved long enough. He needs someone to make him happy again, and you are just the lady to do it."

"Rachel, please. He's still hurting. Let me take care of the romance in my life. Okay?"

"That's the problem. If left up to you, there is no romance in your life."

Adrea picked up a box. "I have to make deliveries."

"Nice escape."

Not really. She'd probably bump into Grayson, since the wedding was at Palisade.

Seven miles of highway passed as she dreaded running into the handsome pastor.

She turned into Palisade's parking lot, took several deep breaths, slowly exhaled, and got out of the van.

"I can help you."

She whirled around and almost dropped a large box.

Grayson—Pastor Grayson took the carton from her.

"Thanks." She was grateful for the extra muscle. Just wished they weren't his. A less attractive package would've been nice.

They made quick work of unloading. With everything inside the sanctuary, he hesitated.

"Need me to hold your ladder?"

"No thanks. I bought a new one."

He nodded and left her alone.

She added more bird-of-paradise to the archway. The orange spiky flowers with blue tongues gave it a funky look, per the bride's request. Adrea stood back to survey her handiwork. Not what she'd pick, but it held a certain charm. Satisfied, she rushed through the other decorations, willing the bride to hurry with her okay. Too late, the handsome pastor arrived.

"So, we'll be seeing one another often." He cleared his throat. "On a professional basis, of course."

"I guess so. Will someone be here in the morning, so I can pick up the arch and candelabrum?"

"Only my secretary. I'm going with Helen in the morning to the treatment center. But I can help you load up before I go."

"That's okay. It'll probably be later in the day before I come."

Just as soon as the bride made her final assessment and before she could change her mind, Adrea made a hasty escape.

At least she wouldn't run into him tomorrow.

———

Mark's monthlong trial had passed in a blur, and the congregation prepared to vote as he and Adrea left the church after Sunday morning services.

Offering what little comfort she could, Adrea took Mark's hand in hers. Pastor Grayson had promised to phone later with the results.

No matter how deeply the church would entrench Pastor Grayson in her life, Palisade would keep Mark close and in a short matter of months she'd gotten used to him being home.

Spring wildflowers carpeted the church lawn, pink primrose, scarlet Indian paintbrush, and the darkest violets, while birds chattered a welcome. Or was it good-bye?

"Guess what?" Mark clutched her hand tighter.

"What?"

"Grace agreed to have dinner with me. Alone."

"So, I don't have to go?"

"Not unless you want to double with Grayson."

She rolled her eyes.

After what seemed like an eternity, they made it to the car. Mark's hands shook as he started the engine.

"How about Dexter's?"

"It's a nice thought, but I couldn't eat a thing. Not even pizza."

"Me neither." She pressed a hand against the butterflies churning in her stomach.

"Let's go home. I don't know why I'm so nervous." Mark sighed.

"Just pray about it. God will work it out. Look at the bright side; even if they don't vote you in, you still got Grace out of the deal."

"I hadn't thought of it that way. Maybe that's why Grayson didn't want to make the decision himself. Maybe he knew from the beginning that Grace and I were clicking, and he didn't want the congregation to worry that I might get the position due to his or his sister's bias."

"Clicking, huh?"

Mark blushed, something Adrea had never seen him do before. For the first time, she realized that her brother didn't just have a crush. He was falling in love with Grace.

Back at the apartment, Mark and Adrea took turns pacing. She would have loved to go for a jog; however, she wanted to be at his side when Pastor Grayson called.

They both jumped when the phone rang.

"Get the cordless. I want you to hear the decision, too."

"Why?"

"So I won't have to repeat the conversation for you."

She retrieved the handset from a pile of magazines on the coffee table. Mark practically pounced on the other phone.

Holding his free hand, she stood by his side.

He took a deep breath and pressed the receiver to his ear. "Hello?"

"The vote was unanimous, Mark. I hope and pray that you'll accept the position of associate pastor here at Palisade," Grayson said. "I'd like to meet with you tomorrow."

Adrea expelled the breath she hadn't realized she'd been holding.

"Okay, just give me a time." Mark wrote the details down and hung up.

Brother and sister hugged. Adrea's stomach growled and they both burst into giggles.

"I'm suddenly famished." She clutched her abdomen.

"Me, too."

"How about Dexter's?" they asked in unison.

—⁓—

After much prayer, Mark accepted the position a few days later. Adrea embraced the decision as God's will, even though Mark's tenure cemented Grayson Sterling's place in their lives. She was proud of her brother, just out of seminary and now associate pastor at a church consisting of 150 people.

On Easter morning, Pastor Grayson announced, "I'm proud to add Brother Mark to our staff here at Palisade and pray that he'll stick around for years to come. He and his sister, Adrea, will be presented for membership after today's service."

The two men shook hands as the congregation clapped. The only member who seemed prouder than Mark and Adrea was Grace.

As they headed to Sunday school class, Grace stopped Adrea. "Grayson said you wanted to teach the children."

"Well, I. . ." She didn't want to tromp on Sara's memory. "I haven't been officially voted into membership yet."

Grayson stopped beside them. "You will be and Mrs. Jones is all set to help you with the transition." He seemed at peace. His tone even, no jaw twitching.

"If you're sure."

"I'll show you the way," Grace offered.

Adrea soon learned the kindergarten class included Dayne Sterling, since he would begin school in a few months. She adored the child. Though the little boy had his mother's fair coloring, except for those emerald eyes, his features and mannerisms reminded her of his father. A reminder she didn't need.

The children responded to her well and before she knew it, class ended.

"I don't think you need me hanging around. You're a natural." Mrs. Jones patted her arm.

"I've always loved kids." Her heart clenched. *Will I ever have any of my own?*

Back in the sanctuary, the lull between services was quiet. A few families dotted the pews, while most of the congregation lingered over coffee in the fellowship hall. Grace stood at the front, straightening the arrangement. Adrea joined her there.

The silk flowers, Easter and calla lilies with fern fronds, and baby's breath looked old, frayed at the edge of each petal, as if someone had washed them too many times.

"I don't mean to overstep or take anyone's position, but if no one does the flowers, I'd love to."

Grace gasped, looking past Adrea.

She turned to see Grayson standing behind her.

"Sara always did the flowers." His voice was strained.

Adrea clasped a hand over her mouth, wishing she could melt through the floor. "I'm sorry. I—"

"No, it's okay." He frowned. "They're just flowers. We can't keep them forever."

"But—"

"They're getting undustable." He touched one of the white lilies.

Grace nodded. "I'll speak with Patty Deavers, the treasurer. She'll give you a check and go over what's in the flower budget."

---

The music began and the church started filling up. How many times could she trounce across Sara's grave in one day?

After services, Patty Deavers held a check toward Adrea. "Grace told me to give you this for flowers."

"Oh yes, of course." Adrea stuffed it into her wallet.

Patty scribbled a note and stashed it in her purse. "I'll get you a copy of the budget. In the meantime, I think Sara spent about a hundred per arrangement, so you'll be fine with that figure."

"Thanks, I'll put something together in the next few weeks."

"Adrea, how are you?"

She turned to see Helen. Wade's mother looked better. Fewer worry lines.

"Good. And you?"

"Wade's back in that horrible apartment in Searcy. I wanted him to go back to Missouri, away from that. . . He's working. So far, so good."

"We've been missing you at the shop." Adrea kissed a perfectly made-up cheek, trying not to think about Wade's blond floozy.

"And I've missed y'all, too. Since my time's freed up now, maybe I can get in a few days a week, like before."

"I've been wondering. . . Do the people here at church know about Wade and me?" *Namely, Grayson.*

"I don't really have close friends here that I talk about Wade with. Pastor Grayson knows about the broken engagement, but I don't think I ever mentioned your name."

Sylvie Kroft shot a disdainful frown at Adrea.

"What did I do?" Adrea pressed a hand against her fluttery heart.

Helen sighed. "Nothing."

—⚬⚬—

Midweek, Adrea was still in her pajamas and doing her makeup when the doorbell chimed. With mascara applied to the lashes of her left eye, but not the right, she hurriedly slipped her robe on before checking the newly installed peephole.

Once she recognized their guest, she wished her brother could answer. Alas, Mark was in the shower. Grayson had caught Adrea in disarray entirely too many times. *What does it matter? There's no future for us.*

With no other choice, she answered the door.

Sadness clung to him like a shroud.

"What's wrong?"

"It's Helen. She fell and broke her hip."

"Oh no!" Adrea pressed a hand to her lips.

"I'm supposed to go by her house and pick up a few things she needs, but I don't know a thing about stuff like that. Grace is busy with a brunch of some kind, so I couldn't bother her with it."

"I'll take care of it. Want some coffee to go?"

Grayson sniffed the air. "Smells and sounds wonderful."

Mark sauntered into the room, already dressed.

"Helen broke her hip." Adrea poured a cup of coffee. "I'm going to pick up a few things for her."

"How is she?"

"In pain." Grayson sipped the hot brew. "The medication is helping."

"I've got two counseling sessions today." Mark checked his pocket calendar. "But I can stay with her tonight and relieve you."

"I'll probably take you up on it." Grayson headed for the door.

"I'll go get dressed." Adrea turned toward the hall.

"Um." Mark pointed to her eyes. "You might want to do something about that."

Her face burned. She'd forgotten all about her half-applied mascara.

An hour later, she arrived at the hospital and hurried up to Helen's room on the third floor. Doctors and nurses scurried about dressed in scrubs and smocks, their rubber-soled clogs squeaking on the polished tile floor.

Grayson sat beside Helen's bed.

"How good of you to come, Adrea." The older woman reached a trembly hand toward her young visitor.

Adrea clasped Helen's hand. "Of course I came. I had to see about my favorite lady. I'm so sorry. Are you in pain?"

"No, dear. Thank goodness Pastor Grayson came to check on me. I was hurting pretty badly and couldn't get to the phone. But they gave me something and now I'm just tired."

"We'll go and leave you alone so you can rest." Grayson stood.

"Please stay." Helen barely managed a whisper. "I love having you both here."

"I'll stay for a while if you stop talking and try to rest. How's that?" Adrea patted Helen's hand.

"Very well, I guess I do need a little nap." Her sad blue eyes closed and within minutes, her breathing evened and she began softly snoring.

Adrea gently withdrew her hand from Helen's limp grasp. Nodding at Pastor Grayson, she turned to go, but he followed.

"What did the doctor say?" she asked.

"It's a clean break and should heal well. They'll transfer her to their rehabilitation center when she's ready. It'll be a long, painful road, but he expects her to fully recover."

"Why did she fall? She's always been steady on her feet."

"She said she tried to get up too fast and got her foot caught in the sheet."

"Poor Helen." Adrea shook her head. "She's frailer than she used to be— even more than just a few months ago. I cook for her sometimes, but I don't think she's eating well."

"Wade's problems have done a number on her."

*On all of us.*

—∽—

Saturday morning, Adrea hurried toward Helen's room.

"Adrea."

Heart pounding, she squeezed her eyes shut and turned around. Wade stood in the waiting room. She greeted him with a forced smile.

He looked like the man she used to know. The circles under his eyes had receded. Groomed hair, neat clothing, sober.

"How's Helen?"

"Comfortable. Mark was here when I arrived."

*Great.* "How'd that go?"

"Civil. I'm sorry about the way I've acted lately."

"I'm just glad you're doing better."

"Much better. I got reacquainted with God and I'm back in church."

Just what she'd prayed for. "I'm glad. Really glad."

"I could still use your prayers. Shell ditched me in Missouri, and I followed her back here." Raw pain shone in his eyes. "She's pregnant. I'm trying to patch things up with her, but so far, she's not interested."

Despite the reminder of the children they'd planned together, his despair tugged at her. She touched his shoulder.

She caught movement out of the corner of her eye. Grayson entered the waiting room.

Wade's jaw twitched.

Her hand dropped to her side.

A frown furrowed Grayson's brow.

Confusion with a tad of disappointment.

He cleared his throat. "Is Helen awake?"

—·—

Grayson, along with Mark, Adrea, and Grace did their best to keep Helen company since her move to rehab. Several members from Palisade visited, as well. Grayson often ran into Adrea there and a few times, they shared coffee.

In the cafeteria, Grayson chose a table near the door, so he could watch for her, as always, looking forward to the extra chance to see her. He drummed his fingers on the melamine table, hoping she'd show before he had to leave.

The scene with Wade and Adrea had played through his mind several times in the last month. Sober so far, Wade had a new job in Searcy. An alcoholic working at a country club? Par for the course of a golf instructor.

Grayson took a swig of the lukewarm, knock-the-top-of-your-head-off coffee.

Hopefully, whatever was between Wade and Adrea was over. Was that selfish? Wade needed her. With Adrea in his life, he might have incentive to stay sober. But she certainly didn't need Wade.

Adrea stepped off the elevator. A breath of late-spring air dressed in a pale green top and white short pants. *What do they call those things? Capris?* Whatever they were, they showed off her slender ankles.

His heart skipped a beat.

"Would you like some bad coffee?" *Great line.*

"I'll just go see Helen first."

"The nurse ran me out."

"All right then." She hesitated at his table, then got her cup and added two creams and two sugars, just like she always did. With no further way to delay, she took the seat across from him.

"Helen's making an amazing recovery."

Distracted by something, Adrea didn't respond.

He followed her gaze.

Sylvie Kroft headed their way.

She stopped at their table, apparently speechless, a rare occurrence for her. Grayson could see the wheels of gossip spinning.

"Well, well." She found her tongue. "Isn't this cozy."

"Hello, Sylvie." *Calm and casual. Nothing of interest going on here.* "We're just celebrating Helen's speedy recuperation. Her therapist plans to release her next week. Isn't that wonderful?"

"Just grand. Did the two of you come here together?"

"No, I had no idea Pastor Grayson was here." Adrea traced the rim of her Styrofoam cup. "We just ran into each other."

"What a coincidence. Why just last week, Mrs. Jones said how nice it was that you two had visited Mrs. Fenwick."

Poor Adrea. Her usually smiling mouth pulled into a tight line. With jerky movements, she set her cup down, sloshing steaming liquid on the table. She shouldn't have to defend the completely innocent situation. Well, maybe not completely innocent.

He often caught himself not thinking of Helen's injury at all, but instead, his mind strayed to the lovely woman sitting across from him. Curbing his thoughts, fearing Sylvie might somehow read them, Grayson took a sip of his tepid coffee.

"We've both been checking on her often. We don't want her to feel lonely."

"That's nice." Sylvie smirked. "She doesn't have anyone except that horrible Wade."

"Several people from church have visited with her since she's been here. I'm really glad we have such a supportive church family." Grayson frowned for effect. "We haven't seen you here before or at the hospital. Is this your first visit, or have we just missed each other?"

Sylvie's coral-tinted lips moved like a gasping fish out of water, then twisted into a fake smile. "Well, I've been busy. I'll leave you two alone to visit or. . .whatever it was you were doing. I'll just go see Mrs. Fenwick now."

"You do that." Grayson smiled.

She glanced back over her shoulder several times until she disappeared through double doors. Sylvie's husband, an alcoholic, never stepped foot in church. Their two children, both grown and gone with lives of their own, never came for a visit. Instead of having empathy for the plight of Helen and Wade, since alcoholism controlled Sylvie's life as well, she took all her heartache and picked apart the lives of others. Grayson prayed for her daily.

Adrea sipped her coffee. "Why does she hate me?"

"It's not you. Sylvie's life isn't. . .easy. She lives next door to Sara's parents, over in Searcy, and I think she got the impression they were the perfect family. Her daughter was friends with Grace and Sara. Sylvie idolized Sara."

"I hope she won't bother Helen about Wade." Adrea downed the last of her coffee. "Maybe she'll have enough gossip concerning us."

"What can she say?" Grayson asked. "We're sitting in an extremely public place having coffee."

"She'll say something. I'm certain of it." She stood and threw her coffee cup away. "I need to get back to the shop, so I'll check on Helen and be on my way."

Grayson watched her go with a hitch in his heart. He always hated it when she left.

He'd been praying about his developing feelings for her, and somehow he got the impression Sara approved. Adrea loved Jesus and the church. She loved kids. She was great with Dayne, older people, and the hospitalized.

*What if I let myself fall for her and she dies? Just like Sara.*

No. Better to stifle such wandering feelings. He had enough people to worry about.

—∾—

After class, Adrea returned to the sanctuary through the side door. A hush settled over the crowd already there. She'd noticed it all morning. Sylvie had done her job.

Helen was sitting in her usual spot. Her first Sunday back. Though she walked stiffly, with a walker, she'd even made it for class.

Whispers swished through the assembly, with several members looking toward the back of the sanctuary. Adrea glanced over her shoulder. Her jaw dropped.

# Chapter 6

Despite the long hair hanging in his eyes, Adrea recognized the man flanked by Jack and Grayson. Wade stumbled down the aisle of Palisade.

Mark hurried toward her. "What's he doing here?"

When Wade tripped, Grayson steadied him.

Wade jerked his arm away. "I can walk on my own."

"I'll sit with you." Mark put a protective arm around her shoulders.

"No, you go on up front. I'll be fine. He's so far gone he may not even recognize me."

"Wishful thinking on your part."

Mark claimed his usual seat beside Grace and Dayne. Adrea hurried to the back of the sanctuary.

Wade sat beside Helen, tears rolling down her cheeks. She didn't need this.

Despite his rough appearance, the congregation welcomed him. Several greeted him and Adrea heard snippets of how much his mother meant to them. With each greeting, Wade seemed more miserable.

Sylvie Kroft kept her distance, but her eyes never left his disheveled appearance.

The well-trained pastor's son ran to meet the visitor and offered his hand. "I'm Dayne Sterling. Nice to have you at Palisade."

Wade started crying.

Adrea's heart lurched.

Grace hurried to retrieve her confused nephew.

Knowing Helen needed support, Adrea waited until the harpist began then forced herself to move forward and claim her usual seat on the other side of Helen. The whiff of alcohol turned her stomach. Wade was so out of it, he didn't notice her presence at first. By the time he did, the congregational hymns had already begun.

During the song service, he jiggled his feet and twiddled his thumbs. Adrea watched him from under her lashes. His palpable nervousness proved contagious. She half expected him to break and run.

Grayson launched into his sermon. "People think they have to clean up before they come to Christ. They think they have to beat their demons before He will accept them. The complete opposite is true. If you'll just trust Him, He'll clean you up. He'll take your burdens away. Jesus Christ will instill in your heart the desire to come clean. Commit yourself to Jesus and He'll wash all your sins away."

Halfway through the message, Wade had the entire pew bouncing as he trembled.

To drive his point home, Grayson quoted 2 Corinthians 5:17. "Therefore if any man be in Christ, he is a new creature: old things are passed away; behold, all things are become new."

The hymn began as everyone bowed their heads. Adrea felt certain at least half the church prayed for the jittering man seated beside his mother. The second verse began and Wade squirmed even more. Several people knelt at the altar.

Adrea continued to pray. Finally, as if he could stand it no longer, just as the song neared its conclusion, he sprang to his feet and staggered toward the altar.

Helen stood and made slow progress with her walker. Two deacons rushed to Wade's side. As his stance tilted precariously, the men steadied him.

Pastor Grayson stepped off the stage and whispered something to Mark, then went to meet Wade. The entire congregation seemed to hold its collective breath.

Finally, Wade made it to the front and knelt at the intricate, hand-carved altar, joined by Grayson and eventually Helen. The song leader started the hymn over and after all four verses, ended again. Wade kept sobbing.

Mark stood. "Pastor Grayson would like the deacons to stay. Tom Deavers will offer the closing prayer and everyone else is dismissed afterward."

After Tom's prayer, the congregation filtered out of the pews and moved to the back of the church. Sylvie Kroft sat rooted to her seat, until Grace offered to walk her out.

In the lobby, Grace stopped beside Adrea. "Since Mark's tied up, Dayne and I can take you home."

"Thanks, but I think I'll wait for Mark." Her heart hammered in her ears.

"It might be awhile and Grayson can take him home. I learned a long time ago, never to ride with my brother. That way I don't get stranded here."

"I'll be fine. I want to make sure Helen's okay anyway."

"What was wrong with that man?" Dayne asked.

"He's real sick, sweetie." Grace patted her nephew's shoulder. "But he came to the right place."

Adrea waved as they left then went to her car and tried to enjoy the peaceful late May weather.

The parking lot cleared, leaving only a handful of vehicles behind. A few minutes later, the church door opened and Grayson ran to his car, followed by Mark and Tom.

Adrea frowned. What was going on?

None of the men seemed to notice her as they passed, with Mark driving.

Adrea didn't know what to do. Go home or wait and see if Mark came back. As she tried to decide, the church door burst open. Wade stumbled out and headed straight for Helen's sedan. Tires screeched as he tore out of the parking lot.

She watched until he was out of sight, praying that no one ended up in his path. Then Helen came out of the church and Adrea ran to meet her.

"Where did he go?" Tears streamed down the older woman's face.

"I don't know, but he took your car."

"Go after him. Please." The urgency in Helen's eyes convinced Adrea to do as asked.

"How will you get home?"

"A deacon will take care of me. Just please go to his apartment. Make sure he arrives safely."

— ∽ —

Adrea climbed the rusty stairs to Wade's room.

With no response to her hesitant knock, she tried the knob. Greasy, but unlocked. Dreading the encounter, she pushed the door open.

He sat on the sagging couch. The refuse around him wasn't as bad as last time, but getting there. A glass of clabbered milk made her gag. She trekked through the strewn-about trash to take the putrid liquid to the kitchen sink, just to get it out of smelling distance. She shivered.

"Wade? Are you all right?"

"What are you doing here?"

"You tell me. Helen asked me to come."

"How is Mom?" His chin quivered.

"She was upset." Adrea perched on the well-worn sofa arm.

"I'm. . .leaving later." He touched her hair and traced her jaw with his fingertips.

She turned away. "Don't."

"If only I'd loved you the way you deserved to be loved, we'd have gotten married and none of this would've happened."

Unwilling to take the trip down memory lane, she studied her chipped, jagged fingernails, fighting the urge to nibble. "So, what happened at the church?"

He ran his hand through his hair and patted the seat next to him. "Come sit beside me. I won't try anything. I promise."

As she scooted over next to him, he fished a flask out of his jacket and tipped it to his lips.

She stood. "I won't stay if you drink."

"Sorry, I just really need it." He put it away.

"No you don't." She reclaimed her seat. Matted cotton protruded from a rip that ran the entire length of the armrest and a spring lodged in her back. "So, you've been drinking and you drove your mother's car. Do you realize how dangerous that is?"

He snickered. "Trust me, I'm well aware of the dangers, but I had to get out of there."

"What's going on with you?"

"I should have owned up to this a long time ago. There's not much time. The cops will get here soon."

"Why?" Her mind raced. What had Wade done?

"What should have been our wedding day was the beginning of the end." She remembered the date with a shudder.

"I took a little trip to Jacksonville."

The nearest liquor store. "Oh Wade."

"It gets worse. Much worse. After I left the liquor store, I went to a bar in Little Rock. I guess I'd parked illegally or something because when I got ready to leave, my car was gone." The more he talked, the faster the long-pent-up words tumbled out. "I walked probably a mile, but I was tired, so I stopped at a hotel. I found a car with the keys in it."

"You stole a car?" She tucked one leg under the other and turned to face him.

"I was just planning to borrow it. I would have brought it back the next day, I swear."

"Couldn't you have gotten a cab?"

"I wish I had." He covered his face with both hands. His shoulders quaked.

Hesitantly, she touched his back and he pulled her into his arms. His sobs shook them both.

"What happened?"

"I hit another car in El Paso."

"You what?" A glimpse of Sara Sterling's image in the newspaper flitted through Adrea's mind. It couldn't be. "Did you stop? Did you call the police?"

"No."

She pulled away from him and jumped up. "You hit another car and you just kept going!"

"I hoped it was a nightmare. That I'd only hit a Dumpster or something." Wade stood and paced away from her.

"But it wasn't. It was a car. With an innocent family inside."

He whirled toward her, guilt etched into his features. "I was scared. I didn't want to go to jail, so I abandoned the car and hitchhiked home. Next morning, I got mine out of the impound lot and headed to my aunt's in Missouri. Shell followed me and we got a place. Been drinking pretty much ever since. Every time I think about it, I see that woman with the car crumpled around her."

"Sara Sterling." Adrea began pacing now. Tears fell as realization set in. *He was drinking because of me. It's my fault she's dead.*

He noticed her reaction. "Did you know her?"

"No. But, I've done her flowers for years." White roses at the cemetery. *Because of me.*

"It's been eating me alive." Wade buried his face in his hands again. "Then who showed up at my door a few months ago and dragged me off to rehab? Like some nightmare. Then to top it off, he and that deacon hauled me to church this morning and there was that kid. Welcomed me, shook my hand, like a miniature little preacher or something. And all I could think was, 'I killed your mama.'"

"You have to turn yourself in."

He didn't answer, just paced some more. The scuffed wooden floor creaked with each step.

"Wade? You plan to call the police, don't you?"

"Sure." He didn't sound convincing. "But somebody at the church probably already called. I made a full confession."

She walked over beside him and touched his forearm. "I'll go with you to the station."

"No, you go home. I'll wait here for them. I killed that woman on my own. I need to do this on my own."

His words made her more confident that he would do the right thing. "Does Shell know?"

He winced. "We were patching things up. I wanted to start fresh, so I told her. She split and killed my kid without even consulting me." Tears dripped from his chin.

A knife sliced through her heart for the innocent baby. No words came.

"Did you hear me?"

"I'm sorry. Truly, I am. Does your mom know about the baby?"

"I was hoping to tell her after Shell married me. Now, it's too late." His chin trembled. "I told Mom about the accident at the church. Take care of her for me. She'll need you to get her through this."

"I will." Despite the gravity of his confession and all the pain he'd caused, she felt sorry for him. She hugged him, but he pulled away.

"You better go."

"Let's pray."

"Me and Jesus got it all worked out."

"That's good to know."

"Go," he said. "You don't need to be mixed up in this any more than you already are."

"I'm sorry, Wade."

He cupped her face in his hands. "None of this is your fault. It was all me. I started drinking because of our breakup, but I gave you good reason to call off the wedding."

Adrea gave him one more quick hug. "I'm proud of you for coming clean." With a tender kiss on her cheek, he ushered her out.

In a haze, she descended the stairs.

Wade killed Sara Sterling. *Because of me.* Now after two years, he confessed. *I can't let him do this alone.*

She turned to go back up the steps. *Boom!* The blast almost sent her reeling. She fell backward but managed to grab the railing and right herself. A knot formed in her stomach.

Two at a time, she ran up the rest of the stairs. Curious, other tenants came out of their rooms. Adrea bypassed them. The door was slightly ajar. With absolute dread coursing through her entire body, she pushed it open. Wade lay on the couch.

The scene didn't really register in her dazed consciousness. There was something horribly wrong with his head. Hands trembling, she dialed 911.

Wade was dead.

—⁂—

But he wasn't. When the police arrived, they barely detected Wade's pulse. Soon paramedics pushed through the crowd. Adrea couldn't watch. Forcing her way through the spectators huddled just outside the open apartment door, she made her way to the steps and sat.

"Oh Lord, please help." Unable to utter a sensible prayer, she rocked back and forth.

More curious bystanders made their way up to the second level, stepping around her.

She stood and turned sideways.

Finally, the paramedics carried Wade out on a gurney.

Her gut wrenched. He was still, his skin a sickening shade of gray, his head swathed in bandages.

"I'm his friend. Is he alive?"

"Barely."

"Are you taking him to the local hospital?"

"We're MedFlighting him to Little Rock."

*Helen.* With clumsy fingers, she dialed Mark's cell phone.

"Where are you?" Mark asked.

"He shot himself."

"Who?"

"Wade shot himself. He's alive, but barely. They're taking him to Little Rock."

"Meet me at Helen's and I'll take y'all there."

"How is Grayson?"

"A mess."

Adrea hung up and dashed down the stairs to her car.

"Adrea!"

She turned to see Birney Wilson, dressed in his Searcy police uniform, heading in her direction. Since she usually only saw him at Mountain Grove, it jarred her to see him in his professional role.

"You okay?"

"Not really." She leaned on the railing.

"Someone said you were with him?"

"Not when he. . .did it. Just before."

"You know you'll have to come to the station."

"Why?"

"You were the last person to see him. . .before." He scribbled something on a small notebook.

"Am I a suspect?" A hard knot formed in the pit of her stomach. "He shot himself."

"We haven't ruled on that yet."

"But I wasn't there. I was leaving."

"Yes, several witnesses said they saw you leaving before the shot. Don't worry, Adrea. It's standard procedure with this kind of case to question everyone in the area."

"Helen needs me."

"It won't take long." He rested his hand on her shoulder. "Ride with me. You're too shaky to drive."

She nodded and followed him to a squad car. On the way, she called Mark again.

---

A tattooed suspect shuffled past in shackles. Adrea stared at the floor.

A man's legs stopped in front of her.

"Adrea?"

She launched into her brother's arms. "Oh Mark, it was so horrible."

"I know, sweetheart." He stroked her hair. "I'm so sorry you were there."

"I can't believe he killed Sara." Her chin trembled. "How is Helen?"

"She's on her way to the hospital. Jack, Tom, and their wives are with her."

"What about Grayson?"

"I took him home. Grace is there."

"How is he?"

"Still a mess." Mark raked his fingers through his hair. "They both are."

"What about Dayne?"

"His grandfather came and picked him up. Stop worrying about everyone else. Tell me why you're here."

"She was a witness." Birney motioned them to his office. Closing the door, he gestured toward two metal chairs facing him. He handed her a cup of coffee and took a seat behind his charcoal metal desk.

Too strong and black. She didn't care. Maybe it would calm the butterflies flopping in her stomach. She took a big gulp and scalded her tongue.

"Do you mind if I record our conversation?" Birney set a recorder on the desk.

"Of course not."

Birney clicked a button. "So tell me, why were you with Wade?"

"He showed up at church. Drunk. After the service, Wade went to the altar. He left upset and his mother asked me to follow him."

Mark leaned forward. "Has there been anything new in the case of Sara Sterling? Any new leads?"

Adrea set the coffee cup down with a clatter and looked out the window at Birney's view, a brick wall.

"I'm not at liberty to discuss that information." Birney steepled his fingers.

"Wade claimed he was the hit-and-run driver." Mark put his arm around Adrea. "He confessed at the church. There were several witnesses, including Grayson Sterling."

"I see." Birney digested the news for a moment.

"He confessed to me, too." Adrea gulped a deep breath. "Right before. . ."

Mark took her hand. "Can her name be kept out of the papers?"

"You have my word." Birney ran his palm along the back of his neck. "Now, let's get into exactly what Wade confessed to."

---

Mark found a space in the hospital parking lot and killed the engine. "I shouldn't have brought you here."

Adrea stared out the window. Several iron benches surrounded a fountain in front of the entrance. "Did Wade tell everyone at church why he was drinking that night?"

"He never needed a reason, did he?"

"It should have been our wedding day."

"So now you plan on blaming yourself?"

"It's my fault." Her words ended on a sob.

Mark pulled her into his arms. "No, Adrea. You can't think that way. Think about why you broke up with him. It wasn't on a whim. And you didn't put the bottle in his hands or make him steal that car."

"No, but I might as well have. Sara Sterling is dead. Because of me."

He gave her a gentle shake. "Don't ever say that again. Don't even think it. Sara Sterling is dead because Wade Fenwick is a loser who blames his problems on everyone else and drowns them in alcohol instead of facing up to his own failures. If you had married him, and thank God you didn't, he probably would have drank to get through the ceremony. You are not responsible for Wade's drinking or Sara's death. Do you hear me?"

She nodded.

On the fourth floor, two deacons and their wives waited with Helen, but no Grayson.

Adrea steeled herself and stepped into the ICU waiting room. A family huddled together, communicating with sniffles and hugs.

"Oh Adrea, how good of you to come." Even under extreme duress, Helen had manners. "I just can't believe it."

"Me, neither." Adrea sat beside the older woman.

"He's still in surgery. I should have known." Helen wrung her hands. "Wade went to my sister June's on February 15$^{th}$. Couldn't get out of here fast enough. I remember being so upset about Sara, but I never imagined the two were connected. I thought he just wanted to make a new start."

"I'm so sorry." Adrea put her arm around Helen's trembling shoulders.

"I'll never be able to face Pastor Grayson again. Or Sylvie Kroft. I'll have to find a new church. Maybe, I'll move away. To June's."

"No, Helen. He wouldn't want you to do that. No one at Palisade would. Everyone loves you and right now, you need your church family. Don't even think about Sylvie. This is your home."

Helen straightened her posture. "Mark, I want you to take Adrea home and go check on Pastor Grayson."

Mark shook his head. "We're not leaving you alone."

"I'm not alone and June's on her way. She's barely over the Missouri line, so it won't be but a few hours before she arrives."

"We'll stay until she gets here." Adrea patted her hand.

---

Adrea wasn't the least bit tired, despite the roller-coaster day. "Drop me here and check on Grayson."

Mark parked in front of their apartment. "That was my plan. You sure you'll be okay?"

With the balcony windows open, her garden beckoned. "I'm fine. Is that Rachel's car?"

"I called her while you were with Helen."

"Does she know what's happened?"

"I filled her in." He kissed her cheek. "I didn't want you to be alone."

She checked her watch. "We missed church?" She couldn't remember the last time.

"Tom Deavers got a fill-in to handle it."

Once inside, Rachel greeted her with a hug.

Adrea went out to sit in the garden and her sister took the cue. Not in the mood to talk. For the first time, the abundant flowers didn't soothe her soul. She cupped a cool yellow rose with jittery fingers, wondering how Grayson was doing.

She went back inside to pace the small living room.

Rachel sat in the kitchen, her elbows propped on the table. "Why don't you take a shower and go to bed."

"I won't be able to sleep, but a shower might relax me."

It didn't work. As the evening wore on, her shoulders ached with tension. In the middle of blow-drying her hair, the doorbell sounded.

When she stepped into the living room, Grayson stood there, shoulders slumped, his face the picture of anguish.

"Sit down." She gestured to the sofa. Realizing what she wore, a blush heated her cheeks. Though the leopard-spot pajama shirt and pants were perfectly decent, not exactly the appropriate attire for greeting one's pastor. "I'll be right back."

"I'll make coffee." Rachel filled the pot.

"Just give me a minute." Adrea hurried to the bedroom to put on her jeans and T-shirt but caught a glimpse of herself in the mirror. Scrubbed free of makeup, her face was pale and splotchy. Her half-dried hair stuck out at odd angles. She brushed it into place and headed back to the living room. The best she could do. Besides, he'd barely looked at her.

"I'll be in your room." Rachel hurried down the hall.

Grayson waited until they were alone. "Sorry to bother you. I'm kind of thrown for a loop and not even sure why I came here. I guess I wanted to talk to somebody somewhat removed from the situation."

Removed. *I caused the whole thing.* "Mark just went to check on you."

"Maybe he can help Grace. I'm not much good to anyone right now."

"I'm sure everyone understands."

The coffeemaker gurgled and spewed as the rich aroma filled the kitchen.

"For over two years, I've dreamt of finding Sara's killer. Dreamt of smashing the guy's face in and breaking his legs with my bare hands. Not very pastoral thoughts."

"You're only human."

"I never imagined it might be someone I know."

*Me neither.* "I'm sure that makes it even harder." Her voice cracked.

"Today, I dragged him to church, with no idea *who* he was. I guess all these run-ins with me spurred his confession."

"Makes sense." That and meeting Dayne.

He covered his face with both hands. His shoulders shook.

Adrea didn't know what to do. She moved to the chair beside him and tentatively touched his arm.

Covering her hand with one of his, he made an effort to pull himself together. She handed him a tissue and he mopped his face.

Grabbing two mugs from the counter, she poured coffee in each, then set the creamer and sugar on the table. "How do you take yours?"

"Just black tonight." Steam swirled from his cup as he tipped it to his lips. "Since Sara died, I've had—the doctor calls them panic attacks. Like in the park that day. Shortness of breath, tightness in my chest, headaches. The first time, I thought it was my heart. Anything sets them off. A passing ambulance, not knowing where Dayne is or Grace. Even my parents."

"That's understandable. Considering what you've been through." So scarred by the loss of his wife, the sight of their child running toward the street brought on near hyperventilation. *And it's my fault.*

He took another sip of coffee. "I know it's irrational, but with the driver

74

off the streets, for the first time, I feel we're safe. Isn't that crazy? I mean, just because one drunk driver tries to blow himself away, it doesn't mean there aren't a million others out there."

The image of Wade putting the gun to his head chilled her soul.

"The doctor said if he survives, he'll be a vegetable. I'm glad he won't be able to hurt anyone else. I know I shouldn't think that way, but I can't help it."

Part of her agreed with him. The other part still grieved the man she'd once loved. A weight settled across her shoulders.

A key clicked in the lock and Mark stepped inside. "There you are, Grayson. I just left Grace. Your folks are there. They're all worried sick about you."

"What about Dayne?"

"Asleep. He doesn't know what's happened. They figure it's your call."

"I went to tell Sara's parents."

Mark winced. "Bet that was tough."

"I can't get Helen off my mind. I should be with her."

"She's worried about you. Her sister made it in and Wade survived surgery. He's stable." He glanced at Adrea. "June talked Helen into going home until morning."

"I'll call Grace, so she won't worry." Adrea headed to her room. "I should have done that already, but I'm not thinking very clearly."

"Adrea," Grayson called.

She turned to face him.

"Thanks."

She nodded then left the men alone.

Rachel sat on her bed, cell phone in hand. "Here she is. I'll call you later."

"Go on home, Rachel."

"That was Mom. They just got out of church. They want to be sure you're okay."

"I'm fine." Grabbing a yellow satin and lace throw pillow, she hugged it to her stomach and plopped down beside her sister.

"Did Grayson leave?" Rachel put an arm around her shoulders.

"No. Mark's home. I left so they could talk."

"What a mess. I never dreamed it would be Wade."

"Me neither." Adrea laid her head on Rachel's shoulder.

—✺—

Parked in the hospital lot in Little Rock, Grayson sat with Sara's white Bible clutched against his chest. He turned to the familiar indentation between two worn pages. The white rose Sara had insisted on taking to dinner that night, forever preserved. The white rose Sara had died holding, placed to mark her favorite Bible verse. With tear-blurred vision, he couldn't read it. He knew it by heart. Isaiah 41:10.

*"Fear thou not; for I am with thee: be not dismayed; for I am thy God: I will*

*strengthen thee; yea, I will help thee; yea, I will uphold thee with the right hand of my righteousness."*

He longed for peace beyond all understanding, but it didn't come. He cupped the white rose in the palm of his hand, careful not to damage the dry crispness.

How he'd delighted in her joy at each arrangement. Other women would probably take the roses for granted. But on each occasion, Sara's pale blue eyes sparkled; she'd trace his jaw with her fingers, and reward him with a kiss.

Pressing his fingertips to his lips, desperate to recall the feel of her that last day, his chest tightened.

He slammed his fist into the dash.

A car door shut beside him. His deacon, Tom Deavers, waved, sympathy shining, then headed in Grayson's direction.

Grayson waved back with a forced smile. He was sick of sympathy. He didn't want sympathy. He wanted his wife. He wanted to smash his fist into the face of Wade Fenwick, who'd stolen Sara from him. Too spineless to come forward. Until now. *Just when I've begun to heal.*

Gripping the steering wheel, white knuckled, he forced himself to step out of the vehicle. "I was hoping you'd still be on duty. Can I see Wade Fenwick?"

"Visiting hours ended at eight o'clock." Tom looked suspicious.

"I'm not here to cause any trouble."

Tom's eyes narrowed. "Follow me."

Inside, they took the stairs, then corridor after corridor, to ICU. Grayson had sat with numerous families in this very waiting area.

"You can go in, for a few minutes."

"Thank you."

Grayson hurried down the hall.

No family, no medical personnel. Wade was alone with a machine helping him breathe. His chest inflated and deflated, with a jerky, mechanical *whoosh*. The overwhelming desire to ram his fist into the helpless man's swollen face gripped Grayson. Visions of movies where the bad guy unplugged the ventilator played in his imagination. His fingers flexed as he surveyed all the tubes and wires.

Sobbing, Grayson sank to his knees. "Dear Lord, he killed Sara. He ruined my life. He ruined my son's life. Oh God, help me. Forgive me. Help me to forgive."

# *Chapter 7*

Just as Adrea finished dressing the next morning, she heard a knock and hurried to answer.

Grace leaned against the door frame, tears flowing down her cheeks. "Oh honey, I'm so sorry." Adrea hugged her and drew her inside.

"I'll get you something to drink," Mark said.

Grace pulled away from Adrea and flew into his arms.

Adrea quietly exited the apartment.

With a few moments to spare, she drove by the church. As usual, Grayson's car was there. The upheaval in his life didn't change his calling.

She made her way to the office and found him, slumped over his desk, facedown. For a moment, she thought he was asleep, but he raised up.

"I thought I heard someone. Sit. What can I do for you?"

With his world blown apart, still he wanted to help others.

"Can't stay long." She claimed the chair across from him. "I'm on my way to the shop. Listen, I know you've got a lot going on and I can't imagine how you're holding it together."

"I'll be fine."

"You've been dealt quite a blow. But Helen needs you. Last night, she was worrying about being able to face you. She mentioned changing churches or maybe moving to her sister's."

Grayson looked heavenward. "I got here at five o'clock this morning and have been praying for strength to go over there. I think I've steeled myself."

"You don't have to be strong for her. Maybe the two of you need to cry together."

He nodded.

—⁂—

Other than telling Dayne that Sara was dead and going to the funeral, this was the hardest thing Grayson had ever done. Helen was probably blaming herself and he wanted to be strong for her, but right now, he didn't have a strong bone in his body.

In Helen's drive, he sat for a long time. The flower beds and grass weren't perfect as they'd once been. Green vines grew wild, jumping their borders. Dead plants jutted among the blooming bushes. Maybe someone from the youth group could help with her yard.

The kitchen light flicked on. With a quick prayer, he got out and walked to the door. Before he could knock, she answered. He'd never seen such anguish in another person's eyes. The sobs started and her whole body shook. Afraid she might collapse; he picked her up and carried her inside.

"I've got you, and God has both of us. His strength will get us through this. Together."

"I can't believe this is happening. Wade caused Sara's death." A wail escaped and she pressed a trembling fist to her mouth.

He deposited her on the couch and settled beside her.

"Our precious Sara killed by a drunk driver. And not just any drunk driver. My son."

Grayson didn't know how to respond. He took her shaking hand in his. "Dear God, get us through this."

An hour later, he drove Helen and June to the hospital. Upon their arrival, Mark and Grace sat in the waiting room. As the afternoon lengthened, various members of the congregation trickled in. The deacons and Sylvie Kroft, of course.

It almost felt like Sara had died all over again. People patted his shoulder, offering comforting whispers.

Helen sat ramrod straight, not a crinkle in her composure. How did she do it?

"Mrs. Fenwick." The doctor's face was grim. "I need to speak with you."

Grayson didn't think his legs would support him, but he managed to stand and help Helen to her feet. They followed the doctor down the hallway.

—∞—

Saturday afternoon, Adrea exited the hospital with Helen's hand tucked in her elbow. Grayson, made of steel, carried her suitcase to the car.

Wade would move into a regular room in a few days, though he would never talk, walk, or function on his own. Even in a wheelchair, someone else would have to prop him there.

Once outside in the bright sunshine, Helen paused at the bench by the fountain.

The trickling water soothed Adrea's frayed nerves. "Would you like to sit down?"

"It's been a week since I've seen the sun." Helen gingerly perched on the bench. "I feel guilty. Wade will never enjoy the sun again."

"You have to go on."

"I know." Helen's watery blue eyes brimmed. "I've done it before. With my husband and my youngest sister. For some reason, I seem destined to end up alone."

Adrea sat and put her arm around Helen's slim shoulders. "You're not alone. You've got Jesus and a church full of people who love you."

"Shell's only been to see Wade once."

Yesterday, Adrea had seen the blond girl at the hospital and had banished the memories that threatened to stir. "She's hurting, too."

Helen's piercing blue eyes searched Adrea's soul.

The moment of reckoning. She'd dreaded it for days.

"He was drinking on the night of the accident because of me."

Helen clasped her hand. "No. We had him so late in life, and I spoiled him so badly, he never learned to handle disappointment. Wade was drinking because that's what he did."

"But he'd been sober for two years. He started again because of our breakup."

"He gave you ample reason to call off the wedding. I love that boy, but I know exactly what he put you through and you didn't deserve any of it."

"Neither did you."

The older woman scanned the azure horizon. "He told me he was going to turn himself in." A sob caught in her throat. "Instead—this."

"I'm so sorry. I should have seen it coming."

"You tried to help him. He should have come forward when it happened."

Instead, he'd waited until everyone had made tentative steps to get on with their lives. Then he'd blown all efforts apart. Grayson knew the identity of the hit-and-run driver, and the knowledge forced him to relive Sara's death all over again. Poor Helen. Even in a vegetative state, Wade was breaking his mother's heart.

Adrea's hands clenched. She could almost hate him, until she thought of his torment when he'd confessed.

"After he told me about what happened, I asked if he wanted to pray. He said, 'Me and Jesus got it all worked out.'"

Helen closed her eyes. A trembling smile tilted the corners of her mouth. "Thank you for being there for him."

—⁓—

Monday morning, Adrea stashed her purse under the counter in the workroom.

"There's some redhead tormenting the salesclerks." Rachel propped both hands on her hips. "Said she knows you from church."

"Sylvie Kroft?" *Surely not. She's never bothered to darken our door before.*

"That's her." Rachel snapped her fingers. "I better go see if I can hurry her along before they lose all patience."

Adrea checked the computer for standing orders.

June 2nd, what should have been Sara's twenty-seventh birthday. Had it only been a few months since Wade had dropped the Valentine's Day roses? Now, he lay in a hospital bed. Sara's killer. Wade would never hold another beer can, never drive a car, and never hurt anyone else. She knew the news comforted Grayson, while he comforted Wade's distraught mother.

Nothing made sense. She felt like she was watching some surreal movie. The man she'd almost married, a shell of himself, all he'd ever be.

She began working with the white flowers, the rose of innocence and reverence, and shed a few tears as she always did. As the arrangement took shape, she thought of Grayson, as usual, and his motherless son. No child should have to take roses to his mother at the cemetery.

Adding more caspia, she turned the arrangement slowly around, looking for any other holes to fill. Would Grayson even remember the roses? Of course he would. He'd comfort Helen, take care of Dayne, and stroll in later. As if nothing were wrong, he'd personally sign the card and deliver the roses to the cemetery. Where Sara shouldn't be.

The showroom door opened, interrupting her thoughts.

"I'm afraid the roses aren't quite ready, Pastor Grayson." Rachel backed into the workroom. "We weren't expecting you so early."

"Could you keep an eye on Dayne, for just a few minutes?" Grayson side-stepped her.

"Sure." Rachel made a hasty retreat. "I'll just be out front."

Grayson waited until the door shut to speak. "You look like you've been crying."

"The arrangement always makes me sad."

"You're crying for Sara?"

"And for you and Dayne. Since the accident, the roses always make me a bit somber. Even more so, now that I know the men she left behind."

"You cried before you knew us?"

"Many times. It's just so heartbreaking. I'd heard Helen speak of you so often. You had the perfect marriage and family. Then it all got ripped away. It's not fair. . . ."

No need to tell him. Grayson knew firsthand just how heartbreaking and unfair his situation.

"No, it isn't. I appreciate your compassion."

Adrea added a whisper of baby's breath to the spray. "They're finished. I'll help you carry them to the car. Are you parked out front?" She picked up the white roses.

Grayson took the flowers but set them back on the counter. "I'm sorry I make you sad."

"Don't worry about me. Are you parked out front?"

"I'm afraid I can't do that."

"What?"

"Not worry about you."

His words robbed her of the ability to speak. Then she realized, it was the pastor's job to worry about his flock.

The showroom door opened to reveal Sylvie. "Fancy running into you here, Pastor. One of the salesclerks said you were here, just when I need a big strong man to carry my fern to the car. You wouldn't happen to have another, would you?" Sylvie's expression filled with pity. "Adrea dear, are you all right?"

"I'm fine. There should be two others out front. Unless they sold this morning. I can order more." *What's she up to?*

"It must be such a shock." Sylvie planted herself between Grayson and the door. "I mean, a mere two years ago, you were all set to marry Wade."

A sick feeling boiled in Adrea's stomach. Her mouth went dry.

Grayson shot her a concerned look.

"Thank goodness you didn't marry him." Sylvie patted Adrea's arm, as if she genuinely felt sorry for the younger woman's plight. "I heard he fathered an illegitimate baby, but the mother took off. So I guess Helen will never see her grandchild."

Adrea cleared her throat. "Actually, the baby died."

"I hadn't heard that." Sylvie frowned, disappointment evident.

*Less to gossip about.*

"Sylvie." Grayson used a warning tone.

"It's such a shame he reacted so badly to the breakup. Why, wasn't Valentine's Day supposed to be the wedding day?"

All color drained from Grayson's face. Adrea had expected the reaction, only it should have been after *she* told him.

"Oh my, you don't suppose our dear Sara got caught in the crossfire?" Sylvie gasped and drew a palm to her mouth.

"I'll escort you out, Sylvie." Grayson took her by the elbow.

She flashed a victorious smile at Adrea.

—⁓—

An hour later, Grayson parked at the cemetery.

Adrea's car was already there.

It didn't surprise him.

With each step, his shoes sank into the soft earth. He trekked the familiar path to Sara's grave. From a distance, he could see Adrea kneeling, both hands covering her face.

At his approaching footsteps, she mopped the tears.

Noodle legs threatened to give way. Thankful for the shade of a sycamore tree, he sank to the white iron bench he'd bought last spring. "Tell me all of it."

"What's the point?" She shrugged.

"I need to hear it from you. I suspected you were once engaged to him."

Her eyes widened. "How?"

"Before Wade went into Mission 3:16, he said something that sounded like more than you simply working for his mother. I knew he was engaged a few years back and that it fell apart, so with the incident at the shop, I put it all together."

She sighed, as if the weight of the Ozark Mountains lay heavy on her shoulders. "When I first started working at the florist, Wade was in Little Rock, drinking a lot and Helen constantly worried about him. By the time we met, he'd been in several rehabs, joined AA, and had been sober for two years."

A robin burst into joyous song, oblivious to the somber mood.

"So she introduced you, a good Christian girl, to straighten him out."

Adrea nodded. "She invited me to tea at her house, and he happened to be there. Then, she tormented him until he came to a cookout at my church."

"And?"

"Wade rededicated his life to Christ. He was like a different person then. Very charming. We had a lot in common and wanted the same things."

"You loved him?"

"Yes." Her tears came again. "We had such plans. Building a house, starting a family, all the things I've longed for."

"Why the breakup?"

Adrea looked off in the distance, her eyes unfocused. "He wasn't convicted on some things. After our engagement, he. . ."

"What?"

"He wanted to be. . .intimate, before the wedding." A blush washed over her sensitive skin.

"I see." His stomach turned.

"But we didn't. I tried to show him the verses in the Bible about such things, but it's like he didn't want to see it."

"So, that's why you broke up with him?" Relief bubbled through him. "Because he pressured you?"

Adrea plucked a piece of lush grass and twirled it between her fingers. "Two weeks before the wedding, Wade was upset because I couldn't have dinner with him on his birthday. I had two weddings and a funeral, but I managed to finish up earlier than expected and decided to go to his apartment to surprise him."

"And?" Grayson prompted.

"Um. . .he wasn't alone." She blushed again.

"I see."

"Of course, he said she meant nothing to him."

"You must have been very hurt."

She nodded. "I called off the wedding and Wade started drinking, on what should have been our wedding day. Valentine's Day."

He shuddered. "Adrea, it wasn't your fault. The only one at fault was Wade. You didn't put the bottle in his hand."

"I might as well have. If I'd married him, Sara would be alive and Wade would be fine."

He touched her forearm and offered her his hand.

She settled on the bench beside him. "You don't understand. He ran the red light because he was drunk. Because *I* broke up with him. That's why Sara died."

Gently, he placed both hands on her shoulders.

Shocked at his touch, her eyes met his.

"Let's get one thing straight. You had no part in Sara's death or Wade's condition."

She didn't respond.

"You were right in breaking off the engagement. He cheated on you. And besides that, he's the one who made the decision to get drunk and then get behind the wheel."

He caught a tear as it trickled down her cheek. "What started Wade drinking this last time? Do you know?"

"He confessed to his pregnant fiancée about Sara. She aborted his baby."

Grayson's gut clenched. How could anyone do such a thing? *Concentrate on helping Adrea.* "So, it was her fault he started drinking again."

"Of course not."

"Why not? If the accident is your fault, then this other girl must be responsible for this binge. If he'd killed anyone this time, it would've been her fault. We might as well blame her for his attempted suicide, too."

Adrea shook her head. "Even though I don't condone what she did, you can't blame Shell for any of this. I mean, she's never been my favorite person, but Wade's bad choices aren't her fault."

"Then I'm at fault for his suicide. Meeting me pushed him over the edge."

"No, you can't think that."

"Why? If the accident was your fault?"

She grasped his meaning and her eyes lit with hope.

Point made, he let go of her. "I'm sorry he caused you so much heartache. But no more guilt about this; you're not to blame."

"I was with him, just before he shot himself." She swallowed hard. "After you and Mark left, he ran out of the church and took Helen's car. She asked me to follow him, so I did. He told me about the accident and his confession, then promised to turn himself in. When I was leaving, I heard the shot. I found him."

"I heard." He cupped her face in his hands. "I'm so sorry."

"I shouldn't have left him alone. I should have sensed his plans."

"Stop taking the blame for things he did that you couldn't have stopped if you'd tried."

She nodded.

His hands dropped away from her.

"I should have told you. I'm sorry you had to hear it from Sylvie."

"Your past is really none of my business." He wanted it to be, along with her future, but he couldn't take the risk.

She swallowed hard. "I hope Sylvie won't tell Helen about the baby. Wade planned to marry Shell, then tell her."

"I'll have a talk with Sylvie. We need to have a discussion anyway."

She stood. "I need to get back to the shop."

"I'll walk you to your car."

"I'm fine. Really." She hurried away.

He wanted to follow, but his feet wouldn't obey. He dug a handkerchief from his pocket and wiped the dust off Sara's headstone, until the marble shone like polished glass.

—∞—

On Sunday, with Mark handling the sermons, Grayson sat beside Helen, with Adrea seated on the other side of her. His attentiveness to Wade's grieving mother increased Adrea's respect for him.

A hush hung over the congregation. Not everyone knew of Wade's confession, but everyone seemed to feel the tension. After the altar call and closing prayer, Mark turned the service over to Grayson.

"I have an announcement to make." He took a deep breath. "As many of you know, Sara's case has been solved."

Audible gasps moved across the congregation and then shushed whispering.

"An individual came forward to claim responsibility. Police checked out his story, and it will hit the papers tomorrow. Helen and I want you to hear it from me." Grayson swallowed. "Wade Fenwick was responsible for the accident."

More gasps and whispers.

Adrea squeezed Helen's hand.

"Helen wanted to leave the church, but I hope I've changed her mind." He rested his hand on the older woman's shoulder. "It's been rough, but we're supporting one another and relying on God to get through this. We both need everyone's love and prayers and we don't need any gossip."

Maybe it was Adrea's imagination, but Grayson's eyes seemed to pause on Sylvie Kroft for a moment. The redhead looked down.

One of the deacons came to Helen and hugged her. Other members followed suit.

Tears blurred Adrea's vision at the show of Christian love for a wounded member of the body of Christ.

—∞—

July 4th, one of the biggest days for the shop. Red, white, and blue carnations perfumed the air. As she completed the fifteenth patriotic arrangement, the showroom door opened.

"Adrea?"

She jumped at the sound of Grayson's voice. Heart thumping, she turned to see him standing behind her. "Did I forget an order?"

"No." Grayson buried his nose in a lush, lacy red blossom. "But these are lovely, as usual."

"It's a very busy day." Adrea turned away, hoping he'd take the hint.

"I wanted to talk to you."

"Oh," she squeaked.

"Adrea, let me be honest with you." He paused a moment, as if gathering courage. "Since the day we met, I've spent an inordinate amount of time thinking about you. As we spend more time together, getting to know each other, I think about you even more."

"Oh," she echoed herself, again unable to form more than the single intelligible word.

"I haven't thought of anyone other than Sara for years, but recently a raven-haired beauty, with the darkest blue eyes I've ever seen, occupies my thoughts."

"I'm sorry." Stupid, but the only thing she could think of to say.

"Don't be. I thought when we were first getting to know one another that you might be interested in me as more than a pastor. But then you began trying to avoid me until Helen's injury and Wade's confession."

*I tried, but you always managed to show up.* Her brain caught up with him and the meaning of his words sank in.

"I avoid you, because thinking of you as only my pastor is difficult."

"Good, we're on the same page." The tension eased from his face. "It's strange. The confession opened up wounds, but it also gave me closure. With Sara's killer off the streets, I feel I can move on. You said it yourself; Sara would want me to be happy. Taking you out to dinner tonight would make me very happy."

"Okay." Her voice quivered. "But can we make it another night?"

"You have plans?" Disappointment resonated in his tone.

"No, not at all. It's just a really busy day here. I'll probably have to work late."

"I'll wait."

And she knew he would. Her heart fluttered.

"This may sound crazy." He grinned. "But I feel the need to be at ease. Some fancy place would probably make me nervous. How about Colton's Steakhouse over in Searcy?"

She grinned. "Sounds great. But what about Dayne?"

"Grace and Mark are taking him to a fireworks display at Harding University. I'll pick you up at seven o'clock? Is that late enough?"

"Perfect." *In every way.*

Grayson brought the back of her hand to his lips. "See you tonight."

Her breath hitched and shivers danced over her skin.

Barely able to function, she heard the showroom door open and close.

"What was that all about?" Rachel's words interrupted Adrea's thoughts.

"Nothing."

"Don't 'nothing' me." Rachel flashed a knowing smile. "It was definitely something."

"Why do you say that?"

"Because he's been coming here for over six years, but today, he asked to see you. And you're positively radiant." Rachel pointed a long-stemmed red mum at her. "Mum's the word. I'll even think of something to tell the sales-clerks. They're busy with other customers, but curious. Now, spill."

Her face warmed. "As a matter of fact, we're going out to dinner tonight." Adrea stuck a leftover blue carnation behind her ear.

"Well, glory be." Rachel clapped her hands.

"What should I wear when going on a date with my pastor?"

"Hmm. Been there, done that. I can provide excellent advice."

The humid weather dictated Adrea's attire. Wearing jeans and a purple top, she was glad to see that Grayson had dressed equally casual in an emerald button-down shirt—the exact color of his eyes—and khakis. Grayson Sterling had her full attention.

Peanut shells crunched beneath the server's feet as she brought their meal. Rawhide curtains graced the windows, with stuffed deer heads and razorback hogs mounted on the walls.

Grayson asked the blessing, then cut into his steak.

"Tell me how you and Sara met."

He paused to refold his napkin. "You really want to know?"

"If you don't mind talking about it."

"I can't remember my life before Sara." Grayson cleared his throat. "We lived in the same neighborhood. She and Grace were friends from the time they were toddlers, and we all went to the same Searcy school from kindergar-ten to graduation. Sara was just my sister's friend, until we all turned sixteen. Out of the blue, I realized she didn't seem like a little girl anymore."

"So the two of you shared a lifetime together, which made losing her doubly hard."

He touched her hand. "You're incredible. Most women would be uncom-fortable talking about my wife on a first date."

His simple touch turned her pulse erratic. "Sara will always be a part of you. You loved her and still do. I understand that and it doesn't bother me. So, did you always know you'd be a pastor?" She took a bite of her loaded chicken. *Mmm. Bacon, cheese, and mushrooms.*

"God called me to preach during my senior year. Sara went off to college and I enrolled at seminary." He paused to wash down the steak with sweet tea. "We married about a year later. She never got her teaching degree. When she got pregnant with Dayne, she quit, which was exactly what her parents feared. We planned for her to go back to school eventually and finish, but she never got that chance."

"She was happy without it."

Grayson looked at her, his eyes full of questions.

"According to Helen, and I could tell by the picture of her. Contentment radiated from her."

"Where did you see a picture?"

"In the newspaper."

"Oh, I'd forgotten." He traced the trickles of condensation on his glass with a fingertip. "Those days are still a fog for me."

"Over the years, I prayed for you and Dayne. I actually visited her grave once."

"You did?"

"Just the one time, a few days after we met. I couldn't get Sara off my mind. Then, I ran into you and Dayne in the park. Afterward, I ended up at the cemetery."

"Wow." His voice was barely a whisper.

"Sara's parents didn't hold it against you that she didn't finish college, did they?"

"Eventually, they realized Sara was happy as a wife and mother. We all thought she'd have plenty of time for college later." He looked past Adrea, lost in thought for a moment. "I'm sorry."

"For what?"

"This is our first date. I didn't mean to talk about Sara tonight."

Adrea placed her hand over Grayson's and her heart raced again. "Don't apologize. I asked."

"Most women wouldn't be so gracious. I knew you were special the first time we met. I can't tell you how relieved I was to learn that Mark was your brother and not your husband."

"You had all kinds of misconceptions, didn't you?" As an excuse to move her hand and calm her heart rate, Adrea took a long drink of iced tea. "Mark and I were the last ones in the nest, after Rachel married, so we grew especially close. Once I graduated from high school, we got the apartment together. For two years, we relied on one another."

"Then Mark left for seminary in Memphis. Must have been hard on you."

"Even though he came home most weekends, it was a lonely four years. What about your parents?"

"Dad pastors at Thorndike here in Searcy." Grayson pushed his salad plate away. "So, did you always want to be a florist?"

"Actually, I wanted to be a vet, but I knew seeing hurt animals would tear me apart, so I settled for my second love of flowers."

"And your favorite is?"

"Yellow roses."

Something near the door caught Grayson's attention. "Great."

# Chapter 8

A drea looked up to see Sylvie Kroft and two new ladies from church. Shaking her head, Sylvie drew her new friends into a huddle.

"I guess my little project didn't work." Grayson shook his head.

"What project?"

"I asked Sylvie to print up two hundred Church Covenant cards, including the part about abstaining from backbiting."

Adrea pushed her plate away. "I'd really like to go."

"Don't let her ruin our evening," Grayson said.

"I'm not. I'm stuffed and you're finished. I thought we might catch up with Dayne and watch the fireworks display."

"He'd love that." He pulled out his wallet and laid several bills on the table.

Adrea waited while he paid; then they stepped out into the humid evening. Again, Grayson took her hand in his and drew it to his mouth. As his lips brushed her skin, fireworks lit the sky. Just like the ones bursting in her heart.

—⁓—

It was a funeral day. But Mrs. Haynes knew the Lord, her children were grown and settled, and she'd longed to meet her deceased husband in glory. That knowledge helped Adrea.

With the rush of Independence Day orders over, Rachel had time to hang out in the workroom. "So did he kiss you?"

"On the hand."

"That's all?"

"It was very sweet."

"Dating a preacher is kind of weird. I mean, they're still men, you know."

Adrea relived the tingling sensation that had moved up her arm at the soft caress of his lips. "He's definitely a man. I'll admit, I looked forward to more than a kiss on the hand."

"So, you just ate and talked?"

"Afterward, we went to watch the fireworks."

"Ooh, romantic."

"We met Dayne, Mark, and Grace there. Besides, half the town showed up."

"Leave it to my sister to squelch the romance." Rachel rolled her eyes.

"It was nice, and Dayne loved it."

Rachel checked her watch. "Time to open. I'd better go unlock the door."

While working on the casket spray, Adrea hummed "Blessed Assurance." A few minutes later, Rachel returned, holding a long white box tied with yellow ribbon.

"What's that?"

"The competition sent you flowers."

As Adrea took the box, she noticed that it came from Crissy's, a florist in Searcy. Anticipating the contents, she removed the ribbon and gasped at the dozen yellow roses inside. Catching her breath, she read the card:

> *Sorry, I had to use the competition. Your favorite flower seems to imply I'm interested in only friendship. The complete opposite is true.*

Adrea smiled, but a niggling doubt tumbled in her stomach. "Do you think it's too soon?"

"That's a hard question." Rachel added a few more red carnations to a casket spray. "Different people heal at different rates. Old Mr. Adams married six months after his wife died and nobody thought a thing of it."

Adrea finished the final spray for Mrs. Haynes by weaving a red ribbon through the carnations and lilies. "It's been almost two and a half years since Sara died."

"Just don't let what other people think determine your life for you." Rachel filled a tall crystal vase with water and put the yellow roses in it. "Let God determine if this thing with you and Grayson is right. As much as you two have been through, you both deserve happiness. And if you can take the tatters Wade left in his wake and mend it together, I say go for it."

"I just wonder sometimes if Grayson is really ready to move on. I mean emotionally."

"Apparently, he thinks he is. Just follow his lead."

—◊◊◊—

Over the next few weeks, most of the new couple's dates included Dayne and sometimes they borrowed Haylee. They enjoyed family gatherings at the apartment, barbecues and picnics, the stuff of Adrea's dreams. Though, the events took place on the apartment lot, instead of in a backyard.

At church, Adrea realized she and Grayson were a hot topic. A few bolder members of the flock congratulated the couple. At least some people approved.

For Adrea's birthday, August 15th, Grayson invited her to his house for dinner for the first time.

"You have to see my room, Adrea," Dayne piped up from the backseat.

"I can't wait. I used to play in these woods with Mark and the Williams' grandson." As they turned into the long, winding drive, Adrea's childhood memories swirled.

Grayson winced. "It's probably not the eyesore you remember. The

Williamses had gotten too old to take care of it. The men at the church have helped Grace and me transform it since we moved in."

"I've always loved this house. Even in disrepair, it always had such charm."

"Grace wanted to have you and Mark over long before now, but she's so busy with her business."

A freshly painted white fence flanked each side of the road for about a hundred yards; then the dense forest faded into a rounded clearing on one side. The stream, with a footbridge and ornate, white iron furniture nearby, gave her imagination flight. A lovely spot for a flower garden.

The second clearing revealed the two-story house. Huge columns pillared the porch, which spanned the entire length. It looked like an old-South plantation. A picket fence enclosed the front and back yards. Perfect. For kids, cats, and dogs.

"Can I have a complete tour? I've always wanted to see the entire house."

"Sure."

A dog's bark echoed from the backyard.

"Can I go play with Cocoa?" Dayne called, an afterthought as he ran toward the side of the house.

"Don't get too dirty."

A spacious living room, large family room, cozy kitchen and dining area, four bedrooms, and two baths. The house boasted numerous windows, high ceilings, and walk-in closets.

Rendered speechless by the beauty of it all, Adrea finally found her voice. "It's the most beautiful house I've ever seen."

"You really like it, don't you? Grace hates it and Sara would've, too." He stared out the kitchen window. "It felt odd buying something she'd hate with her life insurance money, but Dayne loves it and we needed a new start, without all the memories."

"I've always wanted to fix up an old place. Just think of the history and lives lived here." She hugged herself.

"It's really too big for us, but I fell in love with it. I've always loved big, old houses. It took a lot of work, but it's been worth it. We have five acres with a walking trail around the property."

She looked out the sliding glass doors to see a deck across the back. Cocoa danced along a fenced enclosure as Dayne ran toward the house.

A garden, plenty of room for lots of pets, and a real backyard. Heat crept up her neck. *What am I thinking? We've only been dating a month.*

Dayne burst through the back door and grabbed Adrea's hand. "Come see." The boy propelled her down the hall.

His red and blue room housed every airplane imaginable, from the wallpaper and ceiling fan to his bedspread and curtains. Every piece of furniture and fabric resonated BOY. The small perfume bottle he retrieved from his chest of drawers went against everything else in the room.

"This was my mommy's." He held it up for Adrea to sniff. "Daddy lets me keep it so I can smell it when I miss her."

Adrea's eyes burned. The soft, powdery fragrance of flowers captured the essence of what she knew of Sara.

"It smells really pretty." She hugged him and blinked away the moisture. "I'm glad you have it to help you remember her."

Dayne inhaled deeply. "When I smell this, I can almost 'member sitting in her lap."

Unwilling to sadden the boy further, Adrea's tears fell as she turned away. "I really like your room."

—⁓—

"Don't worry. They'll love you." Grayson escorted Adrea up the sidewalk toward a white two-story house in Searcy.

*Meeting his parents? Don't read too much into it.*

His mother, Emma, met them at the door. "Come in. Come in." Her green eyes twinkled, just like her son's. Graham was a silver-haired version of Grayson.

They welcomed her into their large, inviting, older home. Dinner conversation consisted of theological studies. Just like spending time with Mark and Grayson. She willed her heart to slow.

After the meal, Emma gave Adrea a tour of her lovely garden. A lavender clematis vine snaked up a white lattice archway at the entrance of a floral wonderland. A natural rock border lined the flower beds, packed deep with cedar chips. Humongous hibiscus in pale pink and lilac mingled with purple and fuchsia petunias. The whir of hummingbird wings and buzz of honeybees formed an intense rivalry over various blossoms.

"I'm so happy Grayson is finally seeing someone." Emma held both of Adrea's hands in her own as the two women faced each other. "You don't know how we've worried about that boy.

"After Sara's death, at times we wondered if he'd ever manage to keep on living. We never thought he was suicidal," Emma clarified. "Nothing like that, but he just lost his spark. For the last two years, he's only gone through the motions of life, for Dayne's sake. Then that drunk coming forward opened the tragedy all up again."

Adrea swallowed hard. "I guess Grayson told you about my connection to that drunk."

"The way I see it, you were another broken spirit left in the wake of Wade Fenwick." Emma hugged her. "For the last several months, Grayson has had the spring back in his step. Thank you for putting it there."

"Dayne and Grayson have been a blessing to me, too."

"God has brought healing to your and Grayson's souls by bringing you together. God is smiling on me." Emma winked. "First, he brings us Mark for Grace, and now, you for Grayson and Dayne."

"Oh, I don't know. We've only been seeing—"

Grace opened the patio door.

A green hummingbird with a splash of red across its throat flitted away.

"We need you two. Hurry up." Grace motioned them inside.

The three women hurried to the living room where they found the men.

"We have something to celebrate." Mark looked as if he might burst.

Adrea had a sneaking suspicion at the cause of her brother's happiness.

"Grace has agreed to marry me!"

"Whoo-hoo!" Emma threw her arms around her daughter.

"I'm so happy for you!" Adrea hugged her brother. "Have you told Mom and Dad? Mom will be beside herself."

"We're going there in a few minutes," Grace said.

Grayson hugged Grace. "Finally, you're getting a life of your own. That's some surprise."

"I feel guilty for abandoning you and Dayne. We're talking about several months away, though, maybe New Year's Day. And I can still watch Dayne after school and in the summers. I just won't live in that old relic with you anymore."

"Don't think of anything other than your happiness. Dayne and I will be just fine. We'll miss you, but if you want to get married next weekend, do it. Don't worry about us." He lowered his voice. "It's possible the Sterling household will change before long anyway."

Adrea gasped.

Grace, the only one who'd heard, stared openmouthedly, but left her inquiries unsaid.

He put his arm around Adrea's shoulders. "We better get Dayne home."

"Oh, but it's not even dark yet," Emma said.

"Yes, but he skipped his nap today, and he starts school next week."

—⁂—

A few weeks later, Grayson and Adrea took Dayne to see a kiddie movie at the Rialto. Afterward, on the way to Romance, Grayson stopped at the coffee shop on the outskirts of Searcy. They entered the dimly lit café, and Adrea tried to adjust her eyes.

"Let's go somewhere else," Grayson whispered.

Confused, Adrea turned back toward the door.

As Grayson hurried them outside, she caught a glimpse of a middle-aged couple adding cream and sugar to their drinks. Somehow, they looked familiar to her, but she couldn't put her finger on how she might know them. It hit her as Grayson drove away.

"Where are we going, Daddy?"

"You ate such a good supper, let's go to the ice-cream shop instead."

The child didn't argue with that idea.

After Yarnell's Death-By-Chocolate ice cream, they arrived back at

Adrea's apartment. Dayne went to the bathroom to wash his sticky hands.

"That was them, wasn't it?"

"Who?" Grayson's attempt to sound casual miserably failed.

"Sara's parents."

"How did you know?"

"I've seen their picture at your house and besides, she's an older version of Sara. They don't know about me, do they?"

"I'm sorry, Adrea." He hung his head.

"Don't be."

"I've ruined our evening."

"No you haven't."

"I just can't find the words to tell them. But I will. Soon." He clasped her open palm to his lips. "I promise."

—⁓—

September 21st dawned a lovely day, Dayne's sixth birthday, his third without his mother.

Outside, birds chattered as if it were still spring. The showroom door opened and Grayson arrived just as Adrea finished the roses. "Beautiful as usual. This ritual doesn't bother you now that we're dating, does it?"

"Of course not. You know I'm okay with Sara's memory. Where's Dayne?"

"He's entertaining Rachel and the salesclerks. Would you like to come with us to the cemetery today?"

She opened her mouth, but no words came. Her heart hammered.

"Dayne and I discussed it already, and he said it was all right with him."

"Oh Grayson, I couldn't possibly do that."

"Why not? We'd both like for you to come."

"I'd feel like such an intruder."

"You wouldn't be." He tipped her chin up with his fingers until she looked at him. "You've been there with me before, on Sara's birthday."

"Yes, but it was an accident and I felt terribly awkward."

The showroom door opened and Dayne entered.

"Dayne, I told you to wait out front."

"I know, but I wanted to ask Adrea. Are you going with us?"

How could she turn him down?

"You betcha. Happy sixth birthday, Dayne."

"Thanks."

"Just let me tell Rachel I'm leaving."

Dayne wriggled his little hand into hers.

Her heart warmed.

"I already told her." He tugged her toward the door.

*Along with the curious salesclerks.* "Let's go out the back." To avoid watchful eyes.

Soon, they reached their destination. The threesome held hands as Dayne carried the white roses for his mother. A blue jay squawked his disagreement with their presence. A squirrel grasped a hickory nut with both paws and chattered at them, then scampered up a tree.

They made the silent trek through the cemetery, sidestepping occasionally to avoid walking on graves.

In the few months they'd dated, her relationship with Grayson had deepened considerably. She knew for certain that she loved him, completely and irrevocably.

Grayson seemed to feel the same way.

She knew down to her toes, he was the one. No matter what anyone else thought, there was just something right about her and Grayson.

Though she'd loved Wade, she'd never had that right feeling with him.

"We don't talk to her at the cemetery," Grayson explained as they drew close to Sara's grave. "She's not here. We simply place the flowers to honor and remember her."

Dayne solemnly placed the flowers and polished the headstone while his father tidied up around the grave.

Adrea stood off to the side, still feeling a bit awkward, careful not to tread on Sara's memory.

—⁂—

Since it was Saturday, the entire Sterling family, along with Adrea, Mark, and Haylee, gathered for lunch at Dexter's for Dayne's celebration. Sara's parents didn't show up, and Adrea knew it was because Grayson didn't invite them. Their absence bothered her, though she covered for Dayne's sake.

That night at Grayson's home, Adrea stood in the entryway, staring at the table lined with Sara's image. Though Sara's face had embedded itself in her memory, she inspected the Sterling family portrait taken shortly before disaster struck. They looked so happy. The senseless tragedy still saddened her. Even though Adrea would have no place in Grayson's life if Sara were alive.

Sara had been a lovely woman. Her short blond hair, powder-blue eyes, and petite frame perfectly contrasted her husband's darker coloring. The two had been an attractive pair.

Strong arms came around Adrea's waist from behind. Though Grayson was careful not to hold her too closely, her pulse raced.

"I can put these away if they bother you."

"Don't you dare. They're lovely pictures of a happier time." She carefully set the gilded frame among the others on the marbleized tabletop.

"I'm quite happy right now. Thanks to you." He nuzzled Adrea's neck, sending shivers over her.

"I am, too, but you better stop that."

"Thanks for going with us today. I hope it wasn't too much for you."

"It was an honor that you wanted me to go." She wisely pulled away as he continued to cause shudders. "But it bothers me that you left Sara's parents out of today. I could have stayed home, for Dayne's sake."

"We had a party at their house yesterday, after school. Dayne thought it was cool to have two celebrations." Grayson turned her to face him, his hands resting on her shoulders. "They're coming for dinner next week, and I plan to tell them about you."

"It doesn't matter to me whether they know or not. I just don't want them hearing it from someone else."

"The movie's ready," Dayne called from the next room.

Linking his fingers with hers, Grayson pulled her to the family room.

Adrea expected a cartoon, but Sara's face filled the screen. The camera panned out to show a birthday party for Dayne in a contemporary kitchen with stainless-steel appliances. Sara led several children and adults singing "Happy Birthday." The high soprano lilt of her voice riveted Adrea. Grayson apparently had filmed the video, as he wasn't in the happy scene.

Dayne sat in the floor, mesmerized by the image of his mother.

"That's the wrong tape, Dayne," Grayson said gently. "Turn it off and find the movie. We can watch that later if you want."

"We can watch it now if you like." Adrea's voice cracked. "We'll have plenty of time for the movie afterward."

"Are you sure?" Grayson mouthed silently.

She nodded and turned her attention back to the screen. The happy images of Sara trying to encourage a much younger Dayne to make a wish and blow out his candles made Adrea smile.

The scene changed to a backyard of a modern house. Children played numerous games with gleeful howls and giggles. She recognized most of the adults and children from church. While Grayson occasionally offered direction from behind the camera, Sara played referee. The tape ended with a shot of the entire group.

The happy faces of Sara's parents haunted Adrea. Tears trickled down her cheeks.

Quickly, she wiped them away. "Which birthday was that, Dayne?" The banner above the table, in the cake scene, proclaimed it his third. But maybe Dayne needed to voice his memories.

"I was three. It was my last birthday party with Mommy."

"From the tape, it looked like a good one."

"Why are you crying, Adrea?" Dayne asked. "You didn't know her, did you?"

So much for hiding tears. "No, but I've heard wonderful things about your mommy. It makes me sad that you and your daddy lost her."

Dayne ran to Adrea and hugged her. "It makes me sad, too, but I like 'membering her."

"I think that's enough sadness and remembering for one night. Let's watch the movie," Grayson suggested.

As Dayne pulled away and settled back on the floor, Grayson moved closer to Adrea on the couch and took her hand in his.

Halfway through the cartoon, she went to the kitchen to check on the slow-cooker.

A few minutes later, she looked up to see Grayson leaning in the door frame.

She shooed him away. "Go watch the movie with him. I can handle things here."

He stepped close and cupped her face in his hands. "I love you."

Tears welled in her eyes. "I love you, too."

Grayson kissed her soundly, then headed back to the family room.

Her heart skittered in her chest.

The doorbell chimed. With the cartoon on in the back of the house, Grayson probably wouldn't hear. Wooden spoon in one hand, she ran to open the front door.

A familiar couple stood on the porch.

Adrea pressed a hand to her heart. Its hammering echoed in her ears.

Obviously shocked, it took a moment before the woman spoke. "We're Dayne's grandparents, Joyce and Edward Owens. I didn't know Grayson had hired someone. I guess since Grace is getting married, she won't have as much time."

"Grandma! Grandpa!" Dayne zoomed into Joyce's waiting arms.

Adrea turned to see Grayson behind her.

"Joyce, Edward, what a surprise. It's great to see you."

His mother-in-law kissed him on the cheek. "You never told me you'd hired someone. I wouldn't mind bringing over a dish, and your mother would certainly do the same." Joyce turned back to Adrea. "Forgive me, dear. I don't mean to oust you out of a job."

Grayson cleared his throat. "I didn't hire anyone. Adrea is my—"

"Friend." Adrea's face warmed. "Everything is ready. Let me get the pork roast on the table and I'll be on my way. There's plenty for your guests."

"Dayne mentions you often." Edward's eyes narrowed. "You're his Sunday school teacher."

He knew.

"Dayne and I have become great friends." She hurried toward the kitchen.

"There's no need to rush off, Adrea. Why don't you join us?" Grayson followed her and lowered his voice. "Let me get it over with and tell them."

"There's no rush to do it tonight. Just have a nice dinner with them and I'll go." The haunting pain she'd seen in Joyce's eyes tore at her.

"I don't want you to go." Grayson kissed her.

Her heart did a somersault. "And I don't want to go, but they've been hurt enough."

"I planned to tell them next week. Now is as good a time as any."

"When it feels right, tell them." She set another place at the oak table. "Besides, my allergies are flaring up. I've sneezed several times and my throat is scratchy. I need some sinus medicine."

Before he could protest, she exited the kitchen and Dayne rushed into her arms. "You're not leaving, are you? I thought you were gonna eat with us."

"Not tonight, sweetie. We'll do it some other night. You enjoy visiting with your grandparents and I'll see you later."

———

After Adrea left, the atmosphere didn't improve. At least Dayne seemed oblivious to the tension as the former family ate in silence.

Grayson watched his son consume his last bite. "Dayne, go put your pajamas on."

"But Grandma and Grandpa are here."

"Go get ready for bed; then you can visit."

"Okay." With slumped shoulders, Dayne hugged both his grandparents and went to his room.

"I know we saw Dayne yesterday." Edward inspected the intricate pattern on the handle of his fork. "But it just didn't seem right not seeing him on his birthday. We should have called."

"Is it serious?" Joyce's voice trembled as she pushed her plate away.

"What?" *That's it. Play dumb. Procrastinate.*

"Adrea. She's more than a friend."

"I'm sorry I haven't told you." Grayson folded his napkin and placed it over his uneaten food. "I just didn't know how to bring it up."

"How serious?"

"Joyce, it's none of our business," Edward cautioned.

"What affects Dayne is our business. How serious?"

Edward started to say something, but Grayson interrupted. "She's right. You both have a right to know. Eventually, I'll probably ask Adrea to marry me."

Joyce's chin quivered. She stood and ran from the room.

With an apology to Grayson, Edward followed.

———

As soon as the Sunday morning service ended, Adrea hurried for the exit and hoped to slip past Grayson as he spoke with a young couple.

The man and woman left, just as Adrea reached him.

"I tried to call last night. I wish you hadn't left." Grayson's voice sounded strained.

"I went to bed early and Mark was out with Grace." She lowered her tone. "You didn't tell them, did you?"

"They figured it out."

"Were they upset?" Adrea looked around. Clusters of people dotted the sanctuary. Sylvie Kroft's stare bored a hole through her.

"Joyce was, but she'll get over it."

"We'll talk about it later. I have to go."

"I was hoping we could have lunch."

"Not today." She rushed out the exit and to her car.

Forty minutes later, she stood on the stone steps of the Owens' home. Three times, she'd gone to the polished oak door, then back to her car, then back to the door. She stood with her finger inches from the bell, but couldn't force herself to push it.

*I shouldn't have come.*

The door opened. She stood face-to-face with Edward Owens.

"Hello, I thought I saw someone out here."

"I found your address in the phone book. Is this a good time? If not, I understand completely." She turned toward her car.

"It's a perfect time."

"Are you sure?"

"Yes. We need to talk."

"Is your wife still upset?"

He nodded. "It's not your fault. Adrea? Is that right?"

"Yes."

"A unique name. I thought maybe Dayne was leaving the *n* off of Adrian."

"People often call me that."

"Dayne thinks the world of you."

"I adore him." Adrea pleated the folds of her skirt between thumb and forefinger. "Grayson has no idea I'm here. It seemed like a good idea for us to speak, but now it seems all wrong."

"Edward, is someone here?" Joyce called, just before she stepped into the open doorway. Dark circles under her eyes testified to a sleepless night. Her chin quivered.

"I'm sorry, I shouldn't have come." Adrea bolted.

"Grayson said the two of you are serious." Joyce barely got the words out.

Halfway to her car, Adrea stopped and turned to face Sara's parents. "This must be so hard for you. I thought it might help if you knew how much Grayson and Dayne mean to me. They"—Adrea searched for adequate words—"complete me. I love them both, very much."

"Please come inside." Edward beckoned to her. "We need to talk this out and we have rather a—" He gestured to the next house. "Rather an inquisitive neighbor, who should be home anytime."

"Are you sure?"

"Yes." Joyce nodded. "Please come in."

# Chapter 9

Inside the house, pictures of Sara greeted Adrea. While Grayson had one tabletop filled with his wife's image, photos of Sara occupied every empty space on the wall and all flat surfaces in her parents' home. Sara as a fat, frolicking baby. As a wobbly toddler. In grade school, high school, college. Sara as a bride and a new mother, and then with a toddler of her own. The pictures abruptly stopped, as her life had.

"Dayne talks about you constantly." Edward gestured toward the over-stuffed sofa.

She perched on the edge. "I love your grandson very much."

"Grayson said you'd been seeing one another a few months."

Adrea clasped her hands together, willing them to stop trembling. "They loved Sara long before they ever met me and they still love her. Grayson and I will never have what they had. If Sara were still here, Grayson would never have looked at me twice, and I'm okay with that."

Joyce's tears flowed freely now.

"I'm so sorry that this hurts you. Maybe it was wrong of me to come." Adrea started toward the door but stopped and turned back toward the Owenses.

"It's not fair. Sara should have lived to see Dayne grow up. She should have grown old with Grayson. I wish to the depths of my soul that she had, even though it would have changed the course of my life. But Grayson is ready to move on. He loves me, and Dayne loves me.

"Yet, it's not fair to you. You don't get to move on. Dayne and Grayson get someone new to love, but you can't get another daughter. And for that, I'm eternally sorry." Adrea hurried outside to her car.

With trembling fingers, she managed to start the engine.

She scanned the house next door. A head bobbed from the window and hid behind the swaying curtains. The red hair looked familiar. Sylvie Kroft.

—∞—

After evening services, Grayson caught up with her. "Where'd you run off to this morning? I tried to call several times."

"I went to see Sara's parents."

He cocked an eyebrow.

"I shouldn't have." Her hushed tones were for his ears only. "I rattled on and on. I should know by now that any bright idea that takes shape after midnight is a bad one."

"You tried to help and maybe you did. Maybe getting to know you will make them feel better." He grinned. "I honestly don't know how anyone could not like you."

Her heart warmed. "You're prejudiced."

"Definitely." He frowned. "You didn't mention Wade or your relationship with him?"

"No, I figured they could only handle one bombshell at a time."

A niggling unrest struck her in the gut, as if eyes bored into the back of her head. She turned to see Sylvie Kroft's contempt.

Adrea moved away from Grayson.

His gaze questioned her sudden need for escape.

Helen stopped her progress. "What a lovely arrangement. The two of you. It's perfect."

"I'm glad somebody thinks so." Adrea started toward the exit but remembered she'd left her lesson book in the children's classroom this morning.

She crossed the sanctuary and went downstairs to retrieve it. By the time she returned, the church had emptied. She heard voices coming from the lobby.

"I tell you," Sylvie hissed, "she's intent on replacing Sara, in every sense of the word."

Adrea peeked around the wall. The three women stood in a circle.

The kinder of the three, Mrs. Patton she'd learned, spoke first. "I don't think so. They've both been through a lot, and I think it's wonderful if they can find some happiness together. Adrea seems like a real dear."

"Don't let her fool you." Sylvie paused to scan the length of the lobby.

Adrea flattened herself on the other side of the wall.

"First she took the children's class Sara used to teach. Then she took Sara's flower ministry. Now, she's set her cap for Sara's husband and child. Why, she visited Sara's poor grieving parents just this afternoon and tried to worm her way in with them."

Eavesdropping. *What have I lowered myself to?* The white silk roses with sprigs of freesia and Casablanca lilies sat in front of the pulpit. She'd lovingly arranged them to honor Sara.

Clearing her throat, she straightened her spine and walked casually through the lobby to the exit. "Evening, ladies."

She hurried outside, hickory nuts rolling, crunching, and popping with each step.

"There you are." Grayson waited beside her car.

"I forgot my lesson book in my class." Sounded almost natural.

"You okay?" With a furrowed brow, he touched her arm.

"Fine."

"Dayne went with Grace and Mark. How about we stop for coffee?"

"Not tonight." She opened her car door. "I'm tired."

"Edward called me a few minutes ago." He loosened his tie and ran his hand along the back of his neck. "He and Joyce invited us over for dinner next Thursday night."

"Us?" Her stomach twisted.

"They insisted on your presence. I hope you don't mind, but I suggested they come to my house instead. I thought you could cook a nice meal."

"Win them over with my culinary skills." A smile escaped. "You sound like my mother."

"Actually, I thought it would be good for them to see you with Dayne and me at the house. The house where Sara never lived."

The wind gathered brown, curling leaves, rolling and scraping across the asphalt.

"I don't know." An engine started nearby. "School is out for parent/teacher conferences, and the kids are supposed to spend the night with Mark and me. We promised a hot dog roast."

"So, we'll move it to the house. Haylee can keep Dayne occupied while the adults talk."

Sylvie pulled out, without waving. Mrs. Patton waved, when her car passed, but Mrs. Hughes didn't.

Adrea shook her head. "Maybe this is all too soon."

With the parking lot empty, he pulled her into his arms. "Not for me. Please come."

In the comfort and security of his embrace, she'd agree to almost anything. And he knew it.

Playfully, she slapped him on the back. "Oh all right."

—⁂—

Adrea straightened Sara's checked blanket across the redwood picnic table on Grayson's back deck.

"Look. A frog." Dayne held a large toad inches from her face. The creature lowered his warty head and blinked one eye at her.

She laughed "I think he just winked at me."

"You're not afraid of him?"

"I love frogs. When I was a kid, Daddy built my brother and me a frog cage. It had screen all around the sides. Mark put dirt, grass, and sticks in it so they'd feel at home. We kept a pan of water in the corner and spent hours swatting flies to feed them."

"Cool." Dayne petted the frog with one careful finger.

"We'd keep them for a while, then turn them loose and catch a new batch. Sometimes, we had twenty frogs at a time. Maybe we could talk your dad into building a frog cage." The lighthearted fun couldn't quell the knots in the pit of her stomach.

"I don't think so."

"Why not?"

"He's afraid of frogs."

"Your father is afraid of frogs?" Adrea couldn't suppress her laughter.

"Terrified. I love sticking them in his face. It makes him pretty mad. I figured you was afraid of them, too."

"What does he think a frog can do to him?"

"He says when they move their neck like that"—Dayne pointed to the creature's undulating throat—"they're working up a spit. I never had no frog spit on me, have you?"

She laughed so hard, the muscles in her stomach clenched. "No, I haven't."

"Dayne, haven't I told you not to touch those things?" Grayson set a huge pitcher of sweet tea on the table. "One of these days, one will spit on you."

"Adrea likes 'em, Daddy. When she was little, she had pet frogs and says they don't spit."

"She does, huh?"

"I'm gonna ask Mr. Theo to build me a frog cage." Dayne scurried away to show Haylee his prize.

Grayson cocked an eyebrow. "Frog cage?"

"Mark and I used to have one." She shrugged.

Dayne and Haylee chased Cocoa around the yard.

Adrea set the buns, mustard, and relish on the picnic table, with shaking hands.

"Calm down." Grayson stoked the fire. "They wanted you here."

A tingling, burning sensation assailed Adrea's nose and worsened with each breath. She grabbed a paper napkin. "Uh—uh—*achoo*."

"Bless you. That might be more than allergies. Maybe you should go to the doctor."

"Adrea, come help us," Dayne called.

The small plastic pool billowed bubbles. Not only was Cocoa in the makeshift bathtub, but both kids also, their teeth chattering.

"Dayne, I told you not to get in there." Grayson shook his head. "It's too cool and Grandpa and Grandma will be here any minute."

Adrea stifled her laughter and walked over to the kids. "You'll both need a bath."

"We'll take one here." Haylee scrubbed Cocoa's back with a brush.

"I don't think you'll get clean in this bathtub." Adrea surveyed the muddy water. "Okay, Cocoa, let's get you washed up and then the rest of us will go inside to freshen up."

Large, patient, brown eyes peered at her from the bubbles. The smell of wet dog surrounded them. Cocoa shook. Ears flapping, he doused everything within several feet with gritty water and soap. Adrea ducked as the chilly mess splattered across her.

"Dayne, get that dog out of the pool!" Grayson shouted.

Unable to contain her laughter anymore, Adrea gave up. She joined the muddy dog and children in the pool, with icy water up to her shins and teeth chattering.

Grayson's laughter roared across the yard.

Adrea noticed movement at the side of the house. Edward and Joyce.

The laughter died on Adrea's lips.

Following her gaze, Grayson's amusement instantly stopped as well.

"Grandma! Grandpa!" Dayne cried, leaping from the pool. The sopping boy ran toward his grandparents.

In spite of the muck, Edward hugged the child. "You're a mess."

"We're giving Cocoa a bath." At Dayne's words, the dog bailed from Haylee's grasp, ran across the yard, and shook repeatedly. The adults tried to avoid the torrent, while the children cackled with glee.

Finally, Grayson caught Cocoa and Adrea supplied him with a somewhat dry towel.

"Okay, kids, inside and clean up, then we'll eat." Adrea herded them toward the house.

"You won't leave before I get back?" Dayne asked his grandparents.

"No, we'll be here." Edward squeezed the boy's shoulder.

"We're roasting marshmallows and making s'mores for dessert." Dayne jumped up and down.

"That sounds. . .cozy." Joyce tried to join in his excitement.

"Are you sure you won't leave?" Dayne pressed.

"I promise." Joyce stood firm, immovable. "We'll be right here."

<hr>

With Adrea and the kids out of earshot, Grayson shook Edward's hand and hugged Joyce.

"It's always nice to see you. I didn't like the way we left things the other night."

"We came to tell you that we've accepted the relationship." Joyce's voice quivered. "It's hard for us, but you've been lonely long enough." She cleared her throat. "Adrea is a wonderful woman. Seeing her with Dayne, just now, proved it."

"I truly love and respect you both and hate hurting you. I'm sorry."

"Don't be." Edward patted Grayson's shoulder. "You deserve happiness. Sara would want it for you, and she'd want someone to love Dayne, as well."

"I didn't know Adrea had a daughter." Joyce sounded stronger. "But the little girl and Dayne seem to get along well."

"Haylee is Adrea's niece."

"Oh. She was so caring with the child, I just assumed."

*I did, too.* Grayson grinned at the memory. "Adrea is great with kids. Dayne and Haylee are spending the night with Adrea and her brother tonight. They do that two or three times a month."

A polished Adrea emerged from the house, with a scrubbed Dayne and

Haylee, all wearing fresh clothing.

"Thankfully, I just picked up my dry cleaning today and Haylee had clothes packed." Adrea seemed flustered, anxious to explain that she didn't keep clothes at the house.

Joyce took a deep breath and met Adrea on the sidewalk. "Take care of my boys." Joyce offered her hand.

"I will." Adrea accepted the bridge.

"You have my blessing."

Tears filled Adrea's eyes.

Grayson's heart swelled until he thought it might burst. Nothing stood between them now. With the blessings of everyone involved, she could become his wife. Why wait?

*I'll ask her at dinner, tomorrow night.*

Adrea's stomach clenched. With a temperature of 101, the closer she got to the apartment, the darker the foreboding black cloud of smoke hovered in the sky. Surely, it couldn't be.

She topped the hill to see fire shoot from a downstairs window. The firefighters stood around their truck, barking orders, manning the hose.

With the parking lot blocked, she turned into the drive of the next house.

"Everyone got out," her elderly neighbor yelled. "Mark is at the church, right?"

She nodded. The knot in her gut eased.

From the sodden yard next door, Adrea watched the firemen make progress. The flames seemed contained downstairs, but the blaze wasn't under control. Mark's car careened over the hill and screeched to a halt.

Grayson lurched from the passenger's side and rushed toward the burning building. Her brother bolted toward the crowd. A firefighter caught Grayson and did his best to hold him back. With chaos and smoke surrounding her, Adrea pushed through the gathering crowd.

Mark saw her first. His eyes brimmed with tears as he pulled her into his arms.

"I just got here. I'm fine."

"We have to find Grayson." Mark kissed her forehead. "He's a mess."

Holding hands to keep from being separated, they made their way through the pandemonium. Adrea recognized Grayson's dark hair and rushed up behind him. When he caught sight of her, his knees gave way. She knelt on the ground beside him as he moaned incoherently.

"I'm okay, Grayson. Don't worry. Everything is fine."

"Grayson, Adrea is right here. She's fine." Mark turned to her. "We need to get him out of here."

Adrea helped her brother pull Grayson to his feet and walk him back to the car. They settled the distraught man in the backseat, and she climbed in beside him. Grayson laid his head in her lap. Gut-wrenching sobs tore through him.

"Where are we going?" she asked.

"The church." Mark turned onto the highway.

They met another fire truck and it took longer than usual to get to their destination. Grayson was still beyond words as Adrea stroked his hair.

"How did you find out?" She directed the question to Mark.

"Peg heard it on the radio and came to tell us. Since we knew you stayed home sick today, we were both terrified."

"My fever wouldn't break, so I went to the doctor. Bronchitis."

By the time they arrived at the church, Grayson could walk by himself.

Peg, the secretary, rushed to meet them, obviously shaken at the sight of her shattered boss. "Is everyone okay?"

"No one was hurt in the fire, but it took us a little while to locate Adrea," Mark explained.

"Thank God no one was hurt. I'll get some coffee." Peg darted for the hall.

"Thanks." Adrea's voice was little more than a croak.

Mark's eyes were too shiny. "You may need to see your doctor again."

"I'm fine. The smoke irritated my throat since it was already raw from the bronchitis."

Grayson sat hunched over on the couch with his head in his hands.

Peg returned with coffee, creamer, and sugar, then left them alone.

"Well, we can stay in the basement here for a few days until we find a place to rent." Mark ran his fingers through his hair and paced, in fix-it mode. "We have a couple of cots for emergencies. Grace and I can go shopping and get us each a week's worth of clothing until we determine the damage. Write down your sizes for me. I'll call Mom and Dad, Rachel, and Grace to let them know we're okay. Peg is calling a few people from church."

"Make sure she calls Helen." Adrea never took her eyes off the distressed man at her side. "She's at the shop today."

"Grayson, are you all right?" Mark asked.

"Can you handle Sunday's sermons for me?" Grayson mumbled. "I don't think I'll be up to it."

Adrea blew out a breath, thankful to hear him speak.

"Sure."

"Thanks for getting me out of there, Mark. People didn't need to see the local pastor disintegrate."

"No problem. Everyone expects preachers to be made of steel, but we're only human. With everything you've been through, you had every right to fall apart." Mark gave her shoulder a gentle squeeze. "I'll be back soon."

As soon as the door closed, Grayson laid his head in Adrea's lap again. "I can't lose you, Adrea."

"You didn't. I'm fine."

"The mere thought of losing you was almost more than I could bear."

"You're fine. You just had a scare."

Disentangling himself from her arms, he sat up and wiped away the tears, then buried his face in both hands.

Adrea massaged his knotted shoulders.

"I have to pull myself together enough to pick Dayne up from Mom's. It's time for me to go." He sat upright next to her. "I don't think I can handle dinner tonight. I'm so tired."

"I'm not feeling very well anyway. Just take care of Dayne and go to bed early." Adrea traced his jawline lightly with her fingers and started to hug him again.

He quickly turned away from her and stood. Without another word, he left.

Her stomach tumbled.

———

As Adrea made up her cot, footsteps echoed across the tile. She turned to see Grayson, his face haggard and drawn. Yesterday's fire seemed to have put ten years on him.

"I thought you might call last night." Her voice came out high-pitched.

"I meant to, but I fell asleep on the couch. Where's Mark?"

"He went to check out the apartment."

"Good, we need to talk."

"I'm worried about you."

He wouldn't look at her. Instead, he stared at the floor.

A chill skittered up her spine. She wasn't sure if it was from fever or apprehension.

He took a shaky breath. "Yesterday proved once and for all that I'm not ready for this."

"Ready for what?"

"To love someone so deeply that the thought of losing them cripples me. I can't do this again."

"Grayson, what are you saying?" Tentatively, she touched his forearm.

"We shouldn't see each other anymore."

"You're not thinking clearly. You just had a scare, but it's over now."

"I can't risk letting myself love like this again." He turned away from her. "With the possibility of losing again."

"That's life." Adrea spoke to his back. "You've said it yourself: God doesn't promise us how much time we have. We simply have to trust Him, live our lives, and to the best of our ability, glorify Him. He never promised it would be easy, just that He'd be there for the rough times, to hold us together."

"I'm sorry for leading you to believe we had a future together. Just be glad I figured out what a coward I am now, instead of later. I planned to propose to you last night."

His admission jolted through her. It should have filled her with joy, not sadness at all that she had to lose. An iron fist closed around her heart.

She stepped in front of him, forcing Grayson to look at her. "We *already* love each other. It's a little too late to decide you're not ready."

"I'm sorry for hurting you, but I can't open myself up to loss again." His shoulders drooped. "I barely made it the first time and don't have the strength for another round."

"You don't know what will happen. We may live to be a hundred, or you could die long before me. But eventually, we both get eternity. Let God give you the strength. You can't live in fear and close your heart."

"Dayne needs the only parent he has left to be strong and remain capable of functioning, for his sake." His gaze never left the floor.

"So, you're letting fear—of something that may never come—steal your happiness. 'For I the Lord thy God will hold thy right hand, saying unto thee, Fear not; I will help thee,' " Adrea quoted from Isaiah.

Grayson turned away from her again. "I'd rather not love than to love and lose again. I'm not the man you thought me to be. Forget about me; find someone else. You deserve happiness."

Shaking her head, she stiffened her spine and, with as much pride as she could muster, left the room. With nowhere to go, she ran to the fellowship hall and paced the length of the building until she heard a car start and leave. Through sheer willpower, she refrained from crying.

She pushed Grayson's mention of a marriage proposal to the back of her mind, refusing to allow herself to think about it now. She couldn't let the tears start, knowing they wouldn't stop. The emotional strain did nothing to ease her fever and throbbing head.

The door opened and she jumped.

"Whoa." Mark held both hands up, palms facing her. "Don't go through yourself, it's just me. Good news. The flames never reached the upstairs. One of the firefighters told me the house is structurally sound. We probably sustained smoke and some water damage, but that's all. We should get the chance to see what's salvageable in the next few days."

Mark took in her appearance. "What's wrong?"

"Can we get a motel or something?" Her voice cracked.

"Sure, if you want to, but why?"

"Did you see Grayson when you came back?" she squeaked.

"No, his car is gone. What happened?" Worry formed on her brother's face in the shape of a frown.

The tears she'd been holding inside coursed down her cheeks.

"Hey, what's wrong?" Mark pulled her into the shelter of his arms.

"Grayson doesn't—want to—see me—anymore." Her hiccuped words ended on a sob.

"Why? He loves you."

Incapable of answering for several minutes, Adrea's tears soaked Mark's blue cotton shirt. Finally, she pulled away from him.

"The fire scared him and he's afraid he'll lose me. He said he'd rather not love than to love and lose again."

"That's the most ridiculous thing I've ever heard." Mark's eyebrows drew together. "He already loves you."

"That's what I said. He says he can't risk losing me."

"So he'd rather not have you at all?"

The tears began again.

He pulled her back into a comforting embrace.

"I can't stay here, Mark, and worry about running into him."

"How about Mom and Dad's?"

"Maybe tomorrow. I can't deal with everyone's sympathy right now. Please can we find a motel just for tonight, so I can try to pull myself together?"

"Sure." He squeezed her hand.

—⁂—

An hour later, Adrea sat in a spotless Searcy motel, trying to pull herself together again.

Mark pressed his palm against her forehead. "You're burning up. Have you taken anything for that fever?"

"Not lately. I guess my antibiotics are still in the car."

"I'll go get your prescription. I bought some sinus medicine and aspirin along with the clothes." He disappeared into the bathroom and returned with a cup of water and the medicine. "Here, take these. I wish we had a thermometer."

Before leaving, Mark tucked her into her bed as he would a child. Within minutes, he was back with her antibiotics.

For hours, she tossed and turned. Knowledge of Grayson's intended proposal was something she could've lived without. Lying on her back, hot tears coursed down each side of her face, quickly soaking the hair at her temples. Crying swelled her sinuses even more, and she could only breathe through her mouth, which made her throat hurt worse. She rolled over and tried to mask her sniffles by burying her face in the pillow. Soft snoring came from the other queen-size bed; at least she wasn't keeping her brother awake.

When she finally did fall into a fitful sleep, dreams plagued her. Dreams of a raging fire keeping her from Grayson. No matter how hard she tried, she couldn't reach him. As the flames closed in on her, Adrea awoke with a start, drenched in sweat. At least her fever had broken.

—⁂—

Saturday evening, on autopilot, Grayson didn't want to go to the church, but he had to check his messages and clear his calendar. Would Adrea attend tomorrow? Would he get through the service if she did?

At least there were no other cars in the lot, except Peg's.

She met him at the door. "Are you okay?"

Must have been watching for him. He knew she wasn't nosy, just genuinely concerned about him.

"I'm fine. Just tired."

"Coffee's brewing. I'll bring you a cup in a few minutes."

"That would be great, but I'll come get it. You don't need to wait on me. Really, I'm fine."

"I don't mind. Mark and Adrea got a motel, so they're gone."

Her name twisted the double-edge sword lodged in his chest.

"Thanks for letting me know." In his office, he leaned his elbows on the cool surface of the desk and covered his face with both hands. A few minutes later, he heard footsteps.

Expecting to see Peg, instead he looked up into the angry face of Mark.

Grayson stood to greet him, hand extended.

Mark slammed his fist into Grayson's midsection.

He bent double as breath escaped him.

"That's for Adrea." Mark muttered the unnecessary explanation and stalked down the hall.

Gasping for breath, Grayson followed, his stumbling footsteps echoing on the tile.

Halfway to the foyer, Mark turned to face him. "You want more?"

"No, though it is justified." Grayson strained to speak. "Adrea didn't deserve the way I treated her. I pursued her and then decided I couldn't take the heat."

"No pun intended," Mark referred to the fire, but his glare showed no trace of humor.

"I never met a man worthy of my sister, until you. I encouraged your relationship, pushed you toward her. And what did you give me in return? You broke her already broken heart and turned your back on her when she was sick and suddenly homeless."

He couldn't argue with the truth. "I need some time off. Can you fill in for me, say for about a month?"

"You need some time off? What about Adrea? How do you think she feels?"

"Actually, it might help her if I disappear for a while."

Mark sighed. "Okay, but not for you. For her, and when you come back, prepare to find yourself another associate."

"Now, Mark, there's no need for that." Grayson shook his head. "You do a great job here. This doesn't have to affect our church relationship. Let's just forget that you winded me, especially since I deserved more."

"I don't think I can work with the coward who devastated my sister." Mark stalked to his own office.

Grayson didn't follow. He walked outside and tried to come up with an explanation for Dayne on why they needed to pack up and leave.

Adrea didn't go to church. Guiltily, she slept in as October dawned, then met Mark at the abandoned apartment house.

"I'll probably smell smoke for the rest of my life." She sifted through their belongings, a pungent odor hanging heavily in the air.

"It could have been much worse." Mark swept a pile of sodden refuse into the corner. "We could have lost everything, including our lives. God blessed us, sis. No one was hurt and the damage was limited."

"Right again." She found their photo albums nestled in a dry corner and flipped through them. *Thank You, God.* "No more complaints from me."

"We should probably try to find a new place, though. The landlord said the smoke removal might take some time, along with the repairs downstairs. But, I have some good news."

"What?"

"Our not-so-fearless leader is leaving for a month. He feels the need for a sudden sabbatical."

Adrea's breath caught in her throat. *Concentrate on the effect of his absence on others.* "What about Dayne? School just barely started."

"Grace said he worked it out so Dayne can homeschool for the month. His teachers are sending all his schoolwork with them."

"What about the church?" She dropped some pictures, which had never made it out of the store envelope, into a box with the albums.

"I'm in charge until he returns. After that, I plan to look for a new church."

"Oh Mark, don't leave Palisade because of me." She propped both hands on her hips. "God placed you there. Let Him decide when you need to leave. You have Grace to support you now, so I'm planning to return to Mountain Grove anyway."

Mark's jaw clenched. "I can't fulfill my calling under a man I no longer respect."

"You have to get past this. That man is your fiancée's twin brother. You're stuck with him. Do whatever you have to in order to work things out with him. Don't worry about me, I'll be fine."

Mark didn't respond and she dropped the subject, for now.

"Since we're basically homeless, we could move a little farther out of town." Farther away from Grayson. "We could get a smaller apartment. Your wedding's barely three months away, and I won't need as much space after you're gone."

"I won't allow you to run or go off on your own to lick your wounds." Mark touched her cheek with his fingertips. "We'll find something where we both can live happily and maybe you could move in with Grace and me after we're married."

"I'm not moving in with you and your bride." She turned away to dig through another pile.

"We can talk about all of that later. In the meantime, I may need your help charming my angry fiancée after she sees her brother."

Adrea whirled to face him. "What did you do?"

"It was no big deal."

"Mark? Did you hit him?"

"Nothing that will leave a mark." He smiled. "Pardon the pun."

"I'm not amused." She looked heavenward. "You are a preacher!"

# Chapter 10

I t was righteous anger," Mark said.

"You really hit him?" *Please be joking.*

"Just in the stomach, but it took him a while to catch his breath. He's pretty solid. In fact, my hand still hurts."

"Mark!"

"I wanted to knock his head off, but that would cause a bruise and people would ask questions. This way, it was just between him and me." Mark dusted his hands against one another.

"And God—and Grace. How on earth did you preach this morning?"

"I felt great, until now." Guilt flattened Mark's voice.

She plopped into a chair. A smoky odor wafted from the fabric. "Listen to me. I am fine. I'll get over Grayson Sterling. Please don't let this affect your position or your relationship with Grace. You two love each other so much. I couldn't stand it if problems arose between you because of me."

"Grace and I will survive. Don't worry. We'll find another church."

She lifted an eyebrow. "You haven't spoken with her about this?"

"I didn't want to tell her on the phone. She's helping her marvelous brother get ready for his trip. By now, he's probably told her all about the wallop I delivered."

"He'd never do that."

"Why are you defending the man?" The veins in Mark's neck bulged.

Adrea closed her eyes. "Don't ask Grace to choose between you and her twin brother."

"If God calls me to another church someday, Grace will go with me, not stay at Palisade."

"This is different. When that happens, you'd leave because of God's will. If you leave now, you'll make the decision out of anger and force her to choose."

"She'll choose me," Mark mumbled.

"Are you certain? And even if she does, if you truly love Grace, you won't ask her to make that choice."

Mark ran a hand through his hair. "I belted the guy for your honor and you go and make me feel guilty."

"How would you like it if Grace asked you to choose between her and me?"

Mark sighed.

"Do whatever it takes to repair your relationship with Grayson." Adrea touched her brother's arm, desperate to communicate the importance of the situation. "If you want to do something for me, make amends. I didn't want you to hit him, but I want this."

—∞—

Before Grayson left, Mark forced himself to bury the hatchet, though Adrea knew he wanted to bury it in the back of Grayson's head. Since Grace was a little miffed at her brother over his broken relationship with Adrea, she took the news of Mark's punch in stride.

After two weeks at Mom and Daddy's, Adrea and Mark stood with Rachel outside one of only two affordable rental houses in Romance. Nice, freshly painted, and well-kept—but directly across the street from Wade's old house. Where he'd lived during his and Adrea's relationship. Where they'd planned to begin their marriage. Where she'd caught him with another woman.

She tried to concentrate on October's vivid kaleidoscope of yellow, orange, and red leaves.

"We'll find something else." Mark ran a hand through his hair.

The chipper real estate agent pointed across the street. "Remember, that one's available also. Same owner."

"There's got to be somewhere else."

Wind chimes tinkled in the nippy wind. The ones she'd bought Wade? "We'll take this one."

The woman grinned and handed her the key. She counted the cash Adrea gave her and turned toward her car. "If you need anything, don't hesitate to call."

Adrea blew out a big sigh and picked up a box, dug around in it until she found a pair of scissors, and marched across the street.

"What are you doing?" Rachel followed.

Adrea snipped the string holding the chimes. They clattered to the porch in a tangled heap.

"Brilliant. But I still can't believe you're taking the place."

"It's just a house." Unlike her sister, Adrea had long ago made peace with Wade, forgiven him, and even visited him at the nursing home in Searcy. Yet, she didn't need to go back. Only forward. To her side of the street.

"You don't hum or sing while you work anymore. How can you ever be happy living here, looking at that every time you step outside your door?" Rachel motioned at the house full of memories, then dug one of the plants that had survived the fire out of Mark's Tahoe.

"I'll heal. I plan to continue attending Palisade while he's gone. But in a few weeks when he comes back, I'll go back to Mountain Grove."

"Did you find someone to take your children's class?"

Adrea set a box of pictures in the living room. "Mrs. Roberts has recovered from her heart attack, but she felt my youth was good for the children and never reclaimed her post. However, with gentle persuasion, I'm sure I can talk her into teaching again."

"I'm sorry you're hurting, but it'll be nice to have you back at church." Rachel hugged her.

She'd miss the friends made at Palisade, and especially Helen. It seemed just weeks ago, she'd faced changing churches. So much had happened since then. One day, she'd see God's plan in it all.

"Well at least the smoke removal service worked wonders." Mark set a box marked DISHES on the kitchen counter. "Most of our stuff survived. And for the first time since you moved out of Mom and Dad's, you'll have a yard to call your own."

Small comfort.

"And most of your garden came with you." Rachel joined an obvious effort to point out the positives.

"Surprise." Mark set a pet carrier on the floor and opened the door.

Tripod clambered out, big-eyed, taking in the new surroundings.

"Hey, baby." Tripod curled himself around Adrea's ankles. She picked up the less-than-whole feline and he rubbed against her, motor running. "Oh Mark, thank you."

"Since the floors are tile, the landlord said we can have pets. I might even build a fence in the back."

The location of the rental house was farther from Rose Bud and Grayson's stomping grounds. She wouldn't have to worry about seeing him every time she turned around when he came back.

"This is a good move. I'll be fine here."

~⁓~

Adrea stared out the dining room window. The early November wind howled with brown, falling refuse to be raked, bagged, and burned.

Something brushed against her hand. Her breath caught and she whirled around, sloshing coffee.

"Whoa." Mark righted her cup. "How many have you had?"

"Three. It's not helping. Is he back?"

"Yes. And if it's any consolation, he doesn't look happy, either." Mark flashed an impish grin.

"It's not. You didn't hit him again, did you?"

"On the contrary, I pretended to be absolutely overjoyed to see him." He motioned toward his tie.

"Good boy." She made the loops and pulled the burgundy and gray striped silk into a neat knot. "How's Dayne?"

"He seemed a little sad, too. I think he misses you. He asked about you a dozen times."

"I miss him, too."

"It's a shame his father is such a jerk."

"Mark!"

"Well, it is." He kissed her cheek. "Ready?"

"You really should go to Palisade."

"I've got the day off and I choose to go with my family for a change."

She hugged him, grateful for his support.

Ten minutes later, they arrived at Mountain Grove for the first time in eight months. As she stepped inside, it felt like old-home week. Their parents, Rachel, Curt, and Haylee welcomed them, as did all their friends. They met several new people who had begun attending during their absence.

Adrea missed the harp, but it didn't matter at all that Palisade was a prettier church. No one asked why she was back. As usual, Mom had smoothed things for her.

After class, small arms snaked around her waist. Expecting one of the children she used to teach, Adrea was shocked to see Dayne.

"Dayne! Oh, how I've missed you." She knelt to his level and returned the exuberant hug. "What are you doing here?"

"I wanted to see you, so Grace said we could visit your church. I miss you. And Haylee."

"We miss you, too." Tears blurred her vision. She blinked them away. "She's around here somewhere."

"Why did you leave our church? Didn't you like teaching me?"

"I loved being your teacher, Dayne." She stood and tousled his hair. "Really. But Mrs. Roberts is well now."

"I'm glad she's all better since her heart attacked her. I like her and all." Dayne shrugged. "But I liked when you was my teacher, too. Why aren't you and Daddy friends no more? Why don't you come to our house no more, and how come me and Haylee don't get to spend the night with you and Mark no more?"

"Oh sweetie, it's complicated."

Grace and Mark joined the reunion, rescuing Adrea from Dayne's probing questions.

Haylee rushed over. "Can I take Dayne out to the swing set?"

"For just a few minutes, but stay away from the parking lot." Adrea brushed the little girl's bangs from her eyes. "It's almost time for service to start, and it's too cold to be out for long."

"We wanted to ask you something." Grace's voice echoed her apprehension.

"What?"

"We'll understand if you say no." Mark rubbed his chin.

"What?" Adrea repeated.

"Will you be my maid of honor?"

"Oh Grace." Adrea hugged her soon-to-be sister-in-law. "Why would you think I might say no?"

"Because I've asked Grayson to be my best man." Mark chewed the inside of his jaw.

Her stomach twisted. "Well, it's good that the two of you are getting along so well."

"I'm trying to mend fences." Mark hung his head. "For Grace's sake."

"I'm proud of you." She patted his shoulder, then turned to the radiant woman beside him. "Grace, it will be my privilege to serve as your maid of honor."

"Are you sure? I really want you to, but the last thing we want is for you to feel uncomfortable."

"All I'll feel is happiness for you two." She stepped between them and put her arms around both their shoulders. "Did Mark tell you that I want to do the flowers free? Whatever you want, it's my wedding gift to you."

"That is so sweet of you, but it's too much."

"It's not too much. It'll be my pleasure."

"Well, when you get married, you've got a free caterer, at your service." Grace realized her blunder, with a rare blush.

An awkward silence ensued. The choir music began.

"Excuse me," Adrea said. "I better get up there. The song service is about to begin."

"I'll get the kids." Grace hurried toward the door.

After the choir finished, she sat with her parents, with Dayne beside her. She enjoyed the service, but had a difficult time concentrating on Curt's sermon. Instead, her thoughts kept straying to Grayson.

After church, Mark hitched a ride with Grace. They invited Adrea to lunch, but she begged off.

On the way home, she noticed movement along the side of the highway. Two dogs; a starved German shepherd and a skinny bloodhound. She pulled to the shoulder. The larger dog backed away, shivering with fear and cold. It walked with a limp and its right hind leg had dried blood on it. The hound came right to her, limping, its pads raw. Most of its left ear was missing. With very little coaxing, it jumped into the backseat.

"Let's see, you're a hunting dog. We'll call you Coon." The dog nuzzled his velvety muzzle in her hand, looking for anything edible. "We'll go to the store and get you some food, as soon as I get your friend in the car."

The shepherd was a different story. She finally gave up and went to the store. Thirty minutes later, with a raw hamburger incentive, Mouse got into her car.

---

The Thursday after his return, Adrea stopped by Helen's on her way home from work. Expecting the subject of Grayson to surface, her stomach churned.

"Adrea, what perfect timing." Helen swung the door open wide, leaning on her cane. "I just got these out of the oven."

Adrea sniffed the air. Fruit and cake. Blueberry muffins.

Helen slathered butter on two, set them on saucers with delicate blue flowers around the rim, and handed one to Adrea.

"Eat up, while it's still warm." Helen took a bite.

Adrea sank her teeth into the moist, savory confection. "You'll ruin my supper."

Helen shot her a conspiratorial grin. "We're adults, we can have our dessert first. Sit down, dear." Helen fixed her a cup of coffee. "I missed you at church yesterday."

Adrea swallowed hard. "Mark doesn't need me there anymore. I'm going back to Mountain Grove."

"Now, you know I'm not nosy, and I certainly don't mean to drag up a painful subject." She held up her hand when Adrea started to speak. "Let me say my piece. I'm just concerned. I know you and Pastor Grayson aren't seeing one another anymore. And I feel so bad."

"Why?" Adrea sipped her coffee.

"Wade has caused so much heartache for you both." The aged blue eyes grew watery. "I felt so much better about things, since the two of you were moving on. Together."

"None of it's your fault."

"I can't help taking part of the responsibility."

"Did you raise Wade to believe it was okay to drink?"

"Of course not."

"Then you can't blame yourself, Helen." Adrea patted her hand. "He made his own choices."

"Did you know Grayson goes with me to see him? While he was gone, Grace went."

He'd never mentioned it, not even when they'd been almost engaged. "I can go with you anytime."

A knock sounded at the door.

"You're expecting someone? I could have come another day."

"Stop worrying yourself. I'm not expecting anyone." Helen made moves to get up. Though her hip had healed completely, she still moved more stiffly and slowly than before, relying on her cane for support.

"Let me get it." Adrea peeked out the high window in the heavy pine door and immediately wished she could melt into the floor. All she could see was his hair and forehead, but she'd know him anywhere.

Adrea swung the door open and greeted him with a forced smile. "Hello, Grayson."

"Adrea." His voice and raised brows reflected his surprise.

"She still visits me a few times every week. Isn't she a doll?" Helen asked. "Some man will be lucky to get her."

Adrea grasped for a subject change. "How's Dayne?"

"Okay. He enjoyed the trip."

Grayson looked tired and worn, but still handsome.

"Where did you go? Dayne didn't say."

"The Grand Canyon. I always promised we'd go there, but Sara never made it. I decided to make sure Dayne and I did."

The try at casual conversation felt strained. They both fell silent for a moment.

"Well, I really need to get home," Adrea said.

"Please don't leave on my account."

"Don't go just yet, Adrea." Helen patted the sofa to her left. "Sit with me. I'm leaving for Thanksgiving at June's tomorrow and I'll be gone a whole week."

Obediently, Adrea sat.

"I was about to tell you a story. You'll like this one, too, Pastor Grayson." Helen patted the sofa to her right.

"I do love your stories." He sat on the other side of the older woman.

"Did I ever tell you about my older sister, Ruthie?"

"No."

"She passed a few years ago, didn't she?" Adrea concentrated on breathing evenly.

"She's with the Lord now. But when she was young, she met this man, fell for Herb hard, and he worshipped the ground she walked on. Both of them were strong in the Lord, put Him first in everything. They were perfect for each other. Just as the whole town started buzzing about wedding bells, *poof*, it was over."

"What happened?" The story drew Adrea, despite the handsome man across from her.

"Don't know. Ruthie never would talk about it, but I know, until her dying day, she loved Herb. No one could bring up his name without her bursting into tears." Helen paused to wipe away one of her own. "Long about five years after the breakup, she married. She and Ernest raised three kids. Now, he loved her dearly and she loved him, in her way. But, not like Herb."

Grayson cleared his throat.

"Poor Herb never married, pined for Ruthie the rest of his life. Ruthie went on, but she never was as happy and Ernest knew she didn't love him as she should have. Now, why would people want to do that?" Helen held both hands out, palms up. "God gives them someone to love and cherish and they snub their noses at His gift."

Adrea took Helen's hand. "I enjoyed visiting with you, as usual, but I really do need to go. I have to get dinner on, though I'm not hungry, thanks to those scrumptious muffins."

"I put a couple aside for Mark." Helen gestured to the table. "There, wrapped in foil."

"He'll love you for it." Adrea retrieved the goodies.

Grayson walked her to the door as she forced her pace to slow.

"It's always nice to see you. You look well."

"You, too."

Their eyes met and held.

With a wave at Helen, Adrea fled.

—⁂—

Adrea checked the computer. November 18th, Grayson and Sara's anniversary. The order was still there. Would Grayson keep his standing order at the shop or take his business elsewhere?

Rachel stepped through the door from the showroom holding a long white box tied with yellow ribbon. "Do you want this?"

"Yes."

Rachel patted her arm and went to the office.

Adrea opened the box. A single yellow rose. *He must simply want to torture me.* She forced herself to read the card.

> *Dear Adrea,*
>
> *I hope you are doing well. After wrestling with myself about whether to find a new florist, I concluded that you are the best. You truly love Sara. No other florist would do her justice. I won't disturb you when I pick up the arrangement. However, if you feel led to discontinue your services, I'll understand completely. I'm sorry for everything.*
>
> *Sincerely,*
> *Grayson*

"Rachel," Adrea called.

Her sister stepped out of the office. "You rang?"

"Will you call Grayson and tell him that his business is always welcome here?"

"Are you sure? It would be much easier on you if he went elsewhere."

"Yes, it would be, but it wouldn't be right."

With an understanding nod, Rachel went back to the office to make the call.

Adrea resolutely began the arrangement of white roses for Sara. More tears spilled as she cried harder over the flowers than ever before. Only two months before, she'd joined Grayson at the cemetery for Dayne's birthday.

Rachel returned, but wisely said nothing when she saw the tears. She simply took the array to the showroom.

Adrea didn't relax until she heard that Grayson and Dayne had come and gone.

—⁂—

The week after Thanksgiving, Adrea arranged flowers for two funerals. As the back door opened behind her, she assumed it was Rachel, back from a delivery and ready for the next.

"I'm finishing the last spray. Just give me a minute."

"Hello, Adrea."

For a few seconds, she couldn't bring herself to turn toward the voice. Finally, after what seemed like an eternity, she turned to see Grayson, just as handsome as ever.

"Hello." She controlled the quiver in her voice.

"It's good to see you. You look great."

"You, too." A few more lines around his eyes.

"Dayne misses you."

"I miss him, too. It was wonderful to see him at church."

"He said you sang in the choir. Why didn't you join the choir at Palisade?"

"Your church had a large choir already, so I wasn't needed. Mountain Grove wouldn't let me off the hook." It seemed odd speaking of trivial things while her heart hammered.

"You shouldn't keep your talents under wraps." He stuffed his hands into his jean pockets. "Look, I promised not to bother you, but I'm here on Dayne's behalf. Do you think you could occasionally find time for him?"

"What do you mean?" Adrea concentrated on the carnations.

"He misses you. He hasn't stopped asking to see you. I probably would have given in sooner, but the holidays kept him somewhat occupied." Grayson shifted his weight from one foot to the other. "The other day, he said all he wanted for Christmas is to see you."

Adrea's heart clenched. "How sweet."

"You were good for him, and he shouldn't have to lose you simply because we're no longer seeing one another."

"I'd love to see him." She nodded. "How about tomorrow night and then once a week? There's usually nothing happening on Thursday nights unless of course a holiday falls on it, but we can work around that."

"That sounds good. Dayne will be excited. Should I drop him at your place?"

"I can pick him up." *Please don't show up on my porch.*

"At least, let me retrieve him."

"That's okay. We might even go to Searcy anyway, so I can take the Rose Bud route. I'll come to get him at six o'clock and have him back by nine o'clock. That's not too late for a school night, is it?"

"Sounds good. Maybe this will help. Dayne had a hard time with the abrupt ending of our relationship."

*He's not the only one.* "I hope seeing me won't confuse him." Adrea kept a smile plastered on her face.

"We'll have a long talk tonight and make sure he understands things. It's my fault that he had a rough time and I really appreciate this, Adrea. It will help him adjust."

"Maybe Haylee can come sometimes, too, just like old times." *Almost.*

"That would be great. Well, it was good seeing you. Take care."

"You, too." She smiled harder.

Grayson left.

A full minute passed before Adrea could relax the muscles in her face. The spray she'd been working on was a complete disaster. She pulled it apart to start over.

—※—

As soon as Adrea stopped her car in the drive, Dayne rushed to jump in the back. She waved to Grace, who stood on the white-columned porch.

"I wish things were like before," Dayne whined. "I wish we could stay here with Daddy."

"We'll have fun."

"Everything's just different. I missed you on Thanksgiving. I begged Daddy to let me see you at the shop when we picked up Mommy's flowers last time, but he said you were too busy."

Her heart clenched. "You may tell your father that I'm never too busy to see you."

"I wanted you to come to the cemetery. Maybe you can come with us for Valentine's Day."

"Don't count on it, sweetie." Adrea patted his hand as she turned onto the highway. "At least we're getting to see each other now, even though things are different. I've looked forward to tonight all day long."

"Me, too."

The boy's mannerisms so reflected Grayson's that spending time with him painfully reminded her of spending time with his father. "How about Dexter's?"

"Dexter's, Dexter's, Dexter's."

She laughed. "I'll take that as a yes."

At the restaurant, numerous birthday celebrations caused the usual ruckus.

"Dayne," a familiar voice called.

Adrea turned to see Edward Owens scoop up his grandson. "Hello, Adrea. It's nice to see you."

"Yes. You, too." Adrea shook the hand he offered.

"Run and say hi to Grandma. We're just about to leave." Edward motioned to a long table to their left.

Joyce's gaze was riveted to Adrea.

"It's not what you think." She swallowed hard. "Grayson and I are no longer seeing one another."

"I was sorry to hear that. He and Dayne miss you."

"Dayne and I have a date once a week."

"We're here for our friend's grandson. We actually called to see if Dayne wanted to come, but Grayson said he already had plans. I'm glad it was with you. You're good for him and for Grayson, too."

Adrea didn't know what to say.

"Looks like the party's breaking up. I'll send Dayne back in your direction."

"Thank you."

—◦◦◦—

The weeks before Christmas passed in a flurry of activity, poinsettia plants, and church services.

The Welches enjoyed their traditional Christmas celebration with thoughtful gifts and scripture readings. Adrea steeped herself in the whole meaning of Jesus' birth.

The next week brought Mark and Grace's wedding preparations. Adrea spent her time obtaining even more poinsettias of every color from the wholesaler.

Their parents arrived to ride with Adrea and Mark to the rehearsal.

"I just hate to think of you living here." While Adrea primped, Mom perched on the bed, with Tripod curled in her lap, purring a steady hum. "Especially with Mark moving out."

"I'm fine."

"So, nothing's different between you and Grayson?"

"It's old news, Mom. It's over between us."

"This is your mother. I can see the hurt written all over your face. I know how much you loved him."

"I can't talk about it." Adrea's stomach knotted. "I've got to get through this wedding. For Mark's and Grace's sake, I can't think about Grayson."

"Very well, then. Oh, I meant to tell you, the florist shop in Heber Springs is up for sale."

"It is?"

"Mrs. Johnson is retiring. Speaking of retiring." Mom paused to massage her wrist. "My supervisor talked me into transferring instead, to the Rose Bud office. I start training my replacement soon. A real sweet gal, Laren Kroft."

"Kroft. I wonder if she's related to Sylvie?" Adrea checked her watch. "We need to go."

Ten minutes later, they arrived at the church. The rehearsal wore on Adrea as she walked the aisle to stand across from Grayson a dozen times.

Sara's parents arrived to sing a duet for the wedding. Though Edward greeted Adrea warmly, Joyce avoided her. Adrea couldn't blame her. They'd painfully learned Grayson was dating and given their approval, only to watch the relationship falter.

She diligently managed to avoid Grayson's parents.

By the time the rehearsal was over, she was as jittery as a helium balloon with its string caught in a box fan.

The bridal party settled in the large fellowship hall for dinner. Seated at one end of the long table with Grayson far on the other, Adrea made a mental note to thank the bride and groom for their arrangements. Even so, she was glad when the evening ended.

On New Year's Eve, Adrea grabbed her scarlet satin dress, said a prayer for strength, and headed to Palisade.

She spent an hour on decorations. Placing and re-placing each spray, candelabra, and archway until Grace was completely satisfied. After the bride went to prepare for her wedding, Adrea ducked into the ladies' room and changed into her dress. Stepping back into the hall, she saw Emma Sterling headed in her direction.

Kindness radiated from Grayson's mother. Emma would never broach the subject of the broken relationship. Guilt needled Adrea for avoiding Emma at the rehearsal.

Emma hugged her. "It's so good to see you again. You look lovely in that color. It brings out the auburn highlights in your hair."

"Thank you. I thought Rachel got all those." She ran her hand over her hair. "I was so busy last night, I didn't even get to speak with you."

"Graham and I got to sit with your parents at the dinner. They're always so delightful."

"I'm glad. I've enjoyed doing this wedding more than any other." *Except for rubbing elbows with your son.*

"And you did a fabulous job, as usual. Well, I'm off to see the bride." Emma waved.

"That's where I'm headed. See you in a few minutes."

Vibrant red, faded salmon, lush burgundy, and creamy white poinsettias filled the church. Gold ribbons gathered small bouquets festooning the first several pews. Adrea inspected the decor one last time before going to find Grace. On her way, she ran into Mark and Grayson.

Trying to ignore her brother's attractive companion, wearing a chocolate tuxedo, she surveyed Mark's white one. She straightened his tie and hugged him. "You look so handsome. I'm so happy for you and Grace."

"You're quite lovely yourself. Grace and I really want you to consider moving in with us."

"I'm fine and I doubt you'll miss Mouse. He certainly won't miss you."

"Who's Mouse?" Grayson asked.

"A German shepherd. Our new landlord allows pets, so Adrea's been collecting strays. His leg was full of rat shot, and he's terrified of men. He hides under her bed most of the time."

"Doesn't sound like much of a watchdog." Grayson cleared his throat. "I can check on Adrea occasionally, until you get back from your honeymoon."

"That won't be necessary." She answered too quickly. "Coon is a good watchdog."

"Until he bellows." Mark curled his lip, Elvis-style. "Anyone with ears can tell he ain't nothin' but a hound dog."

She wanted to smile at her brother's antics, knowing he was trying to help her relax, but the muscles around her mouth wouldn't comply. "I better go help the bride."

"Tell her I love her." Mark blushed.

"My tie could use your expertise." Grayson stepped close to her. "And my boutonniere, too."

Giggles surrounded them and she turned to see several teenage girls from the youth group staring. One girl pointed up.

Adrea looked up to see mistletoe directly above. Her face warmed.

# Chapter 11

Adrea bolted.

In a small classroom, Grace glowed with happiness and didn't seem nervous at all. Emma buzzed around her daughter, fluffing her train and perfecting the curls Grace rarely wore.

"Mark said he loves you." Adrea blew her a kiss. "He even blushed."

The bride's smile brightened even more. "He's so cute when he blushes."

Rachel squeezed Adrea's hand and whispered, "You okay?"

"I'm fine."

The women trickled out of the classroom as the time for the ceremony neared.

As the music swelled, Rachel walked the aisle, with Curt and Mark waiting at the front. Adrea's turn came and she concentrated on keeping her eyes off the other man waiting there with her brother. Grayson stood at the pulpit to perform the ceremony until their father handed Grace over to Mark. Then the Sterling patriarch, Graham, took over as Grayson slipped back into his role as best man.

The two became one in the sight of God and many witnesses. The well-wishers congratulated, cameras flashed, the servers cut the cake, and all too soon it was time for the bride and groom to leave for their honeymoon.

Mark hugged her. "Yo, Adrea, I wish you'd stay with Mom and Dad."

"I'm fine. Really." Anything but fine; she hadn't really thought about saying good-bye to Mark. It was just like when he'd left for seminary only this time he wasn't coming back, to their rental house, anyway. She held her tears until the happy couple disappeared.

Before helping with the cleanup, she grabbed her coat and went out in the courtyard to gather her composure.

She missed Mark, and coupled with the many encounters with Grayson over the last month, it was all too much.

Frigid air chilled her, but she didn't care. She hugged herself.

—⁂—

Grayson stared down the highway, long after he could no longer hear the clunking trail of cans tied to Mark's car.

The tux did little to keep him warm, but at the moment he couldn't face anyone. He'd lost her. Adrea had avoided him all evening, and why shouldn't she?

"Gray." His mother touched his shoulder. "You'll freeze to death out here."

He turned to face her. "I'm okay."

She cupped his cheek in her hand. "Go home, son. Dayne is having a great time helping with the cleanup. He can spend the night with us."

"I should stay to help."

"We've got plenty of help. Go." She patted his cheek. "I think you've had enough for one day."

With a nod, he kissed her forehead. He'd parked on the other side of the church and decided to walk around.

Someone stood in the lit courtyard. Someone beautiful wearing a red dress.

"Adrea?"

She jumped and with jerky movements, wiped away tears.

He wished the tears were for him, but he knew better.

"You'll miss Mark. I'll miss Grace. I don't know what Dayne and I will do without her."

She took a soggy breath. "Grace still plans to babysit Dayne after school and during the summer."

"She offered, but I want her to have plenty of time for her new husband as well as her business. Mom and Joyce have agreed to fill in."

"I better go help with the cleanup efforts."

"I wanted to speak with you." He stepped closer.

She backed away. "About?" Her breath puffed a cloud between them. "Us."

"There is no us." One delicate hand clutched the patio railing so hard her knuckles turned white.

"I've been thinking about you a lot. I miss you."

"Just leave it alone, Grayson." Adrea made a mad dash back inside.

―⁂―

Sheets of rain assaulted Adrea's windshield wipers, rendering them useless. Traffic putted along blindly. When she could no longer see the yellow line, she pulled over to wait out the onslaught.

For two weeks, she'd avoided Rose Bud and Grayson. But her luck couldn't hold forever. She had to get out of this town.

The escape route continued to percolate in her tired brain. But she'd been the one to talk her sister into their partnership. She couldn't run out on Rachel.

After a few minutes, the deluge ebbed and she edged into the flow again. Just as she parked outside the shop, the sky opened up once more.

She dashed for the door. A gust of wind nearly sucked the ineffective umbrella from her hand, and by the time she made it inside, she was soaked through. Pushing damp bangs from her eyes, she checked the first order of the day and read Rachel's note. All the flowers for both weddings were complete, except for the bridal bouquets. *Hope it stops raining.*

As soon as Rachel entered from the showroom, Adrea made her plea.

"How would you feel about buying the florist shop in Heber Springs?"

"It's for sale?"

"Mrs. Johnson is retiring." Adrea clustered pink roses together in the center of a rounded bouquet. "I don't think I can take another Valentine's Day. Not here."

"Who would run it?"

The hum of the busy showroom grew louder as the connecting door opened, then faded away as it shut.

"I'd move there."

"You're moving?"

She turned at the sound of his voice and found the reason for all her heartache standing behind her.

"Ahem." Rachel cleared her throat. "I'll just be out front."

Adrea turned away from him and concentrated on the roses. "We're thinking about buying the shop in Heber Springs. It's a good business move and someone has to run it."

"What about your family?"

"I'll visit often."

"What about Dayne?"

"I'll still be here for a while, and he'll see me when I'm in town."

"What about me?"

"It doesn't concern you."

"I still love you, Adrea."

The breath whooshed out of her lungs.

"Do you still love me?"

She worked on the roses more frantically, entwining much more baby's breath than necessary.

Grayson moved to stand beside her and placed his fingers under her chin, forcing her to meet his eyes.

Her tears welled.

"Yes, but what good does that do us? You're afraid to love me."

"Grace's wedding made everything clear. By breaking up with you, I lost you, which is what I tried to avoid by breaking up with you. This isn't making any sense."

Her heart did a somersault. "You're making perfect sense, for the first time in months."

"If, God forbid, anything happens to you, He'll be there to put me back together, like He did three years ago. He's shown me that I need to turn all fears over to Him and rely on Him for my happiness, instead of earthly relationships. God has given me the strength to love you. I need you, Adrea. My son needs you."

She pressed a hand to her tremulous lips. "What if something happens to shake that strength? What if you change your mind again? My heart can't take another breakup."

Grayson took her hands. "I need to tell you about the accident."

"You don't have to."

"Yes, you need to know the details. It will help you understand me. People who plan to get married need to understand one another."

Adrea's mouth went dry. She couldn't have spoken, even if her whirling brain could have formed words.

He scooted two tall stools out of the corner.

Obediently, she sat, facing him.

"As you know, Dayne and I were also in the accident. Thankfully, he was in his car seat and came out unscathed. I remained conscious the entire time rescuers worked to cut us out."

Adrea watched Grayson mentally relive the past. His pained expression put an ache in her heart.

"My legs were pinned, so I couldn't move. Dayne was screaming at the top of his lungs, but I couldn't get to him. I could touch him, but couldn't get him out of his car seat to hold him or comfort him."

Tears glistened in his eyes. "Sara looked fine but was unconscious. After a while, her breathing became more and more labored. Though she never came to, she coughed up blood a couple of times.

"She started gurgling. Her breathing grew more difficult and infrequent, until it stopped. A paramedic worked on her through the broken windshield, but it wasn't enough. She drowned in her own blood, with me sitting right next to her. Completely powerless."

Adrea stood and wrapped her arms around him. "I'm so sorry."

"When I saw your apartment building on fire, I felt that helplessness again. That night, I dreamed of the accident, the sound of Sara struggling to breathe, and Dayne crying. This time, after a while, it wasn't Sara beside me, but you. Then the car caught fire."

"Oh Grayson."

They held each other, tears mingling, before he managed to pull himself together.

"Loving you still frightens me, but I can't live my life in fear and lose you. I'd rather love you and risk losing you. I'm tired of wasting time when we could be together."

The showroom door opened. "Oh my." Rachel gasped.

Adrea and Grayson disentangled themselves.

Rachel grinned and backed toward the showroom. "I'll just go find a plant to water."

—⁓—

On Valentine's Day, the showroom door opened and Dayne burst through. "Pretty flowers."

"For a pretty lady."

Dayne flew into Adrea's arms as Grayson joined them. "I'm so glad you and Daddy are friends again."

"Me, too." She glanced at Grayson.

He joined the embrace, his chin resting on top of her head. "Will you come to the cemetery with us today? One last time."

Adrea frowned but didn't ask questions and grabbed her jacket. "Sure."

Fifteen minutes later, they arrived at the cemetery. Adrea's black heels sank into the red clay, but despite the chill in the air, her heart sang. The threesome held hands as Dayne carried the white roses for his mother.

She no longer felt like an interloper when it came to Sara. Instead, Adrea felt as if Sara's torch, to love and care for those she left behind, had been passed on. She willingly complied.

Dayne solemnly placed the flowers and polished the headstone while his father tidied the grave. Adrea stood off to the side with a sense of belonging.

"Son, head to the car. We'll be there in a few minutes."

"Okay." The boy hurried in that direction.

He took both of Adrea's hands. "I've wasted so much time. I never thought I'd be happy again after Sara died, but God sent me you. And I almost blew it." He kissed her forehead. "I've asked Sara's parents to do the flowers in the future. I'll only come on Valentine's Day, and I won't bring Dayne anymore, unless he asks."

"Are you sure?"

"Dayne and I need to move forward." He tucked her hand into his elbow and turned toward the car. "With you."

His words warmed her heart. She snuggled against his side.

***

The next day, Grayson sat at his desk at the church. Footsteps headed his way and he looked up to see Mark.

"Good, just the person I need to see." Mark closed the office door.

He didn't look happy about it.

Grayson offered his hand.

Mark ignored it.

"What's on your mind?"

"My sister."

"Isn't that a coincidence? She's on my mind, too." Grayson smiled, but it died on his lips when Mark didn't match his cheerfulness.

"Look, as long as Adrea is happy, there'll be no interference from me. But if you hurt her again, you'll have me to answer to."

"I'm well aware of that." Grayson rubbed his stomach as if it were still tender from Mark's blow. "I love your sister. I've talked with God about her and placed her in His hands. Through His strength, I can move on."

"You're sure?"

Grayson opened his mouth.

Mark raised his hand to silence him. "Let me finish. You've been through a lot and my concerns may seem callous. But are you certain that you're ready this time?"

"I plan to propose. Our life together can't begin soon enough for me."

Mark nodded. "Adrea deserves to be happy."

"I'll do my utmost to never hurt her again."

The two men shook hands.

—◁▷—

Adrea hummed as she put together a bridal spray. Early March brought preparations for the first spring wedding of the year. The showroom door opened and she turned to find her very own prince.

"Close your eyes." He shot her a devilish grin.

"What are you up to?"

"I'm kidnapping you."

"Sounds heavenly, but I have a wedding today."

"Rachel promised to handle it."

Tears pricked her eyes.

"What?" His hand cupped her cheek.

"I'm not used to having a man care about my schedule or my business."

"Get used to it." He kissed the tip of her nose. "Everything's taken care of. Now close your eyes."

Shivers moved over her as she obeyed. A soft linen cloth draped over her face and she could feel Grayson tying it in place, careful not to pull her hair. Spicy cologne filled her senses.

His arm came around her waist and he walked her out.

"It better not be very far. The suspense will drive me mad."

Adrea lost all sense of direction as Grayson drove. Each turn took her stomach.

"Is it much farther?"

He stopped the car. "Actually, we're here." His car door opened, then hers, and he helped her out.

"Can I see now?"

"Not yet." With his arm around her waist again, he walked her across bumpy ground. "Slight step up."

Level, a sidewalk perhaps.

"Now, three steps down."

Water. The rush of water.

"Romance Waterfalls."

"You've been here before?" He sounded disappointed. "Eight steps down."

"I've done two weddings here, but I always love coming." She touched the blindfold. "Can't I see now? I'm missing all the landscaping."

"Not just yet. Five steps down."

She followed his instructions and the sound of rushing water grew louder, until finally, he stopped and removed the handkerchief.

They stood on the balcony overlooking the waterfall. The water crashed over jutting rocks.

"Even though I've seen it before, I've never seen it with you." She turned to scan the flower beds, kept fresh looking with silk blossoms in the winter.

"Good, I wanted this to be special." He knelt on one knee. "Will you marry me?"

"Oh Grayson."

"Is that a yes?"

"Yes."

Grayson swept her into his arms. He had proven Rachel was right, after all. Men do indeed sweep women into their arms.

"Let's get married on Easter. We usually dismiss evening services. What better time for a wedding?"

Joy welled in her soul. "Can we pull a wedding together that fast?"

"We'll put an army on it, my mom, yours, Grace, Rachel, Helen."

She pulled away to look into his eyes. "At Palisade. A fresh start for both of us."

"We'll create good memories. Together."

—⁓—

Adrea thought back to when Grayson announced their engagement at church this morning. Everyone applauded. After services, well-wishers surrounded Adrea. Sylvie's friends offered congratulations, but Sylvie didn't.

Despite Sylvie's disapproval, it was no longer Grayson and Sara, but Grayson and Adrea. He spoke of his first wife less as he and Adrea developed a history of their own. Their names were now synonymous to those who knew them.

The smell of charbroiled burgers beckoned her back to setting the table. She rubbed her chilled hands together. Crazy. Who else would grill outdoors in the middle of March? But Dayne loved it.

She caught Tripod. "Away from the table, or I'll lock you in the house."

"Have you settled the new shop yet?" Grayson asked.

"I promise it will all be under control before the wedding. I'll find a great manager, so I won't have to go there but maybe once a month."

"Make it happen sooner." He flipped the burgers. "I'm tired of our bicoastal relationship."

"It's only two days a week and not that far." The nagging at her conscience wouldn't let up. "Have you talked to Edward and Joyce about our wedding?"

"Yes."

"And?"

"It's hard on them, but they're happy for us."

"I think we have one more thing to take care of before we can move forward. Do you think your mom or Grace could watch Dayne after supper?"

"Tonight?" He quirked an eyebrow.

"I'd like to get it over with."

—⁂—

By the time Grayson parked in the Owens' drive, Adrea's whole body trembled.

"I can do this." He squeezed her hand.

"No, it's my place." She jumped out of the car and hurried to the door, but he halted her.

"Okay, but do what you have to do. Then go."

"I can't drop my bomb and skulk away. What will they think of me?"

He smoothed her hair. "I don't want anything said in a moment of shock that could hurt for a lifetime."

Adrea shook her head.

"Okay, I'll leave with you, take you home, then come back to check on them." Grayson waited until she nodded, then rang the doorbell.

"Well, how nice to see you," Edward said. "Come in. I hear congratulations are in order."

She was thankful for his always gracious attitude. In contrast, Joyce looked anything but happy.

"Joyce, sorry to bother you without calling first." Grayson hugged his former mother-in-law. "Adrea and I need to clear some things up."

"Oh."

There wasn't any way to ease in to it, and her heart felt as if it would surely burst from her chest. "I was engaged to Wade Fenwick."

"Oh my." Joyce clasped her hand to her heart and reclaimed her seat on the sofa.

Adrea felt the blood drain from her face.

"Let me." Grayson tried to steer her toward the door.

"No, they should hear it from me." Adrea closed her eyes. "He'd been sober for two years when we met. Shortly before our wedding, I learned he'd been unfaithful, and I called off the engagement."

"Do we really need to do this?" Edward pulled his wife into his arms. "I'd just as soon never hear anything about that dreadful man. It's past history; what does it matter?"

"But it does matter." Adrea stared at the floor. "Our wedding day would have been February 14th, three years ago. He started drinking again because of our breakup."

Edward's face crumpled and a sob escaped Joyce.

Grayson urged Adrea toward the door.

"I'm sorry. Truly I am, but I—we—were afraid you'd hear it from someone else and be angry with us for not being honest with you."

Grayson hurried her outside.

Feeling cowardly, she wiped her eyes and looked toward the house next door. A redhead ducked behind the swaying curtains.

Adrea pulled away from Grayson and ran to his car.

—⁓—

On Easter evening, the twenty-six-year-old bride sat in one of Mountain Grove's classrooms. While Rachel wove baby's breath into Adrea's dark hair, Grace applied pale pink nail polish. Emma and Mom fluffed and clucked nervously as Adrea calmly sat in the midst of all the fuss.

When the door opened, all eyes turned, fearing the groom might have decided to do away with traditions. Instead, Joyce stood uncertainly in the entrance.

"Adrea, you look lovely."

"Thank you." She smiled, hoping her nervousness didn't show. "This is my mother, Samantha Welch, and my sister, Rachel. This is Joyce Owens, Sara's mother."

The women exchanged greetings.

Joyce turned her attention back to the bride. "I was hoping to speak with you."

Her stomach did a somersault. "Of course. I think they've done all they can do with me."

Rachel cleared her throat, prompting the other women to begin filing out. "We'll go see how things are coming along."

Adrea looked in the mirror and applied a little more blush. The white satin sapped her fair complexion of all color.

"I owe you an apology," Joyce said.

"You don't owe me anything."

"Yes, I do." Joyce pressed her fingertips to her temple. "I treated you badly at Dexter's and at Grace's wedding. Grayson never told us what happened, until a few days ago. I assumed that you'd broken up with him. But, even if you had, I shouldn't have ignored you."

"You gave our relationship your blessing, and then we broke up." Adrea adjusted her veil with trembling fingers. "It must have seemed like added heartache for no reason. And this new revelation certainly doesn't help matters, but I felt you had a right to know."

"And you were very brave for telling us the truth." Joyce moved to the window. "I trust God's plan and His timing completely. I won't claim to understand why bad things happen in this world."

Joyce turned to face her, as Adrea's tears spilled. "Now, don't do that. You'll muss your makeup." Joyce dabbed Adrea's cheeks with a tissue. "We don't blame you."

"But if I'd married Wade, Sara would still be alive."

"I don't think so. That goes back to God's plan and timing. I believe their lives would have collided, ending Sara's, no matter what you did."

"He'd been sober for two years, until *I* broke the engagement."

"The only thing that would have come of you marrying Wade Fenwick would have been heartache for you. Men don't usually change after marriage. He would have remained unfaithful, you'd have been miserable, and some disappointment could have set him to drinking eventually." Joyce handed her another tissue.

"Or maybe he would have celebrated at your wedding reception and you'd have been in the accident, as well. Or maybe something else would have ended Sara's life, but it would have happened. It was her time to go. God only lent my angel for a short time and then He took her home."

Adrea gulped a sob, and Joyce took her hand.

"I wanted to welcome you to our family today."

Her eyes swam with tears. "That means a lot to me. Thank you."

The two women hugged.

———

After repairing her makeup, Adrea and Joyce stepped into the foyer to find Edward waiting.

"Ah, looks like things are okay." He hugged Adrea. "Wade Fenwick caused you and Grayson a lot of pain. Now, God has brought the two of you together. No more looking back, only forward."

Daddy joined them. "Ready?"

Adrea nodded and the doors opened. The church echoed with the wedding march as Daddy escorted her down the aisle. Yellow roses filled every crevice and perfumed the air. Grace and Rachel, the matron of honor, dressed in yellow satin and lace with hooped skirts, stood with Haylee, the flower girl. A veritable feast waited in the fellowship hall.

Her breath caught at the sight of Grayson standing at the altar, beaming at her. Her very own Prince Sterling, resplendent in a white tuxedo with tails.

Dayne, as ring bearer, tried not to fidget. Best man, Mark, seemed almost as happy as she felt. Jack served as Grayson's groomsman while Joyce and Edward were given a seat of honor next to his mother. Helen sat with Adrea's mom, both dabbing their eyes with tissue.

Adrea's huge satin hoop skirt whispered with each stutter-step across yellow rose petals strewn by Haylee.

Love welled in her heart until she thought she might burst. God had taken the tattered pieces of her and Grayson's hearts and mended them into one.

When Graham declared Grayson and Adrea husband and wife, the sanctuary erupted with a joyful standing ovation.

Tears laced Adrea's lashes.

"You may kiss your bride."

Prince Sterling swept his bride into his arms and did just that.

# WHITE DOVES

# Dedication

To Daddy, my number-one fan. I'll never forget our trip to Dallas when you took me to claim my first important unpublished writing award, babysat my five year-old in the pool all day, and told everyone you met that your daughter was a writer.

I'd like to thank the real Romance, Arkansas, Postmaster, Angie Davis; Postmaster Relief, June Sullivan; and West Point, Arkansas, Postmaster, Debbie Minyard, for their insight into the inner workings of the post office. I appreciate EMT Doug Perry for his help with medical questions.

# Chapter 1

The post office door opened and Laken closed her eyes, waiting to hear Mother's accusing tone. A *whoosh* of June's humidity blasted her with its hot, steamy breath. Nibbling the inside of her lip until she tasted blood, she realized it was the employee door.

"Welcome to Love Station," a male voice said from behind her. "Hope you like weddings. I've got a whole passel of invitations."

Laken turned around. A man swung an overstuffed mail sack from his broad shoulder. Tanned calf muscles rippled beneath knee-length khaki shorts as he bent to scoop up a stray Post-it. He turned to face her. Laugh lines crinkled the corners of olive eyes.

"You must be the new postmaster." He wore a day's growth of beard, the kind that made a woman want to rub her cheek against it. A wind-blown coffee-colored lock dipped low over one eyebrow. He brushed away the stray wave and pressed the back of his wrist against the perspiration beading his forehead.

Until that moment, he looked like he'd stepped out of one of those cheesy soap operas, where perfect male specimens serve up a daily dish of melodrama. But romantic heroes don't sweat—even in Romance, Arkansas's sticky heat.

*Get a grip, Laken. So he's cute.* She tried to concentrate on the paneled walls, the tan commercial tile, the mail instead of the male.

"You're the. . ."

"Mail carrier at your service." He made a low, sweeping bow as if she were royalty, then straightened with a cocky grin and offered his hand. "Your loyal servant, Hayden Winters."

Laken hadn't paid much attention to what the transferring postmaster had said about the carrier, picturing a graying, potbellied Cliff Clavin, not a member of the hunk-of-the-month club. She cleared her throat. "I don't have any servants. Just coworkers. I'm Laken Kroft."

With a genuine smile, he grasped her hand and shook it then deposited another bloated manila envelope on her counter. He strode to his three-sided sorter, pulled the envelopes from each slotted divider, and stuffed them into his tray.

"Do you live around here?"

"I moved from Little Rock last week." She set a flats tray full of magazines next to him. "No packages today."

"Since my parents retired here a few years back, I moved from North

137

Little Rock last month so my nephew could be near them."

She propped her hands on her hips. "I'd like to know how you got to transfer exactly where you wanted to."

"I prayed for God to work it out and waited almost a year."

Her mouth went dry. Well, he was almost perfect. Too bad he had to start talking about God. She went back to stamping, with more determination.

*Clunk-clunk, clunk-clunk, clunk-clunk* reverberated in Laken's ears. With perfect precision, she imprinted the famous postmark barely at the edge of the entwined wedding rings on the fancy postage stamp. Just like the former postmaster had shown her.

"Do you have family in these parts?" Hayden scratched his chin. "Seems like there's a lady at my church in Rose Bud by the name of Kroft."

Laken stifled a sigh. If only her promotion could have materialized somewhere else. Somewhere far away from Searcy and her parents and all the people who knew them.

Already this morning, three customers had figured out her family ties. An imaginary clock ticked in Laken's left temple. Any minute, Mother would show up with a disapproving frown ready to dredge up the past.

Surely Mother had better things to do than drive forty-five minutes just to hassle Laken.

Hayden cocked an eyebrow.

She pursed her lips.

"Never mind. Just trying to make conversation." He stuffed more mail into his case.

Keeping rhythm with the *tick-tock* in her head, Laken clunk-clunked the metal stamp a little harder.

The door from the lobby opened and seemed to suck the cool air from the building. Forcing a smile, Laken turned to greet her next customer. Her smile died.

Over-bright, bottle-red hair and garish watermelon-colored lipstick drew attention to the wrinkles in her mother's face. Too many for a woman not quite fifty.

"Laken, I can't believe you're here."

Something in Mother's green eyes tugged at her. Hurt? No. No one could hurt Sylvie Kroft, even if they ran her down with a mail truck. She'd just come up slinging gossip about the driver.

"I thought certainly Mrs. Jones was wrong." Mother propped her hands on still-slim hips. "How could you, my own daughter, not call or visit for eight years?" Her voice grew louder and more shrewish with each word. "Eight years. Then land a job as postmaster and arrive in Romance without so much as a letter?"

"No one writes letters anymore." Despite her trembly insides, Laken willed herself not to break eye contact. "E-mail is the lament of the U.S. Postal Service."

Laken could almost see the steam erupt from her mother's ears.

"Young lady." With a forefinger, Mother jabbed the air in Laken's direction.

"Ahem." Hayden stepped into Mother's line of view, with a great show of clearing his throat, followed by a forced cough. "Hello, Mrs. Kroft."

Mother flashed a trademark fake smile. "I've seen you at church lately. You're. . ."

"Hayden Winters." He shook her hand.

"You have the young boy in the wheelchair." Mother cocked her head to the side, striving for innocence. "But I haven't seen a wife."

Hayden stiffened, and the light in his eyes dimmed. "Brady is my nephew. My sister died almost three years ago."

"Oh my." Mother clasped a hand over her mouth as if she'd intended no harm. "I'm so sorry. Was it a car accident? Is that what happened to Brady?"

Laken wished the mountain of wedding invitations would swallow her up as Hayden's inner light snuffed completely out.

"Mother, do you need something mailed?"

Her mother frowned. "No."

"Well then, Hayden has a lot of sorting to do, and I'm up to my eyebrows in invitations."

"But I came all the way from Searcy." Mother's mouth opened again. Nothing came out.

"I'm not here just for fun. I'm on the clock and I don't have time to"—*deal with you*—"visit."

Hayden's jaw clenched. "I'm sure your daughter is just nervous since it's her first day."

With an indignant, sharp nod Mother paraded out, head held high. The door thudded closed behind her.

Heat crept up Laken's neck. "Sorry about that."

"It's none of my business." The life in his voice drained dry. Hayden sifted through the mail in his case. "Brady and I love Palisade. I guess you used to attend there?"

"Yes." Her stomach knotted at the memories threatening to surface. She stamped the final invitation and began sorting by route.

"Then it would be like home for you. Of course, I hear there's a great church here in Romance, too, but since my folks live in Rose Bud, they've always attended Palisade."

"I really don't have time for church." *No church for me. No room for any more hypocrites in my life.*

"Well, if you change your mind, we'd love to have you. Better get going. See you later." He picked up his case and strode toward the door but came to an abrupt halt. "Looks like we've got a wedding. Guess I'll stay put. They usually don't take long."

"You'll get behind on your route."

"Who am I to interfere with romance?" The tic in his jaw contradicted his casual tone.

Laken peered out the small barred window in front. A young woman in a short white sheath dress stood beside a man in a black suit. Both faced another man holding a Bible. A blond man, with a discreet ponytail, wore a large camera around his neck. A woman, who looked like she'd just stepped out of *Vogue* magazine, carried a small cage, the top covered by a white cloth.

"So, they just show up?"

Hayden stepped into the lobby. "Some call ahead, especially if they want to get married inside the office. Sometimes, you get to play wedding planner."

Curious, Laken followed him to look out the window in the main door. "Why would anyone want to get married at the post office? I mean, why go to the trouble of getting married in Romance and have the ceremony here? Why not the park?"

"Or a church or the waterfalls?" Hayden's jaw clenched. "Just wait until Valentine's Day. I heard there were eight weddings in Romance this past year. And on top of that, you'll stamp yourself into a frenzy with cards and invitations arriving in droves for the special Love Station postmark."

"Different every year and in use from February first to the fifteenth."

"Very good. You catch on quick."

The young couple gazed into one another's eyes as the preacher spoke. Laken's mouth went dry. No one had ever looked at her like that.

The just-marrieds sealed their love with a kiss, and the foursome bowed their heads in prayer. Hayden did, too, and Laken's muscles tensed. Her throat constricted.

After a few seconds, the prayer ended. The woman with the cage stepped forward and set it in front of the bride and groom.

Laken swallowed the lump in her throat. "They're done."

Hayden raised his head.

The woman removed the cloth with flair, flapping it in the nonexistent breeze.

"What is that?"

"I'm assuming white doves."

The newlyweds took turns reaching into the cage and each pulled out a delicate, sleek bird with alabaster feathers. Laken gasped. In a flurry of wings, the birds of peace flew toward the heavens as the photographer focused his lens.

The doves flew up until they blended with puffy white clouds. She frowned. "Can they live in the wild?"

"They're rock doves. Like a homing pigeon, they find their way home."

She turned to face him. "Not something your typical mail carrier knows."

His throat convulsed. "I used to have a friend who worked for a handler in Little Rock. I better get busy with my route."

Hayden waited until all three cars drove away, then went back to the work area, retrieved his case, and opened the door. "See you this afternoon."

Not your typical mail carrier at all.

—⚭—

With the steering wheel in a vise grip, Hayden tried to concentrate on the road. Of all the dove handlers in Arkansas, it had to be Jan. She looked good, with her glossy blond businesslike bun at the nape of her neck. A perfect silver suit accentuated her lean build and gave her a dovelike appearance, almost matching the birds she'd set free. Nary a bead of sweat despite the temperature. Calm and cool as an iceberg.

The sad thing—even if he'd walked right into her, she'd have remained just as tranquil.

*Think about something else.* What was with Laken and her mother? Despite the scene between the two women, the soul-deep pain in Laken's pretty blue eyes haunted him. He'd seen that kind of sorrow.

In his own mirror.

Anguish still stared him down some days. But Jesus got him through the valleys.

Did she know Jesus?

He traveled the first winding gravel road on his route, then turned back onto Highway 5. Three stops later, he approached a bright blue Mustang convertible on the side of the road. The top was down and steam billowed from under the hood. Another victim of the stifling heat.

It couldn't be. A car just like that had been at the post office, but he hadn't paid attention to which car she'd driven away in. The Mustang looked like something she'd drive. Probably not the preacher. But maybe, just maybe it was the bride and groom. Or even a different car.

Hayden pulled to the shoulder behind the car and grabbed the two milk jugs of water and shop towel he kept handy for this purpose. As he walked toward the Mustang, the driver's door opened and a pair of long, shapely legs appeared. The woman stepped out onto the slightly sloped shoulder of the road, graceful despite her high heels.

Jan.

He swallowed hard.

"Hayden, what are you doing in this godforsaken place?"

"My route." He gestured toward the flashing yellow light on top of his truck. "And there's no place on earth that God has forsaken."

She rolled her eyes. "Still on your religious tangent, huh? Well, I'm melting here. Can you give us a lift out of Hooterville and back into civilization?"

The photographer sat in the passenger seat, with no offer to get out of the car, much less help. Probably her latest conquest.

*Thank You, Lord, for letting me see how shallow she was before it was too late.*

"More than likely, your radiator just needs water." He held up the jug. "This should do the trick."

"Just hurry." She crossed her arms over her chest.

He wadded the towel around the scorching radiator cap. The heat found its way to his fingers, and he jerked away. Three more attempts and he managed to twist the cap off and pour water in. More steam billowed and water hissed as it glub-glubbed into the boiling radiator.

"That should do it." He tightened the radiator cap. "Start it up now."

The powerful engine roared to life.

"Thanks."

He held the other gallon jug toward her.

Her nose crinkled at the dusty container.

"If it gets hot again, have GQ add water."

A sly grin pulled the corners of her mouth upward. "His name is Miles." She accepted the jug, tilting sideways at the awkward weight of it.

*Great, she thinks I'm jealous.*

"There's a station about fifteen minutes up the road in El Paso. Have them take a look and make sure you don't have a leak."

"I will." One perfectly plucked eyebrow rose. "So, how did you get demoted from postmaster in North Little Rock to mail carrier for this hick town?"

"I put in for the transfer. My parents live here, and Brady loves being near them." He waited. Surely she'd ask.

She rested a hand on his forearm. "It's good to see you."

"Brady's doing great." The tic in his jaw started up.

"I was hoping that by now, your parents would've taken the kid off your hands."

Hayden clenched his teeth and took a step back. "I'm glad we ran into each other, Jan. You haven't changed a bit."

"Thanks." Her radiant smile didn't waver as the insult sailed over her head like a white dove. She got back in her car, and with an elegant princess wave, pulled onto the highway.

When her car was out of sight, he shook his head. How could he have ever fallen for her? Had he really been that superficial?

Yes, he had. Until Katie got sick. Until Brady needed him.

Several vehicles whizzed past as Hayden started his engine. Taking a few deep breaths, he pulled back onto the highway and concentrated on getting the mail into the right boxes.

—⁂—

Almost home. Laken sighed. Could the rental house in Romance ever feel like home?

Thankfully, the rest of the week had been uneventful. Mother hadn't returned.

The contract carrier stopped in daily, an older gentleman, all business and in a hurry to get his load to Beebe. The other local carrier, middle-aged Carol, was friendly, outgoing, and prompt. Hayden could be a bit tight-lipped, but when in a talkative mood, he was pleasant.

With no more weddings, Laken's first week on the job ended on a peaceful note.

A white Cadillac sat in the drive of her new home as she pulled in, and a familiar redhead waited on the porch. Laken closed her eyes. So much for peace.

She opened the car door. "Mother, how did you know where I'm staying?"

"Everybody knows everything about everybody in Romance."

*Thanks to your gossip.* Laken bit her lip to keep the thought from becoming audible.

Mother swept a dismissive hand toward the front door. "Really, Laken, couldn't you find anything better?"

Laken gazed at the neat, freshly painted house. "What's wrong with it? It's newly remodeled and clean." And one of the only available accommodations in the tiny town.

"It's beneath you. Don't you know who once lived here?"

"No, but I'm certain you'll tell me more than I want to know."

"Watch your tone with me, young lady." Mother pointed a finger at her. "Wade Fenwick. You remember him, don't you? Slightly younger than you in school."

Laken unlocked the door. "Look, Mother, I'm tired. I just want a crème brûlée cappuccino and a bubble bath."

"You're not even going to invite me in?" Mother followed her in, obviously not needing an invitation. Her haughty glare took in the humble furnishings and the unpacked boxes lining the living room. "Wade was the town drunk, until he tried to off himself."

"I thought Father held that title."

Mother gasped. She drew a hand to her mouth, and her green eyes moistened.

Laken bit her tongue. Why had she been so cruel?

"I don't understand you kids." Mother shook her head. "Your father and I did everything for you. Yet both of you left, in your brand-new set of graduation wheels, without so much as a glance in the rearview mirror."

Laken softened her tone. "It's not like we were the perfect functional family."

"Your father's been through a lot."

"So that makes it okay to be a drunk?"

Mother's palm caught Laken across the left cheek. "Don't ever call your father that again."

Laken pressed her hand to her stinging cheek.

"You can't possibly understand."

"Then tell me, Mother." Laken held her hands palm up. "What is there to understand?"

"I can't." Shaking her head, Mother strode toward the door. "I'm sorry. I shouldn't have hit you. Welcome home, Laken." The door slammed behind her.

Laken locked it and leaned her throbbing temple against the frame.

—⁂—

Hayden neared the Rose Bud intersection and flicked on his turn signal. Maybe his parents wouldn't come outside. He could avoid their blaming attempts for the day and hurry Brady for a quick getaway.

His cell phone vibrated. An unfamiliar number showed. With a frown, he flipped it open. "Hello?"

"Who is this?" a male voice asked.

"Hayden Winters. Who is this?"

Silence.

"Hello."

"I'm trying to get in touch with Katie. She gave me this number."

The breath went out of Hayden, as if he'd been kicked in the gut. He pulled the truck to the shoulder of the highway. "What kind of sick joke are you playing?"

"It's no joke. It's Collin."

The Collin who took advantage of his little sister and left her pregnant and alone. The Collin whose last name Katie never revealed because she knew Hayden would find him and pound his face in.

Heat boiled up inside his chest. "It's a little late to be calling. Where were you three years ago?" *Where were you seven years ago?*

"Being a jerk. Please." A shaky sigh echoed. "Just tell me. Is she okay?"

Hayden's jaw clenched. "No, she's not okay. She's dead."

An audible gasp. "No."

"And you couldn't even give her the time of day when she needed you most."

"I didn't know." Collin's voice cracked.

His temple pounded. "Don't give me that."

"I didn't. I swear."

"She sent you a letter, begging you to come, and you never even bothered to answer."

"You have to believe me. I never got it, until last week."

Hayden closed his eyes. He'd seen a few chewed-up envelopes stuck in the bottom of bar code sorters. But not for three years.

"I believe you have something that belongs to me."

# Chapter 2

B rady is not a possession," Hayden hissed.

Collin sighed. "You know what I mean. He's my son."

"Why now?" His throat convulsed.

"I have legal rights and I want to see him."

"I wouldn't be so sure about that after abandoning him."

"I didn't know he existed." Collin bit out the words.

Hayden swallowed all the hateful things he wanted to say. Collin had just as much ammo. He just didn't realize it. *Stay cool.* Hayden clenched his fist tighter on the steering wheel. "Let me talk to him. Prepare him."

"Of course. Where do you live, so I can make my plans?"

Tempted to hang up, somehow Hayden knew this complication wouldn't go away. "Rose Bud, Arkansas."

"It just so happens, I know exactly where that is. I'll make plans for a visit and be in touch."

He sucked in several deep breaths. A full fifteen minutes passed before he pulled back onto the highway.

Turning into his drive, he killed the engine and pressed a fist to his mouth. "Not now, Lord. Brady's happy. We're settled."

A rhythmic bounce echoed through the evening stillness. Back and forth, Brady rolled his wheelchair across the house-wide porch, dribbling a basketball.

The friends he'd made at church didn't ask about his chair or make fun of him. His easy manner and humor blended right in. He was just one of the guys, and the other kids loved his wheelies and cool basketball tricks he'd learned from therapy and hours of practice. In August, he'd begin the second grade with a handful of friends already made.

If only Hayden were the one in the chair instead. He ran a hand through his hair, stepped out of his pickup, and cut through the line of crape myrtle trees between his and his parents' houses.

But his nephew never complained, never accused. Sometimes Hayden wished Brady would just put the blame where it belonged.

Squarely on Hayden's shoulders.

Brady saw him and stopped dribbling. "I aced registration. Justin and Mike are both in my class."

"Great." Hayden stepped up on the porch and tousled the boy's stiff brown hair. "Been in the gel again?"

"All the kids wear it. You want me to fit in, don't you?"

"There's fitting in, and there's setting your own trend."

Brady rolled his eyes. "That's what Grandma said."

"Grandma's always right."

A barn swallow chirped from her perch in a crape myrtle tree, warning them away from her nest under the eave of the house.

"I think they're about to fly." Wistfulness echoed in Brady's voice.

Soiled siding lined the area under the nest. He and Brady had spent hours watching the mother bird build her little mud nest and marveled at the five fuzzy heads peering over the edge. Then things got messy. Daily, Dad or Hayden hosed off the siding, while the mother bird swooped and twittered. But Brady's sadness at their coming departure tugged at him.

Hayden knelt beside Brady. Might as well get it over with. "I got a phone call today."

"From who?" Brady's blue eyes narrowed. So much like Katie, sometimes it almost hurt to look at the boy.

Hayden's jaw began the familiar tic, and he tried to put some enthusiasm in his tone. "How would you like to see your dad?"

"My dad?" Brady's eyes widened and a smile quivered, but a frown won. "Why?"

"He'd like to come for a visit."

The boy's bottom lip trembled. "I thought he didn't want me."

Hayden's fists clenched. Oh, to sucker punch Collin. "No, Brady. Don't ever think that. It just so happens, he didn't know about you."

Brady frowned harder and a tear spilled. "How could he not know about me?"

Hayden caught the moisture with his thumb and hugged his nephew. "Sometimes adult stuff is complicated. Your mom and dad broke up before she knew about you. So he never knew you were born. If he'd known, I'm sure he'd have come a long time ago, but he just recently learned about you."

"Hey, what's going on?" The screen door opened, and Mom stepped out on the porch, a frown winged over her accusing eyes.

"Hi, Mom. I was just telling Brady that his dad wants to come for a visit." Her chin trembled.

*Come on, Mom, keep it positive. It's just a visit. I hope.* "It'll be good for Brady to see his dad."

Mom nodded. Salt-and-pepper curls danced. When had she started going gray?

"We've already eaten. Want me to warm you a plate?"

His gut rumbled. Home-cooked food. But he couldn't sit across the table from his folks. The blame in their eyes would sour his stomach. "I'll get something at home. Ready, Brady?"

"Yep." The boy wiped his face with the back of his hand and started dribbling again. The rhythmic bouncing continued down the ramp.

Laken's cell vibrated in her pocket and she jumped, further jangling her nerves. Collin.

"Collin." Laken sank into the plaid couch. She pressed her fingertips over quivering lips as a rush of how badly she'd missed him threatened to crush her last semblance of composure. Eight years since she'd seen him. "Why haven't you called me lately?"

"This last week has been rough."

"Same here." She closed her eyes.

"Listen, I'll be in town soon."

"You're coming here?" Her heart leapt. She slipped off her tennis shoes and propped tired, achy feet on the coffee table. "Okay, so let's get together."

"That's why I'm calling. I need your help with something."

"Whatever I can do." Almost like she actually had a family. Someone to talk to. Someone to lean on. Someone who cared. "It'll be good to see you."

"I'll call again when my plans are more definite. Don't tell the parents."

She managed a fake laugh. "Like I talk to them."

"You haven't?"

Her gaze wandered to the bare walls, where no family portraits hung. "Well, I've had two run-ins with Mother since I've been here. It wasn't pretty."

"I bet. I'd like to make it in and out of town without their knowledge."

"Good luck with that." She nibbled on the inside of her lip. "Maybe we could meet in Little Rock."

"No, I have to come there."

She frowned. "What's going on?"

"I'll explain when I arrive. See you, sis."

Tears burned, but she wiped them away. Her stomach growled a reminder that she'd skipped lunch. She wandered into the kitchen and grabbed a Coke and a package of shelled peanuts. The icy soft drink fizzed as she dumped the treat into the glass. She took a swig of her brother's favorite beverage.

*Mmm*, the salty sweetness hit the spot. How many times had they sneaked to her playhouse with their favorite snack, right before supper?

Maybe her sort-of meals alone were almost over. At least, temporarily. Collin was coming home.

Midweek, July opened with a blast of intense heat. Thank goodness Laken didn't have a route to run. In the perfectly cool office, she marveled at how fast the envelopes flew as Hayden and Carol stood at their sorters, casing their routes by address.

"So, Jim and I are going on the trail ride." Carol's amber eyes never left her bin. "Are you bringing Brady?"

"I am." Hayden nodded. "It'll be nice to meet your husband."

"I'm hoping if he meets a few people, I might get him to come to church. He's very shy."

"Really?"

"I scared him to death the first time we met." Carol paused and glanced at Laken. "If you don't have plans, why don't you come for the Fourth of July trail ride and picnic? You could meet people, and it'll be over in plenty of time to go see the fireworks display in Searcy."

Laken's nose wrinkled. She already knew entirely too many in this community. Why did Carol have to drag her into the conversation?

"Oh come on. Do you like to ride horses?"

A smile tugged at Laken's mouth.

"I'd say you do." Carol snapped her fingers. "Your eyes just lit up. Don't try to deny it."

"I always wanted to ride but never got the chance."

"Well, here's your chance."

Laken shook her head. "I don't attend the church, and I'm not interested in getting involved."

"Who said you had to? Come on, Hayden, help me talk her into it."

"Anyone can come." Hayden continued his sorting. "And you used to attend there."

"Really?" Carol shrugged. "So, you could get reacquainted."

A weight settled on Laken's shoulders. "I know what you're up to."

"What?" Carol feigned her best innocent face.

"You talked your husband into coming so you can rope him into going to church. No offense, but I'd rather not be roped."

Carol's lips pursed. "Busted."

"Just come to the trail ride." Hayden finished sorting and carried his case to the side door. "I promise I won't bother you about attending church."

"Me, too," Carol chimed in with a grin. "Just think, one trail ride, and we won't bother you about church. Horses and a picnic lunch. Come on, it'll be fun."

It did sound like fun. A lot more fun than drinking Coke and eating peanuts alone. And though Mother attended the church, she wouldn't come for an outdoor event. She'd never risk sweating.

As Hayden carried his case out the service exit, the lobby door opened.

"Laken Kroft, I can't believe you haven't called me."

She'd know that voice anywhere. A bubble of good memories whooshed through her soul, followed by sadness. Bittersweet. As she scurried out to the lobby, tears threatened.

"Grace, it's so good to see you." Laken shrugged. "I didn't know if you were still around, and I'm still settling in."

Grace hugged her, and the tears won. "I'll let it pass, this time."

Carol cleared her throat. "So I guess there's no need to introduce y'all."

"Sorry, didn't mean to ignore you, Carol." Grace waved. "Laken and I were friends all through school."

"How's Grayson?" Laken swiped at her eyes, but her words came out in a watery whisper.

A frown marred Grace's delicate brow. "He's good. Really. He married a wonderful woman a few months ago, and she's great with Dayne. We all love Adrea. Sara would've, too."

"I should have come home."

"You're here now." Grace linked arms with her. "We have to get together and catch up. In the meantime, I brought you something. Come out to the car for a minute. Carol can handle things here."

The two women walked outside. "What are you doing these days?" Laken asked.

"I married the love of my life in January. Mark is Grayson's associate pastor at the church and Adrea's brother." She patted her flat stomach. "And we just found out I'm pregnant."

A twinge of jealousy jabbed her. "That's awesome!"

"Even better. Adrea is, too, so come January and February, we'll have double cousins. I'll hire another employee then and cut down my hours." Grace opened the back door of a cream-colored SUV.

A mix of savory smells made Laken want to lick her lips. She read the lettering on the window. "You're a caterer, just like you always wanted."

Grace deposited a flat box in Laken's hands. "How about you? Are you married? Kids?"

"No." Laken pushed the familiar longing down deep and concentrated on identifying the contents of the box. "My favorite? Mexican pinwheels."

"Glad your tastes haven't changed. Speaking of which, have you seen your mom?"

Laken took a deep breath. "A couple of times."

"Are things any better between y'all?"

"Not really."

They trailed back to the office.

"I'll pray about it."

Laken frowned.

Back inside, Grace set a cellophane bag filled with blond cedar wood, spruce fronds, and walnuts on the counter. "I brought you a little present."

A woodsy, spicy aroma emanated from the bag.

"Mmm." Carol sniffed. "Walk in the Woods, my favorite Aromatique smell."

"My new sister-in-law owns the local floral shop so I picked it up there. It's a welcome-home gift for Laken, but I bet she'll share the Mexican pinwheels."

The service door opened and Hayden returned.

"Hey, Hayden, I brought Mexican pinwheels."

"My favorite." Hayden rubbed his palms together.

"Laken and Grace are old friends." Carol nabbed a treat. "Small world, huh?"

Hayden raised a brow. "Seems Laken has lots of ties around here."

"Grace, you'll be at the trail ride. Hayden and I were trying to talk Laken into going." Carol popped another pinwheel into her mouth.

"Grace was the natural." Laken patted her friend's shoulder. "I'd probably stink at it."

"Sara was too frilly, while Laken always wanted to get dirty, but her mother wouldn't let her." A smile tugged at Grace's mouth. "Come with us, Laken. It'll be fun. Grayson will be a familiar face, and you can meet Dayne, Adrea, and Mark."

Laken chewed at the inside of her lip. "When is it?"

"Seven on Saturday. I'll be busy with the food, but if you don't mind going early, you can ride with Mark and me. That way, you don't have to show up by yourself."

"Or Jim and I can pick you up." Carol scooted her case toward the door.

Laken shook her head. "I've never ridden, and I have no idea where to find a horse to ride, anyway."

"I know just the mare for you." Hayden grinned. "Pearl, my parents' dappled gray, is the calmest I've ever seen. Brady learned on her and he's seven."

"Perfect." Carol pushed wiry, silvered hair away from her face and grabbed her case. "It's all set then. We'll pick you up at a quarter to seven."

"But I didn't—"

The door shut behind Carol.

Grace slung her purse higher on her shoulder and turned toward the lobby. "See you Saturday. I better get busy making deliveries."

Hayden opened the service door, held it with his foot, and picked up his other case.

"I'm not going back to church." Laken propped her hands on her hips.

"I didn't ask you to, and I won't." He shouldered the door open wider and left.

So why did she feel pressured to go?

—⁂—

The easy comfort between Carol and her husband put a dull ache in Laken's heart. Though Jim barely said two words on the drive to the church in Rose Bud, his adoration for his wife shone in the way he listened to her almost constant commentary, the way he entwined his free hand with hers, and the way he immediately adjusted the air-conditioning when she complained about the heat.

They pulled into the parking lot, and Laken's stomach twisted. A small crowd of people and horses gathered under a large oak tree toward the back of the brick building.

Jim got out of the car.

Carol remained seated. "The trail cuts through the woods and winds back around to the Family Life Center."

Jim came around and opened Carol's car door, then Laken's, too.

Humidity hung in the air as Laken stepped from the cool interior.

"Want some?" Carol sprayed her ankles with an aerosol can.

The fog smelled deadly. Laken's nose scrunched. "Eau de Off. Sure."

Carol laughed.

Hayden met them on the freshly mown lawn. "The pastor wants everyone to gather around back."

What could Grayson have to say? Restroom facility directions? Laken hung back, not certain she wanted to hear, uncomfortable with seeing Sara's husband with another woman.

Several familiar people from her childhood greeted her.

"Hi, I'm Adrea Sterling."

Laken turned around. A pretty, dark-haired woman offered her hand. Grayson's new wife. Her pregnancy undetectable.

"I'm the pastor's wife. We're so glad you came today."

"Thanks. I'm Laken Kroft. Grace, Carol, and Hayden"—*ganged up on me*—"invited me." Her new friends continued toward the crowd, apparently not noticing she'd stopped.

"Oh, you're the new postmaster. My mother, Sam Welch, just transferred to Rose Bud."

"A very nice lady. She showed me around my first morning."

"I'm so sorry I haven't been by yet."

Laken frowned. "Was I expecting you?"

"I own the floral shop in Romance and usually bring all the newcomers a plant, sort of a welcome thing. Morning sickness put me behind." Adrea pressed a hand to her stomach. "Some days it lasts all day, but today, I'm good."

"I'm glad you're feeling better, but you don't have to bring me anything."

"But I want to. Now, you're Sylvie's. . ."

Resisting the urge to scream, Laken swallowed. "Daughter."

Adrea's face reflected only sincere kindness. "I bet your mother is pleased you're home."

"Yes." A bitter taste rose in Laken's throat. An ominous buzz neared, and she stiffened then relaxed as a red wasp flew past.

"Adrea." Grayson curled an arm around his wife's slender waist. "You sure you're feeling up to this?"

"I'm fine." Adrea kissed his cheek.

In his late twenties now, Grayson hadn't changed much.

He stuck out his hand and blinked. "Laken! It's been a long time. Grace mentioned you were in town, and I'm so glad you came." He raised an eyebrow. "Are you here visiting?"

"Actually, I recently moved to the area."

"She took Mom's place at the post office." Adrea waved a persistent fly away. "So, you grew up next door to Sara?"

Laken managed a nod as her heart clenched, even after more than three years. She hadn't come home for Grayson and Sara's wedding. She should have at least come home for Sara's funeral.

"So what church do you attend?"

Something inside her chest tightened, and she didn't know what to say.

"Listen to me rattling on." Adrea smiled. "Excuse me, I think I'll go in where it's cool until time to go. We're glad you're here, Laken."

Laken turned to Grayson. "I'm sorry, I just came to ride horses."

"And that's all we're here for, but if you decide you'd like to come to church, that would be fine, too."

She searched the crowd for her friends. "I better catch up with Hayden. He brought the horse I'm supposed to ride."

"It was nice to see you again."

Someone squealed behind her. "Laken, I'm so glad you came." Grace gave her a quick squeeze. "This is my husband, Mark."

The boyishly handsome man could barely take his brown eyes off of Grace to look at Laken. "Nice to meet you. I've heard a lot about you."

An earsplitting whistle cut through the hum of numerous conversations.

Everyone quieted and Grayson addressed them. "Welcome to our first Fourth of July trail ride and picnic. With this good of a turnout, it just may become an annual event. I'm Grayson Sterling, pastor here at Palisade. Most folks call me Pastor Grayson. We're planning to have some fun. Let's ask the Lord to bless our evening." He bowed his head.

"Dear heavenly Father, thank You for the lovely day You've blessed us with. Thank You for these who have come. Bless our fellowship and our safety. Remind us that all good things come from You. In Jesus' precious name, amen."

Grayson scanned the group. "Now, I planned to make this event all about patriotism, but God impressed a verse on my heart this morning and a mini-sermon. I figure if He gave it to me, there's a reason, so just bear with me."

Laken's stomach lurched.

"Philippians 4:7." He opened his Bible. " 'And the peace of God, which passeth all understanding, shall keep your hearts and minds through Christ Jesus.' " He looked up at the gathering. "Do you ever wonder how people deal with the hurts in this world?"

A weight settled on Laken's chest. She stepped backward, right onto someone's foot, and turned to see Hayden. "Sorry," she whispered.

"You okay?" he mouthed.

"Is that the horse?" She pointed to a gray mare with dark-ringed white specks splashed over her coat.

He nodded.

"I think I'll go get familiar with her."

Grayson's voice rang clear in the hush. "For the Christian, we lean on Jesus in rough times. We trust Him to give us that peace that 'passeth all understanding,' and He never fails to deliver on His promises. But I wonder about the folks who don't know that peace. How do they survive the tragedies and torments of this life?"

Laken turned away and tried to tune him out, to concentrate on the choir of birdsong and the fragrant honeysuckle overtaking a nearby barbed-wire fence, but she couldn't. Grayson's words tugged at something deep inside as she stroked the horse's silken muzzle.

"I charge the members of this church to reach out with Christian love to those who are hurting—those who are believers, and especially those who don't know our Jesus. If there's anyone who doesn't know Him, please make that decision. Today. All you have to do is ask."

The woods beckoned. Laken circled around until the horse was between her and the gathering. No one seemed to notice. Casually, she strolled under the plush, green denseness of the trees.

"If you don't know Jesus," Grayson—Pastor Grayson—continued, "repeat this prayer. 'Dear Lord, I know I'm a sinner. I come to You, with nowhere else to turn. I've tried living on my own steam, Lord, and it's not going very well. I need Your help. Give me new purpose and Your precious peace.'"

Even though Laken tried not to pay any attention, the words sank in. She darted farther into the woods. The sound of her breathing and last fall's dead leaves crunching with each step muffled his voice. Acorns and pinecones rolled under her tennis shoes, and she almost lost her footing.

Deep in the pine, cedar, and oak, Laken tried to erase Grayson's words from her brain. Even when she could no longer hear him, she kept running, until she couldn't remember which direction she'd come from. Her pulse raced from more than mere exertion.

She stopped to catch her breath. Her bright orange T-shirt clung to sweaty skin. The humid air congested her lungs. Looking up, she caught only glimpses of the blue sky in the thick overgrowth. Though still a good hour before dusk, the forest was dark. The trees closed in.

An eerie, bloodcurdling shriek erupted overhead.

# Chapter 3

The barred owl's catlike screech punctuated the close of Pastor Grayson's prayer. Though Hayden had heard the creature before, the hair on the back of his neck stood on end.

A human scream pierced the stillness.

Hayden's heart jolted as he turned to check on Laken and Pearl. The mare shivered, swishing her tail to ward off flies.

Laken was gone.

He frowned. Surely she hadn't taken off in the woods on her own with only copperheads to keep her company. He scanned the crowd. "Carol, have you seen Laken?"

"She was with Pearl the last time I saw her." Carol shielded her eyes and looked around. "Grace, have you seen Laken?"

"Last I saw, she walked over to the edge of the woods."

"Did she take the path?" Hayden scrubbed his palm across his stubbled cheek.

"No." Grace shook her head. "I figured she was looking for shade."

The owl shrieked again.

Hayden cupped his hands around his mouth. "Laken!"

"I'm sure she's just fine." Grace patted his shoulder. "And with this many people milling about, we're sure to find her."

"Brady's riding over with his Sunday school teacher after his riding lesson." Hayden backed toward the trail. "Carol, can you wait for him?"

"Sure." With a nod, Carol turned toward the church.

Hayden loped into the thick woods. Memories of getting lost as a kid assailed him with unseen terrors in the shape of tree limbs clawing at his back. Not to mention the very real copperheads. "Laken!"

"I'm here." Her faint voice sounded far in the distance and way off the path.

Cupping his hands around his mouth again, he shouted, "Are you okay?"

"So far."

The pressure in his chest eased. "Are you lost?"

"Most definitely."

As he turned into the thick underbrush, briars tore at the ankles of his jeans. "Keep talking."

"What should I say?"

Hayden grinned. "Anything. Just help me find you."

"Did the trail ride leave without us?" She sounded closer.

"Not yet." His side ached, but he kept running.

"Guess I should have stayed with the group."

He caught a glimpse of orange to his left, about five hundred yards away. "I see you."

"You do?" He saw Laken turn and peer into the trees. Relief sounded in her voice.

He reached her, stopped, and bent over. With his hands propped on his knees, he inhaled a lungful of humid air.

"Sorry to be so much trouble. I just wanted to get out of the sun."

"I believe you managed that." He straightened as his breathing slowed. "You okay?"

"I'm fine. I hope you know the way back."

"The path is over there." He gestured toward his right.

She fell into stride beside him. "Thanks."

"No problem."

The owl shrieked again.

Laken jumped and grabbed his arm, her nails digging into his bicep. "What is that?" Her voice quivered.

"An owl." He caught a whiff of coconut shampoo from her caramel-colored lengths. She felt nice on his arm, despite her taloned grip. How long had it been since he'd felt like a protector instead of the destroyer?

"I appreciate you trying to make me feel better, but I prefer the truth."

"It's a barred owl, I promise. He sounds close. Maybe we can find him." Hayden stopped and searched the trees overhead. "Some folks call them screech owls, for obvious reasons."

Laken didn't release his arm, but her nails let up.

Scanning the limbs, he spotted the unblinking creature. "There." He pointed. "See him in that big pine? He's white and brown mottled and streaked. Kind of blends in with the bark."

"He's so big." A smile sounded in her voice. "I've never seen a real, live owl. I mean, away from the zoo. He's so beautiful."

"God created amazing creatures."

Her hand dropped to her side.

Not ready to let her go, Hayden entwined his fingers with hers in the guise of leading her back toward the path. Rotting leaves from last fall swished and crunched with each step. "Didn't you grow up around here?"

"We lived in Searcy and started coming here for church when I was eleven."

"Come to think of it, I've lived in a few rural areas and only heard a barred owl a few times."

As they moved away from the owl, it screeched again.

"That's the creepiest thing I've ever heard." Laken shivered. "Aren't owls nocturnal?"

"It's dark enough in here; he probably thinks it's dusk." Hayden pushed a branch out of the way and held it until she stepped through the opening. "Reminds me of when I was a kid on a road trip to visit relatives. We were somewhere in Mississippi at a motel with a pool so packed my sister and I couldn't get in."

He kept his eyes trained on the ground, making sure nothing moved among the bed of leaves in front of them. "It wasn't a very developed area, with lots of woods around. Katie and I sat on the deck, mad, until a barred owl cut loose. Apparently, no one else had heard one before. Within minutes, we had the pool to ourselves."

Laken laughed. "I can't say I blame them."

"What you should worry about in these woods are snakes, tarantulas, and scorpions. Especially snakes. Copperheads love to den up in dead leaves to escape from the heat."

Her hand shook in his grasp.

Oops, he'd really scared her. He softened his tone. "I just want you to understand, straying off the path isn't such a good idea."

"Mother never would let us near the woods growing up, so I don't have much experience."

They reached the trail, but he didn't let go of her hand. A comfortable silence surrounded them, until he saw a few riders in the distance.

She stiffened and pulled her hand loose.

—⁂—

Laken followed Hayden as he stepped to the side of the path. They met horse after horse.

"Oh good, you found her." Adrea rode behind Grayson on a large russet-colored horse. "We decided to start the ride so we could help. I'm already dreaming of the air conditioner at the end of this tunnel."

Several other riders greeted them, glad for her safety.

"Great," Laken whispered. "Everyone's laughing because the greenhorn got lost."

"No one's laughing. They're glad you're safe, and we won't miss the ride."

Laken wiped sweat from her brow and imagined her frizzy hair and melting makeup. "Didn't Adrea say something about air-conditioning?"

"Jack Phillips owns this property. He's a deacon and the adult Sunday school teacher. The trail comes out at his barn. We'll leave the horses there then head back to the church's Family Life Center. Besides being cooler there, people who don't ride can come, too."

The urge to jump up and down fluttered through Laken's brain, but the heat sapped her energy. "I was wondering why y'all picked July to have a trail ride."

"We wanted to move the Fourth of July to a cooler season, but. . ." Hayden's lips quivered with an almost smile.

She laughed. "I guess that wouldn't work very well. Where's your nephew?"

"He hadn't arrived yet, when I left to find you. Carol's waiting for him."

At the end of the trail, a man sat astride a horse, addressing a group of kids on horseback. Pearl and three riderless horses waited with Carol and Jim near the church.

"There's Brady," Hayden whispered. "The one on the paint."

"Paint?"

"The pinto—brown- and white-splotched."

"Oh." Laken spotted the horse with the boy astride intently listening to the man speaking. The child had some of Hayden's features. "That's their Sunday school teacher, Bob Reynolds."

Not a wheelchair in sight. The child looked perfectly capable. "How did he get on the horse?" As soon as the question passed her lips, she bit her tongue, remembering her mother's nosiness and Hayden's reaction. "I'm sorry. I shouldn't have asked."

"It's okay." Hayden swallowed. "Bob built a special ramp he keeps at his place since we board our horses there. He retired from a therapeutic riding ranch in Bentonville, and he gives Brady lessons."

The teacher finished speaking and turned his horse toward the path. The kids followed single file.

"Come on, I'll introduce you." Hayden jogged over to the brown-spotted horse. Its platinum mane and dark-tipped tail bounced with each stride. "Brady, this is Laken."

"Whoa, Spot." The boy slowed his horse and smiled, revealing a gap where his front tooth should have been. "Hi, Laken."

Hayden cleared his throat. "Have fun and—"

"Be careful. If I fall off, it won't hurt my legs." The boy giggled. "See you."

The muscle in Hayden's jaw began a rhythmic tic.

"He certainly has a good attitude about his. . ." *Handicap* didn't fit the unflappable child.

"He's handled it better than any of us." He strode toward the church.

Laken almost had to jog to keep up with his long strides.

—∞—

"Relax." Hayden trailed behind Laken as she bounced on her saddle like a dribbling basketball. He'd hate to see what happened if the horse did more than walk.

"I'm trying."

Her attempt to play it cool, despite obvious discomfort, threatened to tug a chuckle out of him. "Let your body move with Pearl's rhythm. I promise she won't throw you. She barely shivered when the owl cut loose earlier."

Despite his instructions, her posture never relaxed. At the end of the trail, Hayden followed her into direct sunlight.

157

"Are we almost there?"

"See that metal building?"

"Way over there?" Her question came out in a moan.

Her backside probably ached by now. "I can help you down if you'd rather lead Pearl."

"No."

She had to be the most stubborn, determined woman he'd ever met. He liked that in a pretty girl.

Hayden closed his eyes. But strength alone couldn't get her through this life. Laken didn't know Jesus, which meant Hayden needed to introduce the two.

"Why are you so quiet back there? You better not be laughing at me."

"I'm not. Head for the gate up there." All amusement drained from Hayden's soul, leaving behind a void. If she wouldn't accept the introduction to his best friend, he and Laken could have no future.

Where did that come from? He didn't want a future with any woman. After Jan, he'd vowed to never trust another woman.

The last several yards of the ride passed in silence.

As they neared, Jack opened the metal gate for them.

"Give a light tug on the reins."

Laken followed Hayden's command and Pearl stopped near the barn, where numerous horses stood around several large water troughs in the edge of the woods.

"I can't wait to feel the air-conditioning." Laken dismounted, wobbly but without help.

Hayden helped take the saddles off the eagerly drinking horses. "I guess that means you'd like a ride back to the church instead of walk?"

"Your truck's here?"

"Several folks drove here and rode the horses to the church."

"A ride in an air-conditioned vehicle. Utopia."

—✴—

Cars lined the center's parking lot. Cool air met them as Hayden opened the door for Laken and followed her inside. A momentary chill crawled over his heated skin.

"Oh, this is heavenly." Laken took a deep breath. "This wasn't here when I attended."

Determined not to tell her it wasn't anywhere close to heaven, Hayden clamped his mouth shut. He had to take it slow with her. "It's a great place for large events, and the kids love the basketball court."

Three end-to-end tables laden with food buzzed with women uncovering dishes, stirring, and supplying dippers for each bowl. Grace waved to Laken from the middle of the huddle. More tables and chairs surrounded the makeshift buffet line.

Several people greeted Laken with obvious joy at seeing her again.

With a heaping plate, Brady sat at a table with his friends. But his interested gaze locked on the basketball goals at each end of the gym.

"He doesn't like for me to hover." Hayden smoothed sweat-soaked hair away from his face. "I try to give him space, but it's hard."

Laken gasped.

"What?" Hayden followed her gaze. Her mother stood across the gym, openmouthed. "Do you want to leave?"

"No. I'm fine." Laken turned her back on the redhead.

In Hayden's experience, Sylvie Kroft was hard to ignore. What was with these two anyway? Of course, he wasn't one to wonder about others' family issues. He had his own.

Someone clinked silverware against glass, and Pastor Grayson prayed over the meal. At the close of the blessing, a line formed. Hayden ushered Laken ahead of him.

Carol stopped near them with a case of Cokes. "I just heard you're Sylvie's daughter and you practically grew up in this church."

"Let me get that." Hayden took the load from her.

"You're our guest." Carol linked her arm through Laken's. "Come on, you shouldn't be so far back in line."

Laken blushed. "No. I'm fine here."

"I insist, and could you move it along?" Carol motioned toward Hayden's load. "That thing's kinda heavy."

"Don't rush on my account." Hayden grinned. "But you might as well go with Carol. She won't leave you alone."

"You, too, Hayden, since she's your guest."

"Uh, I think you gave the initial invite." Hayden nudged Laken with a gentle elbow. "But Carol's right. Guests go first."

Laken's mouth straight-lined, but she gave in.

Carol led Laken toward where her mother stood farther up in line.

"Really." Laken's eyes widened. "This is so unnecessary."

"Everyone." Carol clapped her hands until the gathering quieted. "Some of you probably remember Sylvie Kroft's daughter, Laken. She's the new postmaster over at Romance. Be sure and welcome her home."

The crowd applauded with a few shouts of welcome.

Red-cheeked, Laken's body stiffened. She glanced toward the door.

Hayden tensed, half-expecting her to flee.

"Laken," Sylvie whispered, her eyes begging. "Please."

—⁓—

The entire room fell silent, awaiting Laken's response. She took in a sea of familiar faces from her childhood, along with a smattering of new families. Grace offered moral support with a wink.

Laken wanted to tell them Romance was the last place she wanted to be, that she hadn't spoken to her mother in eight years, and she was nothing like her mother. She cleared her throat.

"It's wonderful to be here," she mumbled. "Thank you."

Beside her, Hayden blew out a sigh.

The chatter of numerous conversations resumed.

A deep breath filled her senses with the savory smell of fried chicken and baked beans. Foods that would usually make her mouth water, but tension crashed through every nerve ending in tidal waves, stealing her appetite.

Laken concentrated on filling her plate and claimed a seat at the end of a table. Mother settled beside her, with Hayden across from them.

"This is Virgie Patton and Doreen Hughes." Hayden gestured to two ladies.

Mother patted the seat beside her. "My dearest friends."

"Nice to meet you." With a fake smile in place, Laken picked at her coleslaw, the only thing she could possibly stomach.

Virgie took the seat beside Hayden. She didn't fit in with the other two. Her silver hair was natural and unfussed with, her jewelry sedate and modest, her blouse and skirt probably from Walmart.

Doreen settled beside Mother, completing Mother's clique perfectly. Her too-dark hair, fresh from her hairdresser's shampoo and set, curled perfectly around her too-made-up face. Her nails modeled a professional manicure with flashy rings on almost every finger. Her designer perfume hung heavy in the air, complemented by a trendy high-dollar dress.

"So, Laken." Doreen took a sip of her iced tea. "Why are we just now meeting you?"

Laken swallowed hard. "I've spent the last several years concentrating on my career. Unfortunately, that left little time for much else." Why was she working so hard at convincing everyone things were fine with Mother? Like they hadn't been estranged for the last eight years. To save face? Uphold the charade Mother lived?

A wrinkled hand settled on Laken's shoulder. Turning, she looked up into the kind eyes of Helen Fenwick.

Hayden grinned. "Helen. How are you?"

"Fine. I wanted to welcome Laken."

Laken's smile reached her heart. "It's nice to see you again."

Mother's mouth tightened into an outward show of disapproval.

"One of the sweetest ladies I know." Hayden winked at Helen.

The older woman blushed. "I'm glad you're here, Laken. Your mom needs you near." Helen limped past.

Mother leaned close to Laken. "Last year, her son, Wade, confessed to Sara's murder and tried to kill himself. He used to live in your rental house."

The facade slipped. Laken's smile fizzled. Sara's death was painful enough for those who loved her, without dredging up the details for gossip.

"And why did that come up?"

Not taking the hint, Mother continued. "I just wanted to fill you in on what's happened around here. Pastor Grayson had a horrid time dealing with our dear Sara's death, and poor Adrea was once engaged to—"

"Wade." Doreen butted in. "His confession came about the time Adrea and Pastor Grayson were falling for each other. Heavens, I don't know how they ever got past all that baggage."

"The Lord mended their spirits together." Virgie nodded with certainty. "And just look at them now. I can't wait till the baby comes."

How had such a nice lady gotten sucked into Mother's circle? Laken's temple throbbed. She couldn't pretend, not for another moment. Her chair scraped against the concrete as she pushed it back and stood. "I'm afraid I'm not very hungry and I'm developing a headache."

"Probably the heat." Concern tinged Virgie's voice. "Have Hayden take you home, dear."

"No, that's not necessary. Where is the restroom?"

Hayden stood. "I'll show you."

"Take care of her, Hayden." Disappointment shone in Mother's eyes.

With a nod, he ushered her to a hall with restrooms on each side and an exit at the end.

Laken hurried outside. The sun had begun its descent. The warm evening air felt good against her air conditioner–chilled skin.

"I don't need to go to the restroom." The muscles around her mouth ached from forcing a continuous smile.

"You okay?" Hayden raised an eyebrow.

"I just had to get out of there." Laken ran her hands over her forearms, where the abrupt temperature change raised chill bumps. "The heat didn't induce my headache. My mother did. I'm sorry, I hate to make you leave early."

"You're not. I was finished eating. The picnic will break up soon, and Brady and I are going to see the fireworks. Want to come?"

His boyish enthusiasm tugged at her. Laken's heart turned giddy and skipped a beat. Why did he have to be so handsome? And so easy to talk to? She could easily dump her life story on him.

"It sounds nice, but I think I'd just like to go home."

—⁓—

Sunday evening, Brady wheeled himself down the ramp after services. Hayden used to try to push. But self-sufficient Brady didn't want anyone to help any more than absolutely necessary.

A freckled boy with blond hair waved to Brady. "See you later."

" 'Bye, Scott."

"Who's Scott?"

"He's new. He was at the trail ride yesterday."

"I'm glad you made another new friend."

"Me, too. Are you dating Laken?"

Hayden's eyebrows rose at the rapid subject change. "No. She's not a Christian."

Brady frowned. "We sure don't need another Jan."

"Trust me." With a chuckle, Hayden continued toward the van. "The only thing the two have in common is lack of belief." But Jan hadn't revealed her true self until he'd needed her the most. Inside, was Laken just as shallow and self-centered? What did it matter anyway? He certainly wasn't interested in anything other than friendship and introducing her to his Savior.

"Did you tell Laken about Jesus?"

"She's very resistant to anything to do with church, so I'm taking it slow. If I beat her over the head with it, she'll run." Why did Laken have such issues? Her mother never missed a service, and Laken had been raised in church. He'd pray about it and trust the Lord to give him insight on how to help get her beyond the past.

Who was he kidding? He couldn't get past the past.

"What if she dies tonight?"

A chill crept down Hayden's spine. "You're right. I'll ask the Lord to help me figure out how to speed things along."

"Let's ask her to go horseback riding soon."

Hayden chuckled. "Let her recover from this round. Back to you. Tell me more about Scott."

"He came to the trail ride, but he'd never ridden before. I love riding. It's like. . ."

*Like he could walk again.* Hayden silently finished Brady's thought.

At the van, Brady pressed the button that let down the lift and situated his chair. Once at the right level, he hit Stop, maneuvered his chair inside, locked it in place, and slid the door shut.

Perspiration beaded both their foreheads, but Brady wore a smile of accomplishment.

Hayden's cell phone vibrated against his thigh, and he dug it from his pocket, flipping it open without looking. "Hello."

"It's me. Did you talk to him yet?" Collin's tone was all business.

"Yes." He strode to the back of the van, out of Brady's earshot.

"Good. I'll be coming in two weeks."

"There's something you need to know." *Brady's in a wheelchair and it's my fault.*

# Chapter 4

C an we meet first?" Hayden closed his eyes.

Collin's exasperated sigh echoed through the cell. "Just tell me now."

"This isn't something that can be covered over the phone."

"I'm warning you, Hayden. I won't take no for an answer. No amount of cajoling will make me go away. I intend to see my son."

"Fine, but we need to talk first. I'll plan on seeing you midmonth."

"And I'll plan on seeing Brady then."

Hayden climbed into the van. Adjusting his seat belt, he checked his mirrors, cautiously eased forward, and pulled onto the highway. Despite the pricey bumper camera he'd had installed, he never parked where he'd have to back up unless there were no other options.

"Who was that?"

"Your dad." Hayden tried to keep his tone even. He stomped the brake as the car ahead of him came to a dead stop. A few vehicles approaching them passed and the car turned left, with no blinker. "He'll be here in two weeks."

"Does he know I can't walk?" The tremulous voice didn't sound like Brady.

Hayden tried to swallow the lump in his throat. "Not yet."

"Are you gonna tell him?"

"Do you want me to tell him before you meet him?" Did Brady fear seeing his dad look at him with shock or pity?

"Yeah." A moment passed before Brady added, "And tell him I'm really good at doing stuff by myself."

"Okay."

"Do you think he'll still want to see me?" Brady's voice quivered.

"I don't know, Brady. I don't know him."

If Collin changed his mind after learning about Brady's paralysis, Hayden would kill him. *Not really, Lord, but I'd want to.*

"I honestly don't know." *He'd better want to see Brady, and if Collin wanted to know how his son was, he should have read Katie's letter when he received it.* Hayden blew out a deep breath. He wasn't even thinking rationally anymore. "Don't worry. Everything's going to be fine."

Brady scrubbed a hand across his face and nodded.

———

The day after a holiday always brought tons of mail. Not as big as if the day off had fallen on a Friday, but Laken looked forward to it as she parked next to the post office. A nice distraction. She grabbed her cell from the console to see who had called while she drove. A blue highlighted line across the bottom announced: NEW MESSAGE. She pushed a button and listened. "Laken, it's Collin. I'll be there in two weeks."

Her heart somersaulted.

"I'm renting a car, so I'll have wheels during my stay. Your rental house is the old Fletcher place, right?"

Her hands tightened on the steering wheel.

"My flight is supposed to arrive at seven p.m., but you know how that goes. I'm looking forward to seeing you."

"Me, too," she said aloud, flipped the phone closed, and dropped it in her purse. Slinging its strap over her shoulder, she hurried to the building. Would she and Collin still have a bond after not seeing each other for eight years? Or would they have to get reacquainted?

Her fingers trembled as she unlocked the employee entry.

"Good morning." Carol sounded perky as ever. "You okay? You left the picnic rather abruptly."

"I meant to thank you for inviting me, but my caboose is sore." Laken ran a hand down her bruised backside. "Horseback riding certainly wasn't what I expected, and it was embarrassing when I got lost. Especially since Hayden had to play hero."

"What's up with you and your mom?" Carol's hand jerked to her mouth. "Forget I asked. Absolutely none of my business." Caring brown eyes showed concern, not nosiness.

Laken sighed. "It's okay. We don't get along so well, and pretending we do grated on my nerves."

"My fault. I'm so sorry."

"You had no way of knowing." The air conditioner kicked on with a *whoosh*. "I shouldn't have walked out. Surely no one likes her any more than I do."

"Laken! She gave birth to you. That's more than a lot of pregnant women do these days."

Laken hung her head. "She's just always so uppity, clinging to her gossip and the charade that she's high above everyone else. I'd have loved to rip the farce out from under her."

"Your mother's hurting." Carol touched Laken's forearm. "Maybe over your relationship. But whatever it is, I think she uses her persona to hide her pain."

Something in Mother's eyes had reached out to Laken's soul. She hugged herself.

"Maybe y'all could work things out." Carol turned to her sorter. "Jim and I have a grown daughter, and if anything happened to our relationship, it would kill part of me."

"I always envied Sara's and Grace's families. Theirs were so close, so perfect. Mine was just a mess."

"Come to church Sunday. It could be the first step in healing for you and your mom."

*Too many memories to dredge up.* "You promised not to ask." Laken shook her head.

"Sorry, but I like you, Laken. I'd kind of like to see you in heaven someday."

The words jolted through Laken. She opened her mouth, but nothing came out.

Carol scooped up her case and turned toward the side door. "At least Jim fell for the roping. He promised to come with me. See you this afternoon."

Laken leaned against the counter.

All in all, Independence Day had been dismal, except for Hayden. Spending time with him had been pleasant. A smile tugged at her mouth.

She ran her hands over her upper arms.

The side door opened, and the object of her thoughts strode inside.

"Hey." Hayden set his mailbag near her desk. "Brady wants you to go riding with us."

Laken's pulse fluttered. "When?"

"Yesterday." He chuckled. "I talked him into letting you recover from the other day. I was thinking some evening, so it won't be so hot. How about Saturday?"

"Sounds fun." And it did, more fun than she wanted to admit.

—∞—

After a busy workweek, Laken pulled into Hayden's drive as he waited with the horses. "Where's Brady?"

"At Bob's getting in a lesson. The woods behind our house connect with Bob's place, so we'll ride over and meet him." Hayden untied Pearl, knelt beside her, and made a stirrup with his hands.

Accepting his offer, Laken wallowed into the saddle a little easier than the first time.

He turned to his mount, a tan-colored horse with black lower legs, tail, and mane. With one foot in the stirrup, Hayden swung his other leg, landing perfectly astride his horse.

"How do you do that?"

"Just takes a little practice. The first several times I tried, it didn't go so well."

The horse responded to the slight snap of Hayden's reins and click of his tongue.

He made it look so easy. Maybe if she learned a few things, she wouldn't feel so off-kilter. "What kind of horse is that?"

"A buckskin. His name's Buck." He shot her a lopsided grin. "Spot,

Pearl, Buck. Real original."

"So, he's a stallion."

"Was." Hayden chuckled. "Buck's a gelding."

Unfamiliar with the word, she eventually figured out what it meant. Her cheeks warmed. "Oh."

The horses ambled toward the woods. Despite the slow gait, Laken bounced and flounced while trying to relax and remember Hayden's instructions. With each jostle, her still-tender bottom ached more.

The forest canopy enveloped them in a peaceful, ray-blocking blanket.

"Can we stop for a minute? I'm sorry. I'm afraid I'm not very good at this."

Hayden reined in his horse and swung down to help her dismount.

Despite his offer, Laken clambered from the saddle.

"You can borrow Pearl anytime if you'd like to come out and practice." Hayden tied the horses to a tree. "Pearl doesn't get ridden much since Brady graduated to Spot."

"I might take you up on that, after I recover from today, that is." She leaned against a huge oak. "Sorry I cut your fun short the other night. It wasn't you."

"I knew that."

"If I'd stayed one more minute, I think the top of my head would have blown."

"Sounds messy." He grinned.

Laken frowned. "Mother said Wade Fenwick used to live in my rental house. Did he. . . ?"

"No, I think he lived in Searcy when he shot himself."

"Good." Laken shivered. "I mean, I hate that it had to happen anywhere, but it was kind of creepy thinking it might have happened where I live. Poor Helen."

"She's had a tough time of it." Hayden stroked Buck's long neck and the horse nickered. "Her son is in a nursing home now. She visits him several times a week."

"Please don't think I'm anything like my mother just because I asked. Sara and I grew up next to each other. We were good friends. So Mother's info was rather jarring."

"I'm sorry. Her death must have been hard on you."

"It was." Everyone else who loved Sara seemed to be past her death and focused on fond memories. Of course, they'd been here. Being where Sara had last lived, with the people she loved, opened unhealed wounds.

"It electrified my last nerve for Mother to gossip about Sara's death." Laken crossed her arms over her chest. "As far back as I can remember, my mother has spent her time picking everybody's lives apart, like she's Miss Perfect. Isn't there something in the Bible about backbiting?"

"A few things." Hayden settled on a tree stump.

"My parents used to drag my brother and me to church three times a week. Mother was on all the committees and Father was a deacon." Her insides twisted. "We sat through countless sermons about gossip and drunkards. Yet, as soon as we got home, Mother called everybody she knew with the latest scandal and Father drowned himself in the liquor cabinet."

Hayden plucked a fuzzy dandelion and blew the seedlings off the stalk. "Sounds tough."

"On the outside, we were the perfect, upstanding family." She hugged herself tighter. "On the inside, we were a sham."

"That's what you've got against church?"

She huffed out a big breath. "I've seen enough hypocrites to last me a lifetime."

"There are hypocrites everywhere. The only difference is, some are forgiven."

*So, if you go to church, you do whatever you want and God forgives you?* She wanted to know more, but she'd heard enough about God for one day.

"You're not a hypocrite, Hayden." Laken searched his luminous eyes. "You're true-blue, without a bone of put-on in you. You're so together. I bet you had a good, solid, functional family."

He looked off in the distance and his eyes misted. "We were, before Katie's cancer. None of us have been very functional since. My folks can't forgive me for what happened to Brady. I backed into him."

Laken's jaw dropped.

"Two years ago. I was leaving for work, and Brady slipped away from his nanny. He ran out the front door as I backed my SUV out of the garage." Hayden closed his eyes and ducked his head. "He thought I saw him and headed for the passenger side. I'll never forget the thud." Raw pain echoed in his voice.

She swallowed the golf-ball-sized lump in her throat. "It was an accident."

"Yes, but Brady still can't walk. I was the one driving, and they can't get past that." He focused on her, his eyes damp. "Neither can I."

"I'm so sorry."

"Me, too." He blinked several times and stood. "Any togetherness I have comes straight from above."

She bit her lip, not wanting to get into that subject. "He seems very well-adjusted."

"He's the only one who is. I cost Brady his legs. Yet, he doesn't hate me. I blame me. Everyone who knows what happened blames me. But Brady doesn't.

"We better get our horses." Hayden turned away. "By the way, folks here don't know what happened, and I'd rather it came from me."

The urge to touch his shoulder, to provide comfort, rose within her. She shoved her hands in her pockets. "Don't worry. I don't give my mother fodder for her gossip mill."

Hayden spun to face her again. "I didn't think—I just meant—"

"It's not my place to say anything to anyone."

A whip-poor-will's haunting call echoed, announcing the onset of dusk. "Brady's probably getting antsy. Can we walk the horses over, so I'll be able to move tomorrow?"

"Sure." His crooked grin materialized. "Just watch your step. As hot as it is, we should be okay as long as we stay on the path."

His calm reminder about snakes almost made her want to ride. Almost.

His confession rattled her. How could he and his nephew have such a wonderful relationship after the accident? Why didn't Brady blame Hayden?

—⁓—

"Special delivery. Happy Monday." Hayden stepped inside the cool post office, hoisting a large black plastic pot.

"What's this?" Despite the red blotches covering her neck and arms, Laken's eyes lit up at the sight of the towering orange flowers with long, spiky stems.

"You've got poison ivy."

She rubbed the deltoid muscle in her upper arm. "I feel like clawing my skin off. I should have stayed on Pearl. Grace brought me some cream this morning."

He set the pot on the work counter. "Adrea sent this over. She apologized for just getting around to it now, but she's really been sick."

"Poor thing." Laken buried her nose in a vibrant blossom. "I love gladiolas. How did she know?"

"She asked me to describe you, so she could figure out something you might like."

"And you said. . . ?" With a hand propped on one hip, she shot him a saucy grin.

"That you're the strongest, most determined woman I've ever met, but somewhere in there, I've glimpsed a soft side."

The smile faded. "Keep that last part to yourself, will ya?"

"Tough as nails on a chalkboard." He saluted. "She said glads symbolize strength and I knew you liked orange. I've seen you wear it."

Laken swallowed, tracing a lacy blossom. "Beautiful. I'll send Adrea a thank-you note."

"Even with courage as fierce as a lion, you still need Jesus to steer you through this life."

Her head whipped around. "Now you're gonna preach to me?"

"Just trying to help." He opened the door. "I better get my sack." Maybe his words would take root if he left her alone a minute or two. He wrestled the stuffed mailbag out of his truck.

When he returned, she still stood at the counter. "Adrea said she'll stop by soon and tell you how to plant the glads sometime in the spring."

"That's very sweet, but I may not be here by next spring, and even if I am, I don't want to plant anything I'd end up leaving behind."

Hayden's spirits plummeted. "Are you going somewhere?"

"Romance wasn't exactly what I had in mind, so I only accepted this position temporarily, until something else opens up." Laken shrugged. "Even if I end up staying here awhile, I probably wouldn't keep renting forever."

"You've only been here a month. Give it some time." Why did he care? She certainly didn't want him to. And why did his heart flop like a dying fish at her mention of leaving town?

"Contrary to popular beliefs, time doesn't heal everything."

"Where do you want to go?" He managed a casual tone.

She scanned the tiny office. "Anywhere but here."

Hayden shuffled the mail from his sorter into his tray, careful to keep it in order by route. "Romance is a great little town."

"Yes, but my parents are forty-five minutes too close."

"That could be a good thing." He tried to sound enthusiastic, even though his own parental relations were strained.

"My life was much better when I was far away from them." Her shoulders sagged, as if her words weren't quite true.

He'd definitely hit on something Laken had buried deep. Something bigger than she could handle. *Lord, help me make her see she doesn't have to go it alone.*

The side door opened. "Hey, y'all." Carol set down her sack. "What's going on here? You could cut the tension with a butter knife."

"Nothing." His voice blended with Laken's.

"Ooh, honey." Carol winced. "Just looking at you makes me want to scratch."

"I have an appointment at lunch to get a big, nasty steroid shot."

"Good. Guess what?" Carol's enthusiasm was almost contagious.

"What?" Again, he and Laken answered together.

"I told you Jim loved church Sunday. He's coming to Bible study on Wednesday, too."

"That's wonderful." Hayden spoke alone this time.

"Would you like to come, Laken?" Carol clamped a hand over her mouth. "Oops, sorry. I promised not to bother you after the trail ride."

Color crept up Laken's neck, connecting the splotches of her rash. "Even if I wanted to go, my brother's coming for a visit next weekend." She winced. "But keep it quiet."

"Oh, it's a surprise." Carol squealed. "I love surprises."

"It's a total, complete secret. In fact, he's not planning to see our parents while he's here. So please, Carol, not a word."

"All right." With a dramatic eye roll, Carol scooted her case closer to her sorter. "But I wish y'all would get your issues sorted out. This is not what a family is supposed to be like."

*Can't help with that subject.* Hayden grabbed his bag and headed out the door. "Catch ya later." But he and Carol had definitely planted seeds.

—∞—

Longing for a glimpse of her brother, Laken fidgeted as she searched the chaos.

The weekend airport crowd rushed about, burdened with luggage. The endless line of passengers trying to get through security snaked through the bustle. Squealing reunions took place all around her while flight departures boomed over the intercom.

A little girl danced, legs clamped together. "But I gotta go *now!*"

Laken's lungs deflated like a pricked balloon. She turned away from the reminder of family ties she'd never have.

Briefcase in one hand, a man strode confidently past, with his wheeled carry-on trailing behind. She knew that walk. With his light brown hair cropped close, businessman-style instead of shaggy, he looked professional and polished. The way his suit enhanced his lithe body testified to its high cost. Obviously, expensive tailoring had finally replaced his favorite ragged, kneeless jeans. The jeans that had almost given Mother heart palpitations. She'd love this version of him.

"Collin." Laken scurried after him.

He turned around. Recognition dawned in his sapphire eyes, and he smiled. That big toothy grin she hadn't seen in eight years flashed. "You weren't supposed to come."

"I couldn't stay away." She lunged into his arms. "I missed you so much."

"Me, too." He set down his cases to hug her. "Look at you. You're an adult and so pretty."

Tears blurred her vision, and she buried her face in his shoulder.

He patted her back as she tried to control her sniffles.

With slight decorum, she pulled away and traced his lapel with her fingers. "Look at you, Mr. Fancy Businessman. You clean up good."

"Thanks. Let's get out of here."

"Don't you have more luggage?"

"I travel light."

Her heart dropped to her toes. "You're not staying long?"

"My flight leaves tomorrow evening." He managed his two cases with one hand and slung his other arm around her shoulders. "Let's pick up my rental car, and I'll buy you supper."

—∞—

"Here we are." Laken waited on the porch, certain her humble rental house didn't measure up to the accommodations this new Collin was accustomed to. Especially since he'd rented a Lexus. At least she'd gotten everything unpacked and put away. Even a few paintings graced the walls.

With an unreadable expression, his gaze swept the place. "Tell me again why you moved from Little Rock to Romance."

"I got a promotion." Her key clicked in the lock.

He parked his cases in the living room and followed her to the adjoining kitchen.

"Did it have to be here?" With his chin propped on his knuckles, Collin stared at the large painting of the Romance Waterfalls above the couch.

"That's exactly how I felt." With shaky hands, she poured them each a cup of coffee, adding cream and sugar to hers. The spoon slipped from her fumbling fingers, clattering to the linoleum floor. "But I'd have been crazy not to accept the position, and it's actually temporary until something closer to Little Rock opens up."

He knelt to retrieve the spoon, dropped it in the sink, and trailed her back to the small living room.

She set two steaming mugs on the coffee table. "So, tell me about you. How's California and the world of accounting?"

Collin closed his eyes. "Sit down, sis. There's so much you don't know about me."

A sinking feeling settled in her stomach. She dropped to the couch and patted the seat beside her. "Is everything okay?"

He ran his hand through his hair and sat. "My senior year of college in Little Rock, I met someone. It was love at first sight for both of us."

"You never said anything about it."

"She wanted to get married and all I could think about was Mother and Father." A world-weary sigh emanated from deep within him. "It scared the heebie-jeebies out of me."

Laken understood completely. Unwilling to get caught in the trap of marriage, she'd avoided any kind of emotional attachment to anyone. Yet her traitorous heart longed to know a nurturing love, longed for a real family, longed for children of her own. "So what happened?"

"My company wanted me to transfer, so I ran away as far as I could get."

"To California and broke her heart."

"Yes. And on top of that, she was pregnant."

The room spun. She grasped the arm of the couch. Anything to keep her afloat. "How could you abandon your child?"

"I didn't know about him." Collin cupped his face in his hands. "Until recently."

A jolt went through her heart. "The mother just contacted you?"

"Not exactly."

She shook her head. "I don't understand."

"It's complicated, but. . ." Collin stood and paced. The aged hardwood flooring creaked with every few steps. "He's here. Brady is here."

"Brady?" A hard ball formed in the pit of her stomach.

A knock sounded at the door.

"You're expecting someone?"

"No." She'd only had one visitor since she'd lived here, and surely Mother wouldn't have the nerve to come again. "It's probably my landlord." She hurried to answer.

"Good. I'll tell ol' Pete he needs to spruce this place up for you a bit."

Laken opened the door.

Hayden stood waiting.

"What are you doing here, Hayden?"

He held her cell phone toward her. "I found this in the parking lot. Didn't know if you had a home phone or not, so I thought you might need it."

"Hayden?" Collin's voice came from directly behind her. "Hayden Winters?"

Hayden raised a brow. "I'm sorry. Have we met?"

"I'm Collin Kroft."

Hayden's jaw dropped. "You're. . . ?" He pointed at her.

"Collin's sister." She voiced the thought for him.

"You're planning to help him take Brady away from me?"

"What? No." Laken frowned. "I'd never do that."

Collin grabbed her elbow and turned her to face him. "You're planning to help him keep Brady away from me?"

"No."

Hayden sidestepped her. With his muscled frame, stature, and fire in his eyes, he made an intimidating picture. "So, you are planning to try to take Brady away from me?"

But Collin didn't back down. "He's my son."

They stood almost nose to nose, chests puffed out, ridiculous and frightening.

Laken squeezed between the two men. "Why does Hayden have Brady?"

Hayden's breath fluttered across the top of her head. "Tell your sister why I'm raising your son. Tell her how you left Katie alone and pregnant. Tell her how you never would marry her, and how when she begged you from her deathbed to come and care for your son, you ignored her letter. Such a coward, you didn't come to claim your son."

# Chapter 5

Hayden's insides boiled.

"Shut up," Collin hissed. "I didn't know."

Laken elbowed her brother in the stomach and managed to push him away from Hayden. "Stop it, both of you. You're adults, and you should be able to talk without throwing punches."

What a poor witness. Hayden hung his head. "You're right. I'm sorry."

"It seems to me, you both want Brady to be happy. So there has to be some kind of compromise."

"I'm not the compromising type." Collin shoved his hands in his pockets.

"Well, maybe you can learn." Laken took a deep breath. "Hayden, thank you for bringing my phone, but it's time for you to go."

He nodded. "How about breakfast, Collin?"

"I will see my son." Collin ground the words between clenched teeth.

"Yes, but we need to discuss a few things first." Things Hayden didn't want to tell, and Collin wouldn't want to hear.

"Just go, Hayden. I'll talk to Collin, and he'll be a different person at breakfast, even if I have to tranquilize him." She pointed at Collin. "You. Sit."

Collin didn't comply, but he stayed put.

Laken followed Hayden outside and the door closed behind her with a thud. "I had no idea Collin was Brady's father until about two minutes before you showed up."

"Your family doesn't excel in communication, huh?" His vision clouded. "I can't lose Brady. When Katie was sick, she wanted Collin to come for Brady. But he didn't. I did. We've built a life together."

"I'll talk to him, and if you two can be civil, maybe something can be worked out." Laken sighed. "Does Collin know about the accident?"

"That's what I planned to discuss at breakfast."

"Do you want me to tell him?"

With everything in him, Hayden wanted to say yes. He gazed up at the stars twinkling in the inky sky, stomach churning at the coming confrontation. "It's my responsibility."

"I could join you at breakfast."

His eyes sought hers. "You'd do that?"

"Of course. Suddenly, I have a stake in Brady's happiness." Her blue eyes sparkled in the glow of the porch light. "I've never been an aunt before."

"I better get home to Brady. He's nervous about tomorrow." With a lump in his throat the size of a post-holiday mailbag, he hurried toward his truck.

"Hayden, I'm sorry about this."

With a hard swallow, he turned to face her. "Me, too."

"So where is breakfast?"

"At the Rambler Café, over in Rose Bud."

Her eyes widened. "A restaurant?"

"I thought a public place might keep us from coming to blows."

"Not a good idea." She shook her head. "Raised voices airing dirty laundry. Though my mother would see this as a scandal to be kept secret, it will still get out, eventually."

"Hadn't thought of that." Hayden ran a hand along the back of his neck.

"I could cook here." She settled on the edge of the weathered, wooden porch step. "Or better yet, if it's okay with you, at your place. That way Collin would get the chance to see Brady's home, where he's happy."

"All I have is frozen waffles, Pop-Tarts, and cereal."

"I already grocery shopped for Collin, and I love to cook. It's settled. Where do you live?"

Hayden rattled off directions. "You'll never know how much I appreciate your help on this. Puts you in a tough spot."

She straightened her shoulders as if shifting her heavy load. "No problem."

Thanks to her calming presence, his stomach settled. He turned toward his truck. Surely together they could make Collin see Brady needed to stay right where he was.

––––––

Laken rushed inside to find Collin pacing her small living room.

As the door thudded closed, he skidded to a stop. "Let me explain."

"You abandoned Katie even though she was pregnant?" She propped her hands on her hips.

"She didn't find out until I'd already left."

"But she wrote to tell you when she was dying. How could you not go to her?"

He sank into the couch.

"After I moved to California, I jumped into a rebound relationship with a coworker. I cried on her shoulder, so she knew all about Katie. She split a few weeks ago, and as a parting shot, she shoved Katie's letter in my face. All this time, she'd been hiding it."

The words cooled her anger. She plopped beside him and the springs creaked in the cheap furniture. "Oh Collin, I'm so sorry. You really loved Katie?"

"More than life. When I finally read the letter, I held out hope that she'd beat the cancer. That she was still alive." Collin's eyes squeezed shut. "Have you met Brady?"

"Twice." Laken's mouth went dry. "Of course, I didn't know who—he's a great kid."

"Is he happy?"

"Yes. He loves Hayden very much."

Collin stood and paced the room again. The floor popped and squeaked with each step. "I don't want to miss any more of my son's life. Will you help me?"

She followed him. When he turned back toward her, she blocked his path. "I won't help you rip Brady away from everything he knows. We have to do what's best for him. Even if that means he stays with Hayden."

"How can you be on Hayden's side?"

She hugged him, burying her face in his shoulder. "I'm not. I'm on Brady's side."

His arms came around her.

No matter what happened, she knew they'd be all right. She just had to convince him of the best thing to do. And at the moment, she wasn't sure what that was.

—m—

A knock sounded at the door. A large knot lodged in Hayden's throat.

Laken's bright smile greeted him, with a subdued Collin on her heels.

"I've got bacon, sausage, eggs, biscuits, and gravy fixings." The cheeriness in her voice didn't put a dent in the tension surrounding them.

Food was the last of his concerns, but Hayden pointed the way to the kitchen. "Great. Right through there. Collin and I will talk in here."

"No." The word wrenched from Laken. "Y'all come." She adopted an overdone Southern drawl. "I hate being banished to the hot stove while the menfolk visit."

Laken ushered her brother ahead, and Hayden followed her.

"Set the groceries right here." She clattered pans together even though Hayden had them sitting on the stove waiting. The wheelchair-accessible cabinets were awkward for her, too low. She lined a skillet with bacon. The gas burners clicked a steady rhythm until they lit. As the bacon began to sizzle, she whisked the eggs.

Hayden took his usual seat at the oak table and gestured for Collin to sit across from him.

"This is a great house." With the stove in an island, Laken faced Hayden while she cooked. Collin's back was toward her. "I love the rustic siding and plank walls. Was it already here, or did you have it built?"

"Actually, my dad used to be a contractor. He and I built it for Brady. When he turns twenty-five, it's his."

"Speaking of which, can we just get to the subject of my son?" Collin ran a jerky hand through his hair.

A storm brewed in Hayden's soul.

"Hayden, why don't you tell Collin about some of Brady's activities?" Laken poured fat off the bacon into another skillet and spooned in flour.

"He's a great kid. He rides horses, plays catch, basketball. Typical boy." Hayden cleared his throat. "Only, not typical at all."

Collin leaned forward, his expression softened. "Is he a brain? Katie always was."

Hayden's jaw clenched. *Lord, help me with this.* "You'll notice the cabinets are lower than most, and the ramp out front. The entire house, including both bathrooms and all of the closets are wheelchair accessible."

Laken stopped scrambling the eggs.

"All very well and nice." Collin's brows scrunched together. "I guess you plan on getting old and decrepit and using my poor Brady to take care of you."

The back door opened. Hayden swallowed as Brady rolled himself inside. Collin's eyes widened. "Brady?"

Tears rimmed Laken's lashes.

"You're my father."

Hayden's heart took a nosedive.

"Yes." Collin stood and managed a few shaky steps to kneel beside the boy, as if his legs could no longer support him. "Why. . . ?"

"When I was five—"

"I'll handle this." Hayden settled his hand on his nephew's slight shoulder.

"It's okay, let me." Brady peered up at him, trust and respect glowing from the depths of his soul. "Hayden was leaving for work and I wanted him to stay home with me, so I ran out to catch him as he backed out of the garage. He told me a bajillion times to stay away from moving vehicles, but I thought he saw me."

Emotions warred over Collin's face. His mouth went slack. Shock, anguish, and disgust. Hayden had seen them all in his own mirror.

"You ran over him?"

"Brady, I told you to stay at Grandma and Grandpa's." Hayden's jaw clenched so tight, it ached.

"I guess I still don't listen very good." Brady sat straighter in his chair and looked at Collin. "I shouldn't have run behind Hayden. It wasn't his fault. It was an accident."

The weight in Hayden's chest shifted with the different take on what happened. He squeezed Brady's shoulder. "It wasn't your fault. You were five; I should have watched for you."

"But you'd told me and told me to stay away from moving vehicles."

"Who was supposedly watching out for him?" Collin thundered.

"A nanny. After Brady got out of the hospital, my mother stayed with us through the week, until I transferred here a couple months ago. Now he stays with my parents when I work."

Collin pounded his fist on the table. "Katie trusted you to raise my son, and you paralyzed him."

All color drained from Brady's face.

"Like Brady said." Laken turned the burners off and set the meal on the table. Calm in the midst of the storm. "It was an accident. Now let's stop trying to place blame and eat."

Despite the distractions, the meal was magazine perfect. The scrambled eggs wafted appetizing steam, the gravy bore no clumps, the biscuits' golden surface begged for butter, and the bacon was just-right crisp. Hayden's mouth watered.

She set another plate in front of Brady and pulled her chair next to where he parked. "Your father is my brother, so that makes me your aunt."

"Cool." Brady grinned. "I never had an aunt."

"If it's all right with you, I'd like to spend some time with you, get to know you better."

"I'd like that." The boy turned to Hayden.

The plea in Brady's eyes tore at him. "I think it would be best if you went back to Grandma and Grandpa's."

"Please, can't I stay? I can ask the blessing."

Hayden nodded. At least he'd done something right with his nephew.

"I cooked plenty." Laken passed a glass of juice to Brady.

Collin cleared his throat. He bowed his head, only when Laken did.

"Dear Lord, thank You for this food and the good stuff You do for us. Please let Hayden and my dad make friends. Help us all get to know each other and be a real family. Amen."

─◦◦─

Laken's insides hurt, as if a prizefighter had used her for a punching bag.

Brady's innocent prayer for the two men glowering across the table from one another to be a family didn't look promising. How could she get these two on the same page? She had to keep Collin from dragging Brady back to California. Away from the only family he'd ever known. Away from his friends and his home.

Away from her.

The biscuit and gravy weighed heavy in her stomach. All she'd wanted was to get out of Romance, but now with Brady in the equation, she had to stay. She didn't even know him, yet the blood they shared drew her to him. His happiness mattered most.

The scrape of silverware against plates reverberated through the room. Both men were wolfing down their breakfast, while Brady pushed his eggs around and around. Couldn't they see their love for Brady was the common thread?

Maybe she could ease the tension between Hayden and Collin. Maybe she could help them come to a compromise for Brady's sake. Maybe she could assure Brady's happiness and form some semblance of the family she yearned for. Could Brady fill the hole in her heart?

"So, Brady, are you excited about school starting?" She took a sip of her cooling coffee. It would probably make the wad in her stomach swell larger.

The boy's eyes shone. "Two of my best friends from church will be in my class."

"You've made a lot of friends here?"

Brady nodded. "More than I ever had. At my old school"—his shoulders slumped—"the kids made fun of me."

A lump lodged in her throat, and she glanced at Collin, hoping the comment sank in. Was he listening? *Brady's happy here.*

Her brother gulped a swig of coffee.

Laken placed her hand on Brady's back. She could feel him trembling, absorbing the tension between the two men most important to him. "So you like small-town life?"

"People are nice here. The ones at church anyway. I hope kids at school will be, too."

"Don't worry. You'll be the hit of the school." Hayden winked. "Word is, Justin and Mike have your back."

Collin needed Hayden's gentleness. Her brother obviously wasn't used to dealing with children. Each time he moved, Brady's gaze flew to Hayden.

"So, Hayden tells me you play basketball." Collin's tone was all interest. He was learning.

"Yes, sir."

Collin's Adam's apple bobbed. "I'm your father, son. You don't have to call me sir."

"But you don't have to call him dad, either." Laken smiled. "How about Collin for now? You two have some catching up to do."

"Speaking of which," Collin cajoled, "I'd like to spend some time with Brady. How about we go for a walk—I mean—maybe shoot some hoops."

Brady's eyes lit up. "You play basketball?"

"I used to." Collin dropped his crumpled napkin on his plate.

Hayden wolfed down bite after bite, faster and faster as Collin made headway.

The boy's trembling stopped. "I've got a court over at Grandma and Grandpa's."

Collin stood. "Let's go."

Brady looked at Hayden.

"I'm not comfortable with that temper of yours." Hayden's gaze pinned Collin, like a lion protecting his cub.

"I'm not mad at Brady," Collin deadpanned.

Hayden's jaw twitched. "Go show him some of your moves."

"Cool." As Brady rolled toward the door, Collin hurried to push.

"I'd rather do it myself," Brady mumbled.

"Sure." Collin's hands jerked away. "No problem."

The door shut behind them.

Pushing away from the table, Hayden stalked to the sink. Gripping the countertop edge with both hands, he hung his head. "You have no idea how hard it was to let them go."

She touched his arm, rock hard and muscular beneath her fingers. "You did the right thing. Brady wanted to go with him. No matter how badly a parent lets a child down, the child longs for a close relationship. Trust me, I know."

"Why is he here? Why now?"

"His girlfriend hid Katie's letter, until they broke up last month and she tossed it in his face."

"So he moved on, while Katie gave birth to his son." Hayden's voice broke in contradiction to his obvious physical strength. "He can't move Brady to California. He just can't."

"I'll do my best to encourage him to stay here." She traced her fingers in a soothing motion across his back. "That way, even if he wants Brady to live with him, at least they'll be here instead of thousands of miles away."

Hayden turned toward her. "What's keeping Collin in California?"

Laken nibbled on the inside of her lip. "I'm not sure. I know he wants to be far away from our parents. Our dad was verbally abusive toward Collin."

"And you?" His green eyes softened with concern.

Tears stung and she blinked. With all he faced, Hayden still worried about her. "No, he ignored me. Anyway, Collin is the comptroller for a large fragrance company. That's all I'm aware of."

Hayden scratched his chin. "So he doesn't have any other California connections? The girlfriend?"

"That's definitely over, and it was a rebound relationship anyway. I don't think he ever got over loving Katie."

His eyes clouded. "Me neither."

The urge to hug him flitted through her mind, and she turned away. "A comptroller could find work anywhere."

"How do we convince him?"

"We—I mean—you let them spend a lot of time together, and Collin will have to see how happy Brady is here. And how jarring it would be to move him."

"Brilliant. And you can spend time with them both and make sure Brady's okay."

"Collin would never hurt him, Hayden."

"I mean emotionally."

She offered her hand. "It's a deal." Now, if only Collin would catch on to how disruptive claiming Brady would be.

"Could you check on them about now?" Hayden's jaw twitched. "I'll get the dishes, and I'd feel a lot better if you were with Brady. I think they've had enough alone time."

"Why don't you come with me?"

—∿—

Laken followed Hayden to a trail winding through a tall line of lavender crape myrtle trees with a citrus, honeysuckle scent. Even without him, she'd have found her way by the steady thumping of a bouncing basketball next door.

"So, you played basketball in Searcy?" Brady swished the ball through the hoop in the backyard of a house much like Hayden's. Nothing but net.

Collin rebounded and passed it back to his son. "Star shooter. In California, the school close to my condo ranked seventh nationally and second in state this year."

The suggestion was clear. *Come home with me and you can attend a big-time school.* Had Collin been pressuring Brady this whole time?

Brady's shot bounced off the rim, and Collin rebounded.

Hayden cleared his throat. "Rose Bud has a great basketball program."

At the sight of his uncle, Brady's eyes lit up.

Loping toward Collin, Hayden stole the ball and hit a three-pointer. "It's not fancy, but it's a good school."

Collin sprinted toward Hayden.

Laken managed to cut him off and whispered, "Enough about California. And what would Brady think of you if you attack the uncle he loves?"

Collin blew out a big breath. "I was just going after the ball."

"With an intentional hard foul in mind."

Closer to the house, Laken noticed a brooding older couple rocking on the porch in matching white chairs. She waved. "Hi, I'm Laken."

"Laken, I'd like you to meet my folks, Paul and Maye Winters." Hayden rocketed the ball back to Collin in a hand-stinging pass and strode to the porch. "Laken's the new postmaster I told you about, and she's also Brady's aunt."

Laken hurried after him. "Nice to meet you. Sorry to invade your yard." Neither accepted the hand she offered.

"Brady's always welcome." Maye rocked harder.

"Mom." Hayden lowered his voice. "Laken's on our side."

"Actually, I'm on Brady's side. I want what's best for my nephew, and this morning has convinced me that staying here would be best for him."

"Well, in that case. . ." Maye shook Laken's hand, as did her husband. "Let me get you a glass of lemonade."

—∿—

Laken followed Brady through the bustling airport with Collin trailing behind. A staccato voice droned over the intercom, and wheeled suitcases glided over the tile, mixing with the hum of numerous conversations. Security was backed up as usual.

This afternoon, Collin had begun to bond with his son, but tonight, he had to leave. Would he learn to put Brady first in the future? Or would his work always take priority?

The crowd parted neatly to let Brady through. Lots of pitying glances flashed their way, but Brady held his head high.

Collin put his arm around her shoulders. "Thanks for talking Hayden into letting Brady see me off."

"No problem. He's a great kid."

"He is, isn't he?" Collin frowned. "And I had nothing to do with it."

"Hayden loves him. And Brady loves Hayden and his grandparents. He's happy here, Collin."

"I know."

"Won't you just think about moving back here?" She snaked her arm around his waist, not wanting to let him go.

"With Mother and Father just around the corner?" A bitter laugh punctuated his words. "No thanks."

"We could get a place together." Laken shrugged. "I've been here a month and have only run into Mother three times."

"Brady, we'll have to stop here. Only passengers past this point." Collin wrapped Laken in a big bear hug.

Tears rimmed her lashes. "I don't want you to go."

"Trust me, I don't want to go. You take care of Brady until I get back. A week, tops."

She nodded against his shoulder then forced herself to let go of him.

He knelt beside Brady.

Feeling like an eavesdropper, she backed out of earshot, determined to give them privacy.

Hugging his son, Collin spoke to the boy for a few minutes. When he stood, his eyes, too, were shiny.

Brady's shoulders drooped.

Collin waved her over.

"I'd better go." He chucked Brady under the chin and hurried toward security without looking back.

Brady's chin trembled.

"Hey, how about some ice cream?" She squeezed his shoulder.

"I haven't had supper yet. Hayden never lets me have dessert before supper."

"Just this once, I think it'll be all right, but I'll call Hayden to make sure. Maybe he can join us."

"He'll probably say okay if you invite him. He's a pushover when it comes to ice cream." Brady's mischievous grin warmed her insides.

She handed him her cell as they threaded through the crowd. "I don't know his number."

Brady didn't flip the phone open. "I've been thinking."

"About?"

"Miss Sylvie, she's my grandmother, right?"

Laken clutched her hand to her chest. She hadn't thought of that complication. "Yes."

"But my dad hasn't told her about me." Brady's shoulders deflated.

"Our family isn't close. Until this weekend, I hadn't seen your dad in eight years." She held the exit door open. "I guess he wants to tell her about you in person."

"I think I understand. It's kind of like how Hayden loves me and Grandma and Grandpa love me, but they don't get along very well with each other."

So wise for such few years. "It's complicated."

"Can I tell Miss Sylvie who I am?"

Laken winced. "We'd better let your dad do that. He'll be back next weekend."

"How about you come to church with us tomorrow? Maybe that would help you and Miss Sylvie make friends again."

# Chapter 6

Laken sucked in a deep, steadying breath. She'd vowed never to step inside a church again, especially not the one her mother attended. Yet, here she was. Because she couldn't say no to her adorable nephew. She stepped through the door, barely supported by noodle legs.

"Welcome." An usher shook her hand and passed her a bulletin. He looked familiar. "I'm Bob Reynolds. I saw you at the trail ride. You're Sylvie Kroft's daughter, but for the life of me, I can't remember your name."

"Laken."

He snapped his fingers. "Welcome, Laken. We're so glad you could join us today. Some of the classes have let out already, and the rest should be along soon."

"Well, I'll be." Carol clasped a hand to her heart, as if she thought it might escape her chest. "I'm so glad you decided to come." Carol linked arms with her. "You can sit with us."

"Actually, Brady invited me, so I should sit with him."

"Wow, you two became fast friends."

"You have no idea."

"I tried to call you the other night." Carol frowned. "I wanted to make sure your brother made it in okay, but I didn't get an answer."

"Sorry, I didn't check my messages. He made it just fine and flew back last night."

"So you had a nice visit?"

"An enlightening one."

"Laken, you came!" Brady rolled toward them.

"I told you I'd think about it." She dropped a kiss on top of his head and inhaled the fresh minty scent of his shampoo.

"Hayden said you didn't like church, so you might not come."

She scrunched her nose. "The first part is true, but I couldn't say no to you."

"We'll have to remember that." Hayden's hunter-green button-down, black pleated trousers, and contrasting paisley tie complemented his eyes and dark hair. He looked absolutely delicious, and Laken couldn't find her tongue.

"I'm glad you came. You look"—his gaze took in her appearance—"really nice."

From the pleased expression on his face, she was glad she'd chosen the pool-blue sheath. "Thanks. You're not so bad yourself."

He cleared his throat. "We usually sit over here. Brady, lead the way."

"Laken, you're here!" Grace squealed and gave her a quick squeeze as the harpist trilled a soothing hymn Laken knew but couldn't put her finger on. She'd missed the harp, and she had to admit being in church with Grace felt right. "I've got dibs on lunch. You have to go with Mark and me."

Five people stopped them to welcome Laken before they got to the pew, fifth from the front, right side. Brady positioned his chair in the wide aisle by the window and patted the pew beside him for Laken to sit at the end. Hayden claimed the seat on her other side, looking and smelling way too good. His spicy cologne served up a constant reminder of his proximity.

The harpist trilled her last notes, and as the pianist began a traditional hymn, Laken tried to concentrate on her surroundings instead of Hayden. The burgundy carpet, matching cushions on the pews, and white walls shone with multicolored prisms shooting about from the stained-glass windows. All just the way she remembered. The harp dwarfed one side of the stage, and Laken longed to hear more of its soothing trill.

Mother, Doreen, and Virgie walked the aisle and turned into the pew two rows ahead. Before taking her seat, Mother took the opportunity to survey the crowd behind her. She spotted Laken and her jaw dropped. Recovering quickly, a smile tugged at the corners of her mouth.

A real one.

Misty-eyed, Mother blew Laken a kiss.

A knot formed in her throat. The first kiss since Laken was a child.

Maye and Paul hugged Brady, welcomed Laken, and threaded through to sit on the other side of Hayden.

Twice, Doreen turned around, with obvious interest in Laken, Hayden, and Brady. A knowing smile curved her lips.

Laken's stomach clenched. Oh no! Everyone would assume she and Hayden were dating.

—⁓—

Hayden could barely keep his gaze off Laken. Her blue dress deepened the color of her eyes and brought out all the femininity her usual jeans and post office uniform top concealed. Who was he kidding? She was all woman, no matter what she wore, but the dress definitely exclaimed the point. Yet her broken spirit shone from within.

His soul danced. She was here, beside him in church. *Holy Spirit, do Your work.*

During the hymns, he sang louder than usual, holding his book so Laken could see.

Her mouth remained clamped shut.

"How Great Thou Art" echoed through the rafters, and his heavy burdens rolled off his shoulders. If only he could live here, safe and secure from the rest of the world. From Collin.

At the close of the third song, the congregation reclaimed their seats. Laken's shoulder rested against Hayden's, the silky fabric of her short sleeve smooth against his skin. Her soft perfume—just a hint of flowers mixed with her coconut shampoo—filled his senses. *Keep the brain where it should be.* He placed the hymnal in the rack and forced his attention on the pastor.

*Lord, let Pastor Grayson speak directly to Laken's heart.*

Sylvie Kroft stood and moved toward the stage with customary elegant ease.

Laken stiffened.

"Relax, she's singing," he whispered. What did Laken think her mother might do?

The pianist played the intro, and Sylvie's high soprano echoed through the hush in a perfect rendition of "In the Garden."

Covering her mouth with her hand, Laken looked as if she might hurl when Sylvie hit the last flawless note.

—∾∾—

Laken studied her nephew, intent on the sermon, as if his very life depended on the message. The pastor's words began to seep through her barricade. According to him, she needed a Savior and all she had to do was ask.

The same message she'd heard as a kid, sandwiched between her hypocritical parents. And she'd vowed never to be like them. If this Savior was someone her parents knew, she didn't want anything to do with Jesus and His salvation.

Lack of circulation tingled in her foot. She shifted position and uncrossed her legs.

But Virgie Patton wasn't like her parents. Sara hadn't been and Grace wasn't. Grayson and Adrea weren't, either. Hayden was the best person she'd ever known. Laken wouldn't mind being like any of them.

Grayson opened the altar call and her chest tightened. As the pleading song "Just As I Am" droned on and on, surely she'd explode. How many verses could one song have? Unable to stand another second, she stepped out into the aisle. Brady looked up at her and she motioned to the lobby, then scurried to the restroom.

She stared at her reflection in the mirror. Her eyes looked vacant, her expression hard and bitter. The song faded away and voices neared. Coward. Yellow-bellied coward.

Several women entered, and she made a show of washing her hands.

"Dear, are you all right? You look pale." Virgie's brows pinched together.

"I'm fine. I skipped breakfast this morning."

"Well, we can fix that. Have lunch with me?"

*And Mother? No way.* "That sounds lovely. Maybe some other time."

"I understand, dear. You're probably going with your mother."

Laken's brow rose. "No, actually I'm going with Grace and her husband."

"Maybe next week. Carol and I were going with Helen Fenwick."

Three sweet women with no hidden agendas. "That sounds like the most pleasant gathering I've ever heard of."

The door opened and Grace strolled in. "There you are."

"Oops, I'm holding up your lunch guest." Virgie leaned toward the mirror and dabbed on fresh pink lipstick. "I invited her, but you already beat me to it."

"Why don't we all go together?"

"That sounds lovely." Virgie blotted her mouth with a tissue. "Laken, see if you can find Carol and Helen. I'll catch up."

Laken and Grace exited to find the sanctuary cleared out with everyone outside already.

She scanned the parking lot. The steady thump of a dribbling basketball drew her gaze to the court. Brady, of course, with Hayden watching from a distance.

"I want you to meet someone." Grace snapped her fingers. "Dayne, come here."

Following Grace's gaze, Laken saw a blond boy run toward them.

A gasp escaped her. He was all Sara, except for the eyes.

"This is Laken, the one I told you about. The other friend your mom and I spent so much time with growing up."

"Nice to meet you, Laken."

"Dayne loves hearing stories about his mom." Grace tapped her chin with an index finger. "Over lunch, we'll have to remember some exciting tales."

"You're going to lunch with us?"

"And Hayden and Brady, too."

"Cool."

"Are you and Brady the same age?"

"I'll be in first grade, but I'll be seven in two months. We would have been in the same class, but my birthday's too late."

The dribbling stopped, and Laken glanced toward Brady. Mother knelt by his chair.

Every nerve ending jolted. "Excuse me."

Laken rushed over to Hayden. "What's she doing?" she hissed.

"Just asking how long he's played basketball and where we used to live."

"She's up to something." Laken pressed her finger to her lips, straining to hear.

"So, are Laken and Hayden dating?" Mother's light tone carried in the quiet and swirled fire through Laken's veins.

She hurried toward the pair, with Hayden close behind her.

"I don't think so." Brady dribbled the ball faster.

"They seem to spend a lot of time together."

"They're really just spending time with me, since Laken's my—"

"Ready to go, Brady?" Hayden cut in front of Laken.

Mother stood and turned to face them. "Doreen and I were hoping Brady and Hayden would have lunch with us. Laken," Mother's voice quivered, "would you like to come?"

An invitation? Laken had never heard her mother do anything but bark orders. "Sorry. We already have two other invitations."

"Maybe another time." Hayden swatted at a bee buzzing near him.

"It was nice chatting with you, Brady." Mother's tone rang unnaturally chipper.

"You, too." Brady rolled his chair toward the van. "Hey, Laken, you gonna ride with us?"

"Sure." She slowed her stride to let Brady get a few yards in front of them and whispered to Hayden, "We have to talk."

———

Hayden waited in the drive until Brady rolled inside his parents' door and Dad waved an all-is-well. Craning his neck, he looked behind him several times and repeatedly checked his bumper cam as he made the loop in the circle drive and pulled onto the highway.

"Mother needs to know about Brady." Laken's words tumbled in a rush.

"I really don't need further complications." Hayden's jaw ached from smiling and making light lunch conversation at the Rambler. "Can't we just keep it quiet for a while?"

"She'll keep asking questions until she gets to the bottom of it. Brady was about to spill when we showed up."

"I'm being completely selfish." Hayden pulled into the church lot next to Laken's car and punched the steering wheel. "Brady has a right to know his other grandparents, and they have a right to know him."

"I didn't say anything about my father." Her seat belt clicked as she unlatched it. "And I wouldn't advise you to let Brady anywhere near him."

Tired of wearing a brave front, Hayden faced her, despite tears welling in his eyes. "I can't shake the feeling that with every new family member who comes into Brady's life, I lose a bit more of him." Hot moisture traced down his left cheek.

Laken's chin trembled. With tentative fingers she caught the tear. "He loves you. No matter what happens."

"I'm not sure I can handle it"—his voice cracked—"if Collin takes him to California."

Soft arms came around him.

Hayden closed his eyes and reveled in her embrace, pulling her close. Comfort in the arms of a beautiful woman. A woman he cared for. A woman he could fall for. How could that be? He'd only known her a little over a month. He'd carefully constructed a wall, determined not to trust another woman with his heart.

Yet, they'd spent time together on a daily basis, and over the emotional weekend, they'd bonded. But she wasn't saved. Yes, she'd attended church this morning, but she'd made no decision for Christ.

With everything in him, he wanted to hold her tighter, to trace kisses across her cheek until he found her lips.

─∿─

A chill replaced the warmth of his arms on Laken's skin as Hayden pulled away.

He stared off in the distance. "When will you tell your mother?"

"It's Collin's place." Her voice sounded throaty and tight, affected by the close contact more than she'd expected. "He'll be in Friday night."

"Will she want custody of Brady?"

"I doubt it. Mother isn't very child oriented. Besides, no judge in his right mind would send a child to live with my alcoholic father."

Hayden sighed. "Guess I'll prepare Brady for more sprouting on the family tree."

"Actually, he already caught on. He doesn't miss much and wanted to tell her himself."

"Think we can hold him off until Collin talks to her?"

"I'll come to church Wednesday night, just to run interference." She touched his hand. "Try not to worry."

Too late. The nerve in his jaw ticked a steady rhythm as he got out of the truck and came around to open her door.

She climbed out and waved.

Hayden slowly backed out of her driveway, continually checking the bumper cam, craning his neck from side to side, looking behind him.

─∿─

Try as she might, Laken couldn't concentrate on her work. Not with the calendar-worthy hunk of mailman sorting beside her. As his biceps flexed each time he stuffed an envelope into his case, she couldn't get the warmth of his arms around her out of her head. So strong, yet so vulnerable. Secure enough to show his emotions, unashamed in his love for her nephew.

Sitting with him last night at midweek Bible study hadn't helped. So close, yet so far.

Worry carved lines in his handsome face. She wanted to smooth them away. Kiss them away. Laken stifled a gasp. Why did her thoughts keep straying in that direction?

Tension throbbed through him. Two days ago, he'd cried on her shoulder. Since then, they'd barely spoken two words to one another, as Hayden held everything inside. Typical male.

The main entrance door opened.

"Hey, y'all." Grace set a stack of envelopes on the counter. "It was great seeing you at church again last night, Laken. Both Sunday services and

Wednesday night Bible study. You're becoming a regular."

"It was"—Laken searched for a word to describe the unnerving experience—"nice." Only a little white lie.

"Nice to see you, Grace. I better get going." Hayden finished sorting his route, propped two cases on his hip, and hurried out the door.

"What's with him?"

Laken plopped in her chair. "Why can't my heart do what my brain tells it to?"

"Hmm." Grace tapped her chin with a perfectly French-manicured fingertip. "Need more info before I can summon up wise counsel."

"I think I have a crush." A weight lifted from her shoulders at the admission.

"I knew it." Grace pointed at her. "You're into Hayden."

"It's insane. I've known him a little over a month, and if you tell anybody, I'll tell Mark about the crush you had on Collin in school."

Grace grinned. "Actually, I already told him, but. . ." She made a zipper motion across her mouth and held her hand up as if taking an oath. "Scout's honor. So spill."

"He's so gentle, honest, and caring, but it can't work. He's into God and I'm totally not."

"Quite an obstacle." Grace pursed her lips. "Hayden would never go against the Bible. You know, the unequally yoked thing."

Laken's eyes widened. "I didn't say anything about getting married."

"No, but it's unwise to entertain thoughts of a relationship with someone you wouldn't want to marry." Grace fingered one of the envelopes in her stack. "You were raised in church, but I've sensed your discomfort lately. Don't you like Palisade?"

Laken let the chair spin in a slow circle. Where to start? "You know how dysfunctional my family is, but we attended church every time the doors opened. After a while, the whole fake mess turned my stomach."

"I imagine there are a lot of people hiding their truths, but there's nothing superficial about Hayden or his faith."

"I know, but even if we could meet in the middle on that issue, there are more obstacles than we could ever overcome."

"Such as?"

Laken stopped the twirling chair. "My brother is Brady's dad."

"Collin?" Grace pressed a hand to her heart.

"Long story, but he didn't know Brady existed until recently. Now that he does, I think he wants Brady, and I'm caught in the middle." She sprang from her chair and paced the office. "I promised Hayden I'd do my best to get Collin to move here. But, if Collin takes Brady to California, I don't think Hayden would survive." Her words flew as pent-up tension released. "And poor Brady."

"Whoa."

"Now you see why Hayden's on edge?"

"He's crazy about Brady."

"So am I. You know, I always wanted a real family and kids, but I was too afraid of marriage to pursue it. Having a nephew, it's almost like having my own child."

"You're crazy about Hayden, too."

Laken skidded to a halt. "I wouldn't put it quite that way."

"I would." Grace drummed her fingernails on the counter. "We just have to get the two of you on the same wavelength with God and convince Collin to move here."

"Oh, is that all? I'm with you on the second part."

"But you've been coming to church. So maybe. . ."

Maybe nothing. "I came the first time because Brady asked me to. After that, I've been trying to keep him from telling my mother who he is until Collin gets here tomorrow night. I won't fake Christianity." Pressure started to build in her chest, just like during the altar call.

"And I wouldn't want you to. If you'll just keep coming to church and keep an open mind, you'll be amazed at what God can do."

"We'll see." *Go ahead and try, God. You think You can fix me? Have at it.* "Right now I have to concentrate on conquering the life hurdle known as Mother."

"Honor your mother and father. That's from the Bible, you know." Grace turned toward the door then stopped midstride to lean against the counter and peer out the barred window. "Oh look, a wedding."

Not again.

"I wish people would do the whole shebang around here. How's a caterer supposed to get by with all these simple weddings? When you and Hayden get married, will you please let me cater it? Of course, since you're my friend, I'd have to do yours at cost, so that wouldn't help."

Laken blushed. "I don't think you'll have to worry about me getting married." *It won't happen. And definitely not with Hayden as the groom.*

———

With Collin pacing Laken's living room, tension vibrated off Hayden in waves she could almost see. His stiff posture in her kitchen chair belied the casual calm he tried to adopt.

Staring out the window above the sink, Laken tried to concentrate on the pink-and-orange-washed sunset, but a scream welled within her. If Mother didn't arrive soon, it just might escape.

Gravel crunched as a car pulled into the drive, and Laken hurried to peek between the living room curtains. "She's here."

Collin skidded to a halt in the middle of the living room. "Did you tell her I'm here?"

Oozing practiced boarding-school perfection, Mother sashayed across the yard.

"No." Willing Mother to hurry, Laken jerked the door open.

"Laken, I was so glad you called. Is everything all right?"

Mother's mouth opened, clamped shut, and opened again. She ran toward her son, every bit of elegant dignity replaced by elation.

"Oh Collin, I've missed you so." Mother lunged into him.

His arms remained at his sides.

The muscles around Mother's mouth quivered. "You're still angry with me. I tried to shield you from Martin's wrath. I really did." She hugged a little tighter.

Still, Collin didn't return her affection and pushed her away. "You enable him."

Tears pooled in Mother's eyes. "I most certainly do not."

"No, you just shell out the money for as much booze as he can down."

True, but suddenly Laken wanted to spare her mother the indignity of Collin's cold greeting. She touched her arm. "Mother, we have something to tell you."

Mother noticed Hayden. Startled, she backed away from Collin. Color suffused her face. "Hayden, I didn't know you were here. What's going on?"

"I'm here. . ." With a heavy sigh, Collin shut the door. "Because I have a son. Laken and Hayden thought you needed to know."

Mother's hand flew to her mouth.

Just like that, no easing into it.

"Where is he?"

Hayden ducked his head. "I'm sorry, Mrs. Kroft, but I didn't know Collin was your son until this past weekend."

"What does that have to do with my grandson?"

Laken almost wanted to hug her. Almost. "Brady is Collin's son, Mother."

More tears surfaced, and Mother's mouth twisted. "All this time, we've lived in the same town. What about you, Laken? I know we haven't been overly close the last few years, but I can't believe I'm the last one in on this little bomb." Splotches of red marred Mother's cheeks.

Hayden stood and shoved his hands in his pockets. "Laken didn't know until this past weekend."

"But Collin always confides in her. They were always like two peas in a pod. Collin never would have gotten married without Laken knowing about it."

"We never married."

"Collin, please." Mother pressed a fingertip to her temple. "Let's not—"

"Air our dirty laundry." Even under pressure, Mother had to keep up appearances. Cover it up. Keep everything nice and tidy. Hide the family's embarrassing little secrets.

"Your mother is upset enough." Hayden grazed Laken's elbow with a featherlight touch. "T've told Brady all about you, Mrs. Kroft, and he's dying to get to know you better. You can visit with him at my folks' during the day or at our house in the evening."

"That's all fine. I mean, that's great." Mother paced the living room and turned to Collin. "So, Brady's illegitimate. What will people think? We can't let that get out."

Laken rolled her eyes. *Leave it to Mother. The woman just learned she has a grandson and she's worried about keeping up appearances. It would seem sweet if she were thinking of Brady. But Mother only thought of herself.* "In this day and age, no one uses that term anymore."

"It's still important in the right circles, and people will wonder why I didn't know until now that he's my grandson." She tapped an elegant nail against the countertop separating the kitchen. "Maybe we should keep this quiet. Just between us."

"Brady goes by Winters." The tic in Hayden's jaw started up. "I'm sorry, ma'am, but either you accept my nephew or you won't be seeing him at all."

"It's not that I'm ashamed of him. You must understand—it's embarrassing to learn your children keep such life-altering secrets."

"Or when your parents do." Laken pushed the words through clenched teeth.

Mother paled.

Laken's fists balled until her nails dug into her palms.

"Listen, ma'am." Hayden scrubbed his hand across the day's growth covering his jaw. "No one has to know you didn't know. Just introduce him as your grandson. Most folks won't ask questions."

*Polite folks. People not like you.*

"Well, I guess if you're raising my grandson, you should call me Sylvie." Mother turned to Collin. "Just why is Hayden raising Brady?"

Hayden opened the door. "Laken, let's give Collin and your mom some privacy."

Collin's eyes shot her the desperate plea of a drowning man.

Stay and support her brother or run for her life?

Hayden linked arms with Laken, effectively ushering her out.

She stood on the porch, staring at the closed door.

"They'll be fine." Hayden nodded toward his pickup. "Let's go for a drive."

"You go ahead. I'll just hang around here."

"And rescue your brother from his own mess. Come on." Tucking her hand in his elbow, he led her to the truck.

Craning his neck, checking the camera and all three mirrors numerous times, he backed out of the drive. "How long has it been since they've seen one another?"

"Ten years. Now you know why our family has such close ties. You've seen her in action. One minute I feel sorry for her, the next I want to fillet her with words the way she does everyone else."

"Telling somebody off feels good for a minute or two, but regret follows. She certainly isn't an easy person to figure out, but she's hurting."

"I know."

He turned onto the gravel road by the old general store.

Laken snapped to attention, her spine rigid. "Where are we going?"

"My favorite place." He turned through the massive, white-iron, Victorian-style gate. "It calms me. And since you have an enormous painting of the falls on your living room wall, I figured you liked it here, too."

"I was in a coworker's wedding here a few years ago. Her father did the painting for her, and she gave all of her attendants a print."

Hayden parked and killed the engine. "Nice gift."

"Do the owners mind us coming here? Shouldn't we stop at the house and ask?"

"As long as the gate's open, it's okay." He came around to her side.

She stared at the perfectly groomed hedges.

"You okay?"

Laken cleared her throat. "I always thought this would be a great place for a wedding." *If I ever got brave enough to give marriage a shot, that is.*

"I was engaged once." He drew her out of the truck.

Her mouth went dry. She didn't want to think of him with anyone else. "Really? Was it supposed to be here?"

"We never got around to planning the wedding, but I doubt it. I don't think she had a romantic bone in her pinkie toe."

"I'm sorry." She walked under the vine-covered archway with lavender silk wisteria hanging overhead. A few months ago, the blooms had probably been real.

"Don't be. It was a very good thing that it ended when it did. Remember that first wedding at the post office after you came?"

"The white doves. The most beautiful, peaceful thing I've ever seen."

Hayden nodded. "Except that the dove handler was my ex-fiancée."

# Chapter 7

Laken gasped. She could never compete with such perfection. "She looked like a model."

"Her insides didn't match the outside."

Outside, Laken was ordinary; inside she was empty, a tumble of mixed hurts, disappointments, and fears. She sniffed the air, trying to concentrate on the fragrant yellow moss rose, red begonias, and blue bellflowers bursting from terra-cotta pots lining the walkway. "Did you come here with her?"

The heart-shaped flower bed overflowed with coral geraniums, orange daylilies, and other blossoms she couldn't identify. The splash of the falls didn't soothe the whirling in her soul.

"No. She never had time for such frivolity." Hayden took her hand as they walked under the heart-shaped archway and descended the brick steps.

They passed the fountain with the white marble lady pouring her vessel out. Small pavilions dotted each side of the path overlooking the falls. The path narrowed, and Hayden tucked her hand in the crook of his arm as they descended the strategically placed rock steps.

"But you loved her. What happened?"

Disappointment registered with a slight twist of his mouth.

Laken turned to gaze across the falls, seeking calm in the peaceful surroundings, unable to watch the hurt displayed on his face, put there by another woman. The trees and bushes contrasting against the jutting rocks and the blue green pool at the bottom couldn't calm the quake surging inside her. The cascading water didn't sound soothing anymore as the foamy torrent crashed over the rocks.

"If you don't want to talk about it, it's okay."

"Let's just say I fell for someone pretending to be something she wasn't." His fingers grazed her elbow. "What about you? Ever been in love?"

She shivered. Not until now.

He took her hands in his, forcing her to face him. "Tell me."

Still, she couldn't meet his gaze. "I've never let anyone get close enough."

"Why?"

"I don't want to end up like my parents."

Gently he rubbed his thumbs over the backs of her hands. "Despite the astounding divorce rate, there is such a thing as a good marriage."

"If you say so. I never had any example of a nurturing relationship, but deep down, despite the fear, I always wanted children."

"You're great with Brady."

"He fills a void in my life."

Hayden pushed a strand of hair away from her face. "Come to church with me Sunday. I know Someone who can fill that emptiness."

She pulled away. "I know exactly who you mean, and I'm not interested."

"Please, Laken, just give Him a try."

"Look how much He's helped you." She crossed her arms over her chest.

"He has helped me. If not for Him, I wouldn't have been able to function after the accident."

"You still haven't forgiven yourself."

"No, but He has. And that makes life tolerable. On most days, I have peace."

Until Collin showed up. Two squirrels scampered up and around a large oak in a spiral pattern, chattering and swishing their bushy tails. Oh, to be so carefree.

"I just don't see how something you can't even see could help with anything."

"Give Him one more try, Laken. 'The peace of God, which passeth all understanding.' It's waiting in the open arms of God. All you have to do is ask for it."

Something flickered deep in her soul.

"You've tried everything else. You moved away. You started over. You sought fulfillment in your career. Has any of it helped?"

Her heart gave a precarious tilt. "Okay. I'll go."

—⁊⁊⁊—

Laken added sugar to her cappuccino and sat down at her kitchen table. Classical music played softly from the stereo, yet her nerves wouldn't settle. She tried to concentrate on the newspaper. But the drama in her life topped the drama of the headlines, and she couldn't focus.

For the first time ever, Laken dreaded dealing with her brother. He'd been gone when she got home last night and didn't come in until the wee hours. Now she'd get to spend the morning hearing him complain about Mother. Not her favorite subject.

The floorboards creaked in the hallway. She pretended extreme interest in an article.

"Hey."

"Hey." She didn't look up.

"Thanks for sticking around to help last night. I really can't tell you how much I appreciate it."

"I thought you and Mother could use some time."

He plopped down across from her. "I probably would have run, too."

"So, how'd it go?"

"Very messy. She cried, wailed, and yelled. I figured the neighbors would call 911."

Laken winced.

"She finally calmed and called Hayden to ask if Brady could spend the day with us."

"And he said. . . . ?"

"Yes, if you stick with us."

She closed her eyes. "Just the way I wanted to spend my day off—with Mother."

Gravel crunched under vehicle tires, and Laken peered out the window. Hayden's midnight-blue van parked in the drive.

"I guess you told him I'd hang with you since he's here."

"Listen, Laken, I'm not concerned about Mother right now. I need you to help me develop a relationship with my son. If that requires spending time with Mother, so be it. I need time with my son, and I need your help."

The doorbell rang and Collin hurried to answer.

Laken followed.

Instead of Hayden, Mother stood on the porch with Brady rolled as close as he could get. They'd have to build a ramp.

"Hey, Brady." Excitement oozed from Collin's tone. "Wait till you hear what I've planned today."

"What?"

"We're going to a basketball game in Little Rock."

"And Grandma—I mean, Mimi's going with us?"

Brady rolled right into the trap set up for him.

Mother propped her hand on Brady's shoulder. "Darling, I'm thrilled we get to spend the day together, but a basketball game?"

"Not just any old game." Collin checked his watch. "I've arranged for Brady to watch a wheelchair basketball game."

Laken's insides boiled at Collin's obvious attempt to buy Brady's affections.

"Awesome!" Brady's excited shout spurred yapping from the neighbor's dog.

"In fact. . ." Collin strode toward the van. "We better get moving."

Laken frowned but followed. "Did you talk to Hayden about this?"

"He knows we're going to watch a game and loaned us his van."

She stopped walking.

Collin stopped a few paces later. "What?"

"Don't try to win Brady over by being more fun than Hayden." She jabbed Collin in the chest with her index finger.

"Come on, y'all," Brady called, already in the van.

"I can't help it if I'm more fun than Hayden." Collin grinned. "Don't ruin this for Brady. This day is about him."

"Is it?" She hurried to the van. "Mother, you sit up front; I'll keep Brady company."

—⁓—

Turning a slow circle in her bedroom, Laken checked her coral dress in the full-length mirror one more time. So rarely did she wear one, it felt odd, like her slip was showing or something, but it wasn't. With a deep breath, she opened the door and strode to the living room.

Remote in hand, Collin sprawled on the couch and frowned when he saw her. "What are you all dressed up about?"

"I'm going to church. Want to come?"

He snickered. "Are you serious?"

"Yes, I'm serious. Brady goes and he invited me." Last week, anyway.

"Brady may have invited you, but that dress is all about Hayden." Collin gazed off in the distance. "You know, this could work to our advantage. You get Hayden to fall for you and maybe he'd give Brady up without a fight."

"Collin Kroft, I can't believe you said that."

"I should have known you wouldn't help me." His jaw rigid, his tone steely, Collin's gaze pierced her soul. "You're stoking a fire in the enemy camp."

Laken held both hands up, as if to ward off a blow. "That's it. I can't do this." She grabbed her purse and hurried to her car.

With deep, steadying breaths, she backed out of the drive. Pent-up tears singed her eyes, but she wouldn't give in. What had happened to that feeling she and Collin would be solid, no matter what happened with Brady? She wasn't taking Hayden's side and he wasn't the enemy. He'd done nothing but help her and make sacrifices for Brady. Something Collin had never done.

At church, Hayden waited on the steps just as he'd promised. Looking way too good, as usual, in a burgundy button-down and gray slacks.

He caught sight of her and met her in the parking lot. "What's this about Brady playing wheelchair basketball?"

"Hi, how are you this morning?" Sarcasm dripped from her tone.

Hayden ran a hand through his hair. "Sorry. I'm slightly tense."

*Tell me about it.*

"I'm really, really glad you came." Honesty shone from vivid olive eyes.

"Me, too." She sighed. "They were just talking about it on the way home, and I told Collin he'd have to check with you first. I think he's trying to win Brady over with treats."

"Are the games dangerous?"

"I don't think so. It's recreational and noncompetitive. From what the coach said, it's just something for the kids to do and have fun."

"Who is this coach?"

"I don't know. Some retired NBA guy."

"NBA?" Hayden's eyes lit up. "And you can't remember his name?"

Typical male. "I'm not into sports. Anyway, his son uses a wheelchair, so he started this program for kids. There's a small fee to help with expenses."

"Hank Smith?"

"That's it."

"He's one of my all-time favorite players. I heard something about this."

"It's a good sign. Maybe it means Collin's planning to stay here."

197

Hayden shook his head as if to get his brain out of the NBA. "I'm not concerned about the money. I've always done whatever I had to, to keep Brady happy and healthy. What if his wheelchair tips over?"

"It won't hurt my legs." Brady giggled from behind them.

A wince distorted Hayden's features.

Laken turned to see her nephew on the sidewalk, grinning at his painfully honest humor.

Glancing at his uncle, the child's smile melted. He aimed his chair toward the church. "I came out to tell you it's time for service to start."

Her stomach clenched. Already, Brady felt torn between his uncle and his father. And all her peacemaking efforts had fallen flat.

As they stepped inside the lobby, the harpist's melody tugged at Laken. She knew the tune. It was on the tip of her memory. "It Is Well with My Soul." Just like all the other songs she'd heard in this church, she knew all the words by heart.

As Pastor Grayson began his sermon, Laken watched Hayden from under her lashes.

Forgiveness.

Had he asked Grayson to preach to her dysfunctional family? Surely he wouldn't do that, but it seemed every time she came to this church, the sermon aimed right at her.

"While Jesus hung on the cross dying for our sins. . ." Pastor Grayson set his Bible on the pulpit and stretched his arms out, as if he hung there. "He pleaded, 'Father, forgive them; for they know not what they do.' You see, we're all sinners and our only hope is Christ's forgiveness."

The pressure began to build in Laken's chest.

"If Jesus can forgive those who nailed Him to the cross, those who cast lots for His clothes, those who cheered and jeered, who are we to let a hardened heart rule our lives?"

Pastor Grayson picked up his Bible and used it to point at the congregation. "Not only are we to accept Jesus' forgiveness and accept Him as Savior, we're to forgive others. And we're to forgive ourselves. If we accept Christ's forgiveness but can't forgive ourselves, peace eludes us. If Jesus Christ can forgive your sins, who are you to hold on to them?

"If you don't know Jesus' forgiveness and salvation this morning, please come forward. If you harbor bitterness toward others or yourselves, please come forward. Lay your burdens at the feet of our Jesus."

The congregation stood as the harpist began a haunting rendition of "I Surrender All."

"Excuse me," Hayden whispered.

Scrunching forward, she peeked as he stepped out in the aisle, walked to the altar, and knelt.

Hmm, he's saved, so he must be working on forgiving himself for the accident. *Lord, help him to forgive himself.*

*What am I doing?* The music swelled. Her chest tightened even more. She wanted that surrender, that peace, that forgiveness.

*Come on. Out of the pew, sidestep Brady. Forward. March.* The fifteen feet to the altar stretched into miles. Her feet didn't move.

Snippets of prayers she'd heard through the years swirled through her mind.

—∾∾—

As the long line snaked to the lobby, Hayden waited for the sanctuary to clear.

"Hayden."

He looked down at Brady. "Hmm?"

The child's eyes were too shiny. "I forgive you."

Hayden's stomach did a little dip. "What?"

"I never blamed you for my accident, but just in case it might make you feel better, I forgive you."

His knees gave way, and Hayden knelt to his nephew's level, wrapping Brady in a hug as tears streamed down his face. "I think that does make me feel better."

"Where's Laken going?"

Hayden let Brady go and wiped his eyes, just in time to see her scurry out the door. "I don't know. Maybe she's going to lunch with someone."

His mom and dad, with twin disapproving frowns marring their foreheads, waited at the back of the church for Brady to have Sunday lunch with them. "Grandma and Grandpa are waiting for you."

Brady rolled toward them.

With a lump clogging his throat, Hayden followed.

Outside, Brady flew down the ramp, too fast for Hayden's comfort, and rolled down the sidewalk to the van.

Sylvie and Laken stood near her car. Talking.

Sylvie obviously loved Brady. Laken did, too. Something they had in common. Maybe Brady could draw the two women together. Maybe he already had.

" 'Bye, Mimi. 'Bye, Laken."

Laken blew Brady a kiss.

Waiting patiently, Mom and Dad stood by the van while Brady operated the lift. Once he was inside, they climbed in and the engine started. As his family passed, they all waved at him.

He glanced in Laken's direction.

At least she had come. Seeing her loneliness the other day made his chest hurt. Familiar with the threat of ending up alone, the burden she carried made his soul ache.

He got in his parents' Ford. To go home alone. To an empty house. To eat a frozen dinner alone. Might as well get used to it.

Stopping at the intersection, he considered turning toward the Rambler, but he really didn't want to sit there alone, either, so he followed Mom and Dad home. Brady turned around a couple of times to wave, bringing a smile to Hayden's face.

—◊—

Alone with Mother in the parking lot, Laken tried to let the birds' chatter settle her nerves. "Brady's a great kid."

"Yes." Mother nibbled on the inside of her lip. "I so enjoyed spending time with him yesterday."

"He did, too. Listen, Mother, I think we should. . .make up."

"Well, I've never done anything to keep us apart. I've been trying from the moment you stepped back in—"

"Mother. Please, stop talking. I'd like for us to get along. It doesn't matter who or what caused problems for us, let's just forget it and move forward."

"Very well, dear."

Laken took a deep breath. "I love you, Mother."

Mother's lips trembled.

"I love you, too, dear. I always have." Mother hugged her, awkward at first, but both women relaxed in the embrace. "Come home and have lunch with us."

Laken stiffened. "I—"

"Your father would love seeing you."

"I can't deal with his drinking."

"I have something to discuss with you." Mother pulled away. Her eyes bore into Laken's.

"Not more gossip. I can't deal with that, either."

"No, Laken. I want you and Collin both to come to the house. Soon."

"Collin will never come. Never."

"It's of the utmost importance and affects the entire family." Mother's hand shook as she brushed a stray red wisp away from her face. "I need your help, as I don't know where to begin."

Laken's heart clenched. Was Mother sick? Father? Had his drinking finally affected his health?

"I'll talk to Collin and see what I can do. If. . ."

"If what?" Mother's brows drew together.

"If Father will promise not to drink while we're there."

With a sigh, Mother nodded. "I'll see what I can do."

—◊—

Hayden pulled in to his parents' drive to leave the car. Already, Brady was out of the van, practicing his dribbling as usual.

His parents started inside, clearly expecting Hayden to go home as usual.

Maybe they couldn't forgive him, but at least he could try to make things right.

"Mom." Hayden cleared his throat. "Do you have enough food for an extra plate?"

Her mouth tightened into a straight line. "Of course. You know you're always welcome."

"Cool." Brady spun the ball on his finger. "Can we shoot some hoops till lunch is ready?"

"I need to talk to the folks a minute, then I'll come play."

"Cool."

He followed his parents inside.

"This is such a treat, son."

Hayden ran a hand through his hair. "Look. I know y'all can't forgive me. To tell you the truth, I just forgave myself this morning, but I'm tired of the strain between us. I'd like for us to be a family again. For Brady's sake, if nothing else."

Mom's chin quivered.

"We don't blame you, son." Dad clamped a hand on Hayden's shoulder. Truth shone in Dad's eyes.

"So, Pastor Grayson's sermon got through to y'all, too?"

"Hayden, we've never blamed you." A tear rolled down Mom's cheek.

A frown etched across Hayden's brow. "You didn't?"

"Of course not, son." Dad squeezed his shoulder. "It was an accident."

"Then why have things been so tense?"

"Every time we tried to reach out to you, you pushed us away." Mom curled her arms around his waist.

He pulled her in for a hug. "But you never stopped trying." Unable to see past his guilt, he'd become blind to their faith in him. He kissed the top of Mom's head. "I'm sorry."

"You have nothing to be sorry for." Dad wrapped his arms around both of them.

For the first time in years, the house felt like home.

—⁓—

The quiet park soothed Laken's nerves. Two more days until church. She didn't want to go. It was wearing her down. She'd skipped Wednesday night and paid for her cowardice the rest of the week. Hayden questioned her. Carol questioned her. Even Grace had stopped by the post office to question her. And she didn't have any answers.

Tired from the long workweek, all she wanted was to go home. But she couldn't just yet. By now, Collin had arrived. He'd never understand what had happened between Mother and her last Sunday. She didn't even understand it. And she had to think of a way to convince him to visit their parents' home. What was going on there?

But for now, she just wanted to revel in the peaceful surroundings. The concrete picnic table at the edge of the park invited her to sit in the shade. She slipped her sandals off and climbed to sit on top with her bare feet resting on the attached bench.

Hummingbirds flitted about the honeysuckle-draped fence row. Sweet nectar perfumed the air, while crickets chirped and bullfrogs croaked a chorus from the shallow creek running along the back of the walking trail. How long had it been since she'd relaxed enough to hear it?

Gravel crunched in the parking lot. Through the cluster of sycamore, oak, and maples, she saw a truck. A very familiar truck.

Hayden got out and jogged across the park toward her. "Hey, I happened to see your car. You okay? You've been quiet all week."

"I'm fine." She forced a smile.

He took a seat beside her. "I was glad to see you and your mom talking the other day."

"We're better than we have been in a while, but I'm worried about her. She wants Collin and me to come to the house for something important."

"When?"

"As soon as I can convince Collin to go, I guess." *If* she could convince him. She shrugged. "Maybe if Father promised he wouldn't be there."

"He can't be that bad."

"I've never seen him sober and he constantly maligned Collin. Nothing Collin ever did was good enough."

"I'm sorry, Laken." Hayden gazed across the park. "I can't imagine what that would be like. Maybe you can help him."

"I wouldn't know where to begin."

"Bring him to church."

"Yeah, right." She rolled her eyes. "When I was a kid, we attended Thorndike in Searcy. Grayson's dad was the pastor and still is, as far as I know. Dad was a deacon, and he'd managed to hide his problem. But one Sunday, he showed up drunk and disruptive. The other deacons escorted him out. After that, we went to Palisade in Rose Bud, but Father never went again."

"He's ill, Laken, and we're to honor our parents." He took her hand in his. "Since Brady's accident, I've kept my folks at arm's length, certain they blamed me. After last Sunday's sermon, I offered an olive branch and learned they never blamed me. I just wouldn't let them near enough to tell me that."

Something inside her warmed. "I'm glad you made peace with them."

"Me, too." With a satisfied grin, he patted his stomach. "I had the most awesome home-cooked meal after church. Just like old times, before I let my guilt get in the way."

"You forgave yourself?"

Hayden shrugged. "If Jesus can forgive me, who am I to hold a grudge against myself? A lot of good things happened in that church last Sunday."

Tears clouded her vision. "Hayden, I want that surrender, that peace, that forgiveness Grayson preached about."

His eyes sparkled. "You want to accept Jesus?"

# Chapter 8

Yes." Her answer came out wobbly and wet-sounding.

He took her hand and stepped down from the table, then knelt. She knelt beside him. Not knowing where to begin, she hoped God knew.

Hayden's arm wrapped around her shoulders. "Do you want me to pray?"

"I'll do it." The weight pressing on her chest eased. "Dear Jesus, I know I'm a sinner. I know that only Your blood can cleanse me of my sin. Forgive me of my sins." She wiped tears before they could drip off her chin. "I give You my life, trusting You completely for my salvation. I accept You as my Lord and Savior, Jesus. Guide me and lead me. Thank You for dying on the cross for my sins. In Your precious name, amen."

Peace like she'd never known flowed through her soul. "Now what?"

He stood and helped her to her feet. "That's it. Go to church. Tell people about your decision. If you have any questions, you can ask me or you can talk to Grayson if you want. He'll want to talk to you about getting baptized."

It sounded so simple.

"I'll see you Sunday then. For now I better get going." But she didn't want to. She wanted to stay with him, in the peaceful park. Forever. She slipped her shoes on.

"Laken?"

"Hmm." She turned to face him.

"I'm really glad you know Jesus now."

"Me, too." She grinned. "It makes everything better. Thanks for inviting me to church."

"Congratulations." He hugged her.

She snuggled in his arms, her cheek resting against his rock-hard chest. A featherlight kiss grazed her temple. Laken pulled away enough to see him.

His gaze settled on her lips. Spicy aftershave filled her senses. The birds' chorus echoed the song in her heart.

Clearing his throat, Hayden took a step backward. "We better go." He tucked her hand in his elbow.

"I should really check on Collin." She tried to sound natural as his bicep rippled beneath her fingers.

"I need to speak with him. Is it okay if I follow you?"

"Sure." Breathe normal. It was just a little kiss and not even anywhere near her mouth.

203

—m—

Hayden stayed a few car lengths behind Laken, ready to trail her wherever she led. Was this love? Being so near her had turned his insides to squash.

She was saved now. Blood-bought and heaven-bound. He wanted to leap in the air and click his heels together.

Laken had begun anew. Could they make a new start together?

Since she'd given her heart to Christ, he wanted what was left of it. To have and to hold forever. To protect her and shield her from life's hurts. To run his fingers through the silky softness of her hair and kiss all her cares away.

If Brady left, he'd need her to ease his hurt.

She turned into the drive, and he parked behind her.

As they strolled toward the house, he entwined his fingers with hers. It felt right.

The door opened and Collin stepped outside. "Look, sis, I'm sorry. . ." His gaze landed on Hayden, then their clasped hands. "I didn't realize we had company."

Laken pulled out of his grasp.

*We're tearing her in two, right along with Brady.* Hayden cleared his throat but couldn't get around the knot lodged there. "I came to speak my piece."

"Good, I was hoping to spend some more time with Brady."

Hayden's gut twisted, and he forced out the words he didn't want to say. "That's up to him."

"It is?" Collin's brow rose.

"I won't play tug-of-war with Brady." The knot in his throat swelled. He swallowed. "If you want custody, I won't put up a fight."

Laken gasped.

"Is that so?" Collin's voice dripped sarcasm.

"I'm not playing games. I want what's best for Brady, and getting ping-ponged between the two of us isn't good for him." A crushing weight settled on Hayden's chest and he closed his eyes. "If you want to take him to California, I'll ease the transition as much as possible."

Laken's soft hand wriggled back into Hayden's.

He opened his eyes and squeezed her fingers. The tic in his jaw started up.

"I've got some business to attend to in Little Rock." Collin shot him a victorious smile. "I'll be back next Friday for the weekend, then head there on Sunday evening. Since school doesn't start for another week after that, it would be the perfect time for Brady and me to spend some time together."

"So you can leave him in a hotel room with some hired caretaker while you work twenty-four/seven?" Laken shook her head. "I think not."

Collin's gaze drilled holes through her. "When did you get any say in the matter?"

"Stop." Hayden spat the word through clenched teeth. "No more arguing."

"For your information"—Collin pointed at Laken—"I'll do my work from my hotel room, mostly on the phone, and the few associates I'll need to meet with will come to me. Brady will be in my very capable care twenty-four/seven."

Hayden ran a hand through his hair and willed the quaking in his soul to stop. "I don't mind Brady going with you. But his care can be complicated. You'll have to accommodate his needs, bathe him, help him in the bathroom, and get him into his bed."

"It's only a week, and it'll be a test, to see how well we acclimate to one another." Collin crossed his arms over his chest. "We'll be back the following Friday."

"Okay." Hayden squeezed Laken's hand again. "If it's what Brady wants, it's fine by me, as long as you make sure he gets in bed at a decent hour and up fairly early. I've been trying to get him back on his school schedule. I'll head home and run it by him."

"Without swaying him against the idea?" Collin's tone issued a challenge.

Laken propped her hands on both slim hips. "Hayden's word is as pure as gold. He doesn't want Brady pulled back and forth between you. You can trust him."

At least she respected him. Could she trust him with her heart? "I'll call you later." He drew her hand to his lips and brushed a kiss on the back of it.

A pretty blush colored her cheeks.

Collin's glare skewered Hayden.

While his legs would still hold him up, he turned to his truck. Home to convince Brady to spend time with Collin. Eventually permanently.

—⁂—

Laken brushed past Collin and hurried inside.

The door slammed behind her.

"It's worse than I thought." Collin sighed. "You're sleeping with the enemy."

Her jaw dropped.

"But it could have advantages. That's why he changed his mind. You did it for me, didn't you?"

Whirling around, Laken slapped him. "He isn't like that. And neither am I."

"Oh, come on." Collin pressed fingertips to his reddening cheek. "Maybe you're not like that, but he's a man."

"Not your typical man. He's a Christian and I am, too."

"Spare me the details." Collin rolled his eyes and stalked toward the guest room. "I will say this, though—that was a mighty Christian slap." A door slammed behind him.

With a big sigh, she pulled a chair out and plopped at the kitchen table with her face in her hands.

Her cell phone rang.

Tempted not to answer, she checked the number. Mother. "Hello?"

"Laken, did you talk Collin into coming yet?" Mother's anxiety rang clear.

"It's been an eventful afternoon. I just got home." *And we're not speaking at the moment.*

"Let me talk to him."

"Sure." *Better you than me.* She traipsed down the hall and rapped her knuckles on the guest room door.

The door swung open. Collin glared. "What?"

"It's for you."

She jabbed the phone at him, turned, and bolted outside.

—∾—

Early August basted Laken in a sheen of sweat, but she'd rather roast than go inside and face her brother. Barefoot, with strappy white sandals in hand, still wearing her fuchsia and red floral dress, Laken eased down on the porch steps, careful not to snag the material on anything. With an overlay of sheer flowered fabric, it was softer, frillier, and more feminine than what she usually wore. But she'd bought it with Hayden in mind and decided to wear it this morning, hoping the bright colors might improve her outlook.

Though Hayden seemed to approve, the cheery dress didn't help her mood.

She and Collin hadn't spoken since their argument. They'd avoided one another since he stormed out after Mother's phone call. Saturday, he'd taken Brady swimming alone and didn't come home until she was already in bed. This morning, before church, he stayed in his room.

Hayden had worried about her all through morning services and during lunch, but she couldn't tell him what was wrong. If he knew the things Collin had said to her, he'd resent Collin more and worry more about Brady's welfare.

Tears seeped from the corners of her eyes, and she swiped them away.

Why was Collin being such a jerk? He was getting his way.

Poor Brady. Such a big decision resting on such small shoulders. The uncle he loved or the father he barely knew. Laken faced the same choice: the man she loved or the brother who'd grown distant.

She pressed her fingers to quivery lips, remembering the kiss that wasn't even really a kiss, that had sped her heart until it almost leapt from her chest.

The door opened behind her. She straightened, bracing herself for another onslaught.

"Hey." His tone gentle, Collin sat beside her. "I'm sorry."

"I'm sorry for hitting you." She leaned her head against his shoulder.

"I deserved it. I shouldn't have said those things. You're not like that."

"How do you know? We haven't spent much time together as adults."

"I just know." Collin sighed. "I'm sorry you've felt torn between Hayden and me. You obviously have feelings for him."

She sucked in a quivery breath. "I imagine Brady feels the same way. Please don't put any pressure on him. If he says no to next week's Little Rock trip, just accept it and try again later."

Collin nodded. "You're right."

"Hayden's trying. This is so hard on him."

"I'm just not sure I can trust him."

"He's one of the most trustworthy men I've ever met."

"You're in love with him." He dropped a kiss on the crown of her head. "And it has nothing to do with who Brady lives with. Congratulations."

"For what?"

"Falling in love. I loved Katie like that, you know? And I took out all my frustrations on her. I don't know why I hurt the ones I love most."

Like father, like son. She slid her shoes on. "Let's go in and get something cold to drink. I'd really like to change out of this dress, and then we'll fill in the holes of the eight years we missed of each other's lives while we wait for Brady's decision."

He stood and offered a hand to help her up. "Everything?"

"The good, the bad, the ugly." The chill of the air-conditioning swept goose bumps over her. "Did Mother beg you to come to the house?" She hurried to the kitchen.

"It's of the utmost importance," he mimicked as he settled on the couch.

"I'm worried, Collin." She clinked ice in two glasses and poured the sweet tea. "Something isn't right with her."

"She said you two called a truce. And she's already sucking you in?"

Laken handed him a glass and plopped into her favorite armchair. "This is different."

"I know."

"Will you go with me?"

"I'll think about it."

— ∽ —

Hayden sorted his mail by route, stacking the magazines and catalogs in the flats bin. At least it was Monday, the busiest day of the week, lots of mail to keep him busy. Going through the motions, with a gaping Brady-shaped hole in his heart. *He's just in Little Rock.* Not that far, but it was only the tenth. He wouldn't be back until the fourteenth. Hayden had never dreamed a mere week could stretch into eternity.

With a precise nonstop rhythm, Laken stamped mail. "How'd it go? Seeing Brady off last night?"

"I did great, put on a brave face. After he left, I bawled like a baby. The house is way too quiet, way too empty."

The stamping stopped, and she touched his elbow for only a second before returning to her work counter.

He longed for the softness of her arms, the coconut smell and silky feel

207

of her hair. But one little embrace in the office could get them both fired. And this was only the first day of working with her since he'd come to terms with his feelings.

"If it helps any, I spoke with Brady after they got to the hotel last night. He was really excited but missing you already."

Warmth wrapped around Hayden's soul. "It makes the selfish part of me feel better."

"You don't have a selfish molecule in your entire makeup."

"Somehow, you seem to have gotten the wrong impression that I'm Mr. Perfect."

"I'll be the judge of that." She carried her bin to Carol's sorter and began stuffing envelopes into the slots. "Just rest assured that Collin's crazy about Brady."

"Do you really believe he never received Katie's letter until a few months ago?" His voice had a hard edge to it.

"Yes. If Collin had known she was sick, he'd have been by her side."

Hayden swallowed hard. "Then why didn't he marry her?"

At the counter, Laken stacked the mail to be postmarked in a neat pile and began stamping another mound. "Dysfunctional families give you a warped outlook on marriage."

"Does marriage still scare you?" Hayden glanced her way.

Though she didn't stop stamping, her fingers trembled. "A little. But maybe if I found the right guy, it would be different than anything I ever witnessed as a child."

"My parents' marriage was always great. We were one big happy family until Katie died. Then it seemed like everything fell apart there for a while."

"I'm glad things are mended."

"I'll give Collin credit for one thing. At least he didn't take Katie off to California. I treasure those last years with her."

"I'm still trying to derail California."

"I know, and I hate putting you through this. You shouldn't have to stand against your own brother."

"It's no big deal."

"Let me make it up to you. Since you think I'm such a great guy." He stepped over next to her. "Have dinner with me. . ." Tonight, tomorrow, every night? He didn't want to wait, but better make it date night, so she'd know he meant more than a friendly dinner. "Friday night."

Laken's stamping stopped, hand hovering over the stack of envelopes. "Friday night? Okay." Her voice quivered.

*Yes.* Hayden's insides did a little dance. "I was thinking Colton's in Searcy."

"Sounds great."

Hayden grinned and went back to his sorter.

A minute or two passed before her stamping started up again, not quite so rhythmic.

—⁓—

The turquoise tank top gave new depth to Laken's eyes. Hayden could barely keep his gaze off her. Wearing white capris and sandals, with a matching sweater draped casually around her slim shoulders, she was lovely. Inside and out.

His porterhouse steak and baked potato swimming in butter dwarfed Laken's loaded chicken and salad.

Finished with his salad, he downed half his steak while she nibbled. "Aren't you hungry?"

"Yes. It's wonderful."

"Don't you like steak?"

She scrunched her nose. "Not particularly."

"Why didn't you tell me? We could have gone somewhere else."

"I love their chicken. I'm just. . ."

"What?"

"Nervous."

Her admission melted him into a puddle at her feet. He knew the grin on his face was downright goofy, but he couldn't do a thing about it. "With me? We see each other almost every day. Twice on weekdays."

"I know, but this is a date."

His eyes widened. "It is?"

Her eyes saucered. "I mean—I thought. . ."

"Calm down, I'm teasing you."

A blush pinked her cheeks and she giggled.

"Relax. Next time, you choose the place."

An arched eyebrow rose. "Next time?"

He covered her hand with his. "Definitely."

A warm smile put a sparkle in her eyes, but then she frowned and pulled her hand away. "Can I ask you something?"

"Sure."

"One thing I don't understand—Christians still sin, right?"

Where did that come from? *Lord, am I making her think about sinning?* "As long as we're on this earth, sin tempts, and if we give in to it, it sometimes rules us. We pray and strive, but often we fail. When we do, we ask God's forgiveness and restore fellowship with Him."

"I don't think I'll ever understand it all."

"That's why you need to go to church, read your Bible, and pray. We may not ever understand it all. On this side of heaven anyway."

Good, she wasn't thinking about sinning. Instead, she longed to know more. That new believer fire, the fire he'd lost as he'd gotten comfortable and taken his salvation for granted.

"How long have you been a Christian?"

"Not very long, I'm afraid. When Katie got sick, she and I started attending church with Mom and Dad. We both accepted Christ."

A relieved sigh escaped her. "So you know she's in heaven. I'm so glad."

"Me, too. Knowing I'll see her in glory someday makes losing her tolerable."

She nibbled on her lip. "I wonder about my father. We went to church for years, but I don't know if he ever accepted Jesus."

"Ask him. Maybe you can witness to him."

"Me? I have so many questions."

"Fire away. I'll answer what I can. But you don't have to know everything to tell others about Jesus. Just tell them what He did for you."

"You're right."

Right before his eyes, she was becoming a new creature. *Thank You, God, for this woman You've placed in my life.*

——

Hayden caught Laken's hand as they walked to her porch. The rest of their dinner conversation had remained on spiritual things. Seeing hope radiate from her warmed his soul.

He squeezed her hand. "You should have told me you didn't like steak."

"It's not that I don't like it. It's just so iffy. I gave up years ago on trying to get a steak cooked right at a restaurant."

"And what is right?"

"Completely brown, but still moist. I thought that thing you ate might moo at us, so I just order grilled chicken instead. You can't go wrong with chicken."

"Colton's always gets it just right. You need to broaden your horizons." He pulled her close as they neared the door.

"Hayden." She pushed away from him.

"Sorry." All evening, he'd wanted to hold her, but maybe he was moving too fast. Maybe she didn't want to broaden any horizons with him.

"Don't be." She touched his shoulder. "It's just—I don't need any gossip. I'm technically your boss."

Hayden winced. She was right. One of them would have to transfer or they couldn't date. The latter wasn't an option, but he loved the anticipation of seeing her twice a day. Without her and without Brady, his days would dim. "I'll admit working with you today was a challenge."

Her head dipped down.

Though the porch light shadows didn't reflect her expression, he could imagine her blush. With gentle fingers, he tilted her chin up.

"I'm supposed to be temporary, since I didn't want to be in Romance." Her laughter held an ironic ring. "You make me want to take a demotion, so we don't have to worry about things."

"Things?"

Her shy grin sped his heart.

He drew her close again, rejoicing in the soft yielding of her returned embrace. "I'll put in for a transfer and tell the powers that be, it was all me. All you did was look beautiful and I couldn't help but fall at your feet."

She blushed. "Let's just wait and see what happens."

"If anyone has to commute, I'd rather it be me. I'd worry about you on the road by yourself."

"See, my head says tread carefully. If the wrong person happened to drive by, this mail carrier could get me fired. But my heart. . ."

"Yes." He pressed a teasing kiss at the corner of her lips.

She traced his cheek with a fingertip, sending shivers through him. "My heart says, priority male."

A wave of warmth washed over him as he chuckled.

# Chapter 9

His head dipped toward hers.

Her sharp intake of breath revved his pulse.

With a flutter of lashes, her eyes closed.

Softly, sweetly his lips caressed hers. Too soon, he ended the kiss.

As if she wasn't sure her legs would support her, she leaned in to him.

With a ragged breath, Hayden gently pushed her away. "I have to go home. Now."

"Good idea." She giggled.

He unlocked the door for her.

With a wave, she stepped inside.

Finally, he'd given in to the feelings tumbling within him, and she'd gone all soft and vulnerable on him, making him want to hold her closer and longer.

He turned and leapt off the porch, clicking his heels together in the air.

—✦—

It was Brady's first day in second grade. Hayden followed Brady and Scott through the doors of the elementary school. Though it was a different school, the shiny industrial tile, lockers, and classroom doors brought back memories. Justin and Mike waited just inside.

They all bumped fists then the four boys continued down the hall.

Longing to follow, Hayden hung back.

Brady stopped and turned his chair. "You can go, Hayden. I know my way around." So serious, so grown-up.

Swallowing the large lump in his throat, Hayden nodded. "See you after school."

As he walked out and across the parking lot, his cell played "Please Mr. Postman." Laken's ringtone. Knowing she cared made him smile. "Hey."

"How'd it go?"

His insides jellied at the sound of her voice. "He didn't need me. We found his friends, and I was dismissed."

"You poor baby." She laughed. "He was trying to act tough, but he needs you. So do I."

His mouth went dry. "I think I'll come spend my day off at the post office."

"Under the circumstances, not a good idea. My head's clearer than it was last night."

"Lunch?"

"I think we should wait until I move to a permanent position before we go out again." All the enthusiasm drained from her tone.

She was right, but he wanted to see her. Every day, every night, for the rest of their lives. "Dinner Friday night?"

She laughed. "Did you hear what I said? Besides, I can't make it."

"What's wrong?"

"Nothing. I hope. Collin's coming back. I asked for the day off, and we're going to see Mother and Father that morning."

"Still no clue what it's about?"

"None."

"I'll be praying." He leaned back against the headrest, missing her even though he'd see her at work tomorrow. He definitely had it bad. "I have to work Saturday, since I'm off today, but we could do something Saturday night."

"Not if I'm still your boss, but I'll be working Saturday, too. Gotta go, I've got a customer coming." The line went dead.

He hung up. He loved seeing her twice a day but wanted more. *Lord, speed up a permanent position.* But what if the post office moved her far away? Or what if she got demoted because of him?

—⁓—

As Collin drove, nearing Searcy, Laken stared out the passenger window. The farmhouses, pickup trucks, and cedar trees surrounded by leaning hay-fields faded into nothingness in her delirious mind's eye. Hayden wanted to spend time with her. A sensitive, solid, dependable hunk cared about her. A warm ripple bubbled through her stomach.

It had been a long week and weird. Last Friday night, she'd gone out with Hayden for the first time. And what a kiss.

This week, she'd only seen him at work. Funny how she could see him twice a day at the post office and miss him. But at work, they barely spoke, careful not to let any feelings show.

"You're sure Martin hasn't drunk anything today?" Collin's words snatched her thoughts.

"Mother said he promised."

Collin blew out a deep breath. "I'll believe it when I see it."

"So, Brady was awfully quiet about the trip. Everything go okay?"

"Fine. While I worked, he played video games. The system Hayden has is outdated, so Brady got to play lots of new, better games."

Laken rolled her eyes. "You didn't even take him swimming or to a basketball game."

"There wasn't time. By the time I finished work, just getting Brady ready for bed was a major accomplishment." Collin turned into their parents' drive.

Mother's prize roses climbed pristine trellises in front of an immaculate two-story house. The neighborhood children didn't dare play on the grass, which didn't dare grow longer than a quarter of an inch. Nary a flower petal littered the yard, and everyone who stepped foot inside took their shoes off, while the housekeeper constantly toiled at perfection.

A muscled man hoisted a bag of potting soil on his shoulder toward a flower bed. Catching his gaze, Laken smiled, just to be nice. No response. He turned away and set the bag down, then knelt to open it. Probably not used to anyone acknowledging him.

With a glance at the house next door, memories flooded Laken. She'd spent half her childhood there. Sara's parents were warm and nurturing, everything Laken's family hadn't been. Though still well-kept, the house seemed dimmer and duller, just knowing Sara would never visit again.

She, Grace, and Sara had spent hours dreaming of their futures. Husbands, babies, careers. While Sara achieved the first two, for a short time, Grace was over halfway there. So far, Laken had only accomplished the last. Could she grab the rest of her dreams with Hayden?

Staying on the sidewalk, Laken followed Collin single file. They stepped onto the columned porch that boasted an outdoor table with perfectly aligned place mats, like something straight out of a magazine. Laken pressed the glowing button beside the door.

The bell pealed and only moments passed before the heavy mahogany door swung open. A woman in a blue maid's uniform curtsied a greeting. "Why, Miss Laken, Mister Collin, I don't believe my eyes. I heard y'all were both hanging around Rose Bud, but I never dreamed you'd show up here."

"Trust me." Collin winced. "It's not our choice. We've been summoned."

"It's good to see you, Sharlene." Laken kissed the powdery cheek of the woman who'd driven them to school, taken them to the park, and forced broccoli on them while Mother dallied with her roses, her bridge club, and fancy luncheons.

Without being told, she and Collin slipped their shoes off and left them on the throw rug. The foyer hadn't changed. Wood floors stained in a light finish, white walls topped with crown molding. Flowing gold draperies flanked wide windows on each side of the door. The living room began to the right. All done in white and gold, it didn't look like anyone lived there.

To the left, an oversized table with over a dozen matching chairs filled the dining room. Double doors led from the dining area to the kitchen, where Sharlene had helped Collin with homework and taught Laken to cook.

"Your mother and father told me we were expecting guests, but I didn't know the guests were family." Sharlene led the way. "They're both in the drawing room."

"Is it just me," Collin whispered, "or have we stepped into a different century?"

Laken elbowed him. Double doors parallel to the entry led to what most people would call a den. But Mother called it the drawing room.

Sharlene opened both doors.

Mother perched on a white camelback sofa, reading a society magazine. She gave Sharlene no acknowledgment, keeping the lowly servant in her designated place.

Father hunched next to her. Old and beaten. He'd always looked beaten, but he'd aged beyond his years. His once dark hair now silvered, his blue eyes sunken, his skin sallow.

"Miss Sylvie, your guests have arrived."

Only then did Mother's gaze rise. "Laken, Collin, we're so glad you could come."

Compassion slithered through Laken's hardened heart. "Father." She kissed his cheek and caught a whiff of alcohol. Drinking or not, over the years, the sweetly soured odor had embedded in his flesh.

"Sharlene." Mother snapped her fingers. "Bring us a tea tray."

Neither of them liked hot tea, and Mother knew it.

"Laken dear, do you like what we've done with the house?"

Nodding, Laken surveyed the austere white furnishings, white walls, and white carpet with matching billowy curtains. Too cold and too perfect. Where could Brady play? So stuck on faking blue-blooded, upper-crust wealth, Mother missed out on the living part.

Who was she kidding anyway? This house was no place for Brady. Not with Father and his constant drinking.

Sharlene silently reentered the room, and with practiced precision set the tray on the coffee table and poured four cups of steaming liquid. As the double doors closed behind the maid, Mother made a great show of adding sugar cubes, milk, and honey before the taste test. With her pinky at elegant attention, Mother let out a satisfied sigh. "Please, sit down."

Laken sat in a white velvety wingback on Father's side, while Collin claimed its twin beside Mother.

"Why did you ask us to come?" Collin huffed out an irritated sigh.

With a shaky hand, Mother set her teacup back in the saucer with a clatter. "Your father and I have something to tell you."

"So, get on with it," Collin snapped.

Father's gaze skewered Collin. "You and Laken have a brother."

"Excuse me?" Laken whirled toward Mother.

Mother covered her face with both hands. "It's true. I got pregnant between my junior and senior years in high school."

"Who's the father?" Collin deadpanned.

"I am." Father jabbed a finger at Collin. "And you will watch your mouth."

"We were so in love." Mother sobbed. "But my parents didn't approve."

Father grabbed his cup of tea. With his hand trembling much worse than Mother's, he downed the steaming liquid. His face twisted, and, he wiped his mouth with the back of his hand. "Her parents tried to keep us apart."

"But the more they tried, the more determined we were to be together and, well. . ." Mother turned both hands palms up and shrugged. "Needless to say, they weren't happy when I told them I was pregnant. They gave me two choices."

Father jittered more, obviously needing something to drink. "Abortion or adoption."

Laken's stomach sank. How could loving parents pose such a choice? Loving parents couldn't. It wasn't Mother's fault the way she was—cold, elegant, perfect. Laken had rarely seen her grandparents, and the few times she had, they'd seemed stiff and uncaring. Mother's parents had raised her that way, and when she'd messed up their perfect little plan, she'd paid.

"You said we have a brother." Laken's voice quivered. "So obviously, you chose the second option. Where is he?"

"I don't know." Mother's shoulders slumped.

Father wrapped his arms around her, tears streaming down his face.

Laken's jaw dropped. Never had she seen Father show emotion or offer comfort.

"By then, my father was running my grandfather's pharmaceutical company in Little Rock. We moved there to avoid scandal." Mother's words came in bursts between hiccupped sobs. "No one in Searcy knew I was pregnant, except Martin. My parents told me to forget him, that he'd already moved on to his next conquest by the time the baby came. They home-schooled me and kept me out of the public eye until after our son's birth."

"You abandoned him?" Collin spat.

"Not by choice." Mother pressed trembling fingers to her lips. "I wanted him to live."

"Collin, please." Laken closed her eyes. "The important thing is that we have a brother. How will we find him?"

Mother took the monogrammed handkerchief Father offered and dabbed her eyes. "My parents always donated heavily to the children's home in Little Rock that our church in Searcy sponsored. So I had a suspicion they took him there."

"Did they?" Collin's voice cracked, a chink in his steel facade.

"As soon as your mother came back here and we married, we started trying to find him." Father's tone echoed anguish. "But by then, our boy had been adopted out."

"My parents disowned me, so we couldn't afford a lawyer. By the time my grandmother talked them into letting me have my trust fund and giving Martin a job in the family company, our son was six. We decided it would be too jarring for him to fight for custody." Mother cupped Father's cheek in her hand, wiping his tears. "Your father's heart never recovered."

So he pickled what was left of it in alcohol. The grandfather clock ticked in the silence.

"What do we have to go on?" Collin rubbed the back of his neck.

"I spoke with the director of the children's home." Mother dabbed her eyes. "Since your grandparents set up trust funds for you both, Martin and I set up a trust fund for our first son with part of my inheritance and invested the rest. We put the papers, my grandmother's pearl necklace, and a letter in a safe deposit box, with some cash. The director promised to give the adoptive parents the key. Our son became eligible to claim the trust fund on his thirtieth birthday."

Collin chuckled. "I bet the director cashed in on that."

"The home is run by a church, and the director is an upstanding Christian man." Father's glare silenced Collin's laughter. "Besides, no one can claim the trust without our son's original birth certificate."

Mother took a steadying breath. "Over the years I've periodically checked the safe deposit box. Each time, everything was still there. On your brother's thirtieth birthday, I stayed in a hotel in Little Rock and waited at the bank for three days straight. Since then, I've checked weekly. Last month, I discovered it's empty."

Laken's pulse leapt. "Did they give you a name?"

"No, all records are confidential." Mother dabbed her eyes. "I made sure the nurse put both my name and Martin's on the birth certificate, and my parents let me name him. I guess to appease me. His original birth certificate identifies him as Martin Rothwell Kroft Jr., but the director said adoptive parents often rename infants. My letter gave our names and whereabouts. I'm praying he'll contact us. But so far, nothing. I've hired a private detective."

"Drink your tea, darling." Father almost spilled the cup as he handed it to Mother. "It'll help settle your nerves."

"I've put my story on the Adoption Registry." Mother's voice trembled. "But our son will have to register to see it."

The pain in Mother's eyes gnawed at Laken.

A nerve-shattering, echoing gong nearly launched Laken through her skin. Nine more gongs followed as the clock struck ten.

"Basically, we have nothing to go on." Collin stood. "I guess we could put an ad in the paper: Thirty-year-old man with a trust fund, a pearl necklace, and a wad of cash. Have you seen him?"

Laken rolled her eyes. Why did he have to make everything worse? "Let's go, before you twist the fork any deeper." She stood and linked her arm through Collin's, urging him toward the door. "We'll do everything we can to help. And, Mother. . ."

"Yes, dear."

"Thanks for telling us the truth."

Mother blinked away more tears.

"And, Father, thanks for keeping your promise."

He gave a sharp nod. But Laken knew as soon as they left, he'd be in the liquor cabinet.

Laken sat at the kitchen table, cupping her hands around her ceramic coffee mug. The plain wall clock ticked the slow passage of time. Collin hadn't said a word since they'd left Mother and Father. She didn't know what to say to him.

Her cell phone played "Signed, Sealed, Delivered, I'm Yours." Hayden. Her heart warmed, along with her face. So that's what he'd been doing the day he borrowed her phone on his lunch break. She didn't look at Collin, knowing he'd make fun of the song. "Hello."

"Hey. You okay?"

"Yeah." She stepped down the hall and lowered her voice, uncomfortable with Collin listening. "It wasn't bad, just sort of weird. I'll tell you all about it as soon as I get a chance."

"My offer's still good for dinner tomorrow night."

"I'd love to." If only Hayden could come over for coffee and comfort. She could go to his house, but Brady would be there and she didn't want to leave Collin alone. "But I need to hang out with Collin and he'll be in Little Rock again next week, so he's not leaving until Tuesday. I'll see you at church and at work next week."

"Is that all?" Disappointment resonated in his voice. "Couldn't we at least have lunch after church? I need something to look forward to here."

"I'm eating at Adrea and Grayson's to discuss baptism. Besides, we're still waiting on permanent placement, and I think I need to spend time with Mother over the next few days."

"She's not sick, is she?"

"No, but she's having some problems. I really can't talk right now, but surely things will ease up soon. I have to go." She hung up and went back to the kitchen.

"Sorry to put a kink in your love life." Collin paced. "Don't feel like you have to stick close to the house on my account. I think I'll go to Little Rock tonight."

"No, you won't. Hayden can wait." She hated to put him off, but for now she had to concentrate on her semblance of a family.

She plopped into a chair at the table. "My opinion of Mother changed today."

"Who'd have thunk it? An unwed pregnant teen certainly doesn't fit the image she's so carefully constructed."

"Not that. I mean—do you realize if Mother had agreed to abort our brother, she could have lived in a mansion all these years with servants to wait on her hand and foot? Instead, she lived a middle-class lifestyle with one housekeeper and a yard man."

"Yes, but she still enabled Father's lifestyle. After his drinking got him fired from Grandfather's company, her stock provided the funds for him to never lift a finger and enough alcohol to drown all his sorrows."

"Ease up on her. You have to admit, she's had it pretty rough. I mean—emotionally."

His shoulders slumped, and he settled in the chair across from her.

"You okay?" She touched his hand. "What is it?"

"I just feel. . . Ugh, I hate talking about feelings."

Laken grinned. "I won't tell anyone. What's going on?"

"All those years, Father took his frustrations out on me. I wasn't the son he wanted. I was never good enough because he wanted the one that got away. While I was dying to get away."

"Well, this new brother may have the same blood as we do, but nothing can sever our bond of being raised and neglected together." She gave him a halfhearted smile. Despite their differences on Brady's future, they were siblings in the truest sense. They'd shared a lifetime of struggles, triumphs, and disappointments. Mostly disappointments.

"My opinion of Martin changed tonight." Collin's voice cracked. "He's more of a man than I've ever been."

Laken frowned. "All he does is drink."

"Which I don't condone, but he was so devastated by the loss of his son, he grabbed the only escape route he could find. I was too big of a coward to marry the woman I loved, so I broke her heart and abandoned my child."

Laken squeezed his hand. "Once you learned about him, you came back for him. That counts for something."

Collin raised a cocky eyebrow. "Are you beginning to see that Brady belongs with me?"

"I didn't say that." She shook her head. "I agree that you should have a place in your son's life. A close place, but uprooting Brady would be a mistake."

"I don't feel at home here anymore. My home is in California."

"What do you have there, Collin? Here, you have a son." She ticked off the list on her fingers. "Me, along with parents taking tentative steps to make things right, and a close-knit, family-oriented community. What more could you ask for? You could even live here and commute to Little Rock or Searcy. Either way, it's only a forty-five-minute drive."

Collin stared out the kitchen window as the icemaker clattered cubes into the bin. Shaking his head, he muttered, "The cost of moving wouldn't be feasible. I couldn't make near the money here."

"But the cost of living here is less and money isn't everything, Collin. Even if it was, you're two years away from your trust fund. And think of what moving to California would cost Brady. He's just a child."

He checked his watch and stood. "I have to make an important call."

Laken's shoulders slumped. *Lord, help me make him see.*

—⁂—

As Laken's car turned into her drive, Hayden's insides melted. Two weeks ago, he'd kissed her, but he'd barely seen her since, except at work, where they couldn't talk, much less touch.

He jumped up from his seat on her porch steps and hurried to open her door. "Hey."

Swollen, red eyes tore at his soul.

Gathering her in his arms, he kissed the top of her head. "Is Collin gone?"

"I just saw him off. What are you doing here?"

"You've barely said two words at work, and I couldn't seem to get near you. I was hoping you missed me and you might need me."

"I'm sorry I neglected you, but I felt like my family needed me. Trying to keep my distance from you is torment." Her voice wobbled. "I do need you."

"Good, I was worried you might listen to that pretty little head instead of your heart."

She looked up at him with tears brimming. "I have another brother."

"Another brother?"

"My mother, the paragon of virtue, got pregnant before she and Father married." She pulled away from him and turned toward the house. "Can you believe it? All these years, she's broadcasted everyone's secrets while she sat on a doozy of her own."

Hayden took the keys from her shaky fingers and unlocked the door. "You need coffee."

"My grandparents put him up for adoption, but he knows who his birth parents are."

In the tidy living room, Hayden pulled her into his arms. "Maybe he'll show up, then."

"He's known for a month." She snuggled close, muscles tensed. "Maybe he doesn't want to find us, but how will we ever find him? There's nothing to go on."

"Was your father there?"

"He didn't drink a drop, but he smelled like a distillery." She pulled away from him and paced the small kitchen. "His drinking stemmed from losing his son."

Hayden swallowed hard. "I can see how something like that could drive a man to drink."

"Mother hired a private detective." Laken wrapped her arms around herself. "But if we can't get into the adoption records, I doubt he can. We'll probably have to go to court to get them opened, and we still may not be able to do it."

"I'll be there, right by your side, whatever comes our way."

She stopped pacing. "I know, and I can't tell you how much that means to me." She traced her fingertips across his cheek, sending tremors through him. "How's Brady?"

"I think he was bored with Collin." He grinned. "It made the selfish part of me happy."

"Collin just has to see that Brady is better off here." Doubt reflected in her gaze. "I've been praying for him to see that."

If she doubted, how could he keep hoping? He had to prepare himself for losing Brady. And prepare Brady.

"I'm glad you're a praying woman. Really glad." Hayden curved his arms around her waist and brushed a light kiss across her lips. "Brady asked Collin to come to church next weekend since you're getting baptized."

"I hope he won't be too disappointed when Collin doesn't show up."

"Actually, he agreed."

Laken leaned into him, pressing her cheek against his revving heart. "Maybe Collin will hear something to turn him around. I wonder if I could get Father to come."

He kissed the top of her head. "You can always ask."

"Thanks for being here. I did need you."

Symphonic harmony to his ears. He buried his nose in her coconut-scented hair. "There's no place I'd rather be."

———

According to the thermometer outside Laken's kitchen window, September hadn't figured out that summer was over. Still in the lower nineties.

"Hello?" Father slurred a greeting over the phone.

Laken drummed her fingers on the kitchen counter, determination wavering. She sucked in a deep breath. "I wanted to invite you to church with us tomorrow."

"Absolutely not."

"Collin's coming and Brady will be there. You haven't even met him." She sighed. "Father, I'd like to repair things. Wouldn't you like to have a real family?"

Silent seconds ticked by.

"What's that got to do with church?"

Everything. "Don't you ever miss it, Father? You had some good friends at our old church. This one is smaller and everyone is so close. Grayson Sterling is the preacher, so you'd know someone there."

"As I recall, some of my really good church buddies escorted me out of Graham Sterling's church."

If he hadn't shown up drunk, they wouldn't have had to. "Maybe getting back in church would help with—your problem."

"I don't have a problem."

The connection went dead.

Laken jabbed the END button and closed her eyes, pressing the cool flip phone to her pounding forehead. *I'm getting baptized and I wanted you to be there.*

———

Laken tucked a still-damp tendril behind her ear as the altar call began. She'd read over every baptism in the Bible and asked Grayson countless questions.

Though she hadn't really expected it, it would have been nice to see a white dove like Jesus had.

Collin's feet jittered as the altar call lengthened. Mother sat on Laken's other side with Hayden and Brady nearby. If only Father had come. Maybe she should have had Brady call and ask.

*Lord, please touch Collin. With Your love, melt the harsh, bitter wall of cynicism he's built around himself.*

The pleading song ended, and Mark gave the closing prayer. It was over. Collin hadn't made a move. Would she ever get him back in church?

"Collin, I know your flight leaves soon." Mother's voice quivered. "But I was hoping you and Laken could bring Brady by for lunch at the house."

"I'm headed to the airport as soon as I say good-bye to Brady." Collin checked his watch.

"Laken?" Mother's perfectly plucked eyebrows rose.

"Is Father. . . ?"

Mother nodded.

"How about the Rambler Café?" Knight Hayden rode to the rescue. "Brady and I were going with my folks. Why don't y'all join us?"

"That sounds nice." Mother's smile was genuine. "Really nice."

"Can't you come?" Brady's tone pleaded with his father.

Collin checked his watch again and ruffled Brady's hair. "I guess I can swing it."

Laken stole a glance at Hayden. Devastation mirrored in his vivid eyes. Losing Brady just might break him.

—⁓—

The chill in the air had nothing to do with the official launch of autumn. Laken sank into her desk chair, certain her legs could no longer support her. She swallowed hard. "Yes, I understand. Thank you."

She hung up. The transfer had come through. She and Hayden would no longer work side by side or see one another each day.

"What was that?" Carol asked.

Laken swiveled her chair.

Backs to their sorters, Carol and Hayden faced her.

"Hayden is getting promoted to postmaster."

"Woo-hoo!" Carol clapped.

A worried frown winged Hayden's eyebrows. "Where?"

"Here. You're the new postmaster at this office."

Carol gasped and punched Hayden in the shoulder. "You've gone and gotten Laken fired."

# Chapter 10

Laken's heart hammered against her ribs. "Hayden didn't get me fired. I—"

Hayden ran a hand through his hair. "The last thing I wanted was to jeopardize Laken's career."

"Will y'all chill? They didn't fire me. A permanent position opened up. In Rose Bud."

"That's perfect." Carol clapped again. "I was so afraid you'd end up in Timbuktu."

*Me, too.* Relief numbed Laken. Surely, it was too good to be true.

"Only seven miles away." Carol pointed upward. "If I didn't know better, I'd say Somebody wants y'all together."

Hayden's frown eased a bit. "Is it a demotion?"

"I'll be postmaster relief for a while."

His shoulders slumped.

"It was either that or postmaster at Stuttgart, which is more like a hundred miles away." Laken wanted to massage the tense muscles along the side of his neck, but a customer could pop in any time. "And it's okay. Sam's decided to retire at the end of the year. I have a guaranteed promotion then."

"I'll miss you." His groan spoke volumes.

"My cue to leave." Carol picked up her bag while balancing two trays on her hip. "You have my permission to play kissy-face while I load my car and stand guard."

"Carol! Why would you think such a thing?" How did she know?

"I have eyes."

"We're both way too upstanding to play kissy-face in the office—even though I'd like to." Hayden grinned, but it didn't reach his eyes.

"I'm out of here." The door closed behind Carol.

"I also learned you were the postmaster in North Little Rock, took a demotion to be here, and put in for postmaster before I came. Why didn't you tell me I beat you out of a promotion?"

"It wasn't important. Moving Brady was my priority."

"You could have held it against me."

"Instead, I fell in love with you." He winked.

Breathless, she whispered, "I'm glad."

"When do you go to Rose Bud?"

"Monday. They're sending a new carrier from El Paso."

"This will be okay." He sounded unsure, as if he were trying to convince himself. "It's not that far and we'll still see each other in the evenings." His head dipped down. "We might have to make some changes soon. I want more than just your evenings."

Giddy laughter bubbled within her.

The outer door opened and Hayden took a step backward, even though they weren't even touching. Laken reclaimed her chair and turned it away from him. By the time the customer came through the lobby, Hayden stood convincingly at his sorter.

Yes, it was a very good thing they wouldn't be working together much longer.

—⁓—

For the first time in months, when Laken got in her car after work, the interior didn't feel as if it could boil eggs.

Her first day in Rose Bud had stretched long and uneventfully without the anticipation of seeing Hayden twice a day. The four carriers, all older men with constant grandkid news, didn't have much in common with Laken. She missed the easy camaraderie with Carol.

And she really missed Hayden.

As she neared her driveway, his pickup was already there.

With Hayden seated on the tailgate.

Smiling, she turned in and parked.

He jogged over and opened her door.

"What are you doing here?"

"Welcoming you home. I almost came all the way to Rose Bud." He drew her out of the car, scooped her up, and twirled her around. "We don't work together anymore and don't have a thing to hide. I want the world to know I'm crazy about Laken Kroft."

Dizzy-headed when he set her down, Laken clung to his arm and giggled. "What's got you in such a good mood?"

"Let's see, I've got a beautiful woman in my life, I got a promotion, and Brady said Collin's checking into getting a job in Little Rock."

Her pulse jolted. Laken lunged into his arms. "That's wonderful."

"You know, you never did properly congratulate me on my promotion."

"Hmm, I happen to have a pork roast I could pop in the oven and some nice potatoes for baking. It could be done in about an hour and a half."

"Sounds great, but you just got off work. We could go out."

"I love to cook." She sidestepped him.

He snagged her wrist, his gaze centering on her mouth. "That's not exactly the type of celebration I had in mind."

She stood on tiptoe and pressed a tentative kiss on his lips.

"I love you, Laken."

Her vision clouded. "And I love you." She rained kisses over his mouth. Hayden pulled her closer, clearly with nothing tentative in mind.

Moments later, they were both breathless when he came up for air. "We need to concentrate on dinner now. Jobs, life, anything but kissing."

Suppressing a bubbly giggle, she linked her fingers with his as they strolled toward the house. "So, what's the new carrier like?"

"Young, blond, and very pretty."

Laken elbowed him. "Really?"

"She's the biggest flirt I've ever met."

"Maybe I need to meet this girl and let her know the postmaster is off-limits." She squeezed his hand.

"Don't worry. I told her I'm in love with the most beautiful soon-to-be postmaster in the world. That calmed her down." He drew her palm to his lips. "What about your new coworkers? Any men I need to tell to shove off?"

Laken laughed. "They're men, but I doubt they have their own teeth and all they can talk about are their grandkids. But even if they were calendar worthy, you'd be safe." She opened the screen door. "Do you really think Collin will move to Little Rock?"

"I don't know. I can barely stand to think about it, but it's good news compared to California."

Hope blossomed in her soul. "We'll just keep praying."

"You know, on second thought, the way I've missed you today, I think we should go out for dinner." Hayden shot her a lopsided grin.

A blush warmed her cheeks. "I'll freshen up a bit."

———

Over the last several weeks, Laken had spent almost every evening with Hayden. Collin hadn't made as many visits, since his company was in the middle of an audit. Tensions eased, but she felt bad for Brady. How did he feel about Collin not coming to see him so often?

But this morning, Collin was here, at church. That counted for something.

After the closing prayer, Laken noticed Mother headed toward the stage. Her hands trembled, and her posture wasn't as ramrod straight as usual.

"If everyone could stick around a moment, Miss Sylvie has something she'd like to say." Pastor Grayson motioned Mother up to the pulpit.

"I need to apologize to everyone here." A tear trickled down her cheek. "For years, I've done my best to spread rumors and gossip. I know I've hurt countless people."

Laken gasped.

"The truth is—I had my own scandal eating at me. Ashamed, I tried to make sure everyone else's lives out-scandaled mine."

"Let's go up and support her," Laken whispered.

"No way." Collin shook his head. "She made her bed, let her lie in it."

With a sigh, Laken stood and sidestepped Hayden into the aisle.

He patted her arm.

As she hurried forward, Mother's quivery smile forced more tears down reddened cheeks.

Laken ascended the stage and clasped Mother's trembling hand in her own.

"Thank you, dear." Mother turned back to the congregation. "All these years, I bore a pain deep in my soul that nothing has ever fixed. When Martin and I were young, we made a bad decision. My resulting unwed teenage pregnancy horrified my parents."

As her tears flowed, Laken had never been prouder of her mother.

"My son was not a mistake and I wanted so badly to keep him, but my parents whisked me away so I wouldn't sully the family name. He was put up for adoption."

Mother scanned the crowd. "Again, I'm sorry for everyone I hurt in the past, and I vow to be a different person in the future. Thank you for listening. I'd appreciate your prayers as our family unites to find our son. And please pray for my husband."

As Mother finished speaking, Laken hugged her. Someone began clapping and soon the entire congregation erupted in applause.

Collin stood and made his way to the stage, slowly, as if his feet wouldn't quite comply. Laken's stomach did a somersault at the prospect of reconciliation between her brother and Mother. Just before he got to the stage, Collin dropped to his knees at the altar.

Her heart swelled as Pastor Grayson met him. Even better. Acquaintance with Jesus.

—m—

Another two weeks had passed between Collin's visits. Already November, and they hadn't even gotten the chance to talk since he'd accepted Jesus.

Laken hummed as she checked the Crock-Pot. It was kind of nice to have someone to cook for, and she looked forward to a pleasant conversation during their meal. Steaming with savory-smelling stew, plump potatoes and carrots floated to the top. The fork-tender beef sent a rumble through her empty stomach. She spooned a helping into a flowered soup bowl.

"I've made a decision," Collin announced from behind her.

She turned to face him.

Nonchalant confidence rolled off him as he leaned casually against the counter. "I've spent the last several months checking into moving to Little Rock."

Joy welled in her soul. "And?"

"I'm going back to California and taking Brady with me."

She gasped, dropping the glass lid. It clattered on the linoleum floor but somehow didn't break. She scooped it up, rinsed it, and eased it back in place. The escaping steam scalded her wrist.

Turning to face him, with twisting insides, she resorted to begging. "Collin, you can't."

"I can and I will."

"But what about what happened a few weeks ago?"

"Precisely what made up my mind." He straightened to his full height. "God's been patient with me. It's time I take control of my life and own up to my responsibilities. I failed Katie. I won't fail Brady."

"You're missing the point here. You're not supposed to take control. You're supposed to offer it up to God."

He sighed. "You know what I mean."

"Have you considered that by moving Brady, you might just fail him?"

"We've talked circles around the subject. All this back and forth to Arkansas has taken a toll on me and my company. They've built my career, and I owe them my allegiance."

Laken grasped on to his words, hoping her insight might be right. "They heard you might leave and gave you a big raise, didn't they? Maybe some fancy title? What would Brady prefer, his family or a bank account?"

Collin paled for a moment. "I am his father, and I have to think of Brady's future. One day, he might be on his own. A nice savings account will help provide for his needs."

Backfire. Her gaze dropped to the floor. "Have you told Brady? What about Hayden?"

"I plan to tell Brady before I leave for the airport. Hayden said he won't fight me, whatever I decide."

"At least have the decency to prepare Hayden before Brady comes home in tears."

"Or excited beyond words." Collin cocked an eyebrow.

"Let me call Hayden. We'll go over and break the news to him."

"I'll go start the car." The door thudded closed behind him.

Laken gulped a deep breath. Her hands shook so badly she could barely dial.

—⁓—

As soon as he heard a car pull into the drive, Hayden jerked the door open. A chilly wind hit him in the face and curled down his shirt collar.

Laken ran toward him, tears gushing.

"What's happened?"

"I'm so sorry, Hayden." She flew into his arms.

Collin grinned. "I think Hayden will be just fine with you to comfort him."

Fear swept through Hayden. "Why do I need comfort?" He swallowed the hard knot in his throat.

"I'm taking Brady to California to live with me."

Hayden's knees buckled. For a moment, Laken held him up. "When?"

"I figure over the school's Christmas vacation would be the perfect time to transfer him."

"But that's only six weeks away." Hayden splayed his hands in begging mode. Don't make it any harder than it is for Brady. "Why not let him finish

227

the school year?"

"Because that's too long. I want my son with me."

"Fine." *It's all about you, jerk.* "I just want this to be easy on Brady."

"Don't worry, I'll bring him home for Christmas. I'll tell him on the way to the airport."

"You'll tell him here, with me to support him." Hayden stepped from the comfort of Laken's arms with clenched fists. "Come inside."

Collin strode to the door.

"Brady," Hayden called. "Your father's here. He has something he wants to tell you."

"Now?" Laken whispered.

Hayden drew her inside. A cozy fire crackled and popped in the hearth. A half-full cup of coffee sat next to Hayden's open Bible on the end table beside his recliner. Only moments ago, all had been calm and peaceful.

"The longer he has to prepare, the better off he'll be." *Lord, give me strength.*

Laken grabbed a tissue and dabbed her eyes.

As he rolled his chair into the living room, Brady's gaze ping-ponged between Collin and Hayden. "What's going on?"

Collin knelt beside him.

Deep inside, a corkscrew twisted Hayden's gut.

"I want you to come live with me in California."

Brady's eyes widened. A smile almost formed, but his chin quivered. His gaze flew to Hayden.

Forcing his feet to carry him toward Brady, Hayden clamped a hand on the boy's slight shoulder, willing himself not to shake. Be a man. Suck it up.

"Maybe some time with your dad would do you good." So far, so good. No voice betraying the terror roiling inside. "I'll come to California as often as I can, and you can visit me on school holidays. Right, Collin?"

"Of course, I'll fly either of you back and forth, whenever you want. I have tons of frequent-flier miles through my work."

"As long as it doesn't interfere with school. What do you think, Brady?"

A log shifted in the fireplace and sparks flew.

The boy's lips twitched. "I really like it here, but I guess it would be okay. Maybe for a while. You won't have to work all the time, will you, Dad?"

A knife sliced through Hayden's soul. When had Brady started calling Collin "Dad"? Couldn't Collin hear the uncertainty in his son's voice?

"I'll be home every day by the time you get off the bus."

"Bus?" Brady's hands trembled in his lap. "How will I get my chair on the bus?"

"I think most school buses have lifts and a station for the chair." Hayden glanced at Collin. Oh, to knock him across the room. "If not, I'm sure your father will make arrangements."

"Can't you just pick him up from school, Collin?" Laken's gaze shot nails at her brother.

"I couldn't leave the office that early."

"I'll go with you." Laken's tone wobbled.

"You will?" Some of Brady's tension drained away.

"I've got vacation time coming, and I can't think of a better way to use it than to spend it with my favorite nephew."

Hayden blew out a big sigh. *Thank You, God, for this woman.*

She turned to face Collin. "How about letting Brady stay here through the first week of Christmas vacation and you can, too, if you want. That way, you won't have to worry about bringing him back for Christmas. Then the second week, the three of us will go to California. We'll have a week to settle in, and I'll be there for Brady's first week of school so I can drop him off and pick him up."

Hayden nodded. "I think that would make Brady feel much better." Could he do without both of them? Stop being selfish. Right now, Brady needed Laken even more than Hayden did.

"In the meantime"—Laken checked her watch—"it's time to take Collin to the airport."

"You ready, Brady?" Hayden hugged the boy.

"We'll be back in a few hours." Laken kissed Hayden's cheek and gave him a quick hug.

He wanted to hold on to her with one arm and Brady with the other. To never let go of either of them. Instead, he held himself in check and watched them leave. In six weeks, he'd basically lose them both. At least Laken would come back.

---

Laken stood at Hayden's stove. The turkey once glistening with honeyed sauce, now only a boney carcass. The golden brown stuffing, now only a few piles of mush. The candied sweet potato casserole baked to cinnamon perfection, now congealed with a scattering of pecans across the top.

Most of her loved ones waited in the next room. Yet, even after the bountiful meal, Laken didn't feel very thankful. *Sorry, Lord, I know I've still got a lot to be thankful for, but Brady leaving trumps it.*

She unplugged the drain and let the dishwater out.

A month left before they'd leave for California. She had to tell Hayden. Later. Let him enjoy Thanksgiving Day.

His mother and hers had both wanted to help, but she'd sent them to the living room. She needed to cry and bake in peace. Now, she needed to cry and clean in peace. She had to pull herself together.

The door opened behind her. She didn't turn around but tried to inconspicuously wipe her eyes with the back of her hand. Strong arms came around her waist. Relieved, she leaned her head back against Hayden's solid chest.

"It was a great idea to have everyone come here. I wish your dad would have come."

"Me, too, but he wouldn't give up his bottle for just a day."

"I'm still praying for him." Hayden squeezed her tighter for a moment. "You did most of the cooking by yourself. You shouldn't have to clean, too. Let me help."

"No. You go spend time with Brady." Her voice wobbled, and she winced.

He turned her to face him, tilting her chin up with gentle fingers. "You okay?"

"No."

"Me neither." He kissed her forehead. "In a month, two of the people I love most in the world will leave. At least I can look forward to you coming back."

*Might as well get it over with.* Laken sucked in a quivery breath. "But I'm not."

———

Hayden gulped for breath, as if he'd been sucker punched. "What are you saying?"

As her eyes squeezed shut, tears seeped from under her lashes. "I've decided to move to California with Brady."

"No." He kissed each eyelid, desperate to stop her tears, desperate to change her mind.

A sob escaped, and she opened bleary eyes. "Brady will be miserable. I can't let Collin do this. I've tried everything to change his mind, but he's determined. So the only option left is for me to go with them. I can care for Brady while Collin works."

"I can't lose you both." Cupping her face in his hands, he kissed her, bittersweet with longing and loss. The happiness he'd finally grasped was slipping away, his contentment dying away. Though safe in his embrace, already he felt her pulling away.

"It's not what I want." She stepped back from him and shoved her hands in her pockets. "But the only other alternative is going to court."

"I can't put Brady through that. And besides, Collin is his biological father. I'm just his uncle." He jabbed himself in the chest with a forefinger. "The one who ran over him and put him in a wheelchair. Who do you think the judge would give custody to?"

"Hayden—"

"If you'd just stay here, Collin might realize how difficult and time-consuming caring for Brady is. Maybe he'd give in. But instead, you're. . ."

"What?"

The tic in his jaw started up. "Nothing."

"Just say it, Hayden."

"It's just that. . ." He ran his hand along the back of his neck. "You're enabling him."

Laken's jaw dropped. "Enabling? You think I'm enabling Collin?"

"With you, he's got a built-in caretaker. In a roundabout way, you're help-ing Collin take Brady away from me. The very thing you said you'd never do."

"Hey." Collin stepped in the doorway. "Laken, I'm heading to your place. I'm sure Hayden can give you a ride when you're ready."

"I'll see that she gets home." Hayden leaned against the counter for support.

"Listen, Hayden, I know this thing with Brady is hard on you." Collin slung his arm around Laken's shoulders and gave her a conspiratorial squeeze. "But Laken and I, we'll take really good care of him. We've got it all worked out."

His insides boiled. *I'll just bet you do.* Hayden searched her face.

Laken pulled out of Collin's embrace.

The puzzle pieces finally linked together. Laken had told him precisely what he wanted to hear. Just like Jan.

But all the while, Laken had been on Collin's side. This wasn't about Brady. It wasn't about Hayden. It was all about Collin. She'd helped Collin take Brady away, and she'd done it intentionally.

She'd played him and then revealed her true self when he needed her most. Just like Jan.

"I'm ready to go now." Laken crossed her arms over her chest.

"Give us a minute."

"Sure." Carefree, Collin turned toward the living room.

The enemy had infiltrated Hayden's army, and he'd won.

"Suddenly, it's all so clear." Hayden's words came through clenched teeth.

"What?"

"You've been working with him." Hayden slammed his fist on the table. "All this time, I thought you were helping me, that you cared about me. But I guess blood is thicker than love."

Her eyes glistened.

But he wasn't falling for her show. Jan had turned her emotions on and off like a light switch. Laken was no different.

"How can you say that?" She propped her hands on her hips. "You have no idea what I've gone through with Collin. How hard I've fought him. You're the one who handed Brady over to him."

A fresh wave of anger turned his voice steely. "I'm trying to do what's best for Brady. He shouldn't be torn between Collin and me. I just wish I'd figured out the truth about you sooner."

"You wouldn't know the truth if I priority mailed it to you." Laken's tone could have frozen the Romance Waterfalls.

Hayden's soul felt just as frigid. He gripped the edge of the countertop with both hands as she strode from the kitchen.

Just like Jan.

Brady had come between them.

The only difference, Jan didn't want Brady. Laken did.

Why had he deluded himself into thinking he could trust her?

# Chapter 11

Gazing out her kitchen window at the gray winter sky, Laken sipped her coffee and tried to pull her brain away from Hayden's accusations. She'd had a week to twist the knife he'd lodged in her heart. How could he think she was an enabler like her mother? How could he not trust her?

Focus. While the two at the table squared off, she needed to pray.

"Collin, I know I failed you, darling." Mother pursed her lips as if the admission left a bitter taste. "But don't punish me by hurting Brady."

He let out a silverware-rattling sigh. "He's my son. He should be with me."

Tears filled Mother's eyes.

Laken pulled a chair and joined them. "Mother is only trying to help. We all want what's best for Brady."

"Collin, please." Mother's voice squeaked. "I'm sorry. I'm sorry for not being a better mother. For keeping secrets. For letting Sharlene raise you. But please, don't take Brady away from me. I've already lost one son. I don't want to lose the grandson I just discovered."

"Please, spare me." Collin pulled his hand away. "It's too late. I've made my decision."

Laken clasped Mother's trembling hand.

"It's never too late." Mother pursed her lips. "Martin and I both want to have a place in our grandson's life. He wanted to be a real father, he really did. But Martin is sick. Alcoholism is a disease. But for the first time in a long time, I see hope in his eyes. He wants to change."

"Maybe if we could pull together, we could help him." Laken touched Collin's hand.

He pushed his chair back and stood. "I'll pray for him. From California." Collin stalked out the door.

Mother's chin quivered. Broken, she lay facedown on the table as sobs convulsed her delicate shoulders. "I've made such a mess of everything."

"You tried." Laken hugged her.

—⁂—

Brady pushed a green bean in a circle around the fried squash and oven-baked chicken Mom had sent over. "What do you think California will be like?"

For the last week, Hayden had tried to get used to the idea of losing Brady. And Laken. How had all the joy in his life snuffed out so quickly? "Probably kind of like Little Rock."

233

"Only bigger."

"Maybe." Hayden took a swig of sweet tea.

"Do you think any of the other kids at my new school have wheelchairs?"

"Probably. It's a bigger school."

"A lot bigger."

"You'll be just fine. You'll make friends just like you did here."

The clock ticked too loud. Ticking away the minutes, hours, days until Brady left.

Though Laken was still in Romance, the Laken he thought he knew was already gone.

"Do I have to go?"

Hayden tried to keep his tone steady. "Do you want to go?"

"I'm not sure." Brady shrugged. "I love my dad and all, but I'll miss you. And Grandma and Grandpa and Laken and Mimi and my friends."

"Laken's going with you."

"But only for two weeks."

"I think she's planning to stay as long as you do."

"Really?" Brady's eyes brightened.

"Yep." At least she truly loved Brady. Or did she just love Collin? *Lord, let her take good care of Brady.*

"But what about you?"

Hayden swallowed hard. "What about me?"

"Well, you two kind of like each other, don't you? And if me and Laken both move to California, you'll be all alone."

"Don't worry about me. I've got Grandma and Grandpa and church."

"I'll miss our church, too." A worried frown wrinkled Brady's forehead. "Do you think Dad will take me to church?"

"If you ask him, he might."

"I bet the churches in California are big."

Hayden took Brady's hand in his own. "Give California a chance. You may like it and you may not. But go with an open mind."

"Do you think Dad will let me come back here if I don't like it?"

Lord willing. "I think your dad wants you to be happy."

"And Laken, too. You were right about her. She's nothing like Jan."

Hayden swallowed hard. "Did I say that?"

"A long time ago, after the trail ride." Brady took a sip of his sweet tea. "Do you think there's anywhere in California where kids like me can ride horses?"

"I'm sure there is, and your dad can buy you all the gear and haul Spot to California."

"Laken liked riding when we went before. How come y'all never go riding?"

"I guess we just never got around to it."

"Can we go riding before I leave? With Laken? One last time?"

One last time.

A vise tightened in Hayden's chest. "If you'll eat your supper, I'll call and ask her."

"Now?"

"Start eating." Hayden pointed to Brady's plate.

With a grin, Brady popped a forkful of squash into his mouth.

Hayden went to the living room to make the call. As the phone rang, his insides tumbled. She'd refuse to spend time with him. She didn't have to anymore.

"Hello?"

The sound of her voice sent his pulse into a sprint. "Laken, it's Hayden. Brady wants to know if you'll go horseback riding with us before y'all leave for California."

Silence. He counted the seconds, willing her to say no, even though Brady would be disappointed. His heart couldn't take any more game-playing.

She cleared her throat. "I'd absolutely love that."

Hayden sucked in a breath. "I'll be with y'all."

"I'll look forward to it. Just tell me when."

He tried to think clearly. "Saturday is supposed to be in the fifties I think. Around three o'clock?"

"I'll be there."

"See you then." He hung up, certain his chest would explode.

———⟶⟵———

Mother's leather-gloved hands gripped the steering wheel. "What did you need to talk to me about, dear?"

Oh, to have gone to the house, but Laken couldn't face Father's stupor. And Collin was at her house. Reduced to breaking the news at the park huddled in Mother's warm car.

"I may not come back from California. In fact, I probably won't."

"You're moving there." Mother's tone trembled as she turned to face Laken.

"If Collin is determined to move Brady there permanently, I'll move, too."

"But what about your career?"

"I'll be Brady's full-time caregiver. That will be my new career."

"What about Hayden?"

"We're history."

"But you're in love with him."

Laken's stomach clenched. "Yes."

"He's a good man." Mother clasped Laken's hand. "And he's crazy about you."

"He was, but he doesn't know who I am." Laken's vision blurred. "He thinks I've been helping Collin, and that I only spent time with him to get him to give Brady up. I can't have a relationship with a man who doesn't trust me."

"You just need to prove to him that he can."

"How?" Her throat clogged with emotion. "I'll be in California."

Mother's chin quivered. "We just got things in order between us."

"Collin promised to fly Brady and me home as often as we like."

"How will we ever put our family back together if we're scattered all over the countryside? Why is Collin doing this?"

Laken sighed. "He feels like he's let Brady down and he wants to make it up to him."

"Like I let him down."

"You can fly out for visits." Laken squeezed Mother's hand. "And I'll still do whatever I can to help find my brother."

Mother nodded. "I love you, Laken. I haven't always been there for you, but I love you."

"I know." Laken drew her into a warm hug. "And I love you."

—⁓—

Laken tried to match the rhythm of Pearl's stride and soothe the churning in her soul. An uncomfortable silence throbbed between her and Hayden while Brady led them down the path.

Why, oh why did Brady have to wait until tension vibrated between her and Hayden before asking to go horseback riding again?

"Why are we riding at Bob's? There are woods behind your house."

"Since we board the horses here, it's just easier to start from here." Hayden held a fidgety Buck in check until Brady rode a good hundred yards in front of them. "You didn't resign, did you? I mean—in case you return—you shouldn't give up your career."

"Despite what you think of me, Brady is more important than any job." She sighed. "I asked for my whole month of annual leave. Sam's retiring on schedule, and they'll have fill-ins at Rose Bud until I get back or turn in my resignation. I warned my supervisor that I might not come back, but she's not doing anything permanent until I give her my final decision."

"You're holding out hope."

"There's always hope." *Just not for us.* She tried to smile, but it didn't reach her heart.

"Wait up, Brady." Hayden slapped the reins against the horse's neck and shot forward.

Obediently, the child slowed his horse, then stopped. Hayden caught up and they both waited.

She knew better than to try to trot. "Y'all never pick good horse-riding weather. The first time, we cooked. Now a week before Christmas, we'll freeze."

"When it gets dark, we're building a campfire and roasting hot dogs and marshmallows, even s'mores." Brady's eyes shone.

"Yum." She tried to latch on to his enthusiasm and not think past today, not think about leaving the man of her dreams, not think of the man who'd taught her how to really love. The man who thought she'd sided with her brother against him.

Dead leaves and hickory nuts crunched under the horses' hooves.

"Just relax." Hayden's tone soothed. "Let your body move with Pearl's. You're all stiff and fighting her rhythm."

"It's no use. I can't relax."

Brady giggled. "It helps if you can't feel your legs. Let's take the horses for a run."

"No thanks." Laken reined Pearl to a stop. "I'll stay here. Y'all go ahead."

"Race ya." Gently, Brady slapped his reins against Spot's neck and the horse sped off.

"Hey, no fair." Urging Buck into high gear, Hayden followed.

A smile lit Laken's soul as two of the people she loved most raced across the yellowed meadow. Brady won, though she was pretty sure Hayden had let him.

They turned their huffing horses in her direction and meandered back, both laughing. She loved seeing them happy. Would she ever see them relax and enjoy themselves like this again?

By the time they reached her, her smile flatlined.

"Let's go back and dismount, then I'll start the fire." Hayden clicked his tongue at Buck.

She nodded and fell in line behind them.

Back at Bob's, he and Brady took the horses to the barn, then Hayden waited with Laken while Brady went to get the surprise he'd promised her.

"Thanks for being such a sport. Brady loved today."

"I'd do anything for Brady." Her heart sped at his nearness. Why couldn't he have helped with the surprise, too?

"Obviously." His sarcasm rang loud and clear.

Laken rolled her eyes. "Can we just call a truce—for Brady's sake?"

"Everything I've done is for Brady's sake." Hayden ran his hand through his hair.

"And everything I've done is for Brady's sake." She paced the driveway. "What is wrong with you, Hayden? I love Jesus, I love you, and I love Brady. I didn't hatch some grand scheme to help Collin, and I'm absolutely rabid at him for ruining Brady's life and taking mine down with it. If you can't believe that, you're not the man I thought you were."

A white Lincoln turned into the drive.

"Did you invite her?" Laken backed out of the way.

Hayden shook his head.

With elegant poise, Mother got out of her car and sashayed toward them. Her jade-colored puffed coat with its taupe fur-lined collar gave her a vibrant glow. "Where's Brady?"

"He'll be along." Hayden shoved his hands in his coat pockets.

"Brady told y'all he invited me, didn't he?" Mother's nose scrunched. "Since I don't do horses, Bob called me in time for the bonfire."

"We're roasting hot dogs." Laken waited for Mother's nose to scrunch again.

"Oh, I haven't had a hot dog in ages." Mother clasped her hands together, her eyes sparkling in delight. "Are you all right, Laken? You seem rather flustered."

"Let's just say horseback riding doesn't agree with me."

"Maybe next time you and Hayden can ride double. I'm terrified of horses, but I always thought it would be so romantic to ride off into the sunset with the man you love."

Laken's face warmed. Riding double with Hayden. Being so close to him. It would never happen. Without trust, love withered and died.

A loud motor started up in the distance. The sound neared, and Brady rounded the side of the house on a four-wheeler. He stopped nearby and shut off his engine.

"Mimi, you came."

"Of course I did. I couldn't turn down my favorite grandson, now, could I?"

Only grandson that we know of. Laken might have more nieces or nephews through her missing brother. How would she help Mother find him from California?

"Get on, Mimi."

Mother's nose scrunched. "You want me to ride that thing?"

"It's quite safe, Miss Sylvie." Hayden winked. "And Brady's an excellent driver.

"But. . ." Mother visibly squirmed. "What about the brake?"

"It's a hand brake. Come on, Mimi. It's Grandpa's, and I've driven it a jillion times. I'll go slow."

Closing her eyes for a moment, Mother climbed on behind Brady.

Oh for a camera. Mother on a four-wheeler.

Brady started the engine and pulled away, leaving Laken alone with Hayden again.

"Where are they going?"

"To the woods for the bonfire. It's easier to get Brady on and off a four-wheeler than a horse. Let me go get ours."

"You expect me to ride a four-wheeler? With you?"

"Of course not, silly, we're riding a mule."

"A mule?"

Hayden grinned, then jogged away and disappeared around the side of the house.

An engine started up and neared. Oh no, she couldn't ride a four-wheeler with Hayden. Way too close for comfort.

Hayden rounded the house on a golf cart–looking thing.

Relief swept through her.

He pulled to a stop beside her. "Your mule, milady. Hop in."

She swallowed. "I've never been on one of these things."

"It's easier than getting on a real mule. Or a horse for that matter."

True. She climbed in. Seated beside him, she stayed scooted as far away as possible.

Hayden drove behind the house and down a path through the woods. Soon they caught up with Brady. He and Mother were laughing. Mother riding a four-wheeler and laughing.

Time was precious. Time with the nephew she'd just discovered, the mother she'd just bonded with, and the man she'd just grown to love.

From the time she'd come back to Romance, she couldn't wait to leave. Now that she had to leave, all she wanted was to stay.

Thankfully, Hayden had thought ahead. The trees parted into a clearing with wood already stacked in a pile. Tarps and blankets surrounded the soon-to-be bonfire.

As soon as Hayden killed the engine, Laken stepped out of the mule and put some distance between them. At least with the cold, they didn't have to worry about snakes.

Mother climbed off, also. Hayden picked Brady up. Cradling the boy, he deposited him on a canvas chair.

Laken chose a chair and wrapped a blanket around her shoulders while Hayden started the fire. Soon smoke swirled and flames sparked.

Mother set a chair next to Brady's. Grandmother and grandson huddled together, sharing a quilt, while roasting their hot dogs.

The gulf widened between Hayden and Laken as he moved the remaining chair far away from her. She might as well be in California. Already, she missed him.

"I sure will miss y'all when I go." Brady's voice cut through the silence.

The firelight illuminated Hayden. His throat muscles convulsed.

"There'll be lots of visits back and forth." Laken tried to sound enthusiastic. "We'll have so many visits, you won't have time to miss anyone. And we'll go to Sea World and Disneyland. Anything you want."

"I think it might be okay, since you're coming, too." Brady's hot dog caught fire. He yanked it from the flames and blew it out.

Laken's pulse raced as Hayden strode over beside her to stoke the fire with a long stick. Kneeling nearby, he shoved a log farther into the flames. With a wince, he jerked his hand away.

"Did you burn yourself?" Brady frowned. "You always tell me not to touch a log even if it only has fire on one end."

"Smart thinking, but I saw a scorpion."

"Where?" Mother's voice quivered.

The creature scurried toward Hayden's foot. Laken screamed and impaled it with her hot dog skewer. Its tail flailed about, stinger ready, and she shoved it into the fire.

"It's okay, Laken got it. But there might be more in the wood. Brady, I need you to take Mimi to our house while Laken and I put the fire out." Hayden scooped Brady up and deposited him on the four-wheeler.

"But I want to stay."

"Please, Brady, just do what I say." Hayden's words slurred together, and he lowered his voice to a whisper. "Laken, I think you should dial 911. I don't feel so good."

She gasped. "That thing stung you?"

"Shh. Don't scare Brady."

"I hate scorpions." Mother dived for the four-wheeler. "What about the s'mores?"

"Roast them in the fireplace." Laken managed to keep her voice steady.

As the four-wheeler took off, Hayden collapsed in the mule and managed to start it. "Can't get air."

Laken jumped in beside him and jabbed the keypad on her phone.

"911, what's your emergency?"

"My friend just got stung by a scorpion and he can't breathe."

"Miss Kroft, we have your address as—"

"I'm not home. Where are we, Hayden?"

She held the phone to his mouth as he slurred the address, then jerked it back. "Please hurry."

The operator repeated the address back to her. "Ma'am, please stay on—"

Laken flipped the phone shut.

"Just relax. Inhale. Exhale." Tears streaming, she traced his jaw with the back of her hand and helplessly watched him struggle.

"Drive to Bob's."

"I've never driven one of these things."

"Just drive."

Laken mashed the gas and whiplashed them toward the woods.

An angry red welt swelled amongst streaks swirling around his wrist.

"This isn't normal, is it?"

"Maybe allergic." Hayden wheezed and gasped for each breath, so pale. *Oh God, please help him breathe.*

An eternity after they arrived at the house, the ambulance barreled into Bob's drive. Two EMTs jumped out, unloaded a gurney, and helped Hayden out of the mule.

He collapsed on the gurney.

"You're sure it was a scorpion, ma'am?"

"I killed it and cooked it in our bonfire." Laken hugged herself, hovering near as they worked.

"It was huge." Hayden's slurred words were barely audible. "Ouch."

"Sorry, sir, it's the IV."

"Thought it was another."

"Have you ever had an allergic reaction to a scorpion sting before, sir?"

"Never stung afore."

"What's happening?" Laken frowned. "Will he be all right?"

"Your friend's having an extreme allergic reaction. Anaphylactic shock." The paramedic slipped an oxygen mask over Hayden's face, and the gurney jolted as they loaded him in the ambulance.

"Please, can I go with him?" Her words came out high-pitched and panicky.

"I'm sorry, ma'am, but we don't have room. You'll have to follow."

She wanted to argue, but that would only delay Hayden's treatment. Instead, she sprinted to her car and tore out of the drive after the ambulance.

—⁓—

"Hayden, are you all right?"

He couldn't answer. He wanted to see Laken. To know it wasn't his brain playing tricks. That she was really there.

But someone had glued his eyes shut. If he could just get his hands up to his face, he could pry them open, but his arms didn't seem to work either. He groaned.

"Hayden? You're in the emergency room." Laken sounded scared. "You had an extreme allergic reaction to the sting, but they gave you medicine. The doctor says. . ."

As her voice trailed away, a cushion of darkness swirled around him.

"You're going to be fine." Laken touched his cheek. "Just rest."

"Glad. . ." *you're here*, he wanted to add. But his cottony, pillow-sized tongue wouldn't move anymore. The darkness won.

Bright light pierced his consciousness. A weight pressed against his chest. Coconut. Finally, his heavy eyelids lifted. Caramel silken tendrils splayed over him, tickling his chin.

"Laken."

She jumped up. Tear-filled eyes met his. "You're awake."

A nurse came in. "Look who's back with us. I told you he'd be fine."

"What time is it?"

"It's Sunday." Laken checked her watch. "Almost ten p.m."

"Where's Brady?"

"At your parents' house. He's fine."

The nurse checked his monitor. "Your friend's been here ever since we admitted you. The only time she left your side was when the doctor ran her out."

Laken blushed.

241

"You know, it's very exotic to be allergic to scorpions." The nurse grinned. "Maybe not very manly, but definitely exotic."

Hayden's stomach roiled. "I think I'm gonna be sick."

Pretty blue eyes widened. Laken grabbed a trash can.

—⁓—

A melancholy group gathered at the home of Hayden's parents for Christmas Eve. Two days until departure. Collin had flown in and everyone except Father gathered around the loaded Winters' table. Despite the repeat of Thanksgiving's fare, Laken had no appetite.

Hayden still looked ashen a week after his ordeal. The bruise on his wrist from the sting paled in comparison to the one on his other hand from the IV.

She drank her sweet tea. Strain showed on the faces of those she loved, even Collin's. And he was getting his way.

After the meal, Laken and Mother helped Hayden's mom clean the kitchen and load the dishwasher, then joined the men in the living room.

Football blared. Laken's least favorite sport. She didn't understand the rules and didn't care enough to learn. Mesmerized by the game, Hayden's dad, Brady, and Collin didn't even know when the women entered the room, but Hayden's gaze locked on her.

"Maye, thank you so much for inviting us." Mother picked a chair away from the televison. "It was a wonderful meal."

"My Maye can definitely cook." Paul patted his stomach. "That's why I married her. Remember that when you find a bride, son."

Maye swatted playfully at her husband.

"I will." Hayden stood and ushered Laken toward the door. "Your soup was great. Sorry I slept through your visit, but that's all I've been capable of lately."

"I'm glad you're feeling better."

"Let's go to my house," he whispered.

"You need to rest," Laken mumbled. "And besides, I don't want to fight anymore."

"I've rested for a week and who said anything about fighting?" Hayden's breath stirred her hair.

She shivered as he held her coat for her. Her eyes burned at the memory of his closeness. His embrace. His kiss. She blinked until her vision cleared.

The starlit night revealed each exhale in the frigid air. They ducked through the line of dormant crape myrtles. Soon she stepped inside Hayden's house, and he steered her in front of the fireplace as sparks crackled and popped.

He took both her hands in his. Turning her palms up, he kissed each one. "I'm a horrible person for not trusting you, and a selfish lout for not wanting you to move to California."

The firelight flickered in his eyes as shudders moved through her. "So you trust me now? Why? What changed?"

"Can we talk about it later?" He kissed the tip of her nose, and his gaze moved to her lips.

"No." She took a step back. "Tell me now."

Hayden sighed. "It goes back to my ex-fiancée, and I don't want to talk about her."

Wanting to throw herself into his arms and stay there forever, she forced herself to think. "How can we have any kind of future if we can't talk about the past?"

He ran a hand through his hair. "When Katie got sick, I helped take care of her. Jan grew distant. After the funeral, she gave me an ultimatum: Brady or her. She had me totally snowed, pretending she was all about family and children. In reality, she didn't want kids. Not mine and definitely not my nephew."

"So what does that have to do with me?"

"I promised myself I'd never trust another woman again. Then you came along and made me forget my vow." He kissed each palm again.

Pulling away, she shoved her hands into her pockets. "So since I'm female, you decided I must be conspiring against you."

"She claimed to love me and lied to me." Hayden touched her cheek. "But you're nothing like Jan, and I've known that from the beginning." He pulled her into his arms.

She should pull away, but his nearness threatened to turn her brain to Jell-O. Her thoughts fought to the surface. "So what took you so long to let me in on your change of heart?"

"I lost a fight with a scorpion. Did you see the size of that thing? At least two inches. Maybe three." He laughed. "Amazing how such a little critter can bring a man down to size."

"It's not funny." Her voice cracked. "You could have died."

He kissed her temple.

"I was there when you woke up. Why didn't you say anything?"

"I wanted to make sure I could make sense when I said"—he pulled away to gaze into her eyes, sincerity shining in the green depths of his—"I love you and I trust you. Completely. I love you even more for being so selfless on Brady's behalf."

"I don't know about that. Right now, I feel more selfish than selfless. I want to stay right here forever." Her laugh came out watery as her last bit of resistance melted. She curled her arms around his waist and pressed her damp cheek against his chest. "For the next two weeks, I'll torment Collin, try to talk him into moving back here, and pray he'll do what's right."

"I know you will. I'll pray, too." He tipped her chin up with gentle fingers.

As his sweet kiss deepened, she clung to him. Partly because she never wanted to let go and partly because he made her light-headed enough to fall.

He ended the kiss, and Laken's tears spilled.

"Don't cry." He traced her cheek with a gentle fingertip and leaned his forehead against hers. "I'm going with you."

She sucked in a breath. "You are?"

"You didn't really think I'd let two of the people I love most in the world move halfway across the country, did you?"

He pressed something into her hand. Something small, velvety, and square.

—⁓—

Laken's gorgeous blue eyes widened. With a gasp, she looked down at the ring box.

Hayden's hand trembled as he flipped the lid open. What if she said no? Holding the box just so, he made sure the light set the solitaire diamond afire, shooting sparks in every direction.

"Oh Hayden." Her tears brimmed as she stood on tiptoe to kiss him. A kiss full of promise and the future.

"Merry Christmas," he mumbled, ending the captivating kiss, anxious for an answer. "Can I take that as a yes?"

"It's all happening so fast. We've only known each other six months."

His heart crashed against his ribs. "Long enough in my book."

"This feels rushed because of California lurking. If it was a sure thing that I'd come back, would you be asking this question now?"

"Maybe not now." He traced her cheek with a fingertip. "But definitely in the future."

"Don't rush us. I want to make sure everything is right with us. You can't move."

"I'm ready to follow you to Timbuktu."

"But your life is here. You got the promotion you've been wanting. Your family is here and your relationship with them is back intact."

"I moved here for Brady's sake. Now I'm moving to California for his sake." He cupped her chin with tender fingers. "And I just found you. I can't let you go."

One winged eyebrow rose. "What about finances? I know you won't sell the house."

"It belongs to Brady."

"And you won't want to rent it out. So you'll be making payments on it and have to find a place in California, where the cost of living is exorbitant compared to here."

He pulled her closer. "If we get married, we can share living expenses."

"I don't want to get married just to share living expenses."

"That's not what I meant."

"I know. I'm just saying let's slow down." She closed the lid of the box with a spring-loaded *click*.

A piece of him died.

"It's not that I don't want to marry you. I do."

He nodded. "Let's just go to California and see what happens."

"We need to stick to the original plan. I'll go to California. If Brady stays, I'll stay. Then we'll talk about you. For now, let's take it two weeks at a time." She snuggled in his embrace.

Two weeks. Why did two weeks sound like an eternity?

—⁓—

Being at church helped Laken's troubled soul, even though she'd fly to California with Collin and Brady in the morning. Without Hayden.

What had she been thinking? With everything in her, she wanted to accept his ring and marry him tomorrow.

But only a month ago, Hayden had distrusted her. And with only her parents as an example, could she really build a real relationship with anyone?

Glancing to her right, she leaned back a bit to see around Hayden.

Brady caught her gaze and winked, his face scrunching with effort.

Her heart warmed. What if she failed him?

After a series of Christmas carols, the harpist trilled "He Whispers Sweet Peace to Me." Just what she needed. Laken closed her eyes, breathing in His peace. It seemed so right for Christmas to be on Sunday. Especially since she was celebrating Christ's birth for the first time as a Christian.

Hayden squeezed her hand.

Gently, she traced the faint yellowed bruise on his wrist, thankful the paramedics had arrived in time.

From the middle aisle, Mother joined them. Dabbing her eyes, she sat next to Laken.

Laken bit her lip.

A few minutes later, Collin arrived. They all shuffled to the left so he could sit beside Brady at the end of the pew.

As the song service closed and Pastor Grayson stepped to the pulpit, Laken prayed for Collin to change his mind. *Something has to convict him, Lord. Please. Today.*

The pastor ended his sermon and the altar call began. Dejected, Laken squeezed around Hayden, Collin, and Brady. Hayden took her hand and walked with her to the altar. There they knelt together. A shaky hand clasped Laken's as Mother joined them.

*Oh Lord, if there's no way to change Collin's mind, ease Brady's worries. Help him to fit in at his new school and make friends. Help the new kids to be kind. Help Hayden and me not to rush into anything, but to follow Your timing for us. Be with my father, Lord. Give him strength to fight alcohol. I place it all in Your mighty hands. Amen.*

Finally, she stood and turned back to her pew.

Collin was already gone.

As they stepped outside, most of the parking lot had cleared. The thump of a basketball against the backboard drew Hayden's gaze to the court. Collin rebounded and shot the ball again. Once more, it bounced off the rim.

Hayden nudged Brady's arm. "I think your dad wants to play ball before we go home."

Brady's mouth twitched. "I don't want to."

"Listen." Laken knelt beside him. "Let's not make our last day here sad. It's Christmas."

"And it's not the last day." Hayden squeezed Brady's shoulder. "We'll have lots of visits to look forward to."

"I guess." Brady shrugged.

"We've still got presents to open." Sylvie smiled, red-eyed, valiantly trying for cheerfulness. "Aren't you anxious?"

"I guess." Brady shrugged again.

"Okay." Collin jogged toward them.

"Okay, what?" Laken raised a brow.

# Chapter 12

I give." Collin nonchalantly dropped the ball in Brady's lap. "I can't take all these long faces. I'll move here, no matter what it costs me."

Laken gasped.

A weight lifted from Hayden's shoulders. Relief washed over him in waves. *Thank You, Lord.*

Brady's shoulders relaxed.

Sylvie giggled. Giggled?

Collin's hand shook as he raked it through his hair. "I'm not sure if I'll live here and commute or get a place in Little Rock, but the only reason I'm going back to California is to move. And Brady isn't going with me."

"I'm so proud of you." Laken hugged him. "You're doing the right thing."

"I'm not sure if it's right for my career. But it's right for Brady." Collin tousled Brady's hair. "Does this make you happy, son?"

Brady's eyes hadn't been so bright since before Collin started talking about California. "Yes." But his smile was only halfhearted.

"And something else." Scooping up the ball, Collin dribbled it between his legs. "While I'm making myself indispensible with my new company, I'll have to put in extra hours, which means I won't have much time for basketball."

"That's okay. Hayden will be close. He can play with me."

"You're right, but I'm thinking since I'll be working so much, maybe you could keep living with Hayden and visit me, when I'm not working."

Tears filled Brady's eyes.

Disappointment? Rejection? What was that precious little heart feeling?

"Does that sound okay with you?" Collin passed the ball to Brady.

"Yes, sir." Brady's chin trembled as he caught the ball.

Collin kissed the top of his son's head. "We've all got leftovers and Christmas presents waiting at Maye's." He gave a thumbs-up, despite watery eyes. "Mother, can I ride with you?"

"Of course, darling."

Two car doors shut. Minutes later, Sylvie drove by with a stoic Collin.

"We're not going to California," Brady whispered.

"Hallelujah." Laken looked heavenward.

Hayden knelt beside his nephew. "You okay with that?"

Brady's little face crumpled. "I didn't want to go."

"Oh sweetie, you don't have to." Laken stroked his hair. "Don't cry."

"I didn't want to hurt Dad's feelings."

Hayden sighed, relief and peace firmly back in place. "It's over. No one's taking you anywhere."

As the little arms curled around his neck, Hayden's vision blurred.

Laken completed the hug, wrapping her arms around them both.

Right where he wanted to be, in Arkansas, with Laken and Brady. Hayden's tears flowed.

"Hey, Laken." Brady's voice sounded stronger.

"Hmm." She sniffled.

"Will you marry Hayden now?"

She sucked in a breath as laughter bubbled out.

Not exactly the romantic second proposal he'd had in mind. Hayden kissed her cheek. "Well, will you?"

"Didn't I say I needed some time?"

"It's been a few hours."

"Can I give you an answer after I take care of one more thing?"

Hayden's eyes widened. "As long as the answer is yes and it comes really soon."

"I'll do my best to bring a special gift." She traced his jaw with a fingertip, sending a quiver down his spine.

"You don't have to get me anything. A yes will suffice."

"Not for you, silly. For me."

He frowned.

"I have an overwhelming need to start over fresh, with you. And to do that, I just have one more little hurdle. Two hours tops."

Relief surged through him. Not weeks or months. Just two hours. One hundred twenty long minutes. "Guess it'll have to do."

"I'll be there as soon as I can. Brady, go ahead and open your presents, and I'll give you mine when I get there."

—∽—

Laken rang the bell, and almost immediately, Sharlene answered.

"Why, Miss Laken, it's nice to see you again. I'm afraid your mother isn't here."

"I know. Is Father awake?"

"Well, yes, but. . ."

"I know he's drinking, Sharlene, but I need to see him anyway."

"Of course, he's in the drawing room."

Laken sidestepped the well-programmed maid. "I know the way."

"Yes, ma'am. Of course."

She tapped softly on the double doors. "Father, can I come in?"

"Just a moment."

A moment to hide his bottle, his glass, his carafe. If he stuck with his old schedule, he'd only been up an hour or so and only consumed three to four drinks. For him, it was like one wine cooler for anyone else. He should still have his faculties.

"Come in."

With trembling fingers, she turned the knob. Father still wore his bathrobe, his face unshaven. His red eyes revealed surprise. "Laken? Is everything all right? Your mother. . . ?"

"She's fine." He seemed sober. "She went to Hayden's parents' house for leftovers and to exchange gifts. Collin's there, and Brady, too. Collin decided not to move Brady to California."

"A boy should be with his father."

"Collin's moving here."

Father's eyebrows rose. "He is?"

"Listen, Father, I thought you might like to go with me to the Winters'. They're wonderful people, and you can meet Brady and Hayden."

"That's your fella?"

The warmth of a blush crept up her neck. "He asked me to marry him."

"And you said. . . ?"

"I didn't yet, but I'm going to say yes."

"Then why haven't you? Did you leave the poor chap hanging?"

"I think he knows I'll say yes. I felt like I needed to get everything in order before we can begin our life together."

"You think you can get me in order?"

"No, but I know the One who can." She squeezed his hand. "I've been praying for you, Father. I want our family to be the family we never were. I want us to be close and loving. We can't be that if. . ."

"I'm drunk."

Her stomach somersaulted. He admitted it. That had to count for something. "Father, please come to the Winters' house with me."

"I can't. I can't let anyone see me like this."

For years, she'd been ashamed of him. She'd wanted him to stay hidden away at the house. But now, if she could just give him a glimpse of what he'd missed all these years, maybe he'd want to get well.

"What if we find my brother? Do you want him to see you like this?"

Father's face contorted, his lips trembled. "We'll never find him."

"We might. There's always hope. When we do, do you want him to see what losing him has done to you?"

He shook his head.

"Come with me, Father. Please."

Cupping his chin in his hand, he rubbed his fingers over stubbly cheeks. "Let me get cleaned up a bit."

She smiled. "Hurry, they're probably ready to open my presents by now."

—∿—

A bundled Brady waited on the Winters' porch as Laken pulled into the drive.

"That's your grandson."

"Do you think Collin will let me be his grandfather?" Father zipped his coat up.

"I'm praying he will." Afraid Father might not have the courage, she got out, went around to open his door, and waited until he stepped out of the car. He took the sack of gifts from her.

"It's about time," Brady hollered. "I didn't think you'd ever get here."

"Sorry, but I brought a special gift." Laken stepped up on the porch. "Brady, this is your grandfather, Martin Kroft."

"Nice to meet you, sir." Brady offered his hand.

Father shook it. "So mannerly."

The front door flew open to reveal Mother. "Martin, are you all right?"

"He's fine. I convinced him Christmas wouldn't be right without him, so he decided to join us."

Mother lunged into his arms, sniffling. "I'm so glad you came."

The door opened again. "Come in," Hayden said. "You'll freeze out here."

"Hayden, this is my father, Martin."

"Glad to meet you, sir." Hayden offered his hand.

"You've done a nice job with my grandson." Father pumped his arm. "You're Laken's fella, too. Sylvie speaks highly of you."

"I'll admit it. I'm crazy about your daughter, sir."

A blush warmed Laken's face.

"Why's everyone out here?" Maye clucked her tongue. "Come in where it's warm."

"Can we open presents with Laken now?" Brady asked.

Everyone filed in, but Hayden stepped in front of Laken, blocking her path. "We'll be right there."

"He's had three or four drinks, but it's not enough to even give him a buzz. I hope your mom won't mind me bringing him in this condition."

"She'll understand, as long as he's not unruly." He pulled her close. "Don't we have some unfinished business?"

Laken wound her arms around his neck. "I do."

"That was easy." He dipped his head to claim her lips.

She giggled. "California isn't lurking anymore, and you trust me enough to spend the rest of your days with me. I'll marry you anytime, anywhere."

"The Romance Waterfalls on Valentine's Day."

Her vision blurred. He knew her thoughts and the desires of her heart. "You could never forget our anniversary that way."

He captured her lips with a kiss that left her breathless. "Trust me, we'll celebrate every year, every month, every day, every hour, every minute, every second. We better get inside. I'm getting tempted to start the celebration early."

The door opened.

"Presents," Brady whined.

———〰———

With Hayden's arms around her waist, Laken leaned back against him as they peered out the Romance post office window. Outside, a bride and groom in full formal wear exchanged vows on Valentine's Day.

"Adrea said there were nine today, but only three here." A contented sigh escaped Hayden, and his breath stirred her hair. "Two more hours."

She shivered and turned to face him. "Two more hours. Remember the first wedding we watched here together?"

"We were both so broken."

"But God mended us and brought us together."

"Good thing it's past closing time." He kissed her, long and slow, forcing himself to pull back long before he wanted to. He groaned. "There's more where that came from."

She blushed. "Save it for two hours. We've got a wedding to go to—that is if my legs will hold me up after that kiss."

Warm molasses puddled in his stomach. She was just as crazy about him as he was her. How could he ever have doubted her?

She peeked out the window. "They're gone. I'll wait outside."

His soul just might float right out of his body. In two hours he'd marry this woman who turned his insides to mush. Brady would live with them, and happily-ever-after stretched before them into eternity.

At least another hour's worth of invitations piled on the counter. Hayden went over lockup procedures one more time with his replacement for the day and stepped out the side door.

Standing by his truck waiting, she looked like a modest model in a hot rod magazine. Love for him shone in her eyes, making her even more beautiful. He kissed her temple, not trusting himself to let go if he did anything else, and opened the door.

With her hand in his, she climbed up and scooted to the middle. "I hope Grace's matron of honor dress fits. I can't believe she had the audacity to have a baby this month."

"I hope both babies come to the wedding." He cleared his throat. "So, what did you decide about having kids?"

Laken leaned her head against his shoulder and coconut shampoo filled his senses.

"That they better have your eyes."

"What if I want them to have your eyes?" He grinned. "I meant, how soon and how many?"

"Very soon. We should have at least two and cover all the eye color bases."

"A whole baseball team. Now you're talking."

She giggled and punched him in the ribs. "That might be a little much."

———〰———

With all their family and guests packed in and around the two pavilions overlooking the Romance Waterfalls, Laken hadn't realized they had so many friends. Cooing among the gathering were two new members, Adrea and Grayson's little Ashley Sara and Grace and Mark's son, Hunter Graham.

As Grayson said the closing prayer, blessing their marriage, her mind strayed to Hayden. Standing beside her, he looked scrumptious in a gray, tailed tux.

"In Jesus' name, I pray. Amen."

Laken raised her head and couldn't help her gaze going straight to Hayden.

"I now pronounce you husband and wife. Hayden, you may kiss your bride."

The sweet kiss was too short, but tactful for their guests. The assembly erupted in applause as the keyboardist trilled a joyous wedding march. Laken's stomach did a little leap as they turned toward their guests. With her hand tucked in her husband's elbow, she retraced her steps down the aisle.

Though the blossoms surrounding the grounds were mostly silk, it was beautiful. The perfect wedding with the perfect groom. Hayden and Laken Winters. Mrs. Hayden Winters. It had a nice ring.

They greeted their guests in the reception line, with hug after hug. Laken could barely move in the yards of satin dress.

When the line finally ended, they cut the cake topped with white, feathery doves, and went back to the gushing waterfalls for pictures. First with her matron of honor, svelte-as-ever Grace, and Hayden's best man, Brady. Their nephew was way too cute wearing a smaller version of Hayden's tux. They posed alone on the balcony, with the falls in the background, and farther down on the rocks.

After dozens of shots, the photographer called for the family. Father had given her away. She still couldn't believe it. Though he still hadn't sought treatment, he hadn't had anything to drink today. But it was beginning to show as a steady tremor moved through him.

Collin's arm around her waist felt natural, comfortable. She leaned her head against his shoulder and smiled for the camera, thankful for his change of heart. Over the last few months, his bitterness had slowly melted away. He'd moved into her rental house and occupied Brady's weekends.

"Isn't that enough yet?" Collin moaned. "This paparazzi blitz is killing me."

She punched him in the shoulder. "I want to remember everything about this day."

The camera captured their sparring, and he managed another smile for another round of photos.

Maye, Paul, and Brady completed the family pictures of Winters-only shots, then both families together.

As soon as the photographer flashed the last shot, Hayden whispered, "Did you bring your jeans like I asked?"

His closeness sent a shiver over her. "I did, but I'll admit I had something dressier in mind for my traveling clothes."

They neared the gate and more hugs ensued.

Collin engulfed her in a bear hug. "Sorry I've been such a pill."

"You came out of it. And thanks for Hawaii. That's some kind of wedding gift."

"You deserve it."

"Ready, Laken?" Hayden grabbed her hand and pulled her toward the gate.

Just outside the heart-shaped archway, an older woman held something covered with a white satin cloth.

"Oh Hayden, you didn't."

"I did." He grinned, waiting until their guests followed them, then nodded at the woman. She removed the cloth to reveal two white doves inside a wicker cage.

"I'll go first." Hayden cupped a dove in gentle hands.

She reached in the cage, and the remaining bird fluttered into her fingers.

"On the count of three," Hayden whispered. "One, two, three."

In unison, they lifted their hands, releasing the birds. The doves flew toward the heavens in a flutter of white wings.

"Beautiful." Laken breathed the word.

Hayden hugged Brady. "Good job."

The boy accepted a kiss on the cheek from Laken.

"Come on." Hayden grabbed her hand.

Laken blew a kiss to the gathering, and they ran to Hayden's truck in a shower of birdseed, shouted good-byes, and teary-eyed congratulations.

She climbed up into his amazingly clean truck. "No streamers? No shaving cream? No clattering cans?"

"I spotted Brady a twenty to guard our ride." Hayden turned toward Rose Bud.

"Shouldn't we get to the airport? Where are we going?"

"You'll see." He clasped her hand. "I have a surprise for you."

Seven miles of anticipation passed as she peppered him with questions.

Finally, he turned into the drive of his house. "Go change."

Laken scurried inside to the bathroom and quickly pulled on her sweater and jeans.

"Hurry. Our chariot awaits," Hayden called. "I'll be waiting outside."

A few minutes later, she grabbed her jacket and stepped out.

He'd changed into jeans and a sweater, too, topped with a heavy sheepskin-lined coat. Looking like the hero straight out of a cowboy romance novel, he stood with Buck. Hayden mounted the horse with ease then patted the seat behind him.

"This should be graceful." Taking the hand Hayden offered, gingerly, she slipped her foot in the stirrup and tried to throw her right leg over. Hayden had to tug her on up.

Heat washed over her face and she righted herself, trying to get comfortable.

She wound her arms around Hayden's taut middle and whispered in his ear, "Mmm, I like riding double much better."

"Me, too." He clicked his tongue and urged Buck into a trot.

"Where are we going?"

"You'll see and it's not far. Just hold your horses."

Buck trotted into the woods and through a gate. Another five hundred yards or so, and Hayden reined the horse to a stop in the middle of a clearing.

"Why are we here? Remember what happened the last time we were in the woods?"

Hayden swung down and held his arms out to help her off. "Don't worry. I'll avoid scorpion-infested logs if you'll avoid poison ivy, and we'll get to the airport just fine. Bob promised to take care of Buck."

She leaned toward him, bracing her hands on his muscled shoulders.

"I've got you." He swung her around, but instead of setting her down, he cradled her in his arms and started walking.

"Hayden, what are you doing? You'll break your back."

"I've hauled mail sacks a lot heavier than you. Shh, I just carried you over our threshold."

Her eyes widened as he finally set her down. "But you already have a house."

"Yes, but it's Brady's. If you approve, I'll buy this five acres from Bob. He's agreed to finance, so I could make payments, and by the time Brady is grown and able to live on his own, this place will long be paid for. Then I'll build you a house."

Better tell him. "Umm. . ." She nibbled on her lip. "Did I ever mention my trust fund?"

Hayden did a sitcom-style over-the-top hard swallow. "Trust fund?"

"My grandparents set it up for me. I get it on my thirtieth birthday. I'm not sure how much, but probably a pretty penny."

"And why am I just hearing about this?"

She giggled. "I didn't want you to marry me for my money."

"Laken, I—"

Pressing her fingertips to his lips, she grinned. "I'm just kidding."

Gently, he moved her hand. "Shouldn't I have signed a prenup or something?"

"That's exactly why I didn't tell you. I knew it would make you uncomfortable. And I knew you'd want a prenup, and I don't believe in them, because we're forever. I only told you now so you'll know I can help pay for our house."

"I still plan on paying for the house." Stubborn pride oozed from his tone. He winked. "But you got the forever thing right."

Could a man be any more perfect?

No.

She turned in a slow circle and leaned back into him as his arms came around her waist. From this angle, she saw nothing but rolling hills, woods in the background, and the highway in the distance.

"It's perfect. Let's plant my gladiolas here this spring."

"Do you really like it? 'Cause if you don't, we can find something else."

Turning back toward him, she wound her arms around his neck. Her very own calendar-worthy hunk. "I love it, and I love you."

"I love you, trust-fund-I'll-never-touch and all. Got any other bombshells I might need to know about?"

She tapped a forefinger against her chin and grinned. "Not that I know of."

Their lips met and several minutes passed before they came up for air.

"I'm thinking. . ." Hayden's voice was hoarse. "We could head back to my house, spend a little time there, and still get to the airport in plenty of time."

Laken clung to him, weak-kneed. "I'm thinking, I agree."

# WHITE PEARLS

# Dedication

To Mama, for being the unique individual you are, for encouraging my dream and helping me achieve it. You instilled in me a love for reading, helped me go to all those writers' conferences, and babysat so I could meet deadlines.

Acknowledgments: I appreciate Jeannie Webber from the Little Rock, AR, Children's Home Administration Office, Carrie Korzen and Tina Thomas of the Rose Bud Post Office, and Nick Stark, owner of the Darden-Gifford House in Rose Bud.

# Chapter 1

Great, just what Shell needed to spoil the view from the balcony. A church full of Holy Rollers across the street. At least the old plantation sat back off the road a good two hundred yards. The Bible-thumpers wouldn't be able to spy on her. With an exaggerated eye roll, she ran her fore-finger and thumb back and forth over the faux pearl necklace she wore.

She stood at the railing and surveyed the grounds of the crumbling, two-story relic. Transform this place into a happening bed-and-breakfast? On the edge of town in tiny Rose Bud, Arkansas?

But the place had charm. It had obviously once been a grand estate. Oh the balls and cotillions this house must have hosted. Oh the grand, fine ladies who'd lived here. Grand, fine ladies who looked down their snooty noses on the likes of Shell Evans.

"Shell Evans." A hoarse male voice came from behind her.

She stiffened. Probably a carpenter. How did he know her name already? She'd barely gotten here. Already the gossiping tongues wagged. *Wade Fenwick's floozy is in town.* She could almost hear the whispers. Paranoid. Of course, her boss had told the man her name.

"Who wants to know?" She smiled, trying to sound confident as she turned to face him.

Ryler.

Her jaw dropped. Her heart skittered into overdrive. Her knees turned spongy and she leaned back against the railing.

"The landscaper."

If only this could be an April Fool's joke.

A massive brick of a man—but she knew how gentle he could be. Despite his imposing size, he was easy to look at. Same model-worthy, sculpted bone structure with tousled dark waves almost brushing his shoulders, and haunt-ing moss green eyes. Eyes that bore into her soul and seemed to hold all of life's hurts in their endless depths.

Hurts she'd once tried to ease. Instead she'd almost lost her heart. "Darrell hired you?"

Something cracked. The railing gave way, and Shell screamed. Ryler grabbed her arm and jerked her toward him. They landed in a heap by the door with her face buried in his solid chest. She pushed away from him.

He helped her up. "You okay?"

"Fine. Thanks."

The balustrade where she'd stood was gone, leaving twisted, splintered wood in its wake.

Yellow pollen dust smeared her pink T-shirt and jeans. She swiped at it with shaky hands, and managed to pat most of it out.

Ryler coughed and cleared his throat. A few gasps later, he caught his breath.

"Are you sick?"

"Allergies. All this pollen. If it's green and grows in the spring, I'm allergic to it."

"And you're a landscaper?"

"Gotta make a living somehow." Ryler ran a hand through his dark waves, sending them tumbling in disarray.

Shell swallowed hard.

"I don't remember you having allergies before." But she remembered everything else. His deep voice that sent shivers over her spine, his touch that shot lightning through her veins, and his kiss that turned her into a quivering, brainless idiot.

"It was fall. I'm good in fall and winter. I'm usually better than this, but I forgot my medication last night." His gaze scanned the grounds. "This place has a lot of possibilities."

"It'll take a lot of work, but it's doable." The porch swing beckoned to her still wobbly legs, but she didn't trust the rotting wood and rusted chains. "You know, I'd understand if you want to back out of this. I'm sure you can find another job." *Please do. Just walk away.*

"Probably, but we're both adults. I'm starting my own business and something as upscale as restoring the grounds of a former plantation will look great on my résumé." He coughed and cleared his throat.

She hugged herself and managed a smile. "Whatever you think."

"I think I've seen enough." No returned smile, no handshake, no catch ya later. He strolled through the doorway and was gone.

Why? Why? Why? Of all the landscapers, why the one who'd almost made her believe happily-ever-after could be possible. Six months. A whole half a year without him. Yet one glance and her heart had done a giddy tap dance.

Darrell stepped through the doorway. "What happened?"

"I leaned against the railing."

His eyes widened and he gently took her by the shoulders. "Are you okay?"

"Fine."

He wagged a finger. "No leaning on anything until the carpenters do some work."

"I thought you said it was structurally safe."

"In 1982, a tornado hit Rose Bud." With a shrug, Darrell checked his watch. "Some of the outbuildings got blown away, but the house survived. Just think of the history. Famous architects of the time, DeVoss and Carr designed it for the original owner, J. S. Darden."

"When did you get here?" Shell's frustration came out in her tone.

He raised an eyebrow. "Just a few minutes ago."

"I must have been inside opening windows. It needed airing out."

"We parked around back by your apartment."

"You mean my slave quarters." She rolled her eyes. "Leave it to you to buy an old plantation and house me in the slave quarters."

Darrell laughed and his brown eyes almost closed like they always did when he smiled. "Actually the servants' quarters are upstairs. There's a separate stairway from the dining room. And technically since the house was built in the late-1800s, they were no longer slaves, but servants. But think of all the history. When I saw it for sale, I had to have it. It'll be fun restoring this place back to its original glory."

If only his unconcerned, worry-free attitude could make her forget Ryler's presence. But her nerve endings were alive at the prospect of working with him. "Is this an April Fool's joke?"

"Wish I'd thought up something." Darrell snapped his fingers. "But I forgot what day it was. Seriously, I wish I could oversee this renovation project myself, but then I'd miss my lovely wife."

The only upstanding, happily married man Shell had ever known, Darrell was one of the few she was sure would never hit on her. He and his wife, Eva, were the stuff romance novels were made of.

"You have to admit it's beautiful." Darrell strode to one end of the balcony. "Ryler's here somewhere. The landscaper."

"I sort of ran into him."

"Good. He's planting a garden on all four sides with a fountain in the middle of each."

"You said three months, Darrell? This place will take at least six, maybe even a year. I'll never get to go home again."

"Three. Maybe six if we hit snags, definitely not a year." Darrell framed the front yard with his hands. "Just imagine. A garden view from every window. Freshly painted siding and new glass in the broken windows, restored interior walls and flooring. . ."

The breeze blew pollen dust tornadoes across the long drive.

"Darrell, I'm not sure about this." Three months—six months. Either way, too long. What was she doing here anyway? Why wasn't she with Chance in Conway? "It's a bigger job than I expected."

"You have my blessing to go home every weekend to Chance if you want. And there's a church right across the street if you decide to stay here."

261

"You know I don't do church, and I'd rather spend every evening with Chance." She bit her lip.

"I can't keep up. How old is he now?"

"Fifteen months."

"You could bring him here with you."

She closed her eyes. "You know that's not possible."

"Nothing's impossible. You could stay on, run this place for me, and raise Chance here."

Except she couldn't raise him.

"Come on, Shell. This place needs your touch."

And she owed him. "Three months. That's all I have to give."

"That's my girl." He patted her shoulder. "So now do you see the potential?"

"It's a great old place." *It's the landscaper that's the problem.* "Three months, then I'm out of here."

"That's all I need. But think about what I said. This little town would be a great place to raise a child." Darrell checked his watch. "I've got a meeting to get to. I'll come back tomorrow for an official tour and we'll go over the plans. Will you close the windows and lock up for me?"

"Sure."

"You can whip this place into shape, Shell. I have complete confidence in you."

The only person who ever had.

Without a backward glance, he left. Moments later, his black cherry Cadillac convertible rounded the house. With a wave, he drove away.

Slinging her purse over her shoulder, she hurried through the house and retraced her steps, closing windows as she went.

The musty smell was better than when she'd first arrived. She closed the last window, locked the storm and regular doors, and stepped out on the front porch.

"Guess I'll see you tomorrow."

Shell jumped and whirled toward the gravelly voice.

"Sorry, didn't mean to startle you."

"I thought you left."

"I was checking out the grounds." He jammed a baseball cap on his head and tipped it at her. Dark waves flipped every which way under the rim. "Better get used to me hanging around. You're stuck with me, for at least six weeks."

Only half the time she'd be here. A relieved sigh welled up within her, but she stifled it as he waved and jogged toward the back of the house.

Moments later, a charcoal SUV rounded the side of the house and pulled onto the highway. If it was Ryler's, it was definitely a step up from the battered royal blue pickup with the roaring engine he'd driven six months ago.

Her breathing leveled out to normal.

The splintered railing lay in front of the steps. Her stomach clenched. She could have ended up there in a broken heap. Picking up the rotted wood, she threw it in a pile next to the porch and scanned the house.

Six weeks. Six weeks of working with Ryler. The crew could whip this place into shape in three months. They had to. She had to get home to Chance.

Inhaling the fresh spring air, she tried to let the peaceful surroundings calm the quaking inside and imagined the repairs, flower beds, and bushes. Yes, it definitely had potential.

A breeze wafted the tall, amber hay surrounding the house on three sides. Dense woods stretched into eternity behind her apartment separate from the house. Typical of rural Arkansas, hayfields surrounded almost every house, although downtown Rose Bud was just around a curve.

The porch spanned the entire front, with filigree trim and the balcony above it. The window with stained glass panels Darrell had bought in Botkinburg graced the eave overhanging the terrace. His only splurge from keeping everything original. So excited with his antique find, he'd had the window installed months ago when the roof had been replaced and the apartment remodeled.

Double French exterior doors would be perfect for the front entries on both stories, but Darrell wanted the originals with the double arched windows left intact.

Her purse vibrated. She dug out her cell and flipped it open. Darrell.

"Hello?"

"You okay?" Darrell's favorite Christian radio station played in the background.

"Fine. Why?"

"You seemed kind of—funny, so I wanted to make sure you weren't hurt."

A lump lodged in her throat. "It wasn't the fall. I wasn't expecting to see Ryler here, so it kind of rattled me."

"You know him?" Concern echoed in his tone.

"We got acquainted when he was working on the golf course."

"And that's all you're going to tell me." The music faded out. "He did wonders with the golf course, so I thought he'd be perfect for the job. But you're giving me second thoughts. Will you be okay working with him?"

"It's fine. He's gone already and what are you? My boss or my father?"

"Just trying to look out for you, Shell. Somebody needs to. Have you made it to the apartment yet?"

"On my way."

"Call Eva when you get there. She's dying to know what you think."

"I'm sure it will be fabulous. Even if it's not slave quarters."

He chuckled. "Take care, Shell. And if Ryler gets out of line, he can answer to me."

Her heart was the only thing out of line.

As she hung up, a child's giggle echoed through the air, followed by a playful squeal. Now she was hearing things. Painful reminders.

She turned toward the sound. A mother with a toddler and an infant walked toward the house across a narrow hayfield. Great, just what she needed.

Scurrying to her apartment, she rounded the side of the main house. With a screened porch on the side, and a small afterthought of a porch over the door, the back of the main house wasn't nearly as ostentatious as the ornate front.

Separated from the house by the driveway, her apartment sat directly behind it, with an aged wooden garage on the far end. Its door looked permanently jammed about a foot from closed. She shuddered. No telling what kind of creatures had made their home in there.

Coffee. Darrell promised her apartment was fully furnished and stocked with everything she'd need. Two cups, maybe three, then she'd go over the plans and blueprints and be ready for Darrell's arrival in the morning. And Ryler's.

She opened the trunk of her car and pulled out the largest suitcase, then sifted through the keys Darrell had given her.

So much for slinking into town without a splash. Who was she kidding? This job would take forever. No way could she spend months on end here without the locals finding out who she was. Six weeks of those months on end, working with Ryler.

Oh well, at least she wouldn't have to hear her sister and brother-in-law constantly talking about God and church and inviting her to attend.

The aged lock of her temporary lodgings clicked. Inside, the apartment was roomy with sunny yellow walls and white wicker furnishings. Eva had done a nice job with the contemporary, bright, and cozy decor. Given the chance, Shell would have chosen a less hokey color, but it was nice enough. And after Shell finished the job, it would serve as a nice honeymoon suite.

She stepped into the bedroom and hoisted her suitcase onto the bed. After unzipping the lid, she dug through her clothing, found the framed photo, and set it on the night table. She ran her fingertips over the precious face, her chin trembling.

Weekend trips to Conway. Lots of them over the next several months. Home was only forty-five minutes away and she'd left something there.

Her heart.

And the only male she'd ever trusted with it.

—◊—

Ryler parked in front of the glass lobby of the post office. If he'd known the manager for the B & B project was Shell, he wouldn't have taken this job. He should have known. Shell was never far from Darrell. White-knuckled, his hands tightened on the steering wheel.

But she was supposed to be in Conway. And now, he couldn't quit—couldn't let her know that working with her would be hard on him. Hard on his heart.

How had she gotten back under his skin so quickly? He jerked the SUV door open.

She was beautiful, but he'd had his share of beautiful women. Was it the pain in her eyes that had drawn him to her again? He didn't need to dabble with anyone else's pain—he had enough already.

Pushing thoughts of Shell down deep, he concentrated on the task at hand. Meeting his sister. Shortly after his birthday, he'd finally found the courage to unearth his mother's letter from his father's Bible, read it, and head to the bank with the safe deposit key. And his life had pole-vaulted even more out of control.

He'd found his birth mother but hadn't revealed his identity to her yet. Her highfalutin ways made him want to run the other way. Until he learned about his siblings. Siblings who possibly didn't even know about him.

With his stomach churning, he stepped inside the post office lobby and swung the second door open to reveal white walls and commercial tiled floors. Mailboxes lined a long wall and several U-shaped areas. The work area was to his right.

He blew out a breath. She was alone.

Turning from her computer, Laken flashed him a friendly smile. "May I help you?"

His tongue glued to the roof of his mouth. He swallowed. "I just moved to Romance."

"Welcome. I used to live there. It's a great little town."

"I'm trying to decide whether to get a post office box there or here in Rose Bud, since I'll be doing some work in this area, Searcy, and Little Rock."

"Hmm." She tapped her chin with her index finger. "It depends. Is the Romance office close to your house?"

With a shrug, he grinned. "Beats me."

"Where do you live?"

"In a rental house on Highway 5."

Squinting, she cocked her head to one side. "By any chance is Pete Callaway your landlord? Number 124?"

He frowned. Was she on to him? "How did you know?"

"I used to live across the street. My brother lives there now and he mentioned someone new moving in." She shrugged. "Besides, it seems everybody ends up in one of Pete's two rentals when they first come to town."

Across the street from his brother? He couldn't have planned that if he'd tried.

She grabbed a scrap of paper and drew an *X*, then a line and another intersecting it. "Okay, your house is here. The office in Romance is down this road, I'd say about a mile and a half past your place."

Ryler tried to concentrate on her directions. "It's not on the way home either way."

"We can set up a box here or my husband can help you at the Romance office, or you might want to put up a mailbox at your house."

"Your husband works at the Romance office?" Married? Was he an uncle?

"He's the postmaster there. I used to work there, too, but as things developed, I transferred." She blushed.

Her coloring was different from his. Her hair a coppery brown, while his was quite a bit darker, a shade or two from black. Her eyes were blue, while his were green. But there was something about her smile. Something he'd seen in the mirror.

She frowned, obviously uncomfortable under his scrutiny. "Maybe you should check with my *husband*."

Did she think he was hitting on her? Ryler grinned. "I'm sorry. I didn't mean to stare. You seem familiar to me."

"I had the same thought about you. Are you from around here?"

"I've lived my whole life in"—he hesitated, considering a lie—"Little Rock." Would she figure it out? Did he want her to? Did she even know he existed?

"I used to live in Little Rock. Maybe we ran into each other there." She visibly relaxed then snapped her fingers. "I know. You were working at my parents' home a few months ago. Martin and Sylvie Kroft in Searcy. I'm Laken Winters."

His gut clenched. "You have a good memory. Ryler Grant."

She'd waved to him and he'd ignored her, assuming she and the man with her were just another pair of snooty visitors and she had been doing her good deed of the day by acknowledging the hired help. Only later did he learn from the Krofts' young, flirty neighbor that they were Laken and Collin Kroft—he had a sister and a brother.

"I think I'll go ahead and get a box here." The perfect way to get to know Laken without her knowing who he was.

"Sure." She handed him a form. "Just fill this out. You can do it now or take it with you if you want." She rattled off the box sizes and prices.

He'd better go before he got her suspicious again. What if she heard he'd been asking around town about her? "I appreciate your help. I'll be back tomorrow."

"Have a nice day." She turned back to her work.

Forcing his feet to move, he headed toward the lobby.

Shell strolled in, her platinum hair blowing in the slight breeze. A strand fell across her eyes. His fingertips tingled, longing to brush it away from her face. Of all the leggy blondes he'd known, this one was dangerous. He should have taken her offer. Reneged on the job and run as fast as he could. Far away.

"Hello again."

"Hey." He stepped back out of her way.

Her flowery-citrus perfume filled his senses. The perfume he'd bought her. He'd thought he caught a whiff of it at the soon-to-be B & B but decided it was his imagination. But no. She was definitely wearing the perfume he'd bought her. What did that mean?

"Shell Evans?" Laken cried.

Her nearness sank into his bones.

"Laken Kroft."

"Winters now. I got married last February."

"Don't tell me." Shell rolled her eyes. "Married in Romance on Valentine's Day."

"Guilty." Laken laughed. "What about you?"

"I've never married."

Ryler swallowed hard.

Both women looked at him, as if wondering what he was still doing there. Spying. That's what. On both of them. He laid the form on the counter and grabbed the pen waiting there. "I decided since there's not much to it, I'll fill it out here."

"What about you, Ryler?" Laken raised an eyebrow.

He cleared his throat. "What about me?"

"Are you married? Any kids?"

Typical happily married female. She'd just met him and was trying to fix him up with her buddy. She didn't know his heart had already experienced Shell Evans and never recovered. "Nope. I guess y'all know each other."

"Laken and I went to the same school in Searcy." Shell's laugh dripped sarcasm. "Though in decidedly different circles."

"I never paid any attention to circles." Laken smiled.

"My boss, Darrell Norton, set up a P.O. box for me." Sarcasm gone, still Shell's frigid tone could chill a cold-house rose. "I'm supposed to pick up the key."

"Sure." Laken bent to search under her counter. "So, let me introduce y'all."

Ryler concentrated on filling out the form, as if he wasn't listening to their conversation.

"Too late. My boss hired Ryler to transform the grounds at the Darden-Gifford House. We're renovating it into a bed-and-breakfast."

"Oh, I've always loved that place." Laken handed her the key. "What kind of work do you do?"

"I'm supposed to be an apartment manager, but when my boss has a new project going, I play remodeling supervisor and interior decorator, too."

He gripped the pen tighter until his fingers turned white. Darrell was never far from Shell.

Turning toward the exit, Shell waved. "I'll see you around, Laken. And, Ryler, I'll see you bright and early."

As the door closed behind Shell, Laken propped her elbows on the counter. "She's pretty, isn't she?"

Ryler swallowed but couldn't find his tongue.

"She's not married—you're not married."

He held both hands up, palms facing her. "I'm not looking to get married."

"I don't think she has a very high opinion of herself."

"Why? She's gorgeous."

Laken pointed at him. "I knew you thought she was pretty."

He cleared his throat and handed her the completed form. "On that note, I think I'll go."

"Hang on. Here's your key." She handed it to him.

"Thanks." He hurried out.

Yes, Shell was as beautiful as she'd ever been.

And Darrell was still part of her picture. He'd always seemed overly concerned for her when Ryler had worked the golf course in Searcy.

Had things progressed between them? Was Darrell housing his mistress in Rose Bud?

What did it matter? Things with Shell were long over. But his bruised heart didn't know it yet.

And right now, he needed to concentrate on the Krofts.

—◊—

"You taking up residence up here?" Darrell's voice came from behind Shell.

Standing a few feet from the balcony railing, she inhaled a deep breath but didn't turn to face him. "It's peaceful."

And on this project, she needed lots of peace.

"Just don't lean on the railing again." Darrell tucked Shell's hand in his elbow. "Let's officially tour this treasure."

That being-watched feeling crept up her spine. Her gaze canvassed the lawn.

Ryler's stare bored a hole through them as he squatted amidst a pile of rocks and potting soil.

Shell turned away and opened the door. With the musty smell carried away by the breeze, she inspected the house more thoroughly. Propping her chin on one fist, she surveyed the landing flanked by twin bedrooms with plank walls and floors. A few bits of aged wallpaper and scraps of dingy newspapers covered the walls, with glimpses of insulation between the wood.

"The closets line an entire wall. We'll cut them in half and expand out to install a bathroom in each room."

Ugly metal flues jutted from the wall in each room. "Please tell me you don't plan on putting in woodstoves."

"I'd like to, but it wouldn't be very feasible. Central heat and air work much better."

"We could find black iron potbellied stoves with electric logs for looks."

"Now you're getting a feel for the place."

Sheetrock and carpet would get this place in order. But Darrell wanted the house restored, not remodeled.

"I want the original wall planking sanded, and the cracks between each piece of wood filled. At some point there was paneling, which left all the nail holes. Those will have to be filled, too, and then the natural wood can be polyurethaned."

A fresh coat of neutral paint would save the wide, baby pink baseboards. The paneled walls in the landing could be stripped to their original wood, leaving more nail holes and cracks to fill.

Darrell opened the door opposite from the balcony to reveal narrow steps. Flipping on the light, he gestured her ahead of him.

Shell climbed to the attic. The long room boasted the fancy window above the balcony. "Plenty of room to add a closet and another bath."

"I figure the only bathroom downstairs in the entry can serve as a communal powder room for all guests, but we'll need another for the staff."

She ticked off each one on her fingers. "How many bathrooms do you plan to add?"

"Three upstairs, one in the attic, one in the downstairs bedroom, and one for staff. Space won't be a problem since each room is rather large."

No. Just time.

A fast plumber. Was there such a thing?

Oh, why had she let Darrell talk her into this project?

Because if not for Darrell and Eva, Shell might have ended up like her mother.

"That's all up here." Darrell ushered her in front of him.

Shell led the way down from the attic and down the main staircase.

The lone bedroom downstairs was the largest. Plenty of room for the proposed bathroom. She strolled through the spacious, once fancy living room.

"See the transom windows over the doors? All original for circulation. The fireplace is original, too."

The blackened fireplace needed to be torn out and replaced, but Darrell would never agree. She continued into the dining room with the large bay window and faded white wainscot and into the large kitchen with ancient cabinets.

"We'll cut off part of the pantry for a staff bathroom. The original pump is out on the screened porch." Darrell opened a door off the dining room to reveal a narrow stairway.

Servants' quarters. She climbed the passageway to a bedroom. With no hallway, she had to walk through the first room to get to the second identical one. Scraps of newspaper covered the walls in the second room. Squinting, she made out a date: February 1, 1890. Closets lined the dividing wall in each room, back to back.

"Why are there newspapers on the walls?"

"To keep the wind from blowing through the cracks. They didn't have insulation back then. It was blown in later."

Shell shivered. "Glad I didn't live back then."

"You're definitely not the rough-it type." Darrell grinned. "There's really no way to put in a hallway, so this will be a suite. This first room will be a sitting area. The closets are back to back, so we'll take part of both for the bathroom, and expand out into each room a bit. The second room will be the bedroom."

"It all sounds doable. You've thought of everything."

"So how are the Chance withdrawals?"

She swallowed hard. "Doable. Barely."

"Tell me again why he's not with you."

"You know why."

"I've heard your reasons, but as much as you love him, he should be with you. You're his mother."

"Savannah is his mother."

"She's his aunt. You're his mother."

"She's his legal guardian. Why can't you see he's better off with Savannah and Jake? This way, he's got a good life with two stable parents." *Without me. Without the specter of his father.*

She descended the stairwell, retracing her path to the front entryway. Halfway through the living room, a hand clamped over her elbow.

Gently, Darrell turned her to face him. "I just don't—"

The front door opened and Ryler stepped inside the foyer.

Her breath caught.

Darrell let go of her.

Ryler cleared his throat. "Darrell, when you get a minute, I need to compare notes with you on the fountains."

Not wanting to get any closer to Ryler, she turned sideways to let Darrell pass. "You go ahead. We're done."

"I'm meeting Eva for lunch, so I'll have to head back to Searcy soon."

"It won't take long." Ryler backed out and Darrell followed.

Blowing out a deep breath, Shell hugged herself. Close encounters of the Ryler kind.

—∞—

The balcony beckoned and Shell stepped out the windowed door. Standing in the middle, away from the railing, she listened to the constant squeals and giggles from the steady stream of toddlers next door. She hugged herself. Next door wasn't just a house. It was an in-home day care.

Day two of trying to avoid Ryler. All morning, she'd directed carpenters, picked replacement glass, and chosen a just-right white paint for the siding. Several men on scaffolding surrounded the house, measuring, prying rotted wood, sanding cracked paint, and scraping old caulk from window frames.

Her gaze kept drifting to Ryler as he unloaded sack after sack of potting soil and mulch. He heaved another bag and the muscles in his arms rippled. Oh, the feel of those arms around her. She shivered. It would have been easier on them both if he'd had his products delivered in bulk, but Darrell didn't want enormous piles in the carpenters' way.

After dumping his load in the pile near the house, Ryler turned and caught her eye.

Busted.

He pushed dark chocolate waves out of his face. "When you get a chance, I need you to choose plants and tell me where the beds will go."

"I don't know a thing about plants."

"No problem. I do."

No grin, no expression. The most animated she'd seen him so far was yesterday at the post office. Did he have a thing for married women? Or was it only Shell he shut down with?

"Can you come up here?"

"Sure." He grabbed something from his truck and jogged toward the house.

Working side by side with Ryler, picking plants, edging, and fountains. Would she be capable of rational thought as they hovered over catalogs, their heads huddled close together, while her heart leapt around like a giddy teenager? *He's just a man.*

Within minutes, he strolled out onto the balcony and shoved a catalog at her. "This will help. I'll need you to choose what kind of edging you want, too. I like using lots of native rocks throughout the beds. It gives a masculine look and not all B&B visitors will be women."

Don't think about how his hand almost touched hers just then. "Good point. What about water fountains? Darrell wants one on each side of the house."

"They're in the back of the catalog. Who's that?"

Shell looked up from the catalog and he gestured toward the long drive leading to the house.

A couple crossed the street. The man carried a casserole dish and a plant, while the woman pushed a stroller.

Great, shove a baby in her face. Shell rolled her eyes. "Probably the welcoming committee from the church."

"Pack of do-gooders."

At least they were like-minded on one issue. "I wish they'd stay on their side of the road."

"Me, too, but we better make nice. They could be potential customers."

By the time Shell and Ryler made it downstairs, the couple was almost to the porch.

Shell got a better look at the woman and stifled a gasp.

# Chapter 2

"Welcome to Rose Bud." The man set the plant on the porch rail and stuck his hand toward Ryler.

Luckily this rail was sturdier than the one upstairs.

The two men shook hands.

"Miss Evans, I'm not sure if you'll remember, but I'm Pastor Grayson Sterling and this is my wife, Adrea."

Grayson Sterling? Sara Sterling's husband. A chill crept down Shell's spine. The last time she'd seen him, they were nine and she'd dubbed him the preacher's brat.

"Hi, Shell, it's good to see you." Adrea smiled. "We brought you a plant from the floral shop. I hope you like white tulips."

Beneath all her sweetness and light, accusation dwelled in Adrea's gaze.

Killed with fake kindness by the woman whose fiancé Shell had once stolen. She wasn't sure she had the stomach to play this game. Mustering up a fake smile, she took the terra-cotta pot. "Thank you."

"You can plant them this fall if you like." Adrea gestured toward the dish. "Grayson's sister is a caterer, so she made the sandwiches. There's enough for the entire crew. Probably tomorrow, too, if you keep them refrigerated."

Ryler frowned. "Don't we need to pay you?"

"Not at all." Grayson waved away the suggestion. "Sis catered a big wedding last night and brought us a few leftovers."

"We'll certainly put them to good use." Ryler grinned. "Much obliged."

"I've always loved this place." Adrea surveyed the house. "So, you and your husband are overseeing the work?"

"We're not married." Shell and Ryler echoed one another.

"Oh." Adrea blushed.

"I'm the landscaper. Ryler Grant. Shell lives in the apartment. By herself."

Awfully intent on having nothing to do with her other than work.

"I'm so sorry. I saw you both up on the balcony and assumed. . ."

"We were discussing beds." Shell's tongue tangled. "I mean—flower beds."

"How fun. I own the floral shop in Romance, so, Ryler, if you'll stop by, I'll give you my wholesaler's card. They're very reasonable."

"Great. Hey, maybe you could help Shell with your flower knowledge."

"That's not necessary." Shell swallowed. Adrea's brand of perky set her teeth on edge.

"But you don't know a thing about flowers and if Mrs. Sterling helped, I could concentrate on the fountains, edging, and soil."

Less time spent together. And get this job done quicker. But working with Adrea? Or Ryler? Adrea? Ryler? Adrea?

"I'd love to help." A wail emerged from the stroller and Adrea scooped the baby up, a poof of pink ruffles, a shock of dark hair, and an angry red face. She nuzzled in her mother's arms and calmed. "Unfortunately, it's almost time for Ashley's nap and then I have errands to run. I'm working the rest of the week, but I could stop by early next week."

"Perfect. We'd really appreciate it."

"I love big old houses." Grayson scanned the balcony. "I heard the apartment used to be slave quarters."

Shell mustered up a tour guide smile. "I thought the same thing, but the house was built after slavery was abolished and the servants' quarters are upstairs. Apparently, the apartment was built later than the house."

"Are you remodeling the apartment, too?"

"It's already done on the inside and when we finish the transformation, I'll move out so it can serve as the honeymoon suite."

"How romantic." Adrea turned a dreamy-eyed gaze toward her husband. "Maybe it'll be finished in time to spend our next anniversary here."

Shell suppressed a gag.

"Maybe." Grayson kissed her temple, then the baby's, and tucked Adrea's fingers in his elbow. "Oh, almost forgot. We're having a yard sale the last Friday and Saturday of this month to benefit the Arkansas Children's Homes. We've got nice things people donated. Furniture, artwork, dishes. You name it, we got it."

"I might have to check out the dishes." Ryler grinned. "I'm tired of paper plates."

"Good, maybe we'll see you then." Grayson patted Adrea's hand. "We're also having a Mother's Day picnic over at the church next month."

A knife twisted in Shell's stomach. She'd never get to celebrate Mother's Day. "I'll have to check my calendar."

"Y'all are welcome to come and my sister's helping with the food, so you won't want to miss out." Grayson listed all the various services and times at the church. "If you don't have a church home, give us a try."

With a wave, he pushed the empty stroller down the drive as Adrea cooed to the tiny bundle she held.

"So, how do you know them?"

"It's a long story." A sordid one.

Something crinkled. Shell turned to face him.

A wad of aluminum foil filled the empty spot in the container. Ryler's sandwich already had a bite missing. "Mmm, I'm starving."

"I'll tell the other guys before you eat them all." She grabbed a sandwich for herself and rounded the house.

Scaffolding framed the side with several men at various heights. She cupped her hands around her mouth. "Lunch is on the porch, guys."

The foreman started down his ladder. "I brought mine. I didn't know lunch was part of the pay."

Shell didn't answer. Ryler could explain. She just wanted the quiet of her apartment.

Careful not to scuff her heels, she tiptoed across the gravel drive. So, Adrea ended up married to the preacher whose wife Wade killed. And they had a baby. Both of them came out just fine after Wade literally wrecked their lives.

A smirk played across Shell's lips as she remembered sneaking up behind Wade, wrapped only in a towel, and the horrified expression on Little Miss Goody-Two-Shoes' face.

Entering the apartment, she hurried to the kitchen. Ice clanged from the dispenser and diet soda fizzed as she poured it into the glass.

Memories chased one another and her smile faded away.

With a shudder, she hugged herself. She hadn't been to see Wade since his mother put him in the nursing home in Searcy.

Why did women like Adrea always get happily-ever-afters while Shell ended up alone? Not that she wanted a preacher—just the happily-ever-after part.

How many demons from her past could she face in one day? A child's laugh echoed through the open kitchen window. Her demons were laughing at her.

A loud *whir* started up outside, signaling that the men had inhaled lunch.

She took a bite of the sandwich. Chicken salad and it was probably really good, but her taste buds were dead.

—◆◆◆—

Ryler sank onto the foot of the bed. His bed, but the rental certainly didn't feel like home. He hadn't had a home since he was eighteen. The drab white walls closed in around the queen-sized bed that almost filled the room, leaving barely enough room to turn sideways and walk around it.

He looked toward the ceiling, rolling his head from side to side. Tense muscles and tendons popped and ground against one another in his neck and shoulders. Ill at ease at home—ill at ease at work.

She hadn't worn his perfume in four days. Instead she'd worn a light, powdery floral scent. Proof that she hadn't worn his perfume that first day because she missed him but because she liked the smell.

Maybe having Adrea help Shell with the flowers would keep her at a safe distance. The more he saw her, the more he wanted to beg for another chance.

But he'd never been the begging kind and Shell Evans wouldn't drive him to his knees.

He opened the third drawer of the dresser and pushed his T-shirts aside. It was still there. The envelope with the deposit slip and statements from the bank. Twenty thousand dollars earning interest in his account.

What kind of person left that kind of cash lying around in a safe deposit box for thirty years? Guilt? Love? Regret? He ran his hand through his hair.

Never had he held that much money. It would come in handy with building his company.

Maybe having struck out on his own would impress Shell and she'd reward him with a flirty smile. But it would mean nothing. All of her smiles were flirty.

Possibilities brought a grin to his lips as he remembered how soft she felt against him when she literally fell into his arms. Who knows, maybe another fling would get her out of his system. A nice distraction while he checked out the Krofts.

What if Laken and Collin weren't worth knowing any more than Sylvie was? He'd move on. With no ties to bind, no roots, it didn't matter.

Carefully, he put the envelope back in the drawer and covered it with clothing.

No. He'd sworn off women. The last thing he needed was Shell dallying with his heart again until she got bored and cast him aside. No more women.

But why did she have to come in such an attractive package?

A knock sounded at the door. Ryler slammed the drawer shut. Who could that be?

He hurried to the door, picking up a stray sock and remote on the way and stashed them behind a throw pillow on the couch.

A young boy in a wheelchair greeted him, with Collin standing behind. Ryler's jaw dropped. Who was the boy? Maybe he had a nephew.

"I'm Collin Kroft and this is my son, Brady. I live across the street." Collin gestured a thumb in that direction. "Thought we'd introduce ourselves to the new neighbor."

*You mean your brother. Do you know about me?*

Collin frowned. "Maybe now isn't a good time."

"Ryler Grant." He offered his hand and Collin shook it.

"Welcome to the neighborhood. Let me know if you need anything."

"And if you like to play basketball, I do, too." The boy grinned.

"I'll bet." Ryler smiled.

"I'm really good." Brady rolled his chair back and forth in quick succession. "I play on a wheelchair league in Little Rock."

Why was Brady in a wheelchair? A lump lodged in Ryler's throat. To be so young and confined to a chair.

"Well, we won't keep you. Let's go, Brady. Ryler's probably busy."

"Actually, I'd like to see you shoot a few hoops, Brady. I could use a break from unpacking." Ryler held up his index finger. "Hang on a second."

He hurried inside and scooped the basketball from the closet then sprinted back outside.

"There's a hoop in the back."

"Cool." Brady rolled himself around the back of the house. From fifty feet away, he lobbed the ball through the air with perfect spin and arch. *Swoosh.* Nothing but net. If there'd been a net attached to the rusty hoop.

"You're very good." Ryler leaned against the back porch. "Are y'all from around here?"

"I grew up in Searcy, lived in California for the last several years, and moved to Romance a few months ago to be close to Brady."

Divorced and the boy apparently lived with his mom. "I met your sister at the post office today when I got my box and she told me you were my neighbor."

"Laken's a gem. What kind of work do you do?"

"I'm a landscaper. You?"

"I'm a comptroller at a fragrance company in Little Rock." Collin leaned against the porch beside Ryler, crossing his arms over his chest. "Are you working steady?"

Ryler nodded. "I worked on a golf course in Searcy, and I actually worked on your folks' place a few months back. Your sister remembered seeing me there."

"I knew you looked familiar. So, why settle in Romance?"

"I like the area." Ryler kicked at the gravel. "Right now I'm working the grounds of a B&B in Rose Bud."

Brady effortlessly swished another goal.

"I heard Shell Evans was heading that up." Collin smirked. "The old Darden-Gifford place."

"You know her?"

"Half the guys in Searcy know her, if you know what I mean," Collin whispered.

Ryler's throat constricted. His hands fisted. How well did Collin *know* Shell? Why did it bother him to hear her talked about that way? Because there was something vulnerable about her. Used and discarded. Just like him. Only she'd discarded him, too, so why should he care?

"I shouldn't have said that." Collin cleared his throat. "She may have changed. Lord knows I have. Or have I? Sometimes I wonder. I became a Christian a few months back. Unfortunately, there's a lot of the old man left inside of me, but I'm working on him."

*Okay, don't have a clue what you're talking about.* Even though his adoptive parents had taken him to church, the more Collin talked, the more confusion clouded Ryler's brain. *What old man?*

"I've got an early commute in the morning, so I better get Brady home. He's got exercises to do and we haven't eaten supper yet. Want to 'bach' it with us? My sister sent over a pot of veggie soup."

Tempting, but he'd had enough sibling exposure for the day. "It sounds great, but I better get back to unpacking."

Collin clapped his hands to be heard over the constant thud of the dribbling basketball. "Come on, Brady. Let's go."

"Bye, Mr. Grant." Brady passed the ball to him.

"Bye, Brady. Come play ball again some time and please, call me Ryler." *Uncle Ryler? Uncle Martin? Martin Kroft Jr.?*

They disappeared around the side of the house. Ryler went in the back, stashed the ball in the closet, and sank into the couch, cupping his head in his hands.

He'd officially met both of his siblings now. Still, he only had questions. Why had Sylvie thrown him away, but kept Collin and Laken?

His father's Bible sat on the coffee table. Riley Grant, the only father he'd ever known. Flipping near the middle, he found the letter. Carefully, he unfolded it.

*Dearest Ryler,*

*If you're reading this, it means your father and I are in heaven. We can't bear to think of you all alone. I'm sorry, son. We should have told you about the adoption all along, but we were selfish, and afraid that if you knew, someday you'd try to find your biological family and leave us. We hope this news isn't too jarring. Just know that we couldn't have loved you more if you were our own.*

*Please, son, find your family, with our blessing. Your birth mother left the safe deposit key at the children's home. In the safe deposit box, you'll find twenty thousand dollars, a letter from your birth mother, a strand of pearls she wanted you to have, and trust fund papers. Please use the money to open your adoption records and claim your inheritance. For your future.*

*Your loving parents,*
*Riley and Loretta Grant*

He traced his fingers over the precise scrawl. Could he trust her words? His mother had been the ultimate optimist. She could put a sweet spin on the worst disaster. She'd probably had complete faith that Ryler would come home. Right up until her last breath.

He closed his eyes.

Could he trust Sylvie? Trust the woman who gave him away at birth?

Trust the woman who lived in her upscale neighborhood while his adoptive parents struggled to keep food on the table and never touched the stack of bills now padding his bank account?

He refolded the letter and set it back inside the Bible. A yellow streak on the page caught his eye. A verse his father had highlighted.

*"Trust in the LORD with all thine heart; and lean not unto thine own understanding."*

—⁂—

With each car that neared, Shell tensed from her perch on the balcony.

Six fifteen. Any minute perky Adrea would show up with flower advice. Maybe she'd forget. Not a chance. Women like Adrea kept their word.

A silver G5 sports car turned into the winding drive. The perfect little perky car for perfect little perky Adrea.

Blowing out a sigh, Shell closed her eyes. She cut through the landing and marched down the stairs, sidestepping carpenters, tools, and lumber. The constant *whir* of production rang in her ears.

As Shell opened the front door, Adrea stepped up on the porch.

"Listen." Shell propped her hands on her hips. "You don't have to do this. I can muddle through the catalogs and Ryler can give me any flower info I need to know."

"But I'd really like to help. I'm excited to be in the planning stage of such a large undertaking."

This woman couldn't be for real. No one was that nice, that happy. "I haven't had the chance to check with my boss. I can't guarantee a consulting fee."

"I'm not here for money. I just love gardens."

Shell stifled a sigh. "Let's just get it out in the open. I know you hate me." With just cause.

"I don't hate you." Adrea grinned. "Okay, there might have been a time when I did. But that was another lifetime ago. I brought you white tulips. Do you know what they symbolize?"

"I'm not much on flowers." Shell cocked an eyebrow. "That's why you're here, remember?"

"I knew it was you overseeing the restorations here before Grayson and I came over last week."

Shell's mouth went dry. "How?"

"News travels fast in a small town. I purposely brought you white tulips because they symbolize forgiveness."

"Forgiveness." Shell's tone symbolized sarcasm. "You think I need forgiveness."

"I wanted you to know that whatever happened between us is in the past—I don't hold it against you." Adrea clasped Shell's hand. "And if I did anything that hurt you, I hope you'll forgive me."

Pulling her hand away, Shell swallowed hard. Adrea couldn't be blamed for anything.

"Mrs. Sterling." Ryler jogged around the side of the house. "Great timing. I have the garden plans. Ready to get started, ladies?"

—⁂—

Shell's heart ached for Chance, even though she'd spent the last two weekends with him. To have those plump little arms around her neck.

Sitting cross-legged on the balcony with landscaping plans surrounding her, she couldn't focus. If only Savannah and Jake had agreed to officially adopt Chance. Then there would be closure. Like this, Shell could reclaim him anytime. Savannah and Jake even encouraged her to. And Darrell.

Chance was better off without her. Without Wade Fenwick's shadow haunting him.

And to top everything off, there was Ryler. She tried to ignore him working below. Ignore the muscles bulging under his shirt, ignore the impressive expanse of chest, ignore those intense eyes.

How could a man who spent so much of his time playing with flowers be so manly?

*Think about the project.* So far, the plumber was amazingly fast. Soon the bathroom fixtures would be in place and the framework for the walls would go up. The crew showed up daily, working hard and steady. Already, the house looked better, though most of the grounds were covered with fresh dirt.

"Hey."

So much for not thinking about Ryler. She looked down from the balcony.

"I picked up something extra from the wholesaler. Come see what you think."

Frowning, she hurried through the landing and down the stairs. They'd gone over Darrell's budget. There wasn't room for anything extra.

Standing by his truck, he motioned toward the bed. "What do you think?"

A pristine, white porch swing sat in the back of his truck, surrounded by scalloped terra-cotta edging and stepping-stones.

"I've seen you staring at that porch swing. Since you seem to spend most of your time up there, I thought you could use a perch in your makeshift office."

Sweet gesture. But what did he want in return? "It's beautiful. But the budget. . ."

"The wholesaler gave me a deal on the edging since I bought so much, so I used the difference on the swing. It can go back if you don't want it. But I figured future guests could enjoy it."

"You're right. Definitely keep it."

"The guys will need to replace some boards on the ceiling, but they can have it up in a few days. I'll get this unloaded and make another trip for the first load of plants."

Movement in the drive caught her attention. The preacher again. Shell rolled her eyes.

More food, but at least Mrs. Perky and the wailing baby weren't with him.

"Lasagna anyone?" Grayson held two trays stacked on top of one another.

"Mmm." Ryler hurried down the drive.

Reluctantly, Shell followed.

"My sister catered a dinner party last night. Most of her well-to-do clients don't do leftovers, so Grace ends up with extra food."

"You really shouldn't bring everything here." *Can't you just stay on your side of the road?* "Think of all the hungry children in China."

"I took most of it over to the homeless mission in Searcy. My secretary heated these up for y'all."

Shell's mouth clamped shut and she took a dish. "Thanks. The men will love it."

"I wanted to remind y'all about the yard sale Friday and Saturday. And the picnic next Saturday. We really want y'all to come. Your whole crew."

No way. She planned on spending Mother's Day weekend with Chance. And even if she wasn't, there was no way she'd spend it with a bunch of Holy Rollers.

"We'll see." She set the dish on the porch and headed to her apartment. "Lunch, guys," she shouted. "I'm going to get plates."

Drills and saws stopped buzzing. Men descended ladders and scaffolds and hurried to the porch.

"Y'all are all invited to a picnic at the church next Saturday. My sister's helping with the cooking."

Shell ducked into the safety of her apartment, tempted not to go back, but she had to take the crew plates to eat on.

She knew how the religious nuts worked. Come to our yard sale. Come to our picnic. Suck people in and make them feel obligated. Then before they knew it, they were in church. She'd fallen for it as a kid and her mother had let her go. Anything to get Shell out of her hair.

Shaking her head, she focused on steeping the cold brew tea bags in the pitcher.

But Shell wasn't good enough for church either. She didn't fit in. The church kids' parents didn't want their little angels hanging with the likes of her.

*"Do you know who her mother is?"* Sylvie Kroft's whispers echoed through the entire congregation.

A tap sounded on the door. "Hey, need some help?"

Her chest tightened. Her home. A boundary Ryler had never crossed, even during their relationship.

"Um, sure. Come on in." She stacked paper plates, napkins, and plastic forks on the table.

His huge frame made her living room seem small. Masculinity overtook everything despite the feminine, flowery decor.

"If you can take these, I'm in the process of making sweet tea real quick."

"Now you're talking." He grabbed the stack of paper products but paused in the doorway to her bedroom.

Crossing another boundary. "Excuse me?"

"Sorry. Couldn't help but notice what a neat freak you are. I never even make my bed and you've got everything just so. How long does it take to arrange all those frilly little pillows?"

"I like my surroundings neat." The only thing she could control. She had to get used to seeing him daily, without her heart threatening to flutter out of her chest. Become immune to him. If that were possible. "After work, would you like to come by and have coffee with me?"

"Having coffee was how it all started with us." Knifelike words delivered in a stone-cold tone. "This time around, let's keep it business only. Just business."

Even though he'd misunderstood, his rejection stung. "Exactly what I had in mind. Listen, I don't like being uncomfortable around someone I work with. So, I thought maybe we could become friends."

"Friends?" He frowned. "I guess we could give it a try."

"Good. I'm tired of the tension." Sucking in a relieved breath, she removed the cold brew bag from the pitcher. She dissolved the sugar in hot water and dumped ice in.

Grabbing Styrofoam cups, she carried the pitcher out, only to have Ryler take it from her.

The men stood in a pack around the lasagna, ready to pounce.

Ryler stuck two fingers in his mouth and delivered an earsplitting whistle. "Hey, ladies first. She made us sweet tea."

No one had ever called Shell Evans a lady. It sounded kind of nice. Except that Ryler knew she wasn't a lady. And he wanted nothing to do with her.

—⁜—

Ryler entered the post office. Laken pushed aside a stack of envelopes, ready to wait on customers. The *whir* of the air conditioner kicked on.

"Hey." She flashed him a genuine smile. "I'm glad you stopped in today."

"Lots of mail?"

"No. I wanted to ask you something." She disappeared for a moment, then handed him three envelopes. "Hayden and I are having a few friends over for dinner Saturday night and we wanted to invite you. You can bring a date if you want."

The perfect chance to spend time with her and meet her husband.

"What's the occasion?" He sifted through his mail.

"Just newlyweds settling down after three months and having our first dinner party. Actually, a backyard barbecue."

"Let me guess. You invited Shell and you want me to round out the twosomes?"

"I said you could bring a date." She grinned. "And I told Shell the same thing."

His gut sank. "Is she bringing anyone?"

"I don't know. Why don't you ask her? She might agree to be *your* date."

He pointed at her. "I knew you were up to something."

"Who me?" She shrugged innocently. "Collin and his new lady will be there. I haven't met her. Have you?"

"Aha. This whole thing is actually a setup to get your brother to bring his lady friend to meet you. And it's less pressure on him—and her—if you have several people over."

She propped her hands on her hips. "How'd you get so smart?"

"Let's just say I've dealt with a few women in my life. I know how they think." Except Laken seemed different. Could her motives be pure?

"So, will you come?"

"Sure. Sounds great."

Spending time with Shell would cost him. Especially if she brought a date. But spending time with his sister—priceless. "See ya then."

"Do I need to bring anything?"

"Just Shell." She grinned.

Shaking his head, he left. Why not? Maybe he'd ask Shell—since they were friends and all. Who was he kidding? No sane man would want to be friends with Shell. Still if he asked her, then he wouldn't have to deal with her showing up with a date.

Seven miles of highway passed while he rehearsed asking her.

As he pulled into the drive, the words still weren't flowing.

Shell stood in the front yard, inspecting a truckload of glass as the workers carefully unloaded it. Her plunging neckline held everyone's attention. Despite his gaze riveting on the shadowy depths, he wanted to tell the rest of them to keep their eyes to themselves.

She signed off that nothing had arrived broken or damaged. Reluctantly, the workers returned to their jobs, and the truck pulled away.

Staring at her clipboard, she turned toward the house.

He cleared his throat. Now or never. "Shell."

"Hmm." She stared at her clipboard for several more seconds before looking up.

Forcing his gaze to stay on her face and not drift downward, he swallowed. "Are you going to Laken's Saturday night?"

She scrunched her nose. "I don't know. I'm not sure why she asked."

"I think she's just being nice, trying to help us not feel like such outsiders."

"But she and I weren't really friends growing up. I mean—she lived in a nice neighborhood and I lived in a trailer park." She frowned. "She invited you, too?"

"I thought we might go together."

"Together?" One eyebrow lifted.

# Chapter 3

U nless you have a date?" Ryler's insides twisted.

The power tools buzzed to life. The compressor hissed, followed by the *ka-thwack* of a heavy-duty nail gun. Shell jumped. "What happened to just business? They might think we're dating or something."

"Just trying to implement that friends thing you mentioned, and I've never been one to care what anyone else thinks. Besides, I think Laken was trying to set us up."

Shell's fingers tightened on the clipboard. "Really?"

"Now, don't go getting all mad. This way, she'll give up. If we come together and she sees there's nothing going on, she'll chalk us up as just friends. Which is what we are." *Yeah, right.* "Besides, I hate walking into a place where everybody knows everybody, and I don't know a soul."

"I guess that would be okay." Turning her attention back to her clipboard, she hurried to the house as if she couldn't wait to get away. But she'd said yes.

Spending time with Shell, under the guise of friendship. What was he thinking? All he wanted to do was rekindle their past relationship. To kiss her, hold her, and love her. But she was done with him. Maybe spending time with her in a working relationship and as a friend would be better than the last several months without her.

Or pure torment.

—⁂—

Shell scanned her wardrobe. Nothing without a plunging neckline. And he was business only. Then why had he asked her to go with him? Did he really want to be friends? She hadn't meant real friendship—just an easy working relationship.

Not that it mattered. She pulled out a sleeveless purple blouse, and buttoned it higher than usual, then wiggled into her least faded jeans. Turning a circle in front of the mirror, she evaluated the outfit. Not come hither, but not dowdy either. She slipped on her favorite low-heeled gold sandals. As she finished her look with gold hoop earrings and a matching necklace, she heard the crunch of tires on gravel.

On second thought, he might be all business, but let him struggle with the view. She undid the top two buttons and grabbed her purse. Sprinting out to meet him, she slowed to a walk. *Don't appear too anxious.* The only thing she was anxious about was getting this evening over with. Why had she agreed to go?

Because deep down, she hoped to surpass "just business." To reclaim what they'd once had. To let her guard down and allow herself to love him. To know he loved her in return. But stuff like that didn't happen in real life. Not in hers, anyway.

"Hey." She climbed into the truck.

His gaze stayed firmly on her face. "Glad you could make it."

A prick of disappointment jabbed her stomach. Was he really immune to her charms? And why did it bother her so much for Ryler not to be interested anymore? She'd broken up with him. He was her past. Not her future.

He pulled onto the highway as silence vibrated between them. Flicking on the signal, he turned left at the intersection.

"If I got my directions right, the house isn't very far after Doc Baker's veterinary clinic. We should be getting close. I bet that's it." He pointed to a rustic house with a long porch across the front and a ramp leading up to it.

Several vehicles were already in the drive. Who were the other guests? Shell had been so preoccupied with one particular guest, she hadn't really thought about the others.

They got out of the truck and strolled toward the house. The door opened and a man she didn't know greeted them.

"You must be Ryler and Shell?" The man extended his hand. "Hayden Winters, Laken's husband. Glad y'all could make it. Everyone else is already out back."

Hayden ushered them into the cozy living room with dozens of family photos displayed on the walls. They followed him through the kitchen, equipped with unusually low cabinets, to the sliding glass doors.

A large deck spanned the back of the house, and it had a ramp similar to the one in front. Charcoal and lighter fluid flavored the air. Shell scanned the group already there. Adrea, the preacher, and Collin Kroft. Her heart lodged in her throat. A redheaded woman, a man she didn't know, and a vaguely familiar brunette woman.

Laken's gaze lingered on Shell's blouse for just a moment. "I'm so glad y'all made it."

Shell stiffened as Laken greeted her with a hug.

"This is Shell Evans and Ryler Grant. You both know my brother, Collin." *Too well. Complete, total jerk.*

"This is his friend, Jill. Adrea and Grayson said they'd met y'all. Now this part gets complicated." Laken gestured to the sandy-haired man. "Mark is Grayson's associate pastor and Adrea's brother. His wife, Grace, is Grayson's twin. Shell, you probably remember Grace from school and when we attended Thorndike."

Grace. How could she have forgotten?

A round of hellos and nice-to-meet-you's echoed through the crisp spring air.

So, Grayson had followed in his father's footsteps and Grace had carried on the tradition by marrying a preacher.

Great, dinner with not one but two preachers.

Hmm. Scurry to the bathroom and make clothing adjustments or give them a little test. See if these Bible-thumpers could keep their eyes above-board. Shell smirked.

"So, Shell." Collin's lips pursed, forming a thin line, and he kept his gaze on her face as he handed her a red plastic cup. "I hear you're overseeing the work at the old Darden-Gifford place."

"When we finish, it'll be a happening bed-and-breakfast."

He turned to his redheaded companion. "Jill is an architect. She'd love the place."

"Oh, how nice." Small talk with Collin grated on her nerves. But the Collin she knew couldn't possibly be any more comfortable than she was with the two preachers. That knowledge brought a smile to her lips.

"I need some big strong men to move the picnic table off the deck to the yard." Laken clapped her hands to be heard above the chatter. "And some ladies to help carry all the fixin's outside."

All of the women trickled inside, but Shell didn't hurry to help. She wasn't a lady and surely Laken had enough assistants. As the men tackled the table, Collin stayed by her side.

Her insides twisted as she sipped from her cup. Sweet tea.

"You know. . ." He ran a hand through his hair. "I owe you an apology. I treated you badly in the past."

She choked and spluttered.

"You all right?" Ryler called.

With a cough, she retrieved enough breath to respond. "Fine."

Collin sighed. "You're worth much more than you realize, Shell. Don't sell yourself short."

Her eyes stung. "You don't know anything about me," she snapped. "What? Are you a preacher now, too?"

"No, but I did become a Christian a few months back. Obviously, I've got a long way to go, but I'm trying to be a better person."

The low moan of a dog's howl echoed in the distance. A symphony of barks and yaps joined in.

She turned away and watched the men heave the table into place.

Thankfully, Ryler came to her rescue. "You sure you're okay?"

"Fine, my tea just went down wrong." She linked her arm through his, grateful for his presence.

With a confused frown, Ryler turned to Collin. "Where's Brady tonight?"

Clearing his throat, Collin's gaze flew to an approaching Jill. "He's staying with Hayden's parents."

"Who's Brady?" Jill threaded her fingers through Collin's.

His jaw clenched. "My son."

Jill's eyes widened. "You have a son? You're divorced?"

"Actually, we never married."

"I guess you planned to tell me all this at some point?" Jerking her hand out of Collin's grip, Jill crossed her arms over her chest. "I think I'd like to go now."

Jill stalked around the side of the house, with Collin and Laken scurrying after her.

Laughter bubbled up inside Shell. Any minute, she'd lose the battle.

—◦◦◦—

Ryler felt for Collin, but if he didn't want trouble with his date, he shouldn't have hit on Shell. His own brother's date. But Collin didn't know that part.

His stomach twisted. What kind of man was Collin? What kind of brother?

He'd certainly gotten a rise out of Shell. Had they been involved in the past?

What kind of family was this? Ryler ran a weary hand through his hair. What he wouldn't give to be able to sneak inside and check out all those family pictures he'd seen in the living room. Were there any of Martin Kroft Sr.?

"Hey. Where'd you go?" Shell elbowed him.

"Nowhere."

"There for a minute, I'd have sworn you were in another galaxy."

"I guess I didn't expect you to know almost everyone here. I guess y'all went to school together?"

"Unfortunately."

"What's Thorndike?"

"The church in Searcy, where Grace and Grayson's dad preaches." She gazed off in the distance, obviously distracted by memories. A smile tugged at the corners of her lips, but a frown marred her forehead. "I attended for a short time. So did Laken and Collin."

Didn't see that coming. Shell in church?

"Did Collin say something to upset you?" *Nice way to ease into it.*

"Actually he apologized for something that happened a long time ago." She sighed. "Something best forgotten."

"Let me guess." Ryler's teeth clenched. His insides tightened and heat scalded his airways. "He broke your heart."

Her sarcastic laughter crackled with tension. "No. But he wanted to. I was dating his best friend and Collin made a play for me."

His hands balled into fists. Why did Collin's audacity make him so angry?

Ryler didn't have any claims on Shell. He didn't want any claims on her.

Or did he?

Ryler worked at keeping his tone even. "Not hitting on your buddy's girl is an unspoken rule between friends."

"Collin sort of went by his own rules."

"But he apologized. Seems kind of odd." Why did he feel so protective of her? At the beginning of their relationship, he'd set out to use her just as Collin had.

"Says he's a Christian now." She rolled her eyes. "He gave me this big song and dance about how he's changed, but I'm not falling for it."

Laken rounded the side of the house. "Two guests down. So much for our first successful party."

"It wasn't your fault." Hayden drew her to his side. "Burgers are ready. Who wants cheese?"

At least Laken didn't play any games. He grinned. Other than match-making anyway.

———

Ryler pulled into his driveway and killed the engine. Though he'd already dropped Shell off, her perfume still lingered in the cab.

The black Lexus sat across the street at Collin's.

Despite the warning flares in his veins, Ryler jogged over.

The porch light illuminated Collin sitting on the top step. "Know anything about woman troubles?"

His brother—the traitor. He'd better be talking about Jill.

"I guess I complicated things for you tonight."

"It's not your fault. I should have told Jill the truth. But how do you tell a woman you care about that you're a failure?"

He cared about Jill. Not Shell. "You're a comptroller. I wouldn't say you're a failure."

"In my personal life, I am. I was too cowardly to marry the love of my life. After I left, Katie learned she was pregnant and had our son. Alone." Collin huffed out a big sigh. "Then she got sick and wrote me a desperate letter, but my new girlfriend hid it for three years. It's a long story, but in the meantime, Katie died and her brother, Hayden, had to step in and raise the son I didn't know I had."

Collin had followed in their mother's footsteps and abandoned his child. Was it a family tradition? At least he hadn't knowingly abandoned Brady. "That's pretty deep."

"Try living it." Collin ran a hand through his hair.

"We've all done things we're not particularly proud of, but I've seen you with Brady." An itch drew Ryler's attention to his arm. A mosquito. He smacked it. "He's crazy about you."

"I've only been in his life about a year and he still lives with Laken and Hayden during the week."

*Why? Not up to the challenge of raising a special needs child?* Ryler shrugged. "You're repairing things with him. That's honorable. And if Jill's not interested in kids, that's her problem."

"She loves kids, but I wasn't honest with her. She's big on honesty, and at the moment, she's not taking my calls."

"If you really care about her, go to her place." Another mosquito buzzed his ear and he swatted it away. "Don't leave until she lets you explain. The least she can do is hear you out."

"You're right." Collin stood. "A shrink would charge for that kind of sound advice."

"It's on the house."

"What's up with you and Shell? Are y'all seeing each other?"

"We just work together. She didn't have a date and I didn't either, so we came together."

"That's all there is to it?"

*Unfortunately.* Ryler nodded.

"In case things change, I'm sorry for what I said about her. She seems different than she used to."

"Trust me. Nothing's going to change." No matter how badly he wanted it to. With a wave, he jogged back across the street.

The tensed muscles in his shoulders relaxed. At least Collin wasn't interested in Shell.

—⁊⁊⁊—

As the workers carefully popped the old glass out of an upstairs window, Shell held her breath. Showers of glass rained down from the scaffolding despite their caution, and thankfully none of the men stood underneath.

"You should stay farther back until they finish." Ryler spoke from directly behind her.

Her breath caught. She didn't turn to face him. Three weeks of working with him and his nearness still snatched her breath away. "I wish you wouldn't sneak up on me like that."

"I was afraid some of the glass might hit you and tried to rescue you, but I didn't make it."

"I don't need rescuing."

"Hello?" a cheery voice called.

Shell groaned. She'd recognize that voice anywhere. Sylvie Kroft, Laken's mother, the biggest busybody on the planet.

With a sigh, Shell turned around. Sylvie still wore her hair too red and her lipstick too bright. Gems graced almost every finger. Real, no doubt. Less made up, she might have been an attractive woman.

"Sylvie?" Shell forced her lips into some semblance of a genuine smile. "To what do we owe this pleasure?"

Sylvie's mouth shaped into an *O*. "Why, Shell Evans, as I live and breathe. You're all grown up and pretty as a picture."

Shell frowned. A compliment? What was Sylvie up to?

"I just took some of Grace's leftovers to the homeless shelter and Meals on Wheels, but Pastor Grayson wanted me to bring these sandwiches over."

Sylvie and good deeds. It didn't compute.

Her too-red eyebrows drew together. "You're the young man who worked on my lawn a few months back."

Ryler's jaw clenched. "Yes, ma'am."

"I heard something about this place being turned into a bed-and-breakfast." Sylvie handed a tray to Ryler. "Such a grand old place. I'd have liked to have seen it in its day."

*Be nice to a potential customer.* Shell shrugged. "Maybe you will. The owner is restoring it according to original photos."

"I'd love to get a tour sometime."

What game was Sylvie playing? She cleared her throat. "Maybe when more work is done. Right now, it's rather an obstacle course."

Although, it might be fun to invite Sylvie to the balcony and encourage her to lean against the railing.

"Mr. Grant will do a marvelous job here." Sylvie clasped her hands together. "I can't wait to see this place in all its former glory."

"Well, we appreciate the sandwiches. I'll go grab something to drink and tell the crew." Shell rushed toward her apartment.

"I best be getting on my way," Sylvie called. "Bye, dear."

Shell managed a stiff wave. Dear? Since when had Sylvie Kroft called Shell Evans anything besides trash?

—⁂—

Ryler trudged to his bedroom and fished the large, black velvet box from the third drawer. Flipping it open, he stared at the pearl necklace then dumped its contents on the bed. With trembling fingers, he unfolded the letter for the hundredth time.

> *Dearest Marty,*
> *Your father and I never wanted to give you up. Please use the money to find us.*
> *The pearls have been passed down through six generations. Only part with them if you must.*

The letter went on, but he'd never been able to read any further.

Uninterested in her excuses, his gaze scanned to the end.

> *Martin and Sylvie Kroft*
> *Searcy, AR*

He traced his fingers over the long, slanted, flowery signature. Just like she'd signed his check for the yard work he'd done a few months ago.

His hands fisted, half-wanting to wad the note and rip it to shreds. Instead, he refolded it, careful to follow her original creases, then he tucked it back in the lid of the box, with the trust fund papers in the name of Martin Rothwell Kroft Jr.

*Martin Kroft. Marty Kroft.*

He'd never laid eyes on Martin Kroft Sr. But the Krofts' young, flirty neighbor had spilled everything she knew. Martin Kroft—his father—was a hermit. And an alcoholic.

Trust fund? How much? It didn't matter. Money definitely didn't equal happiness. His adoptive parents may have struggled financially, but they'd been wealthy in love and happiness. Until his graduation. Until they'd told him he was adopted. The night he'd been so angry, he'd left and never gone back.

Until three days later, after they died in a house fire.

Scooping up the necklace, he rolled the perfect, polished pearls between his callused thumb and forefinger. Were they real? A jeweler would know. He hooked both hands through the strand and pulled in opposite directions. Break the string and watch them fall. Show Sylvie Kroft what he thought of her heirloom. But, if they were real, it would be a shame to destroy them.

Releasing the tension on the necklace, he replaced it in the box and closed the lid, with a spring-loaded final *snap*.

—∞—

Half a dozen people milled around as Ryler surveyed yard sale items under the huge oak tree beside the church.

He stopped in front of a large painting. A waterfall surrounded by rocks and greenery. So real, he could almost hear the water splashing.

It could almost quell the storm brewing in his soul after yesterday's close encounter with Sylvie Kroft. He sucked in a deep breath and let it seep out slowly. *Don't think about her.*

An elderly man tried to dicker with one of the workers.

"All proceeds go to the Arkansas Children's Homes," Adrea called.

Exactly why he'd come, since he'd spent the first weeks of his life there. But he'd also needed to clear his head. And escape Shell. Just get through the morning, then he'd have a nice long break since she planned to go home for the weekend again.

Even back when they were seeing each other, she'd always run off to Conway every weekend. What kept dragging her there? A man? No, surely she hadn't cheated on him. Maybe her family lived there. People who cared? People she cared about?

Scanning the glassware, video cassettes, and books, he tried to rid his thoughts of her. Lamps, trinkets, and stuffed animals lined numerous tables with clothing racks sagging beneath their loads.

Why did he care? He couldn't give her the opportunity to use her feminine allure to tie him in knots and then cut him loose again.

Seeking peace, he strolled back to the soothing painting.

"That's just down the road." The familiar voice came from his left.

He looked up then did a double take.

Sylvie Kroft stood beside him. Her green eyes, so like his own, bore into Ryler. "The Romance Waterfalls in the painting. They're real and quite lovely. You should go sometime."

"Maybe I will." His throat muscles tightened. Tell her soon or flee?

"Even though it's a print, it's a ridiculously good buy."

"Yes, ma'am." His jaw clenched. Hug her or spit in her face?

"The flower beds you planted are just starting to bloom. You did an outstanding job."

A compliment? Before, she'd only barked orders and complained. "Thank you, ma'am."

"What are you doing in Rose Bud?"

"I like small towns."

"Mother, are you done?" Laken's voice came from behind him.

He turned to face her.

Laken smiled. "Thinking of buying it?"

"Just admiring."

"My friend got married there a few years back, so her father painted the original and made copies for all her wedding attendants. This one was mine."

"Why is it here?"

Laken rolled her eyes. "They're getting a divorce. She didn't want the original anymore, but she couldn't just throw it away since her father painted it. So, she gave it to me and I donated my print to the church."

"Honestly, young people these days." Sylvie sighed. "The slightest difficulty or argument and they're off to see the divorce lawyer."

"All too true." Laken checked her watch. "We need to check on Father. Nice to see you again, Ryler."

Was something wrong with their father?

"You two know each other?" Sylvie wagged a finger between him and Laken.

"I met your daughter at the post office."

"Little wonder. She practically lives there."

"Are you coming to the picnic next Saturday?" Laken tucked her hand in Sylvie's elbow.

"I've been invited." But he'd stick out like a sore green thumb.

"Then you should come. Meet some more people and the food is always great."

"We'll see."

"Hope to see you there." Laken waved and the two women headed to Sylvie's white Lincoln.

Was it his imagination or had Sylvie's attitude come down a peg or two since he'd worked for her? Though she had enough money to set up trust funds, she didn't live in a mansion. Yet she'd strutted around the two-story as if it were a grand palace.

Laken didn't put on any airs. Since she once lived across the street from his rental house, obviously status wasn't important to her. Was there a trust fund for her, too? If so, would it change her? If Ryler let them know who he was, would the money change him? Did he even want it? Did he want them?

"I saw it first." Shell's voice came from his right.

He turned to face her, and his chest did that weird quivery thing it always did when she was near. Her white jeans showed all her curves and they were topped with the plunging neckline of a yellow blouse. Her blond hair was pulled high in a neck-baring ponytail, revealing huge silver, hoop earrings. Why didn't she realize she'd be just as eye-catching in an enormous, shapeless housedress like Aunt Ginny wore?

"Saw what first?"

"I'll take it." She pointed at the painting.

"I believe I saw it first," Ryler deadpanned. "But you're in luck. I was just looking."

"Good. It would be perfect above the bed in my apartment. I mean, in the honeymoon suite. Oh, but I'm not sure I could leave it there. I may buy it for myself."

A yellow-and-black-striped butterfly flitted about the white flowered bush beside the church, giving him something to look at other than her. "I hear it's a real place over in Romance."

"I better go pay for it before somebody else snatches it up."

"I'll take it to the apartment for you."

"Wonderful. Thanks." She pulled a key off her chain. "I have a spare. Stick it and the painting inside the front door for now. I'm on my way out of town."

"Sure." He loaded the painting in his truck. Tempted to stay until she left, just to be near her, he started the engine instead. *Lovesick sap.*

Away from Shell's appeal, Ryler drove across the street, forcing himself not to glance back at her in the rearview mirror. Gravel crunched under his tires as he traversed the long driveway, circled around behind the big house, and parked between it and the apartment.

Ryler unlocked her door and slid the painting inside. As unwieldy as it was, she'd never be able to hang it herself. He jogged to his truck and dug out the necessary tools.

Back inside, he hesitated before entering her bedroom. Was he invading her privacy? No, he was doing a nice thing for her.

Yet during their three-month relationship, she'd spent countless nights with him, but never invited him to her place. What did she have to hide?

Whatever it was, it was none of his business now.

He spread a clean drop cloth over her headboard and fancy pillows. Propping the painting on the headboard, he checked for studs, then moved to the foot of the bed and eyeballed it. Centered perfectly and on studs, too. That didn't happen very often.

After slipping off his work boots, he stepped up on the bed. Holding the painting with his knee, he drove a screw into the wall. The gun jerked as the screw bit into the stud. He slid the large landscape into place.

Again, he stood at the foot of her bed to make sure it was still centered. Perfect. Carefully, he folded the drop cloth over without spilling any of the dust, took it outside, and shook it. Back inside one final time, he smoothed her flowery bedspread and made sure the numerous pillows were still in place.

The frame on her nightstand caught his attention. A toddler dressed in blue. Who could he be? Obviously, someone very important to Shell. Ryler's chest tightened. Did she have a new man in her life? A new man with a child looking for a mother?

—⚍—

Sunday evening, Shell let herself in the apartment. Already, she missed him. Every time she went home for the weekend, Chance had grown, learned new complicated words, and discovered new foods. And she was missing all of it. Who was she kidding? Even at home, she missed all his firsts.

She rolled her suitcase to the bedroom, dumped the dirty clothes out by the hamper, and sorted the laundry into three piles. A good shove sent the suitcase under the bed, and she started out to get the laundry basket.

The waterfall painting hung over her bed. She stopped in midstride. Just where she'd wanted it. Only Ryler could have hung it there.

Her gaze flew to the picture on her nightstand. Her stomach jolted.

Maybe he hadn't noticed.

And even if he had, Chance could be anyone to her. A nephew. A friend's child. Her heart.

Gently, she picked up the picture, kissed her fingertips, and pressed them to his cute toddler grin. Her vision blurred. Only an hour ago, she'd held him and experienced his drooling kiss. How could she miss him already?

—⁓—

Shell waited for Ryler to notice her. But he didn't.

On his hands and knees, he placed large boulders around the fountain and scattered about among the greenery, rosebushes, and blooms. Though each rock was placed just so, it looked natural when he finished.

"Ahem."

He sat back on his heels and turned to face her.

"Thanks for hanging the painting for me. It's exactly where I wanted it."

"I was hoping you wouldn't get mad at me for going inside when you weren't home."

"No, I appreciate it."

"Originally, I slid it inside the door, but then I thought about how bulky it was and I just didn't see how you'd ever be able to hang it by yourself." He pushed a stray wave out of his face. "How was home?"

"Fine." Her voice quivered. "I really didn't want to come back here."

He looked down, almost as if her admission hurt him.

No, she was imagining things.

His eyes squinted and his face contorted with a sneeze, then another, and another.

"Bless you. You forgot your allergy pill again?"

"No, it just hasn't kicked in yet." He fished a tissue from his pocket and swiped at his reddened nose.

*Cute Rudolph impression.*

"Did you plan on going to the church picnic Saturday?"

"On Saturdays I go home."

Ryler winced. "I hate to be the bearer of bad news."

"What?" Her teeth clenched.

"The foreman said the heat-and-air guy called to say he can come Saturday to do the estimate, or it'll be two months before he's free again."

"Two months?" She stomped her foot. "We can't wait two months. We need to get the work done way before then." Her tone registered high and panicky.

"I told the foreman I thought you'd want the guy to come Saturday, so he arranged it."

Her shoulders slumped. "So much for home."

"I suggested you'd probably prefer him to come as early as possible. He said it would only take a few hours and the foreman arranged for him to be here at ten, so maybe you can still go."

Another sweet gesture. Why? His green eyes shimmered in the sunlight. And why did he have to look so good?

"And I was thinking." He shrugged. "After he consults with you, he can do the inspection while we're at the picnic."

She frowned. "Why do you want to go to the picnic so badly?"

"I don't. But I was thinking if we go, the preacher might leave us alone."

A heavenly thought. "Good thinking. And, Ryler, thanks."

"For?"

"For getting the heat-and-air guy to come early. I really need to be home this weekend." She might not get to actually celebrate Mother's Day, but at least she'd be with Chance.

"No problem." His gaze swept past her. "Speak of the devil."

Shell turned to see Grayson coming down the drive, holding two foil pans.

A heavy sigh escaped her. They had to get rid of him. Maybe attending his picnic would do the trick.

—⁓—

Purposefully, Shell had picked the too-short shorts to wear to the church picnic to see if the Holy Roller men could keep their eyes off her legs. Most of them could, but a few stole a quick glance, then looked away. The older women's mouths puckered in disapproval and a few shook their heads.

And though no one said anything about her attire, unease grew in the pit of her stomach. Not just from the constant mention of mothers.

Why had she let Ryler talk her into coming? So, she couldn't go home for another hour. Mental note: No more scheduling workers on Saturday for her to babysit. She should have stayed on her side of the street doing just that.

But if attending the picnic would get Grayson off their backs, this torment might be worth it.

With the meal finished and cleanup done, everyone gathered at the side of the church. Under a large oak, metal chairs lined the carpet of purple, yellow, and white wildflowers.

She tugged at the hem of her shorts as she sat down. Useless. With her heels, she looked like some ridiculous bleach-blond caricature of Betty Boop. Should have worn something else. Something with a bit more coverage.

Why? She'd never been ashamed of flaunting her attributes before. But these people seemed so genuine.

Warmth rippled through her as she caught Ryler staring at her legs. It wasn't the first time. Maybe the shorts hadn't been a bad decision after all. She didn't fit in with the church people, and neither did Ryler. Two of a kind.

She caught his gaze, but he looked away.

Only a week ago, he'd invited her to dinner at Laken's. Since then, he'd been all business. Maybe they weren't two of a kind. Maybe he was above her, too. Maybe he thought her beneath him, just like everybody else did.

And wearing the shorts had only proven everyone right about her.

She needed a new image. A new wardrobe. Buttoned up, longer hemlines, and polished. She'd prove to these holier-than-thou hicks that there was more to Shell Evans than a warm bed partner.

After all, she hadn't warmed anyone's bed since Ryler had wormed his way into her heart.

Pastor Grayson cleared his throat. "Wow, look at this crowd. I'm so glad each and every one is here today. I'm especially glad to have so many visitors. If you have your Bibles, turn with me to John 8:32."

Bibles? No one had said anything about Bibles. Pages rustled as people flipped through to find the right chapter and verse.

"John 8:32, 'And ye shall know the truth, and the truth shall make you free.' Truth and freedom go together, but we only achieve freedom by putting truth into practice.

"Brothers and sisters, humble yourselves and turn to Christ. Accept His truth, that He is the living Son of God who died for our sins. Give Him the ugliness, the lies, the filthy rags of our lives. Only if we accept His truth, can we attain freedom through Him. Freedom from death and hell."

A gasp followed by a tearful cry came from the back of the crowd. "Oh my."

Shell turned to look behind her.

Six rows back, Helen Fenwick sat with a phone pressed to her ear, and tears rolling down her cheeks.

Shell hadn't noticed her at the gathering until now. But she'd surely noticed Shell and sat in the back to avoid her.

Adrea rushed to Helen's side. "What is it?"

"Wade's"—Helen's voice quivered—"dead."

# Chapter 4

Nausea boiled in the pit of Shell's stomach as gasps and whispers swept through the crowd.

"I always keep my phone on vibrate in case the nursing home calls. I didn't think. . ." The tearful mother's words ended on a sob and she clamped a trembling hand over quivery lips.

Grayson looked as if he might hurl. "I think we should pray." He began the prayer, pleading for strength for Helen, but the tremor in his voice proved he needed it himself.

A crushing sense of loss slumped Shell's shoulders. She stood and fled, not even stopping to check for traffic as she bolted across the highway. Her heels scuffed against gravel, but she didn't care. She stepped in a hole, and the pain of an almost sprain shot through her ankle, but she kept running.

In her apartment, she slammed the door and leaned against it. Wade. Dead.

It couldn't be. Just yesterday, Adrea had dumped him. He'd started drinking again, then convinced Shell to move to Missouri—to start over—

A knock jarred the door against her back. She jumped.

—∿∿—

"Shell, you okay?" Ryler pressed his ear against the door, expecting her to ignore him. After all, he'd claimed to be all business then asked her to Laken's dinner party, and this picnic. She must be as confused about him as he was her.

"I'm fine." Her voice cracked.

He winced. "No, you're not. Let me in."

"Really, I'm fine." *Watery sounding*.

"I'm not leaving until I can see you're really okay." Ryler pounded on the aged wood again. What was he doing? Exactly what he'd advised Collin to do with Jill, if he cared.

The lock clicked.

He pushed the door open.

Pacing the living room, she didn't acknowledge him.

"I guess you knew the old guy who died?" *Duh*.

"He wasn't old." She hugged herself. "I was engaged to him once."

Ryler's gut twisted. She'd loved someone. Someone other than him. Maybe that's why she'd never been able to commit. "But I thought he was in the nursing home."

"It's a long story and one I don't want to get into right now." Tucking a silky strand behind her ear, she hurried to her bedroom. "The heat-and-air guy is almost finished and I'm going home for the weekend. Now."

"You okay to drive?"

While she dug a suitcase out from under her bed, he stood in the doorway, appreciating the scenery. *Jerk, she's upset and you're checking her out.*

She nodded, set the case on the bed, and started stuffing clothes inside. "Will you lock up after the workers leave? I'll be back late Sunday evening."

"Want me to drive you, since you're upset and all?"

"No."

Her answer came too quick, as if she were hiding something.

With a shaky hand, she raked her hair back from her face. It fell about her shoulders like a silky curtain in some shampoo commercial.

"I'm fine. But thanks for caring." She frowned, as if his caring confused her. It did him, too.

"I'll let you be then. See you Monday." He turned to go, but a thought hit him. "Do you want to go to the funeral?"

She bit her lip and fresh tears filled her eyes.

*Stop looking like that, woman.* It made him want to kiss all her hurt away.

"I'm not sure yet."

"If you want to. . ." He cleared his throat. "I could go with you—I mean—just so you don't have to go alone."

"That's very sweet," she squeaked. "I'll think about it while I'm gone and let you know."

*Turn toward the door. Run. Run while you still can.*

"All right then. Safe trip." He hurried outside and around the big house.

Settling on the iron bench in the front garden, he could see the church lot had cleared already.

Why had he followed her? Why did he care if she cried? Why did he care if she was hiding something?

Because he still loved her. Just because she'd dumped him, his feelings hadn't died.

—◆◆◆—

In the JC Penney dressing room, Shell smoothed the black sheath over her flat stomach and turned sideways in the mirror. The high neck, short sleeves, and hemline barely above her knees was unlike anything she'd normally buy. But the only little black dress she owned would just solidify the further impression that Shell Evans was nothing more than a bimbo.

Not dowdy, this dress still showed her curves, but left everything else to the imagination. Perfect for the funeral. She almost looked respectable.

With satisfaction she shrugged out of it and back into her jeans and shirt. On the way to the register, she picked several cotton camisoles in different shades. The blouses she owned all had low necklines. But with something underneath, they'd be totally decent. She paid and strode out of the store feeling better about herself already.

The least she could do for Wade was show up at his funeral fully clothed. Funeral. She shuddered.

Did she want Ryler to go with her? Did she need him to?

He hadn't reissued the offer, so maybe she'd just leave it at that.

"Why, hello, dear. Fancy meeting you in Searcy."

Sylvie Kroft.

Shell turned to face her. "Hello."

"I saw you at the picnic Saturday, but I was on kitchen duty, so I never got to even say hi to you. I'm a member at Palisade."

*And that's supposed to impress me?*

"Listen, Shell, you probably know me as a gossip, but I've repented of my tart tongue. I'd like to apologize for hurting you in the past. You were just a child when you came to Thorndike, and I personally ran you out on a rail. For that, I'm truly sorry."

*"Don't you know who her mother is?"* Sylvie's voice hissed from the past.

"Okay." Uncertainty echoed in Shell's tone.

"Really, I'm not in the gossip mill business any longer. Do you have dinner plans?"

Shell couldn't think of anything she'd rather do less. Having her legs waxed perhaps? Not even that.

"No ulterior motives, I promise. I'll even buy and you can pick the place."

*Might as well get a free steak out of the deal.* "How about Colton's?"

"Oh, I love that place." Sylvie clasped her jeweled hands together. "The first time I went there with a friend, I was kind of iffy. I mean peanut shells? On the floor? But I guess it grew on me and the steaks are excellent."

"I'll meet you there." Shell checked her watch. "What time?"

"Now, if you're finished shopping."

"I am."

"All right then." Sylvie beamed. "I'll see you there."

She could just drive home. Stand Sylvie up. After all, it was probably a trap. She wanted information. Probably about Wade. After spreading rumors for years, Sylvie couldn't possibly have changed that much.

"Please show up." Sylvie's tone pleaded. "I imagine you don't trust me. I've given you ample reason not to, but I'd like to make it up to you."

Like a steak could fix it all.

"I'll be there." She wasn't a child anymore. If Sylvie tried anything, she could stand up to this woman and tell her what she really thought of her. Once and for all, put Sylvie Kroft in her place. Her hands balled into fists. The way someone should have done years ago.

Traffic on East Race inched as usual and Shell caught every red light. Even though the strip mall wasn't even a mile from the restaurant, it took ten minutes to get there.

Shell steeled her backbone, ready for a fight at the slightest jab.

Waiting inside the door, Sylvie looked relieved to see her.

"Oh good. I was worried. . ." She clamped her mouth shut. "I'm glad you could join me."

Not sure if she was glad, Shell didn't say anything.

Since it was an off night, the waitress had no problem finding them a table. Peanut shells crunched under their feet as they followed. Crying-in-your-beer music played loud. With dead, stuffed animals, branding irons, and spurs decorating the walls behind her, Sylvie didn't blend into their surroundings at all. They sat across from one another in a booth with mirrors lining the wall beside them.

Sylvie patted Shell's hand. "How are you doing since Wade's death? Oh dear, I still have a lot to learn about tact, don't I? I'm not being nosy. I promise. I just know it must be hard on you. You loved him at one time."

"Or I wouldn't have stolen him from Adrea." Shell's veins boiled. "Is that what you're getting at?"

Sylvie's watermelon-tinted lips pursed. "You don't trust my motives, and I don't blame you."

The waitress came and they both ordered sweet teas.

With a shaky, bejeweled hand, Sylvie tucked her hair behind her ear. "Let me tell you something. When I was seventeen, I wasn't married and I got pregnant."

Shell's jaw dropped.

"That's right. Martin and I weren't married and I got pregnant. Back then, it was still somewhat of a scandal in well-to-do families like mine."

"So, Collin. . . ?"

"No, before Collin. My parents were horrified. They moved to Little Rock to avoid the humiliation and forced me to give my son up for adoption."

Shell's heart twisted. "You don't even know where he is?"

Shaking her head, tears filled Sylvie's eyes. "For years, I was so ashamed and tried to make sure no one found out. I latched on to any rumor I could find and spread it like wildfire. I guess I thought if I kept enough gossip circulating, no one would find out about my secret."

"I'm sorry." Shell swallowed. At least she knew where Chance was. "No mother should have to give up a child."

"No." Sylvie's voice was barely a whisper. "We're trying to find him now, but we haven't had much luck. So, now with my bombshell, maybe you might trust me. Are you okay? Do you plan to go to the funeral?"

"I came to Searcy to buy a new dress for it." Her voice quivered.

"I think you should go. Funerals are for the living. If you don't go, you might never have closure. What about the visitation? I think it's tonight."

"No. I thought it might be too hard on the family for me to show up."

Sylvie patted her hand. "You should go if you want to. Adrea is over what happened and I imagine Helen is by now. They're both very forgiving souls. You can trust me on that. I've hurt them both. They should never give me the time of day, but you'd think nothing ever happened."

Visitation? Standing around looking at Wade? Dead Wade. No way.

"Do you really think they're over the past? Or just covering how they really feel?"

"Adrea and Helen aren't the type who can cover their feelings, and I honestly don't think they could harbor ill will toward anyone. For very long, anyway. We should all be more like them." Sylvie laughed. "I never would have dreamed I'd say such a thing."

The waitress brought their teas and took their order.

When she'd agreed to the meal, Shell had planned to order the most expensive item on the menu just to stick it to Sylvie. But now she ordered what she actually wanted. Sirloin tips. She could almost taste the savory meat, onions, and peppers. Baked sweet potato with sugar, cinnamon, and butter. Yum. Why didn't all restaurants offer it instead of the traditional potato?

She waited until the waitress left. "So, why the change in you?"

"For a long time, God's been poking me in the ribs every time I cause people problems. And for a long time I ignored Him." Sylvie's chin trembled. "I guess it got to where the pokes were so frequent, my ribs bruised. And I wanted everyone to pray for me to find my son. Why would anyone want to pray for me if all I did was cause them pain?"

Sylvie sucked in a quivery breath. "That part sounds selfish, but I long for him so. Sometimes, my arms literally ache from wanting to give him a hug."

Shell's throat convulsed as she tried to swallow the large lump there. "I'd like to make a new start. I'm tired of everyone hating me and looking down on me."

"I don't know anyone who hates you or looks down on you. It could be your imagination." Sylvie sipped her tea.

"You, of all people, know what my reputation is. I didn't even have anything decent to wear to the funeral." *All my clothes have plunging necklines and thigh-high hems.*

"Did you find something?"

"I did. It's nothing like I've ever owned. I think Wade's death made me realize life is short. Just because my mother is a certain way and raised me a certain way, I don't have to follow in her footsteps."

Up until now, her life was like that old country-and-western song "Looking for Love in All the Wrong Places." If there was love out there waiting, she wanted to find it in the right place. Maybe with Ryler. Could he return her love?

If she could reinvent herself, could she be Chance's mother?

"If you don't mind me asking, how is your mother, dear?"

"She got out of jail a few months ago." *Solicitation.* Such an innocent-sounding word. Her gaze lowered to the table. *At least I never did that.* "I think she's back in on drug charges."

"You poor dear. I'm sorry. Truly I am." Sylvie patted her hand. "You know, speaking of a new image, I've been thinking about getting a makeover. Maybe a softer look would warm up my image. Red isn't my natural color. My hair is actually brown with auburn highlights like Laken's."

"So, you're going natural."

"Actually, I've been thinking I might go a soft blond." Sylvie scanned her appearance in the mirror beside them. "According to my hairdresser, as we age, our skin fades and our hair along with it. So maybe a light shade would make me seem kinder, gentler, less of a busybody."

"Mine's mousy brown, but I've been thinking of going with more of a slightly darker shade." *Less bleach–blond bimbo.*

"If you're sure about not going to visitation, I'll call my hairdresser and see if she can get us in this evening."

"Now?"

"I tip well enough, so she usually drops everything to get me in. I'll buy. Operation makeover, change our image, here we come." Sylvie offered her hand.

With a smile, Shell shook it, just as the waitress brought their food.

⁓

Mid-spring called for no pantyhose. Some man who'd never had to wriggle into them had surely invented the things.

As Shell pulled the dress up over her shoulders, a knock sounded at her front door. "Just a minute."

She tugged the dress in place and hurried to the door, zipping as she went. "Who is it?"

"Ryler."

Smoothing her hands over her hair, she slipped peep-toe heels on, clasped her fake pearl necklace, and opened the door.

"Hey." His eyes widened. "You look. . .great."

"Thanks." She took in his appearance. Tan Dockers and a seafoam green polo. His eyes blended with the shirt. "You're mighty spiffy yourself. Going somewhere?"

"To the funeral. That is—if you need me to."

Shell swallowed to dislodge the knot in her throat.

"I know we didn't say anything else about it. But I thought I'd come prepared. No pressure." Ryler held his hands up, palms toward her. "I stashed work clothes in the truck."

Not walking in alone would be nice. "I'd appreciate it if you'd go with me. A lot."

"Walk or drive? The parking lot's filling up, but those shoes look painful. Nice, but painful." He grinned.

"They're really not bad." She peered around him but couldn't see past the big house. "Let's walk. I don't plan on going to the cemetery." There was only so much she could take.

He offered his arm. "Did you do something different with your hair?"

She tucked her fingers in his elbow and they headed down the gravel drive. "It was weird. I went to Searcy last night to buy this dress and I ran into Sylvie Kroft."

Ryler cleared his throat. "I did some work for her once."

"I knew her when I was a kid. She was the meanest, most hateful woman. She delighted in unearthing skeletons from people's pasts or families and telling everyone all about it. I couldn't stand her." A piece of gravel turned under her heel and she clutched Ryler's rock-hard bicep.

"But last night, she was like a different person. She apologized for hurting me in the past and told me her life story with a few secrets of her own."

"What kind of secrets?"

"A lady doesn't tell another lady's secrets, now does she?" She lifted an eyebrow. But she wasn't a lady, no matter how conservatively she dressed. "She's changed and is really quite nice. We shared a very enjoyable dinner and then went and got a makeover. We both decided we needed a new image."

"Sounds like an eventful evening." He covered her hand with his. "You really look great—I mean—you did before, too, but now your hair's more. . ."

"Natural? The hairdresser put darker streaks in so it would look highlighted instead of bleached." Her words probably sounded like Greek to him, but his compliments made her nervous. His biceps made her nervous. His presence made her nervous.

"Whatever. It looks real. . .nice."

As they neared the highway, pleasant small talk could no longer distract her from their destination. She sucked in a shuddery breath. "I wish I didn't have to do this."

"Nobody said you had to. We can turn around and march right back to your apartment."

"I need to do it."

"The lady's wish is my command."

*Lady.* That word again. As if they were both playing a game.

They stopped at the highway and checked for traffic then strode across.

"Oh, Shell, there you are." A newly soft-blond Sylvie stepped from her car. Ryler stiffened.

"I brought something for you." Sylvie handed her a large velvet box. "I thought these would set off your dress, so I decided to let you borrow them for today. I see you thought the same thing."

"You really shouldn't have." Shell flipped the lid open to find a strand of pearls. For a moment, she couldn't find her tongue. Her hand went to the costume strand she wore. "Are they real?"

"They're cultured, which isn't the ultra-pricey, rare kind, but yes, they're real. Our family has a tradition. My grandmother and mother each had pearls and they passed them down to me. These are mine. They'll go to my youngest, Laken, someday. My mother's necklace will go to Collin." Sylvie's chin trembled. "My grandmother's strand went to our oldest son."

Ryler cleared his throat. "We better get inside, ladies. Or we won't be able to find a seat."

"Here, Ryler. You do the honors." Sylvie gently scooped the pearls from the box and handed them to him.

With shaky hands, he accepted.

Why was he nervous? Was it the value of the pearls? Or did Sylvie rattle him?

"I really couldn't borrow your family heirloom." Shell shook her head.

"Yes, you can. I insist. Now, hold your hair out of the way, dear."

Shell did as instructed, removed her necklace, and turned her back toward Ryler.

His breath fanned the back of her neck and she shivered. Eternity passed as he fumbled with the catch. Finally, it fastened into place.

"Perfect." Sylvie clasped her hands together. "Now, take a deep breath. My grandmother used to say, 'Nothing's as bad as you think it'll be except for funerals, but they don't last long.'"

Ryler's jaw clenched. "Listen, Shell, with Mrs. Kroft here, you've got all the support you need. I'll just go."

"No." She grabbed his arm.

"I'll leave y'all alone." Sylvie stashed the necklace box in her car and went inside.

"I can't tell you how much I appreciate you coming with me." Tears stung Shell's eyes. "I'd really like you to stay."

He tucked her fingers in his elbow.

Side by side, they entered the church. Shell hadn't been in one since she was nine.

Burgundy carpet with matching padded pews. A huge harp sat on one side of the stage with a piano on the other. Prisms of light bounced off the stained glass windows.

The coffin sat in front of the pulpit with part of the lid open. Shell averted her eyes from the waxy figure inside. Her stomach clenched as an usher tried to direct them to the front.

"Please, I'd rather sit toward the back."

Ryler nodded and ignored the usher.

Three pews from the back. Far enough that she couldn't see inside the coffin. Maybe she could do this.

"I've never been to a funeral," she whispered.

"Never?" His eyebrow lifted. "I've only been to one."

"Whose was it?"

He swallowed. "My parents'."

"Both of them? How old were you?"

"Eighteen. House fire."

"I'm so sorry." She threaded her fingers into his and squeezed his hand.

"Me, too."

Haunting organ music played as the church filled to capacity. Wade had not been this popular. What was the deal?

Two men in dark suits strode to the front of the church. One moved the flowers from the casket, while the other tucked in satin fabric and shut the lid.

Shell flinched.

Wade was in the box—with the lid closed.

Ryler squeezed her hand.

With solemn dignity, Grayson escorted Helen, her sister June, and Adrea to the front pew. Mark and Grace joined them there as Helen dabbed her eyes. Once everyone was seated, Grayson climbed the few steps to the stage and sat in one of the large wooden chairs facing the congregation.

Soon the music faded away and Grayson stood. "I'd like to thank everyone for coming today. What a great show of love and support for Helen. She'll need each and every one of you over the next several months. Let us pray."

Shell tuned out. So, these people weren't here for Wade, but for his mother.

"Amen." Grayson read the obituary, insignificant details of Wade's life, and his family, which wasn't much to speak of. Most had preceded him in death. "The thing about death is we never know when it's coming. When Wade woke up Saturday morning, he didn't know it would be the last time he awoke in this life."

He didn't know anything. The last time Shell had seen him, he'd been in a hospital bed, curled to one side, with drool running down one side of his mouth.

"Thankfully, Wade had accepted salvation years ago and shortly before his injury, he rededicated his life to Christ. And we know that God is just."

What? When did that happen? In between bars? In between women? In between rehab stints? While he'd been engaged to Adrea and sleeping with Shell? Why was Grayson sugarcoating Wade's life? How could he stand over the coffin of the man who'd killed his wife and act like Wade was a saint?

"I promised Helen I'd share a simple plan of salvation. If anyone here doesn't know Jesus as their personal Savior, make that decision today and leave here with the assurance of heaven."

Shell's heart pounded in her ears. Pressure welled in her chest. She'd felt this way before in church. When she was a kid. She concentrated on the burgundy fabric lining the back of the pew in front of her.

"Pray this prayer with me: Dear Jesus, I know I'm a sinner. Thank You for dying on the cross for my sins. Please forgive me. I'm making a new start. I trust You completely and accept You as my Lord and Savior, Jesus. Amen.

"Folks, with that simple prayer, you can make a difference in where you spend eternity. Heaven or hell? You must make a choice. If you don't make a decision, then the decision is already made for you. Where will you spend eternity?"

The words echoed in Shell's ears. As the service ended, she could hardly breathe. The pianist started playing and the ushers reopened the casket then stepped toward the aisle. The people in the pew just behind Helen stood, then one by one, they walked to the casket.

Shell jabbed Ryler in the ribs. "What are they doing?"

"It's customary."

A few people paused at the casket, while others barely glanced.

"I can't," she whispered then jumped up and ran to the lobby. Standing room only, she wove her way through the crowd and out the doors.

Fresh air filled her lungs and her breathing eased. As fast as her heels would carry her, she scurried across the road and straight to her apartment.

A few of the workers called out greetings, but she didn't respond.

Inside, she sank into the couch, covering her face with her hands.

*"Where will you spend eternity?"*

Could Wade really go to heaven after all the things he'd done? After all the people he'd hurt? After killing Sara Sterling? After attempting to kill himself?

―⁓―

Ryler's fist hovered at the frame of Shell's door. *Haven't we played this scene before?* For the second time, she'd fled from the church and ran blindly home. Both times, he'd followed. Why?

He knocked. "It's Ryler. You okay?"

"I'm fine."

"You don't sound fine."

"That's because I'm not." She opened the door.

Tears shimmering on her cheeks tore at his insides. "You loved him?"

"I didn't know how to love then." Hugging herself, she paced the small living room. "I just can't believe he's dead."

"I heard it was pneumonia."

She shivered. "But he'd been dying for two years."

"Something about an attempted suicide."

She whirled to face him. "How did you know that?"

"I heard somebody say something at the gas station the other day."

"I bet they all blamed it on me."

Ryler frowned. "How could you have had anything to do with it?"

Her chin dropped to her chest. Her shoulders shook and a sob escaped.

Why did she always have to cry around him? It was like she knew he couldn't take it.

He pulled her into his arms, her sobs shaking them both. As he stroked her hair, she soaked his shoulder. The sobs eased and she trembled against him.

So soft, so beautiful, and her perfume could drive a man insane. He buried his face in her hair, grazing his lips across her ear.

She pulled away enough to gaze up at him, her full lips begging.

As if drawn by an irresistible magnetic pull, he lowered his mouth toward hers.

She stood on tiptoe.

# Chapter 5

Heat swirled through Ryler's veins as their lips met. As if the last six months apart had never happened. Striving for control, he traced kisses over her jaw.

"Let's move this party to my bedroom," Shell whispered, deep and throaty.

He pulled away to look into her eyes. The tears were gone, but the damage to her makeup remained. Inside and out. Her lips trembled with vulnerability.

He took a step backward. "You're upset."

"So?" She shrugged. "Make me feel better."

"I've done a lot of horrible things in my life, but I've never taken advantage of a woman."

She stepped close to him. "It's not taking advantage when I'm willing. Quite willing." Her smile promised pleasure.

Closing his eyes, he took another step backward. "You're not thinking straight and I'm leaving. Now."

"Jerk. You're just like all the rest."

He winced. "I used to be. If I still was, I'd be in your bed by now. Then I'd sneak out after you fell asleep." But he was trying to be a better man. The kind of man his parents raised him to be. "I want to stay. Believe me, with everything in me, I want to stay."

"So, stay."

"I can't. You're in no shape to know what you want. Or don't want." He took another step toward the door. "But you shouldn't be alone. Pull yourself together and meet me in the office. We'll talk."

"Talk?" She propped a hand on her hip.

Why, oh why, did nobility have to hit him now? He'd never done a noble thing in his adult life. She'd offered herself and he was leaving. Offering to talk instead.

But he didn't want to be just another regret on her long list. And he didn't want to hurt her. She'd obviously been hurt enough.

"I'll be in the office. Come on up when you're ready." He winked and hurried out the door.

Regret tugged at him. Oh, how badly he wanted to turn around and give in to her.

But for the first time in years, he knew he'd done the right thing. His parents would be proud. Knowing that put a warm bubble in his chest.

Still. Maybe a cold shower. . .

—⁂—

Shell pressed her fist against quivery lips. Why had Ryler left? He'd never turned her down. No man ever had.

Rejection weighed heavily on her shoulders. Yet, it was weird. He hadn't wanted to leave. It wasn't that he didn't find her desirable. It was almost like he'd left because he—cared.

The last thing she wanted was to talk, but she couldn't let him know his rejection bothered her. She had to pull herself together fast.

She doused her face with cold water and changed into her jeans. Her white plunging V-neck transformed into decent with the new aqua camisole underneath. Though she managed to get rid of the tear streaks with fresh foundation and blush, the red-rimmed puffiness around her eyes refused to go away.

But Ryler already knew she'd been crying and the crew knew she'd been to a funeral, so she had a good excuse.

She slid her feet into white sandals, closed the door behind her, and hurried to the big house. Power tools hummed on the other side now. Unseen, she entered through the back door, darted to the front entry, and climbed the stairs.

"There you are." Ryler swayed slowly on the porch swing and patted the seat beside him. With one finger, he drew an imaginary line down the center. "No crossing this line. We're just talking."

She grinned. No matter what the situation, his humor always eased her worries. One of the many, many, many things she liked about him. She perched at the far end of the swing.

"Feel any better?"

"Not really. Tell me about your parents—I mean—if it doesn't bother you."

"They were great. I was the center of their universe. We went to church every time the doors were open. They spent every spare minute coddling me and each other." He frowned. "But we had a falling-out just after my eighteenth birthday and I left."

"For how long?"

"Three days after I left, they died."

Shell gasped.

"It was the stupid Christmas tree lights. They never woke up."

She closed her eyes. "I'm really sorry."

"Our argument seems so insignificant now." He ran a hand through his hair, sending waves tumbling. "But then, I was young and hotheaded. I felt like my entire life was a lie and I could never forgive them for it."

Hindsight. She knew all about it. And now guilt ate at him.

"All those hours I spent angry with them. Wasted. They were just trying to protect me. If only I'd been there."

"It's not your fault." Her fingers itched to touch his arm.

"I'm a light sleeper, so I probably would have woken up."

"Or you might have died with them." A cold chill crept down Shell's spine.

"I think I could have lived with that better." A smile tugged at his mouth. "You know what I mean."

*I couldn't have lived without you better.* "It must have been really rough."

A sparrow perched on the rail under the feeder but noticed them and swooped away.

Ryler nodded. "I made it. How about you?"

Shell huffed out a big breath. "I never knew my father." She wasn't sure if her mom even knew who he was.

"I'm sorry."

"It's no big deal." Her voice broke. With a wince, she shrugged. "I have an older sister, Savannah." *She doesn't know who her father is either.* But they were probably two different men since the sisters didn't favor one another at all. "Mom was originally from Savannah and loved the beach, so that's how she chose our names. It isn't Michelle or Shelly, just Shell."

"A unique name for a unique lady."

There was that word again. She wanted to roll her eyes, especially after what had happened back at her apartment between them.

"It must have been nice having a sibling."

"Painful, too." Her teeth sank into her bottom lip.

"You didn't get along?"

"We were extremely close." So close that when one of them went through something bad, the other ached, too. And there was a lot of bad stuff. Her mind transported to the distant memory. "When I was ten, Mom's boyfriend raped Savannah. She was twelve and he was coming after me next, but Mom got home in time to stop him."

Ryler's sharp intake of breath shook her back to the present.

"I didn't mean to tell you that. It just sort of popped out. I've never told anyone."

"Did the pervert go to jail?"

Closing her eyes, she nodded. "DHS almost took us away. But my sister and I didn't want to be separated, so we lied about how stable Mom was and what good care she took of us."

After that, she seemed to pay more attention to them. "Savannah was in therapy for years, but she's happily married now and raising my"—panic clamped Shell's mouth closed—"my nephew, with another on the way."

Gleeful laughter echoed from next door.

His hands balled into fists. "Did any of your mom's other boyfriends ever try anything?"

"When I was seventeen, but I hit him in the head with a beer bottle and jabbed the broken neck of it at him until he left." He didn't come back and Mom blamed Shell.

Ryler touched her hand.

"You crossed the line." She grinned.

"No child should be raised like that." Ryler swallowed hard.

"I left after that. Savannah had just gotten married and I lived with her and her husband for about a year and finished high school."

"Did you ever see your mom again?"

"No, but she calls Savannah every time she lands in jail." Shell picked at a hangnail and flinched when it got into the quick. "All her years of hard living took a toll on her looks, so she turned to other means of making her living. She's been arrested for solicitation numerous times and lately drugs. *Solicitation*. Isn't that a harmless-sounding word? I can't say that I've been a saint, but I never did that and I've never drank or done drugs."

Ryler squeezed her hand. "You learned too young that most men only want sex, and you confused that with love. I haven't been a saint either, but I only loved once. And too late, I realized she didn't love me."

Could he be talking about her? Or someone else? Her lips twitched and she pressed her hand to her mouth.

"Sex doesn't equal love, Shell. Don't let anybody tell you it does. I'm sorry if I ever made you feel used."

No. That last bit about making her feel used proved he'd never loved her. If only he could.

"I'm hot." She pressed her wrist against the sweat beading her brow. "I mean—it's hot out here."

"If you don't mind me rifling through your house, I'll get you a glass of tea."

"Sounds great."

"Then we'll talk about Darrell's latest idea about the front waterfall." He disappeared through the door.

Why had she told him all that? What a day. Her first funeral. Her first rejection. Her first confession.

Maybe it was the calming balcony. His soothing presence. The *whir* of power tools assuring no one would overhear the conversation.

Or maybe loving him brought out her vulnerable side.

At least she hadn't confessed everything.

~∿~

Ryler stared at the white foam of water cascading down the jutting rocks into the blue-green pool below.

Beside him, standing on a natural balcony, where numerous couples had recited their wedding vows, Shell gazed out over the falls. "Isn't it beautiful?"

Not as beautiful as she was. The only woman he'd ever loved, and he'd almost told her the truth two days ago.

A slight breeze blew her hair in a silken tumble. Red nails peeped at him from matching high-heeled sandals. Her jeans had a hole in the knee, giving him a tantalizing glimpse of her leg now and then. Her red top, edged with white lace, set off her tanned skin. One delicate hand gripped the railing. If he moved his fingers over a couple of inches, he could touch her.

Emotions tumbled within him as violently as the gush of water over the falls.

*Concentrate.*

"Darrell wants the Romance Waterfalls in the front yard of the B&B?"

"On a much smaller scale, of course. I thought it might help if you saw the real thing."

He couldn't care less about the falls. All he cared about was the woman standing so close to him. He wanted the chance to kiss her again. To show her what a real kiss could be. He'd blown it the other day.

Next time, it would be less about passion. More about love and respect. Like he'd never kissed anyone. Despite their past intimacies, with her, it hadn't been all sex. At least not for him.

Her laugh made him dizzy. Her fighting spirit made him want to fight for her. Her strength made him feel invincible.

He wanted more from her. A lifetime?

"It'll take months and make this job last forever."

"I've got time." He swatted at a persistent gnat.

Time to win her heart.

"Yeah, well, I don't. All I want is to finish this job and go home."

"I'll work as quickly as I can. You'll be here another six weeks anyway, working on the interior."

How had she woven her silken web around his heart so completely? So quickly? Her wounded soul cried out to him. Begging for a healing love. And for the first time, he felt he had it to give. And for the first time, he was certain, if he could win her love, she'd never abandon him.

She needed a real love as much as he did. If only he could fill the hole in her heart. He'd lost her once, and couldn't stand to think of losing her again.

"Hello?" She punched his shoulder.

"Hmm."

"What do you think?"

"About what?"

"About how long will this take?"

How could she be so unaffected, when he could barely breathe with her so near? Because she didn't feel the same way. What was he thinking? She'd already abandoned him once.

He cleared his throat. "I'll take plenty of pictures and see what I can come up with. An extra month or so should complete the whole project."

A regret-filled sigh escaped her.

Obviously, she was looking forward to him wrapping up and leaving her alone.

She turned away from the railing. "What are those droopy lavender flowers on the fence where we first came in?"

"Wisteria. It's a vine."

"I think we need some at the B&B."

"I'll see what I can do. They don't bloom very long, but they're very fragrant."

"And pretty. Let's walk down to the bottom, so we can get the full scope of the waterfall."

As she started down the natural stone steps, he grabbed her hand. "Watch your step." Electricity shot up his arm. Any excuse just to touch her again. However fleeting their time together might be.

—⁓—

Shell clutched the chain of the swing with one hand and leaned forward to peer through the newly installed balcony railing. The last day of a long workweek.

Playing in the dirt as usual, Ryler whistled a happy tune while spreading black plastic sheeting where the falls would go in the front yard. A pile of large natural rocks waited.

The terra-cotta scalloped edging and matching stepping-stones led to the fountain, surrounded by numerous rosebushes and plants. Pink, red, yellow, orange, and purple wilted blossoms soaked up the sunlight, struggling with their new home. But Ryler promised he could coax them to life.

Closing her eyes, she leaned her temple against the hand clutching the chain. Try as she might, she couldn't forget the heat of his kiss, the feel of his arms around her, the respect he'd treated her with.

She just wanted to go home.

To Chance.

Away from Ryler.

Oh, for this job to end, this constant contact with him to be over, these odd feelings he stirred within her to stop.

But instead their time together had been extended.

Power tools created a constant *buzz* and *whir* in the background. Shell heard the noise in her sleep. There was something relaxing about the sound.

"If you're asleep, I hate to wake you."

Shell jumped.

Sylvie Kroft stood in the doorway of the landing. "I'm sorry. I hated to let you get a crick in your neck."

"I wasn't asleep. Just thinking." Shell reached under her hair to unfasten the pearls. "I forgot to give you these. I've been a nervous wreck about them and decided the safest place for them was around my neck. I wasn't trying to keep them."

"I know that, dear, and that's not why I came." Sylvie took the necklace, tucked it in her handbag, and sat next to Shell. "I saw how upset you were when you left the funeral the other day, and I haven't seen you since. So, I thought I should check on you."

"I've never attended a funeral before. I didn't know you were supposed to walk by the casket." Her voice cracked. "I couldn't do it."

"Barbaric practice if you ask me." Sylvie's nose scrunched. "So hard on the family. And in my busybody days, I used to go to funerals just to see how good or bad people looked. I told Martin to close my casket and seal it shut whenever it's my turn."

Shell shivered. *Where will you spend eternity?*

The power tools stopped in unison. Quitting time.

A child's giggle echoed in the sudden silence.

Another shiver sent goose bumps over Shell.

"That must be tough. Listening to the tinkling laughter of a child on a daily basis."

Shell frowned. Could Sylvie know?

"I know your baby died and I'm truly sorry. Though my son lived, I know what it feels like to lose a child."

Tears singed Shell's eyes. "How did you know?" Or think she knew.

"I never told anyone about your loss." Sylvie patted her arm. "That's not gossip fodder, even for a former gossip-maven like me. I assume it was a miscarriage, but you should be able to have other children. What did the doctor say?"

"I think that's enough." Ryler's steely voice came from the doorway.

"I'm not trying to stir up any trouble." Sylvie jumped up. "Since I was once forced to give up a child, I thought I could help Shell."

"It's not helping and it's time for you to go. Shell's had enough drama lately."

Shell wiped a tear. "She didn't mean anything, Ryler. Sylvie's been very kind to me."

"It's okay. I should go. Truly, I only want to help." Sylvie patted Shell's arm and turned toward the house.

"I just bet you do," Ryler snarled at the retreating woman's back.

"What was that about?"

"I've heard all about her. She's not being nice. She's digging for ammo to use against you."

"I don't think so. I honestly think she wanted to help. Did you know she has another son and she doesn't even know where he is? Her parents made her give him up."

Ryler ran a hand through his hair. "That's her take on it."

"I've seen the pain in her eyes. Her arms ache to hug him." Shell hugged herself. She knew the ache Sylvie spoke of. "She thought our experiences were similar enough that we might mourn together."

"We're clearing out," the foreman called from beneath the balcony. "See ya in the morning."

"Thanks." Ryler waved.

He turned back toward her. "I'm sorry about your baby. I didn't know."

Shell tried to hold back the tears, but they rimmed her lashes. She'd already had one meltdown in front of him in the short time he'd been back in her life. She blinked several times, but her vision didn't clear.

As the last of the convoy of work trucks pulled out of the drive, Ryler sat beside her and pulled her into his arms once more.

In his arms, she could no longer hold it together. Her shoulders shook and sobs knifed through her. She wanted to tell him everything, but what would he think of her?

Pulling away from him, she stood, and walked toward the railing. "He's alive."

"What?"

Wiping her tears with the back of her hand, she turned to face him. "My son didn't die."

Ryler's gaze narrowed. "Where is he? Why does Sylvie think he died?"

"It's a long story."

"I've got time."

Might as well tell him all of it. She stared down the long drive toward the church. "When I first met Wade, he was engaged to Adrea. He was an alcoholic but had been sober for two years."

"They broke up and you helped him pick up the pieces?"

"I wish." She shook her head, disgusted. "I broke them up. She came to see him and I was supposed to hide in his bedroom, but I made sure she saw me."

He frowned, disappointment written all over his face.

*But he loved her. Not me. And he couldn't get over her.* "They were supposed to get married on Valentine's Day. Instead"—she trembled—"he went on a binge, ran a red light, and had a head-on collision."

"Was anyone hurt?"

"Grayson Sterling and his first wife, Sara, were in the other car. She died." Ryler winced.

"Wade left the scene, didn't tell a soul he was responsible, and asked me to move with him to his aunt's in Missouri."

"Did he tell you what happened?"

"Not at first. He ran to Missouri supposedly so we could start over. A few years later, I found out I was pregnant. I guess he wanted a clean slate, so he confessed." *Which freaked me out.* "I left, but he followed me back here. At that point, I just wanted him out of my life, so I told him I'd aborted the baby."

Ryler's jaw clenched. "But you didn't."

"I planned to, but I couldn't do it."

"I'm glad." He squeezed her hand.

"Me, too." She closed her eyes. "Anyway, Wade made a confession at the church, then shot himself in the head. He's been in a vegetative state in the nursing home ever since."

"And your son?"

"My sister's raising him."

"You gave him away?" Dropping her hand, Ryler backed away from her. His accusing green eyes sliced through her.

She cowered under his gaze. She'd been wrong about him. She'd thought he was different, but he was just like everyone else in this judgmental town.

Shaking his head, Ryler whirled around and stalked to the door. He slammed it behind him so hard she thought surely the glass would break. It didn't.

But her heart did.

—∾—

Ryler flicked his turn signal on, needing a sane presence. No cars sat in the post office lot. He parked and killed the engine.

Half a day lost, dealing with Shell. And she was just like his mother. She'd thrown her son away. An inconvenience. At least she'd let him live.

How could he have been such a fool? He'd sworn off women. Vowed he'd never let anyone near his heart ever again. But Shell had crooked her finger and he'd fallen over himself to get close to her all over again.

He should have known he couldn't trust her when she'd so easily taken up with Sylvie. Two of a kind. He opened the truck door and climbed out.

Laken was the only sane one in the family. How had she turned out okay?

A blast of humid air propelled him inside. He inserted the key into his mailbox and pulled out a handful of bills then continued to the clerk station.

"Hey. How are you today?" Her bright smile couldn't calm the storm in his soul.

"Okay."

She tapped her chin with her fingernail. "You don't seem okay."

"How's Collin? Did he and Jill work things out? I haven't managed to catch him home lately."

"They're fine. He said you gave him advice that worked."

"Good. She seemed like a nice lady." He shuffled the mail in his hand. "Can I ask you a question that's really none of my business?"

"You can ask. I may not answer."

"Why does Brady live with you and Hayden?"

Laken nibbled on the inside of her lip. "After his sister's death, Hayden became Brady's guardian. Collin didn't know Brady existed until last year. He blew into town intent on moving Brady to California with him. Collin's always been a bit on the selfish side." She raised her hands up, palms toward him. "But I didn't say that."

Ryler grinned. "I didn't hear a thing."

A relieved smile tugged at her mouth. "He's changed, though. God's changing him, and he finally realized how unhappy Brady was with the idea and relented."

"So why doesn't he live with Collin now?"

"Collin usually doesn't get home from work until seven each evening, while Hayden and I are home shortly after five." She tapped the countertop with a fingernail. "This is weird. I'm spilling my guts and I hardly know you. Yet, somehow I feel comfortable with you."

"I'm glad." He could barely push the words through his constricted throat, as the truth lurked on the tip of his tongue.

"Might as well keep spilling. Hayden and I are talking about me quitting work when the baby comes." A blush crept into her cheeks as she patted her stomach. "We just found out. You're the first person to know outside of family and close friends."

His throat swelled even more. Outside of family. His little sister was pregnant. "Now see, that's what parents are supposed to do. They're supposed to do what's best for their child. Not give them to someone else to raise."

She frowned. "You think Collin should work less and Brady should live with him?"

"I was thinking of someone else, not your situation. But I just don't understand why anyone would give up their child. It's not supposed to be that way." He jabbed his finger at the air. "Parents are supposed to put their kids first."

"Sometimes putting the child first means giving them up. And sometimes the parent isn't given an option."

The door opened and a woman Ryler didn't know came in.

"I better get going." He turned toward the lobby.

"Don't forget your mail," she called.

"Oh right." He nabbed the envelopes he'd left on her counter. "And, Laken, thanks for being here."

She frowned then raised one eyebrow. "You're welcome. I guess."

—⚬⚬⚬—

Shell's heart revved as she turned into the familiar drive. Home for the weekend.

Chance appeared at the window, a huge grin erupting on his face as he bounced up and down.

Her feet wouldn't move fast enough and she sprinted to the neat, brick house.

Savannah opened the kitchen door.

"Annie! Annie!" Chance cried.

He launched himself into her arms, and her vision blurred. She lifted him high in the air, twirling, and he giggled his musical laughter. Oh, to have him call her Mommy instead of Auntie.

He snuggled close, wrapping his plump arms around her neck. "Missed you."

"I missed you, too, Chance. I think I heard something about a new back tooth?"

Chance pulled away and opened wide but stuck his finger in to show her and blocked everything from view.

She laughed and dropped a kiss on his plump cheek.

"Hello, Shell." Savannah leaned against the counter, grinning at the reunion, her six-month pregnancy pooching. "We didn't expect you until tomorrow."

"I couldn't stay away from this munchkin. Not for one more minute." She traced her fingers across the bottom of Chance's bare foot sending him into giggle spasms.

"Chance, go get your new tractor to show Auntie."

Shell set him down and he vaulted toward his room as fast as his chunky legs would carry him.

"You okay?" Savannah frowned.

"I just missed him."

"What happened? Something with Ryler?"

"I told him about Chance."

Savannah's brows rose. "And."

"He walked out, disgusted that I gave Chance away."

"He doesn't understand." Savannah rested one hand on her stomach and propped the other on her hip. "You know, Jake and I were talking last night. We thought being Chance's guardians would be a short-term thing. He's your son. Not ours. We love him and we'd miss him, but we'd never fight you for custody."

Shell's eyes narrowed. "You don't want him now that you're pregnant?"

"You know that's not true." Savannah's eyes glistened.

"I'm sorry." Shell sank into an oak chair. "I shouldn't have said that."

"We love Chance. We have since the day he was born, but he's your son."

"I know and you've been there for him when I haven't." She covered her face with both hands.

A chair scraped against the tile floor and the table wobbled as Savannah sat across from her. "It's a very delicate balance, loving him, raising him, but always wondering if you'll come back and reclaim him."

And she shouldn't have put them in that position. She shouldn't have left Chance hanging in the balance.

"He's getting older. Understanding more. If you're going to reclaim him, it needs to be soon. The older he is, the harder the transition and the more confused he'll be."

"I need to get this job finished." Straightening her spine, Shell pushed the hair away from her face. "I'm thinking about asking Darrell to find someone else to finish the bed-and-breakfast. I should be here with Chance. Then things can get back to normal."

But her heart would never be normal again.

Savannah reached across the table, covering Shell's hand with her own.

---

Ryler climbed out of his truck and waved at Collin across the street. "Hey, neighbor."

"Got a minute?"

"Sure." Crickets and bullfrogs created a symphony in the cooling evening air.

Collin jogged across. "Jill and I went for a walk after evening church service tonight. She agreed to marry me."

"Congratulations."

"Thanks. She's a Christian, she loves me, and she's crazy about Brady."

"Sounds great."

"Except for one thing." Collin settled on the porch step.

"What's that?"

"She wants to quit working, legally adopt Brady, and have him live with us."

Why couldn't the people surrounding him raise their own kids? "And you don't want that?"

"It's exactly what I want." Collin sighed. "But number one, I want to make sure it's what Brady wants. And numbers two and three, Hayden and Laken are very attached to him. Especially Hayden. And number four, Brady is very attached to them."

"If he lives with you, he'll probably spend the weekends with Hayden and Laken." Ryler shrugged. "He'll still be close. It's not like you're taking him out of state or anything. How does Brady feel about it?"

Collin frowned, as if he wondered if Ryler knew about California. "I think he'll be fine. He and Jill get along great. And a child should be with his parents."

"I'll have to agree. In your case, your girlfriend kept you in the dark about Brady." Ryler couldn't hide the bitterness in his tone. "The people who make me sick are the ones who give up their kids because it's an inconvenience to keep them."

Collin raised one brow. "You're very passionate on the subject. Ever thought of adopting?"

"I think a child should have a mother and father figure and I'm not interested in providing the mother figure."

"Alrighty then. Don't guess you'll want to come to my wedding."

"Actually, I'd be glad to. Just don't ask me to make it a double." Ryler smiled, hoping to take the edge off his steely tone.

"We're putting off the wedding until next year. Maybe you'll meet the perfect woman who'll change your mind by then."

Actually, he'd already met her. Or he thought he had. Had he? "Don't hold your breath. Why wait so long?"

"Beats me. I'd get hitched tomorrow." Collin rolled his eyes. "But she wants to do the whole Valentine's thing in Romance."

"How cheesy can you get?" Ryler chuckled.

Collin frowned.

"Sorry." Ryler's grin flattened and he clapped Collin on the back. "I'll back you up, bro." His eyes widened. Tiny slip. Called his brother, bro. No reaction from Collin.

Ryler blew out a big breath. That was close.

—◊◊◊—

Clutching the doorknob, Shell closed her eyes. Monday morning. Her first encounter with Ryler since she'd told him the truth.

*Just do it. Open the door. Face him. Work with the carpenters. Get this place finished and go home. It's in the home stretch. Five more weeks.* She couldn't bow out on Darrell with only five weeks left to completion.

The plumber was finished. The new bathrooms had walls. Now it was up to the woodworking guys.

She turned the knob.

On his hands and knees beside the back fountain, Ryler looked up then quickly averted his gaze.

Willing herself not to run, she nonchalantly strode to the back porch of the big house and scurried inside. She sidestepped workers, calling out greetings, and climbed the stairs.

The porch swing beckoned. So what if he'd bought it for her? There was no reason not to enjoy it. Vibrant scarlet, fuchsia, and purple petunias flourished in the boxes Ryler had installed on each side of the railing. Three emerald-winged hummingbirds with splashes of red across their throats flitted about from blossom to blossom. Shell sat and opened the catalog to pick paint colors and decor for each room.

"Hey."

She jumped.

Ryler stood in the doorway of the landing.

"Are you following me?"

"Sort of. I need to ask you something."

"Didn't we already figure out what to do with the flower beds and pick all the fountains?"

"It's not about that."

"If it's not about this place, I don't think we have anything to discuss."

"I have to know." Ryler ran a hand through his hair. "Why did you give him away?"

# Chapter 6

Shell's blood boiled and she jumped up from the swing. "I didn't give him away, and I don't think it's any of your business."

Sucking in a deep breath, Ryler shoved his hands in his pockets. "I need to know and you probably need to talk about it. Would you rather go to your apartment?"

"And have all the workers think. . ." She rolled her eyes. "I wanted Chance—that's my son's name—to have a chance."

"Why couldn't he have a chance with you?"

"His father was Wade Fenwick," she snapped, as if that were a death sentence.

"So?" Ryler shrugged.

"So—" Shell laced the single word with sarcasm. "I didn't want my son raised with the stigma of being the son of the drunk-that-killed-the-preacher's-wife. I was the town slut's daughter, and I'm still trying to live it down."

"I think you're doing a good job."

"You do?" She snorted a derisive laugh. "Two days after we met, I was in your bed." A rare blush warmed her face.

"But you seem different now. You dress different, you look different. More—"

"Respectable."

"That's it." Ryler gently gripped her shoulders. "I don't think anyone thinks of you as the town slut's daughter, and I don't think anyone thought of Wade as the preacher's wife's killer. Grayson officiated his funeral. I think this town, at least that church over there, knows how to forgive and forget."

"Maybe." Her skin tingled at his touch.

Ryler's hands dropped to his sides. "All those weekends I wondered about, when we were together, you were with Chance. I thought you had another man on the side."

"There was never anyone else." *There still isn't.* "My sister managed to rise above our stigma. She and her husband are raising Chance right. In church and in a stable, two-parent family. He's thriving."

"Who are you when you visit?"

"Annie." Her laugh sounded more like a sob. "That's how he pronounces Auntie. I moved to Conway to be close to him and got used to seeing him almost daily. This place, being separated from him, it's killing me."

"What do you say we go to church this week?"

Her gaze met his. "Why?"

"To find out, once and for all, about this Jesus business." He splayed his hands palms up. "Now don't look at me like I've lost my mind. Just think about it. He seems to give people comfort. And it seems you could use some. To be honest, so could I. What do you say?"

Comfort. Could something unseen give her comfort? She'd tried everything else with no results. "I'll think about it."

He gave her shoulder a gentle squeeze and footsteps echoed across the balcony. The door opened and closed.

It took every ounce of willpower she had not to scurry after him.

―⁓―

Shell tugged at the dress. Even with the camisole underneath, it wasn't right. Like a second skin and way too short. With a sigh, she wriggled out of it and pulled out her new black dress. People wore black other than to funerals. But her stomach twisted. Wade's coffin, closed with him inside. *Where will you spend eternity?*

With a shiver, she stared at the few dresses she owned. Nothing appropriate. Oh well, she had a good excuse not to go. Except that she'd told Ryler she would.

Shoving hangers aside, she searched for something that wasn't there. A white skirt caught her attention. She must have grabbed one of Savannah's by mistake when she packed.

She pulled it out and held it up. The cottony, gathered softness would fall mid-calf.

On the hanger next to it, hung an identical skirt in black.

*Savannah.* Both skirts and a slip had wound up in her suitcase after their discussion of the funeral and how she'd bought a new dress she'd probably never wear again.

Perfect. They were the same size. Shell grabbed the white skirt. Her peach top with a plunging neckline turned respectable with the white camisole underneath. She spun in front of the mirror liking the way the gauzy skirt whirled around her calves.

The doorbell rang. She smoothed her hands over her hair, slipped on high-heel white sandals, and scurried to answer.

"You're going?" Surprise echoed in Ryler's tone.

He looked good in his turquoise polo and black jeans. *Stop looking.*

"I said I would. Just let me grab some jewelry." She hurried to the bedroom. Silver necklace and earrings set off the airy, summery outfit.

*Thanks, Savannah. Nice save.*

With one more appraisal in the mirror, she hurried back to the living room.

Ryler checked his watch. "We better go, especially if we're walking."

It felt nice being on his arm as they stepped out. The hot sun blazed down on them. Thank goodness her hair was straight. The slight wave she managed to hot roll into it wouldn't last long, but at least it never frizzed.

The charcoal gray Chevy Equinox sat in the drive, next to her car.

"Is that your SUV?"

"Did you think I drove my banged-up work truck all the time?"

"It's all I've ever seen, except for that first day here." She shrugged.

"I always kept the SUV in the garage. I never took you anywhere in it, did I?"

"We usually stayed in." With one thing on their minds. She cleared her throat. "It's hotter than I realized. Maybe we should have driven. I bet the air-conditioning works great in that nice rig."

"We're almost there now. You look really nice. Like a summer breeze."

"Thanks. My sister loaned me this skirt, but I think I'll keep it." Especially since he liked it.

—⁓—

Ryler tried not to think about how good Shell looked as they stepped inside the church. Maybe he'd take her out for lunch after the service.

He'd never even taken her out to dinner. For three months, she'd spent almost every night with him, but he'd never taken her on a date. No wonder she hadn't loved him. She'd probably felt used. But then she'd used him, too. Could they start over? Could he show her she was more to him than a bed partner?

One excited church member after another greeted them.

With each kind greeting, his insides quaked even more. He wasn't like these people. He might have been if he'd never left home. His parents had been consistent church members. But after they died, he certainly hadn't stayed on the straight and narrow path. He'd never officially been on it.

Finally, the music started and the rush of people headed toward their pews. The harpist trilled her strings. He'd seen the harp during the funeral but assumed it was only for looks. He'd never figured harps existed in a real church. Weren't they just for heaven?

"Ryler, Shell, come sit with us." Sylvie motioned toward Laken, Hayden, Collin, and Brady.

Third pew from the front. Ryler cleared his throat. Shell seemed happy with the offer and took the seat beside Sylvie. He settled on the other side of Shell. If only she knew they were sitting with his family.

He ignored Sylvie and concentrated on Shell. Not hard. Every time one of them moved, her shoulder grazed his.

The worst that could happen, he'd wasted a perfectly good opportunity to sleep in. But sitting beside Shell might be worth it. Her maddening perfume, sparkling eyes, and curtain of blond hair filled his thoughts.

As a congregational hymn began, Shell grabbed a book out of the rack in front of them and sang along. Her soft soprano melted him further. *Amazing Grace.*

A rush of memories crashed around him—sitting between his parents, singing hymns, the sermons, Sunday school class. His dad explaining salvation to him. Feeling loved. By his parents and by Someone bigger. He'd been on the verge of giving in to that love when they'd told him the truth. But then he'd turned his back. And after they died, he'd turned his back on God, too.

When the second verse began, Shell turned the page, then with a frown, flipped back to the original.

Pointing to the next verse below the first, he showed her the right place. She started singing again.

The song ended and Pastor Grayson stepped to the pulpit and opened his Bible. "Turn with me to John 10:10."

Pages flipped and rustled as Ryler's heart raced.

" 'The thief cometh not, but for to steal, and to kill, and to destroy: I am come that they might have life, and that they might have it more abundantly.' "

The pastor said a prayer and then continued. "I don't know why bad things happen in this world. I don't know why kids are neglected, abused, abandoned, or orphaned. I don't know why families have a falling-out and never see one another again. I don't know why some folks live to a ripe old age and some folks get cut short."

Ryler swallowed.

"I don't know why tragedies and disasters happen. I don't have the answers. But what I do know is that no matter what happens in this world, God can get you through it. I'm living proof. Four years ago, I was at my lowest."

The message sank into Ryler's soul. Everyone had problems, traumas, and issues. Shell, the pastor, Collin. Even his parents had struggled with three miscarriages. While he and Shell dwelled on pain and the past, Grayson and Collin had moved forward. They didn't dwell on the bad stuff. His parents hadn't either.

"My first wife died with me sitting right beside her." Pastor Sterling paced behind the pulpit. "Helpless. I was eaten up with grief, but I had a son to raise. God gave me the strength and, when I was ready, He brought Adrea into my life. What a blessing she's been to Dayne and me. And now we have a new little girl to cherish.

"A few weeks ago, I preached the funeral for the man who accidentally killed Sara. Four years ago, I'd have never dreamed I'd have the strength to do such a thing."

The people in this church gave their pain to God, like Ryler's parents had. He'd had eighteen awesome years, then turned bitter and blamed God.

He could have had a lifetime of woe. And he still had a whole other set of parents he could get to know. If he could only muster the courage to tell them who he was. Maybe Sylvie had changed. Maybe Martin could get help.

"If you have loved ones who've passed away and they were Christians, you can see them again. Accept Jesus. His truth will set you free." Pastor Grayson finished his altar plea.

Ryler could barely stay seated until the music began. He rose to step around Shell, but she made the first move. He followed her.

At the altar they both knelt. Soon Pastor Grayson joined Shell, while Mark knelt with Ryler.

"Do you want to accept Jesus, Ryler?"

"Yes." Ryler's voice quivered as joy swooshed through him. "And I understand salvation. My parents were Christians."

"All right, then. Just stay until you're finished. I won't bother you." Mark stepped away.

"Dear God, I'm sorry for breaking my parents' hearts. I'm sorry for turning my back on You, and ignoring You. Forgive me for the mess I've made of my life. Help me to turn it around, to rely on You for strength and to live the way my parents would have wanted me to. Mold me into a new creature. Be with Shell and me, Lord. If we're right together, give me strength to treat her like a lady and honor her.

"Help me find the grace You've shown me in dealing with my biological parents, Lord. Help me to honor them. Most of all, thank You for dying on the cross for me. Thank You for saving my soul." He stood and wiped the tears from his face.

Sylvie and Laken knelt at the altar also, along with Collin and Hayden. Tears streamed down the women's faces. Praying to find Him? Praying for their father? Probably a bit of both.

Shell was already standing in their row again, singing along with the hymn "Have Thine Own Way, Lord." Her eyes glistened and a tremulous smile lifted the corners of her lips. As a few others lingered at the altar, she held the hymnal so he could see. Her other hand rested on the pew in front of her. Thankful they'd made such a monumental decision together, he covered her hand with his.

—⁂—

The last of the church members wished them well and left. Still in the sanctuary, Shell turned to Ryler. "I can't believe I did that. I didn't even want to go to church today."

"But aren't you glad you did?"

She nodded. "I had no idea what to do or say. Grayson had to explain everything and he even said the prayer for me. I just repeated it in my head and at the moment, I don't understand anything. My brain is spinning." The man who was hurt most by her and Wade's antics had led her to Christ. Her vision blurred.

"You don't have to understand, as long as you accept His grace. You'll understand more as you keep attending church and read your Bible."

"You seem to know all about it."

"Not all about it, but my parents were Christians. I was in church until I was eighteen."

"I only went to church maybe six months out of my whole life and it seems like a lifetime ago."

"Just stick around and you'll catch on." Ryler linked his fingers with hers. "You got any of those leftover sandwiches Grace sent over yesterday?"

"Two or three. I tried to get you to take them."

"Let's go on a picnic."

Pastor Grayson and Adrea stood inside the lobby door as the last of the congregation trickled outside.

"I'd be glad to answer any questions anytime." Adrea hugged her.

She seemed so sincere. How could someone forgive so completely?

"At this point, I don't even know what to ask."

"Just know I'm willing to talk."

"We'll set up a meeting soon and talk about baptism, too." Grayson shook their hands. "We're really glad y'all came this morning, and please come back."

They strolled out the door and across the street, with her hand tucked in his elbow.

"I'll run home and change. I thought we'd have a picnic at the park. Do you want to meet me there or at my place?"

"I don't know where your place is." She leaned against his side as her heel wobbled on the gravel drive.

"I'm on Highway 5, number 124."

Shell shivered. Across from Wade's old house.

"Are you cold?" Ryler frowned. "It's got to be at least ninety degrees."

"I'm fine. I'll meet you at the park." She never wanted to see Wade's house ever again. Not even from across the street.

"All right. See you there and don't forget the sandwiches. I'll bring snacks and drinks."

—∽—

Birds chirped and sang as Ryler spread a fuzzy taupe blanket on the wildflower carpet of purple, yellow, and white. His muscled arms rippled with each movement.

*Find something else to look at.* Shell turned away from him.

A few families dotted the park, but they'd chosen a secluded corner behind a large sycamore tree.

She emptied the sacks they'd brought. "This would be the perfect picnic

329

if we had one of those wicker picnic baskets like you see in the movies."

"The food's just as good from a brown paper sack." He handed her a bottled sweet tea. "This morning can change our lives. It's like a do-over. Our pasts are forgiven. We get a new chance to live differently."

"A fresh start."

A couple rounded the walking path, hand in hand.

"Can I ask you something?"

"I won't promise to answer."

"Fair enough. Why did you break things off when I asked you to move in with me?"

Shell swallowed hard. *Because I was falling for you, so I thought I'd leave before you got the chance to leave me.* "I wasn't looking for. . ."

"Mr. Forever. Just Mr. Right Now. Same here, only Ms. of course. But it didn't work out that way for me. I didn't mean to fall for you, but I did and this job brought you back into my life." He took her hands in his. "My feelings haven't lessened, Shell. And I don't want you to walk away again."

Why hadn't he told her that then? Could she trust him with forever? Her mouth went dry.

"You don't have to say anything." He drew her into his arms. "I haven't been with anyone since you."

*Me neither.*

His kiss was soft and tender, as if he treasured her. Not about sex. Dizzy, she leaned against him for support. Despite the gentle, undemanding caress of his lips, fire swept through her veins as it always had when she was in his arms.

With a groan, he pulled away enough to gaze into her eyes. "I want to do things right."

"Right?"

"We can't have sex."

"Huh?"

"We're Christians now. God created sex for marriage only. I want to live right. The way my parents raised me to live."

He grabbed his Bible. Sitting cross-legged, Ryler kicked off his shoes. His knee-length shorts revealed muscled calves.

*Concentrate on the Bible.*

He flipped through the pages. "Here it is. First Corinthians 6:18–20."

Shell sat next to him, head huddled close to his and read along with him.

" 'Flee fornication. Every sin that a man doeth is without the body; but he that committeth fornication sinneth against his own body. What? know ye not that your body is the temple of the Holy Ghost which is in you, which ye have of God, and ye are not your own?' "

The text blurred as hot tears filled her eyes. "How do you know where to find stuff?"

"My youth pastor drilled this into our brains. And before I moved from Little Rock, I visited with my aunt. Our visit got me thinking about where I came from. Since then, I've been reading the Bible."

"Go on, read more."

" 'For ye are bought with a price: therefore glorify God in your body, and in your spirit, which are God's.' What it's saying is that every sin is outside the body, except for premarital sex, which is a sin against our own bodies. When we became Christians, the Holy Spirit entered into us."

She cringed at the places her body had been. "So, everything we do with our bodies, we're taking Jesus with us."

"And we were bought by the blood He shed on the cross for our sins, so whatever we do, we should glorify Him. Sort of like making Him proud or doing things that lets other people see His love inside us."

"I don't think I've ever done anything that would make Him proud." Shell shook her head.

"But we've got a clean slate." He squeezed her hand. "Today, we start over."

"Thanks for showing me. I'm glad you know all this stuff." She drew away from him a bit. If she could get far enough away, maybe she could resist him. *Yeah, right.*

"I was on the verge of accepting Jesus as my Savior before I left home."

"Why didn't you? It seems like you'd have needed Him more than ever after your parents' deaths. You were all alone."

"You're right, but instead, I turned my back on God. For a long time, I refused to care about anyone. Until you."

She wanted to tell him she felt the same way, but would he stick around? No other man in her life ever had.

"I want us to be honest with each other. Starting with the reason I left home." He took a deep breath. "My parents told me I was adopted."

Shell gasped. Could Ryler be sylvie's missing son?

"I wish they'd just told me from the beginning."

She leaned her forehead against his shoulder. Offer comfort without seducing him. "Maybe they wanted you to feel you truly belonged with them."

"Whatever their reasons, I shouldn't have left."

"Do you know where your biological parents are?" The Krofts?

His jaw tensed.

"You should try to find them. You've got a whole other family out there somewhere. You don't have to be alone."

He stiffened and pulled away from her. "Just replace the parents who died with another set? Like buying a new car."

"That's not what I meant."

"Good." The word came through clenched teeth. "Because my parents could never be replaced." Ryler stood.

331

She jumped to her feet. "I just meant—you might even have siblings."

"Riley and Loretta Grant are my parents. I don't need another set because I had perfection." He ran a hand through his hair and stalked toward his SUV. "But I didn't realize it until it was too late."

"Ryler, wait."

He didn't even turn around.

Shoulders slumped, she sank back to the blanket.

No, he wouldn't stick around. He was like all the rest. One wrong word, one wrong gesture, one wrong question, and they bolted. Like a racehorse, but in the wrong direction. Away from her.

—⁂—

The porch swing stopped. Shell pushed off with one foot to set it swaying again. Paint fumes burned her nasal passages, even out here. The nonexistent breeze of early June didn't help matters. With all the doors and windows open, surely the smell wouldn't last long.

The reds, golds, and sage tones she'd chosen gave each room a romantic, soft feel with their billowy curtains and sleek antique furnishings. The rest of the furniture would arrive next week, with the bedspreads to follow. Then the final touches of mirrors, paintings, and wall hangings. It was all coming together quite nicely.

Except for the constant distraction named Ryler. A week had passed since their argument and they'd barely spoken two words to each other since.

"Hey, Shell."

How did he always do that? Call her name, just when she was thinking about him.

She stood and stepped over to the railing.

Covered in dirt, he looked better than any clean man had a right to, despite the frown marring his forehead.

"What?"

"My helper won't be here today, and I can't find anyone to replace him."

She closed her eyes. So close to completion. So close to going home to Chance. So close to leaving Ryler behind.

"I've already set the date for the grand opening." Even though Darrell conveniently hadn't found a manager yet. She threw her hands up. "I've called Grace about the food and ordered the flowers from Adrea. This place has to be finished, including that monstrosity of a waterfall. If I have to do it myself, it will be done on time."

His frown grew more intense. "Glad you feel that way. You better go put on some clothes you don't mind ruining."

"Huh?" Her mouth moved, but nothing else came out. She propped her hands on her hips. "I didn't really mean—" She sighed. But if it would get this job finished. . . "I'll be right there."

She hurried down the stairs and out the back door to her apartment.

Something she didn't mind ruining. . . She pulled her most faded jeans from the hamper. Yesterday, she'd accidentally leaned her hip into a freshly painted wall. They'd do.

The oversized T-shirt she slept in, with an old iron-on mostly peeled off, and grass-stained tennis shoes completed the lovely outfit. She pulled her hair into a high ponytail.

Ryler's mouth flattened into a thin line when he saw her. "You look like a teenager with your hair like that. Very fitting."

*Whatever.* "What do you need me to do?"

"If you'll dig the holes, I'll wrestle the rocks in." He handed her a trowel, careful not to touch her.

"Okay, how deep?"

"Not very. See this rock?" He flipped over a flat boulder, half the size of him, with ease.

"It's thicker on one end." He strode past her. "It's going right here. I need this area dug out, so it's level. You might break a nail."

She rolled her eyes and jabbed the trowel in the ground inches from his foot. "I'll live."

"If you stab my foot, I won't be able to finish the job on time."

And she'd have to put up with him longer.

Tension roiled in the humid air as Ryler left her to digging and started on the other side. As far as he could get, away from her.

—⁂—

The stiff cleaning brush Shell usually used on the bathtub would surely scrub the hide from her fingers. She added more soap. Still a line of embedded soil remained under the few nails she had left.

Pounding at the door made her jump.

Drying her hands, she hurried to peer through the peephole.

Ryler.

"Shell, can I come in? I've been thinking about what you said last week. About contacting my parents."

She jerked the door open. "And?"

Clean and shaven, he'd changed into fresh jeans and a hunter green T-shirt that strained over his shoulder muscles.

"I'm sorry I stormed off like that." He paced her small living room. "You were only trying to help."

"It doesn't matter."

"Yes, it does." He strode over to her. "I still want that future with you. Just know it will include my temper."

Gently, he gripped her shoulders. "Can we talk?"

Her breath stalled. "I'm not sure. Lately, every time I talk, you bite my head off."

"I'm sorry." He hung his head. "Being adopted—it's a sore subject with me. It reminds me of how badly I hurt my parents when I left, and now I feel guilty even thinking about contacting my biological parents."

All her anger evaporated. "Like you're replacing them, you said. How did the Grants feel about your biological parents? Do you know?"

"My aunt gave me a letter they wrote in case anything ever happened to them. They wanted me to find my family, so I wouldn't be alone."

She cupped his cheek in her hand. "So what do you have to feel guilty about?"

"My biological family lives in this area. That's why I came to Searcy and that's why I moved to Romance."

Her eyes widened. "Here? Do you know who they are?"

The muscles in his throat flexed. "The Krofts."

She gasped and her jaw dropped. "Oh Ryler. They don't know who you are."

"I moved to Searcy to decide whether to reveal my identity. Or not." He ran his hand through his hair. "And to tell you the truth, when I first met Sylvie, I decided not. But then I learned I had siblings."

Her gaze dropped to his massive chest. "So you moved to Romance."

"To watch them from afar."

"That's why you invited me to Laken's dinner party." Her eyes met his. "It wasn't about me."

"If it wasn't about you"—he grinned—"I'd have gone alone. But I wanted to make sure you didn't get a date with anyone else. Who knew you had a past with my brother?"

She rolled her eyes. "Nothing happened."

"Yeah, but he wanted it to."

"Not anymore." She traced his jaw with her thumb, his nearness working on her pulse. "Ryler, you have to tell them. Have you decided?"

"I have. I think you're right. Sylvie has changed." He captured her hand and pressed his lips to her fingertips then leaned his forehead against hers. "Will you come with me to tell them?"

She shivered and all resistance she possessed dissolved. "Only if you'll kiss me again. It might help me decide."

He backed up. One brow lifted. "Decide what?"

"Whether we might have a future? Or not?"

His lips sought hers. Again, soft, sweet, and gentle. Like no kiss she'd ever known.

A kiss to savor and remember. Because she'd already decided.

Even as his kiss melted her into a puddle at his feet, she knew.

He was a Kroft and Shell Evans didn't run in the same circles as the Krofts. She'd go with him to tell his family—offer him strength, but there could be no future for them. From her disreputable beginnings and sordid past, she couldn't span the gulf between them. Ryler Grant's past was a bit sordid, too, but his blood ran in the right circles. Even though his mother had befriended her, they weren't of the same class. And they never would be.

—⁓—

Ryler looked toward the porch ceiling and rolled his neck from side to side, grinding tendons against tensed muscle.

"It'll be fine." Shell squeezed his hand. "You're doing the right thing."

"I'm glad you came with me." Beside him, at the most important crossroad in his life. *Lord, give me strength.*

"Me, too. I can't wait to see Sylvie's face. She'll be so happy."

"You don't think she'll be disappointed? I mean—I'm not polished and savvy like Collin." He raised his arms. "Even in this ridiculous sports coat. I should have worn my jeans, like I usually do."

"You look better than Collin could ever hope to look." She straightened his collar. "You're real and you're her son. That's all she'll care about. Want me to ring the bell?"

"Could you?"

She jabbed the button. "But I won't tell them. You have to do that yourself."

Wanting to bolt, Ryler closed his eyes. Run. Squeal tires out of here and never come back.

The door opened and Hayden frowned. "Ryler, is everything all right?"

"Fine. Is everyone here?"

Shell squeezed his hand again.

"Yes. And very curious." Hayden stepped aside so they could enter. "But I'm afraid Mr. Kroft won't be coming down. He isn't feeling well."

Drunk. Ryler's gut twisted and he tried to concentrate on the decor. Classy and expensive, but not over the top. It still didn't make sense. If he had a trust fund, then Collin and Laken likely did, too, yet Martin and Sylvie's home wasn't overly grand or ostentatious. Had Martin drank away the fortune? And where had the money come from to begin with?

"They're waiting in the drawing—I mean the den. Right through here." Hayden tapped on the door, then swung it open. "Your guest has arrived—with a guest."

Sylvie sat on a throne-like white chair. Hayden claimed a seat beside Laken on the matching couch, and Collin sat in the twin chair.

"Why, Shell, what a pleasant surprise." Sylvie's brows drew together. "Ryler, it's always nice to see you, but I must admit, I'm confused as to what this meeting could possibly be about."

Sucking in a deep breath, Ryler paused. Where to start? He fished in the inside pocket of his sports coat. "It's about"—pulling out her letter and the pearls, he held them up dangling from his trembling fingers—"these."

# Chapter 7

With a gasp, Sylvie jumped up. "Where did you get those?"

Ryler swallowed the taste of bile rising in his throat. "Out of my safe deposit box."

"You're"—Sylvie's chin quivered—"our son?"

Laken clasped a hand over her mouth.

Closing his eyes, Collin grinned, as if to say, *Why didn't I figure it out sooner?*

"Hayden, Collin, go get Martin." Sylvie tried to blink away tears. "Bring him down even if you have to carry him."

"Now, wait a minute." Hayden put a protective arm around Laken's waist. "I don't mean to seem ugly, but how do we know if Ryler is the real deal? For all we know, he could have stolen the key or found it in the trash."

"I know." A sob escaped Sylvie and she pressed her knuckles against her trembling lips. "I should have known the moment I saw him. Maybe a part of me did. He's Martin made over, as a young man. Except for the facial structure and the eyes, which I see every day in my mirror."

Ryler felt like a child as they talked around him. *I'm right here in the room.*

"I'm sorry." Hayden shook his head. "I certainly don't mean to steal the potential joy out of the situation, but I think we need proof before we tell Martin. If this is a mistake, it might kill him."

"It's no hoax." Ryler's jaw clenched. "I have a letter from my birth parents telling me who my biological parents are. I have twenty thousand dollars, which I haven't spent a penny of, that I found in my safe deposit box with Sylvie's letter and the pearls. I'd be happy to take a blood test."

"That's not necessary." Collin shook his head. "Mother's right. Look at him."

"You've been in town for months." Hayden rubbed his stubbled jaw. "Why are you just now telling us who you are?"

Ryler's Adam's apple worked. "I wasn't sure I wanted to be a part of this family. Parents who gave me away. Siblings who possibly didn't know I existed."

"We didn't give you up by choice." Sylvie's voice shook.

"I'm sorry, Sylvie, I'm only trying to protect this family."

"Protect this family or your share of the inheritance?" Ryler's tone had a steely edge to it.

"I'll never touch Laken's money," Hayden growled.

"Stop it." Laken's voice cracked. "This isn't getting us anywhere."

Sylvie patted Hayden's arm. "I know you're worried, but I'm convinced. Ryler has Martin's hair, my features, and my grandmother's pearls. We'll have a paternity test before we tell Martin, but it's a technicality. Now, please leave us. I'd like to speak with my son. Alone."

"You okay?" Shell whispered.

He closed his eyes and squeezed her hand. "I need to speak with Shell. I'll be back."

His wobbly legs worked well enough to get him outside. "I'm fine. Thanks for being here, but I guess I'll do this part on my own."

"I'll wait here."

"It's hot and this could take awhile." He handed Shell the keys to his SUV and kissed her temple. "If it goes long, go home. I'm sure Collin would take me by your place to pick up my rig."

The door opened and Collin came out, followed by Hayden and Laken.

Collin punched his shoulder. "I should have known. Welcome to the clan, bro."

The brothers bumped fists.

With a sniffle, Laken flew into his arms. "I'm glad you're here. Don't mind Hayden, he's just concerned."

"Someone has to keep on top of the emotion." Hayden offered his hand. "But for the record, I believe you."

"No hard feelings." Ryler shook hands with his brother-in-law. "We'll do the blood test and put everyone's minds at ease. And for the record, I'm not here for the money. I'd just like to know my family."

Laken pulled away and gave his shoulder a squeeze. "I'm so thankful you're home."

"Me, too. I think."

"We're going to hang out in the family room if you'd like to join us, Shell." Collin opened the door.

"Thanks, but I'm fine here."

"Please. . ." Laken hesitated at the door. "Join us, Shell."

"I need some fresh air."

They went back inside, leaving only Shell still there for support.

"You should wait inside with them. They don't bite."

"Collin might. Go." She sat in a chair at the table on the porch. "I'll be right here."

He blew her a kiss and stepped back inside.

Sylvie met him in the entryway. "I was so afraid you wouldn't come back." She lunged into him with a hug.

His arms remained at his sides as a flurry of emotions warred within him.

"I'm sorry." A woman's confused voice came from his left.

Sylvie jerked away.

The maid stood in the dining area. "Excuse me, ma'am. Will you and your guest need anything?"

"Yes. I'd like a lovely glass of sweet tea. What about you, Ryler?"

"That sounds great." Maybe it would dislodge his tongue.

"We'll be in the den. And please tell Martin I still have guests." She tucked her hand in his elbow, as if they were old friends. They retraced their steps.

After shutting the double doors behind them, she sat on the couch. "Ryler, I want you to know we didn't throw you away. And Martin and I have never made any arrangements for what would happen if you didn't claim your inheritance." She patted the seat beside her. "Hayden loves this family and he's only watching out for us. Please don't hold it against him."

"He's protective of his family. I can respect that." He took a seat at the other end of the couch, clasping his hands in front of him. "Why did you give me away?"

"I was sixteen when I met Martin." A heavy sigh came from deep within her. "My family didn't like him because he came from the wrong side of the tracks, so to speak. You see, I come from a very well-to-do family. The kind of people who have mansions and hordes of servants. The kind of people who look down on the ordinary working class."

"They didn't want you involved with someone beneath you." Ryler frowned.

"They wouldn't even let me see him." Sylvie dabbed her eyes with a tissue, her bracelets jingling with each movement. "My parents threatened to cut me out of the family fortune if I didn't stop seeing him."

"But you didn't stop."

"No. Money had nothing to do with how Martin and I felt about each other. For the first time in my life, money didn't matter. We snuck around, stealing time together whenever we could. Many nights, I snuck out of my bedroom."

"And you got pregnant."

Sylvie's eyes closed. "Martin begged my parents to let him marry me. You can imagine how horrified they were. Not only had I been sneaking around behind their backs, but I was pregnant by a commoner. They whisked me off to Little Rock before anyone found out, hoping to save the family name. And they gave me two choices." Her voice broke. "Abortion or adoption."

A hard swallow couldn't dislodge the boulder in his throat.

A knock sounded at the door. "Your tea is ready, ma'am."

"Come in, Sharlene. Just leave the pitcher here and please see that we're not interrupted, except when the nurse arrives."

His father required a nurse?

"Yes, ma'am."

"Thank you, dear." Sylvie took a sip of her tea.

Ryler drained his glass and set it back on the coffee table.

"My, you were parched." She poured him another glass.

"I guess I should thank you for letting me live."

More tears filled her eyes. "I never considered anything else. I begged and pleaded, but my parents wouldn't budge. I chose life for you."

But without her and Martin in it.

"As soon as I turned eighteen, I came back to Searcy and married Martin. We wanted to find you, but my parents cut me off and we didn't have the money to hire a lawyer. We tried to get on with our lives, to move forward. We had Collin and then Laken, but there was always a Martin Jr.-sized hole in our family and in our hearts. But you know most of this from my letter."

Pressure built up in his chest, as if he might explode. "I never read the bulk of it. Just the beginning and your names."

"Why?" A frown creased her forehead.

"No offense, but I already had parents."

Her hand shook as she sipped her tea. "Finally, when you were six, my grandmother gave me my trust fund. We hired a lawyer, which led us to the children's home in Little Rock. But by then, you'd been adopted. The director assured us that you were in a good, stable Christian home."

Ryler swallowed.

"Martin and I cried and prayed over the decision and came to the conclusion that we couldn't rip you away from everything you'd ever known. Were you happy with your adoptive family?"

"My parents were awesome." Weird discussing his parents with his mother.

Her mouth twitched.

"Sorry. It must be odd for you to hear."

"No, I so hoped you were happy and loved. I'm glad you were. Do they know you found me?"

"They died shortly after I turned eighteen."

"Oh my." Sylvie clasped a hand over her mouth. "I'm so sorry. Did you know you were adopted?"

He nodded. Why go into the rest of it? "My aunt gave me the key after their funeral, but I wasn't emotionally ready to deal with any of it. She insisted I had to open the box by my thirtieth birthday."

Her chin quivered. "Since my parents set up trust funds for Laken and Collin, Martin and I used most of my inheritance to set up your trust. We put the pearls and the money in the safe deposit box and lived on my shares Grandmother left me in the family company. The director of the children's home promised to give the key to your"—Sylvie swallowed hard—"parents."

"Over the years, we longed for you. Sometimes my arms literally ached, I wanted to hold you so badly. I so wish we could have raised you. Everything would have been so different."

But he'd had a blessed childhood and didn't regret a moment of his time with the Grants. Meeting his biological mother still felt like a betrayal to them, yet it was what they wanted. Tangled emotions bubbled inside him.

"Instead, I coped by becoming a snooty busybody, while Martin started drinking and it steadily got worse and worse. He's better. As your thirtieth birthday approached, we hoped your adoptive parents would give you the trust fund papers. It gave us hope."

A loud gong. Ryler jumped as the grandfather clock gonged five more times. They'd been at this an hour. No wonder he was exhausted.

He gulped another swig of tea. "What do you mean, he's better? Is he getting treatment?"

"No, but for the first time ever, he's thinking about it." Sylvie pinched the pleat of her slacks between her thumb and forefinger. "But I think the possibility that you might come home made him realize he has a problem. He doesn't want you to see what losing you did to him. We've all been going through the motions of life, waiting for you."

Hearing her side of the story seemed so surreal. For twelve years, he'd hated the mother he thought had abandoned him. Only to learn she was forced into it. "You wanted me?"

"More than anything. From the moment I realized you were there." She pressed a hand to her stomach.

Ryler moved over beside her and hugged her. "You're not angry that I didn't tell you who I was sooner?"

"I'm just glad you're here. Welcome home, son." She trembled, sobbing into his shoulder.

A knock sounded. "Ma'am, the nurse is here."

"Give us a moment, then send her in." Sylvie reluctantly pulled away from him, dabbing at her eyes with a tissue.

"Are you ill?"

"I took the liberty of calling for a paternity test. Don't worry. It doesn't even require blood anymore. They stick some sort of swab in your mouth. And the results will be back in three days."

"Sounds painless enough."

She cupped his cheek in her hand. "For the record, I know exactly who you are, but this will ease everyone's concerns and it wouldn't hurt to have proof in hand in order to get your adoption records open so that you can claim the trust fund."

"But I don't want the money."

"Well, it really doesn't matter. It's your money. Now don't look a gift horse in the mouth, and prepare to be swabbed." She patted his cheek. "So handsome. Just like your father."

A tap sounded on the door.

"Come in."

The double doors opened and a nurse dressed in a scrub uniform entered.

—⁓—

Why had a nurse been summoned? Unease grew in the pit of Shell's stomach until she was as jittery as the sycamore leaves dropping from early June's heat-scorched trees. The rapidly darkening sky cooled the evening air only slightly.

The door opened and she jumped up.

Ryler looked as if the faint breeze could knock him over, but the hurt in his eyes had eased a bit.

"You okay?"

"I can't believe you're still here."

"I told you I'd stay."

He checked his watch. "But that was over an hour ago."

"Why did the nurse come?"

"Paternity test."

"Sylvie doesn't believe you."

"No, she believes me, but she wants to make sure everyone else does."

"So, you didn't see your father?"

"No. She's with him now, making up some excuse about strep throat so the nurse can get his DNA." He took her elbow and steered her down the steps. "Let's go."

"You're ready?"

"Sylvie wanted me to stay, but I need to process everything I learned." He ran a shaky hand through his hair. "I can't absorb anything else today."

"If you don't mind me driving your SUV, you can relax on the ride home."

"Just what the doctor ordered. I never knew life could be so exhausting."

"Are you and Sylvie okay?"

"We're good and the test will come back in three days. We're not telling anyone who I am until then." He entwined his fingers with hers.

"I've been wondering, will you go by Martin Jr. or Ryler?"

"Definitely Ryler."

"Good. You don't seem like Junior and Ryler is a really cool name."

As they climbed into his steamy vehicle, he punched the air-conditioning to blast off, and leaned his head back against the rest. "Thanks. I was named after my dad—the other one."

Shell concentrated on the traffic until they were out of the city limits, then stole a glance at him. Fast asleep.

—⁓—

Despite the previous evening's turmoil, Ryler had slept hard, and three cups of coffee later, he was still bleary-eyed.

*Why, Lord?* He gripped the steering wheel harder, navigating the hills between Romance and Rose Bud without even thinking. Why did he feel so guilty? Torn between two families?

The past didn't matter now. It couldn't be changed. He'd lean on God to see him through. And Shell.

She cared about him. For whatever reason, she couldn't bring herself to admit it, but he was almost certain she loved him.

Flipping his blinker on, he waited for the oncoming vehicles to pass, then turned into the bed-and-breakfast. It was beginning to look like one, with sparkling glass in every window, fresh balcony railing, and newly painted pristine siding. With the exterior complete, a few finishing touches inside remained.

The grounds were taking shape. Flowers and rosebushes flourished now, with only the front fountain and a few walkways left to finish.

His gaze rose to the balcony.

At the railing, Shell's eyes riveted on him.

A smile reached his soul. He waved, jumped out of the truck, and jogged to the big house.

Up the main staircase, he took two steps at a time.

At the landing on the second floor, she waited. "You okay?"

"I am. Sorry I conked out on you during the drive home last night." He cleared his throat and glanced at the workers nearby. The steady hum of power tools with hisses, ticks, and booms covered their conversation. But just in case, he steered her toward the swing.

She settled on the left. "You were emotionally exhausted. With good reason. I was worried you'd fall asleep driving to your place."

Claiming the other end of the swing, he kept his distance. Nothing to stir gossip among the carpenters. He'd once worsened her reputation, but from now on, he'd honor Shell, not sully her.

"I've never felt so torn in my life." Leaning forward, he cradled his head in his hands. "In a way, I wish I could have been raised by Martin and Sylvie, with my brother and sister. Sylvie would have been a better person and spared countless lives from gossip. And Martin might never have become an alcoholic."

"It's normal to feel that way."

"But it's a betrayal to my parents."

"It's not, Ryler." She rubbed his back in soothing circles. "It's a difficult situation. If Sylvie had given you up because she didn't want you, it would be different. But this way, you wouldn't be human if you didn't wonder 'what if?'"

He straightened up. "You're right. And I am oh, so human." Human enough that her touch electrified him. He leaned back, forcing her to move her hand and stop the havoc her comfort wreaked.

"Have you heard from any of your new family?"

"I'm having supper with Sylvie tonight at Colton's over in Searcy. Hayden called and apologized again for being suspicious of me."

"Your willingness to take the paternity test must have convinced him."

"Tomorrow night, I'm having dinner at Laken and Hayden's with Collin and Sylvie. I was hoping you'd join me."

"Absolutely not."

He frowned. "Why?"

"You need time with your family—alone. Especially with your mother."

"My mother." He ran his fingers through his hair. "It's weird. My mom died twelve years ago." And now, he had a new one.

"She won't try to replace your mother."

"I know, it's just weird. And even though I know who I am, Hayden said something that bothered me."

"What?"

"What if my papers got mixed up at the children's home? What if I'm not Martin Rothwell Kroft?"

Shell's eyebrow lifted. "Rothwell? Oh, I think you definitely look like a Rothwell. I think I'll call you that from now on."

He grinned. "Try it and I won't answer. It was Sylvie's maiden name. Seriously, what if?"

"You've got her eyes. The very thing that first attracted me to you. I mean—well, you knew I was attracted to you. Obviously."

Ryler captured her hand. "Come with me to dinner at Laken's tomorrow night."

"You're a big boy. You can handle it. Alone. And besides, we're having dinner with Grayson and Adrea the next night, so I'll see you then. When do you get the test results?"

"Friday afternoon." He'd need a distraction. "Let's take half the day off and run away. Do something distracting."

"Such as?" She scooted closer to him and laid her head against his shoulder.

He laughed. "Nothing sinful."

—⁂—

Grayson and Adrea's large home reminded Shell of the B&B, but it wasn't as old. Large rooms and high ceilings gave it a spacious feel, yet Adrea had kept it cozy with warm furnishings and family pictures. After supper, Grayson, Dayne, and Ryler cleaned the kitchen, while Shell followed her unlikely hostess to the living room for coffee.

Adrea settled on the couch, cradling a cooing Ashley on one shoulder. *Might as well get it over with.* Shell chose a chair across from Adrea and cleared her throat. "I've meant to tell you something. I'm sorry for hurting you." That sounded weak. *More like, I did my level best to destroy your life.*

Adrea closed her eyes for a moment. "It's all in the past."

"Yes, but I am sorry. I wasn't for a long time. In fact, I gloated about it." Wade had been a game to her. "I'd seen you with Wade around Searcy and you were the kind of woman I'd always wanted to be. Upstanding, moral, classy. . . I couldn't be, so I thought it was fun to steal your fiancé. I don't know how you can ever forgive me."

Adrea patted Ashley's back in a steady rhythm. "I was hurt by what happened and for a time, I was very bitter. But I turned it over to God. Once I did that, I got past the bitterness and got on with my life. Then, I could see your pain."

Shell shook her head. "Poor Wade got caught in the middle and I led him to his doom."

"Wade made his own decisions and you couldn't make him do anything he wasn't willing to do. I just wish he hadn't hurt himself or anyone else." Adrea stared off into space for a moment then readjusted Ashley on her other shoulder.

Oh, to hold Chance whenever she wanted. On a daily basis, part of her life. She hugged herself.

"So did Grayson answer all your questions about baptism?"

"Yes. I can't believe how my life is turning around."

Adrea smiled. "You have a new chance to be upstanding, moral, and classy. I never thought of myself as classy, but thanks for the compliment."

"Maybe the moral part, but I don't feel upstanding or classy."

"We need to work on your self-image." Adrea stood, grabbed her hand, and dragged her to a large gilded mirror. "Look at yourself. What do you see?"

Shell stared into her own blue eyes, at the natural-looking blond hair, the modest clothing. "I see a bimbo trying to pretend she's someone else."

"Oh Shell. You're beautiful. Inside and out. Look at yourself the way God sees you. You're innocent and precious in His sight. Made in His image, a daughter of God, and co-heir of Christ."

"I don't feel worthy."

"He sees you as worthy. When you humbled yourself to accept Jesus as your Savior, you became worthy. You have to let go of the past, Shell. He has."

Shell took a deep breath and closed her eyes. Let go of the past. If only she could.

———

Cleaning the kitchen reminded Ryler of helping his mother.

With a final swipe across the countertop, Grayson dumped the dishcloth into the sink and sat at the table. "Dayne, you may go play with Cocoa now."

"Thanks, Dad. See you later, Mr. Ryler." The boy launched out the back door and excited barks greeted him.

Ryler claimed the chair across from Grayson. "I'm having a problem, Preacher."

"What's that?"

"Well, you see, Shell and I, we knew each other before. And now things are different and. . ."

"Whatever you tell me goes no further, but"—Grayson grinned—"I'm no good at fill-in-the-blank."

Ryler sucked in a deep breath. "We had a relationship for about three months and we were. . .intimate. On more than one occasion. My fault completely." Not completely, but he'd gladly save what he could of Shell's rep by taking the blame. "We haven't"—he cleared his throat—"done anything since we ended up working together here, but we've had a couple of close calls."

"And now you're both saved, but you still want to be intimate."

"Well no, I mean not really. We know it's wrong. We don't want to."

"But your flesh does." Grayson cupped his chin in one hand, leaning an elbow on the table.

"Definitely. We've read verses together. Shell—she hasn't had much church, so I showed her some verses on fornication. She didn't even know what it meant."

"It's good that you're reading the Bible together." Grayson nodded. "A very good start. And it's awesome that you want to live differently now. It never ceases to amaze me how unmarried people who get saved in the morning can go to bed with their significant other that night, just like they did the night before."

"But the Bible says it's wrong."

"You're right. I don't know if they don't realize that, they don't care, or they don't think it applies to them because they've already been intimate. Anyway, I'm impressed with both of you."

Ryler ran his hand through his hair. "Every time she's near, I want to throw her over my shoulder like some Neanderthal, haul her up the stairs of the B&B, and love her for the rest of my days." Ryler winced. "I mean emotionally."

"Of course." Grayson laughed. "And physically."

"Sorry, that was probably too much information."

"It's okay. I'm human, too."

"But what do I do about it?"

"You keep coming to church, keep reading the Bible together, and pray about it." Grayson sipped his coffee. "Don't have dinner at her place or yours. Take her out in public. Don't stop somewhere secluded to sit in the car and talk after dark.

"Take her directly home, say good night to her under the porch light, and get out of Dodge. If you go to the park, don't get over behind that big sycamore tree. You know they call that Lover's Lair for a reason."

Exactly where he'd taken her. At least they'd read the Bible together there.

Ryler swallowed. "I feel like a teenager."

"Women can make you feel that way." Grayson steepled his fingertips. "Besides the physical, how do you feel about Shell? Do you care about her?"

A boulder lodged in his throat. "I love her."

"How does she feel about you?"

"I'm not sure. Sometimes I think she cares. It's almost like she's scared to really feel. Afraid she'll get hurt or something."

"If you love her, show her you're not going anywhere. Show her she can trust you. You have a commitment to God to treat her with respect and honor her. Let God give you the strength."

"I was hoping for an easy solution, like a chastity belt or something."

Grayson laughed. "If you try everything and you're still tempted then marry her."

"I'd love to, but I'm not sure I can get her to agree."

"In God's sight, you're already married."

"Huh?"

"You became one flesh."

"But I've—um—in that case, I've married a lot of women." Heat warmed Ryler's neck. "But I've never been legally married."

"And you can't make it right with all of them."

"Shell's the only woman I've ever loved."

"Then do right by her."

"I will."

"And save the staircase thing for your honeymoon, but don't throw her over your shoulder. Women don't like to be hauled. Go Clark Gable. Only, less forceful."

—⁓—

The drive to Shell's had been mostly silent, as if they both had so much on their minds they couldn't think of anything to say. He'd walked her to her door, but there'd been no physical contact and she'd scurried inside with a mumbled good night.

Ryler pulled into his driveway, his headlights illuminating a figure sitting on the porch steps.

Collin.

He killed the engine and stepped out of the SUV.

"Hey. I was hoping we could talk."

"About?"

"All this time, you knew. We're brothers. Why didn't you say anything?"

"I wanted to get to know you first." Ryler shrugged. "And I wasn't sure if you and Laken even knew about me. I didn't want to show up and blow your worlds apart." Been there.

"Admit it, you were scared of Mother."

Ryler chuckled. "She was kind of scary when I worked for her, and I'll admit at one point, I wanted to fade away, but I couldn't. Knowing I had a brother and sister, I couldn't just leave."

"I'm glad. I think, maybe this family can really be a family. For the first time." Collin ran a hand through his hair. "Growing up, I never measured up for Father. He was really tough on me."

"And Laken?"

"He ignored her."

Ryler frowned. Maybe he didn't want to get to know Martin Kroft after all.

"I know now, he was hurting. He could never look past the son he'd lost to see the son and daughter he had."

"I'm sorry."

"It's not your fault."

"It's not yours either."

"You're right." Collin stood. "I better get home. I promised I'd call Jill and tell her how it went with us."

Ryler's gaze narrowed. "She made you come over here."

"Jill doesn't make me do anything." Collin grinned. "Other than follow her around like a lovesick puppy. No, I came because I wanted to. I'm calling her because our semblance of a family blows her mind and she's worried about me."

Must be nice to have someone worry.

"Don't let what I said about Father scare you off." Collin offered his hand. "With you in the equation, maybe we can all heal. Together."

Hmm. Shake, hug, or just say *See ya*.

Collin hugged him and they clapped each other on the back.

Despite the manly stiffness of the embrace, Ryler's eyes filled with tears. Thank goodness it was dark and the porch light was burned out.

Pulling away, Collin gave him a final *thud* on the back and jogged across the street.

—∞—

Chair legs scraped against the tiled floor of the Rambler Café then quieted as the lunch crowd headed back to work. Shell's stomach fluttered, partly because of Ryler's nearness and partly from anxiety over the expected phone call.

Today was the day. The day they'd learn once and for all that Ryler was officially a Kroft. Officially out of her league.

Trying to concentrate on something other than him, she stared out the front window as numerous cars and pickup trucks pulled away.

The waitress brought strawberry cheesecake on one dish with a plump berry resting beside the generous slice.

"Could we have another plate?" Shell asked.

"This is fine." Ryler winked at her.

Her heart swooned.

"If I was twenty years younger, honey"—the waitress propped a hand on her hip—"I'd eat from the same dish with him."

Ryler's eyes widened as the waitress left them alone.

Shell stifled a giggle.

"What? You think I've got germs or something?"

"We're sitting on the same side of the table. If we eat out of the same dish, it becomes—"

"An official date. You okay with that?"

She wanted to be. If he wasn't a Kroft. If he could just stay Ryler Grant. "What did you and Grayson talk about last night?"

He blushed. Ryler Grant blushed. Or Martin Rothwell Kroft? Or whoever he was.

"Guy stuff. What did you and Adrea talk about?"

"Just girl stuff." She scooped up a bite of the cheesecake dripping with sauce.

Gently, he picked up the fruit by the cap. "Wait, do you want the strawberry?"

"Sure."

He held it in front of her mouth.

Her breath caught. "I can feed myself."

"Humor me."

As she bit the strawberry in two, his gaze stayed on her lips. Self-consciously, she chewed and swallowed. "I've never done anything so cheesy in my life."

"It may have been cheesy, but I really shouldn't have done that."

"Why?"

" 'Cause it made me want to kiss you, and we're in a public place."

She looked down and popped the bite of dessert dripping from her spoon into her mouth.

"Now you've got whipped cream on your lip, which makes me want to kiss you even more."

His cell vibrated.

Her gaze flew to his. "Answer it."

With trembling fingers, he slid the phone open. "Hello?"

Her heart launched into double-time as she watched his expression.

He swallowed hard. "We'll be right over."

"Sylvie? What did she say?"

# Chapter 8

S he said my father wants to meet me." Ryler's voice cracked.

Her stomach took a nosedive. *Don't let any disappointment show. Be happy for him.*

Wrapping her arms around his shoulders, she hugged him, even though the news sealed their fate. "Oh Ryler, I knew it, but it's nice to officially know it."

"Tell me about it."

"I can't go with you."

"You have to."

"You're meeting your father for the first time. You do not need me tagging along."

"I need all the moral support I can get. Please come. You can wait outside or in another room, but I need you there."

He needed her.

Her heart tumbled.

He didn't need her. He needed some debutante with blue blood to match his.

But for today, she'd be there for him. And tomorrow. She wouldn't think about tomorrow just yet.

She grabbed the bill and took his hand. "Let's go. We'll stop by the B&B and get my car in case you want to stay for a while."

—⁓—

Ryler gulped a deep breath, his hand hovering over the doorbell.

"It'll be fine." Shell rubbed her hand over his back. "You're about to meet a man who's longed to see you your entire life. He loves you."

"What if he's drunk?"

"I'm sure you've seen a few drunks in your life."

He paced away from the door, leaning one hand on the column of the porch. "What if he's angry that I didn't come forward sooner?"

"Relax." She hooked her hand through his elbow and propelled him back to the door. "Take another deep breath and ring the bell. Am I going to have to do it for you again?"

His finger moved toward the button but the door opened.

Sylvie greeted him with a tremulous smile and a hug. "I'm so glad you're here."

What to call her? Sylvie didn't sound right, but neither did Mom. Laken and Collin called her Mother. Mother? An outsider in his own family.

349

"Your father's waiting in the den. He hasn't had anything to drink today."

"Did you tell him I was coming?"

"No. I told him Laken and Collin were and he knows they'll only come if he doesn't drink."

Shell pushed him toward the double doors.

"You expect me to walk in and drop my bomb with no warning."

"Son, he's waited for this bomb for thirty years."

"Go on." Shell kissed his cheek. "I'll be here when you get back. Don't make him wait any longer."

Ryler sucked in another deep breath and strode toward the den.

"Shell, everyone else is in the family room, if you'd like to join them. Once Martin and Ryler have had some time together, we'll see you there."

Needing extra strength, he turned to face her.

She flashed him a brave smile.

Ryler pulled the double doors open.

Martin Kroft sat on the white sofa. Tall and thin, with stooped shoulders and shaky hands. Yellow-white hair, sallow skin, dark circles sank under dim blue eyes.

"Do I know you, young man?"

"Not yet, sir."

"You remind me of someone." He shook a finger at Ryler then pressed a trembly hand against his lips. "My father. You remind me of my father when he was young. The spitting image. Sylvie?"

"Martin"—with a quiver in her voice, Sylvie took Ryler's arm and propelled him forward—"this is our son."

The older man's eyes widened and a sob escaped him. "How did you find. . . ?" He threw his arms open wide.

Ryler didn't need another father. He already had one. But somehow he felt drawn to the beckoning arms.

He sat beside Martin Kroft on the couch and quivery arms encircled him. Sobs echoed in his ears and pressure welled inside his chest. A low moan escaped him as Sylvie wrapped her arms around them both, her tears soaking into Ryler's shoulder.

"You're home. My boy is home. I'm so sorry. I didn't want you to see me like this."

—⁂—

The double doors opened and Shell jumped up, clasping her hands in front of her, then behind her.

Ryler came out first. His red-rimmed eyes tore at her.

"Thanks for waiting." He reached for her hand.

Sylvie latched on to his other arm as if he might get away.

"You okay?"

"Sylvie, can you give us a minute? I promise I won't leave."

Sylvie let go of him. "I guess I really should see about Martin. It's been an emotional afternoon. Especially for him. You two talk here and maybe when he's ready, we can all join the others together."

"You okay?" Shell repeated as the double doors closed.

"I think so. He cried like a baby, so I did, too."

She cupped his cheek. "How is he?"

"He's a shell of what he should be. The drinking has taken a toll on him."

"Maybe having you here will give him incentive to get help."

"Maybe. I can't tell you how much I appreciate you being here." He brushed a soft kiss across her lips and pulled her into his arms.

The double doors opened and they jerked away from each other.

"Well, who do we have here?" an unfamiliar voice asked.

Martin Kroft had all of Ryler's height, but none of the muscle. Rail thin, with sickly yellow skin and faded blue eyes. But he'd once been a handsome man.

"This is Shell Evans."

"Your lady?"

Ryler grinned. "I'd like her to be. Right now, just call us friends, for her peace of mind."

"Nice to meet you, Shell." He extended a shaky hand toward her.

He needed a drink. Bad. "Nice to meet you, sir."

"Through here." Sylvie led the way.

Two taupe couches and several chairs furnished the large family room. A huge TV dwarfed the central wall. Soft gold walls, hardwood floors with a glossy sheen, and a large area rug with splashes of red gave the room a cozy feel despite its size.

Jill hovered near Collin, as if she felt as out of place as Shell did. The total-honesty policy must include news of new brothers.

"Ryler, welcome to the family." Hayden offered his hand. "Sorry about all that other stuff."

"So, now that we have proof"—Laken frowned—"will Ryler still have to petition the court to open his adoption records?"

"Why?" Ryler shrugged.

"To claim your trust fund, of course." Collin took a sip of his tea.

Trust fund? Ryler had never said anything about a trust fund.

"Ahem." Hayden coughed. "Do we need to get into this now?"

"Shell and Jill are close enough to family." Laken covered her mouth with one hand. "I do hope Collin told you about his trust fund, Jill."

"He did." Jill threaded her fingers through Collin's. "He's learning about not keeping secrets."

Apparently, Ryler hadn't.

351

"I couldn't ask her to marry me without telling her about the trust fund." Collin squeezed Jill's hand. "Might as well reveal our warts and all, so she'll know what she's getting into."

"I didn't come here for money." Ryler's fists clenched.

Laken touched his arm. "That's not what I meant."

"No one thinks you're here for money, son." Sylvie latched on to his arm again. "You could have petitioned the court and claimed your inheritance without contacting us. But you must claim it. Your father and I want you to have the money."

But if Shell kept hanging around, everyone would think she only wanted the money.

"What if I don't claim it?"

Martin shrugged. "I guess if you don't, it'll eventually go to the state. But it's your money, son."

"Number one, money's never been important to me. Number two, if I claim the money, I feel like it will always cause doubts. Someone will always wonder if that's all I came for."

"Only if you take the money and run." Martin took a glass Laken offered. With his trembling, he almost dropped it. He drained it and set it on the coffee table.

"And Ryler wouldn't do that." Sylvie patted his arm.

"If I leave Romance, I won't take a dime with me."

"See. But you won't be leaving Romance, son. Unless you want to move to Searcy. Your father and I couldn't bear to lose you again."

"Listen, I don't know what my plans are right now. It's been a long day, so I think Shell and I should be going. We both have an early day tomorrow."

"Can you have supper with us tomorrow night? Just Martin and me?" Anxiety shone in Sylvie's eyes.

"Probably." He patted her arm. "I'm not going anywhere. I'll call you."

Sylvie nibbled on the inside of her lip and gave a slight nod.

Martin hugged him again.

He ushered Shell through the house and headed to their separate vehicles.

"I wish we'd ridden together."

"I thought you might want to stay longer and you probably should." Hurt and disappointment warred within her. "It's kind of sweet the way Sylvie clings to you."

"And suffocating." He opened her car door for her.

"She's got a lifetime to make up for." She positioned the door between them. "So, did you plan to tell me about the trust fund?"

"Eventually." He grinned. "I'm still getting used to the idea of it."

"Your family doesn't approve of me."

"Why would you think that?"

"They think I'm a gold digger, just like my mother."

"They probably don't even know your mother." His lips brushed hers. "Sylvie loves you. I love you, Shell."

Tears burned her eyes. Words she'd never heard before. Words she could get used to. But could he really love "trailer trash," as the kids in school had called her? Until her mother had found rich men to upgrade their living status.

"Trust me, everyone in Searcy knows my mother and her penchant for taking up with rich men and milking all she could from them. It was only after her youth faded that she turned to prostitution and drugs."

"You don't seem to be hurting for money, Shell." He gestured toward her vehicle. "You drive a nice, late-model sports car, you've worked for Darrell for years, and I imagine he pays you well for your expertise. Why would anyone worry about you wanting my trust fund? I haven't even claimed it yet, and I'm not sure I will."

"I just think you should have told me about it." Sarcasm dripped from her tone as she settled in her car and fastened the seat belt. "Since you love me and all."

"Maybe"—his teeth clenched—"I need you to admit you love me back before I'm willing to share everything with you."

She started the engine and gunned it. That was something she wasn't willing to admit. If she admitted she loved him, then she'd have to try to keep up with the Joneses. And she'd learned long ago, she couldn't. Shell Evans wasn't of the same ilk.

—⁓—

The phone rang for the eighth time. Pacing his kitchen, Ryler ran his hand through his hair. No cool ringtone. No-nonsense ringing, like Shell. *Come on, pick up.*

Would she even answer? He didn't like the way she'd left.

Finally, he'd blurted out his feelings for her. But she hadn't returned the sentiment.

"Hello?"

"Shell, I'm so glad I caught you. Are you going to Conway this weekend?"

"I'm packing now."

"Will you be back for church Sunday?"

"I was planning to go with Savannah there. Why?"

"Laken called to make sure I'd be at church Sunday. Martin's coming." Her gasp echoed over the handset. "Wow."

"Tell me about it. Laken said he hasn't gone since she was eleven." He paced into the living room. "I was hoping you'd be there."

"I'll come back Saturday night."

"Good. I feel a lot more comfortable with you than I do with them."

"You're one of them, Ryler. Let that sink into your stubborn brain."

"I'm trying. Thanks, Shell. Sorry to cut your time with Chance short."

"It's okay. Three more weeks and I'll be back home with him anyway."

Three weeks. Only three more weeks of working with her, seeing her daily. He couldn't let her leave him. Not again.

"I'll see you Sunday then. Safe trip." He wanted to say he loved her, but he didn't want to scare her any further away.

At least she didn't sound mad. But distant. As if, in her mind, she was already gone.

He'd just have to change her mind.

Something clattered at the front door. Another clatter.

Ryler frowned and hurried to open the door.

Brady sat beside the porch, with a basketball in his lap and a crushed aluminum can poised in his fist. "Hey."

"Hey." Ryler's chest felt all fuzzy.

"Dad says you're my uncle."

"It's true."

"I thought we might play some basketball, if you have time."

Ryler nodded. "You're on."

"I'm playing basketball with Uncle Ryler," Brady called.

*Uncle Ryler.* His heart warmed. He glanced across the road.

Collin waved then went inside.

"So, Dad says you just found out about us." Brady swished the ball through the hoop.

Ryler jogged to rebound. "A few months back."

"I think Dad wishes you'd grown up with him and Aunt Laken."

"What gives you that idea?" Ryler lobbed the ball back to Brady.

"I heard him talking to Aunt Laken on the phone, about how everything would have been different if they'd found you sooner. Kind of like if my dad had learned about me sooner."

"I guess so."

"Sometimes I wonder if I'd have always lived with Dad, would I be able to walk?" Brady swallowed hard. "When I was little, I ran out and tried to get in the truck to go to work with Hayden and he backed into me."

Ryler stifled a gasp.

"That probably wouldn't have happened if I'd lived with Dad. But then I think about how God's got it all worked out and we just have to trust Him." Brady swished the ball through the hoop again.

"If I'd lived with Dad, he might have been so sad over Mom, he couldn't have taken care of me good. I might have wandered into the road and died. Then he'd have felt guilty and maybe he couldn't have dealt with guilt the way Hayden has. Maybe if you'd always lived with Mimi and Poppa, your other parents would have been really sad and lonely. And maybe Poppa would've still started drinking, but he wouldn't have ever had a reason to stop."

"How'd you get so smart?"

"I heard Pastor Grayson preach about it once. He said when bad things happen, that God might be saving us from something worse. Like maybe his first wife died the way she did because she was going to get cancer or something and suffer a lot. I thought it made sense."

"It makes a lot of sense." Maybe Shell hadn't been together enough to raise Chance. Maybe some jerk she'd dated would have mistreated her innocent son. Maybe Shell had done the best thing she could at the time.

———

Martin Kroft Sr. had kept his promise. Sunday morning, Shell sat surrounded by Ryler's entire family.

Outnumbered and outclassed.

As Grayson finished his sermon, the music began.

Ryler, Laken, and Collin went to the altar first. In a huddle, they knelt as Shell dabbed at her eyes. Sylvie stepped into the aisle and Martin followed her. Brady rolled himself down the aisle, as well. A few others knelt.

As the song wound down, only the Krofts were still at the altar, with Grayson and Martin whispering back and forth. They all stood and faced the congregation.

Collin crooked his finger at Jill, who joined him and Hayden went up to stand with Laken. Ryler gestured to Shell.

*Me? You want me up there with you?* She shook her head, quick and sharp. He gestured again.

Shell rolled her eyes and went to stand with him.

His arm came around her waist.

"The Krofts have a new family member they'd like you to meet." When he finished speaking, Grayson sat in one of the chairs on the stage.

Sylvie stepped to the microphone. "Several months ago, I asked everyone to pray for Martin and me to find our oldest son. Your prayers worked." Sylvie's voice quivered as she took Ryler's hand. "This is our son, Ryler Grant."

Excited gasps and whispers moved through the crowd.

Martin Sr. stepped up beside them. "Hello, everyone, I'm Martin Kroft, and I'm an alcoholic."

Tears coursed down Sylvie's cheeks and Laken hugged her father.

Shell wiped her eyes with the back of her hand.

"All these years I've drank to get over losing our son, and in the process, I lost the two children I already had. I'm sorry." Martin's watery gaze locked on Collin. "I want to stop. I want to live. I want to get to know my kids. All of them."

Collin moved closer and put his arm around Martin's shoulders.

Sniffles from the crowd filled the silence. Shell scanned the faces. Not a dry eye in the house, except for a few oblivious children.

"Please pray for me." Martin started back to his pew, flanked by his family.

Shell bypassed the pew and went straight to the ladies' room. Staring in the mirror, she imagined how out of place she'd been up there. Laken with inner kindness shining from her eyes. Collin, a work in progress, but changing. Sylvie, a new creature—and Martin on the verge of a new life. Yet, even after all the years Martin and Sylvie had been together, he obviously didn't fit.

Laken, Collin, Sylvie. They were all flawed, but their purebred class oozed from every pore. All that oozed from Shell was wrong-side-of-the-tracks mutt.

The door opened and an older woman with hair too dark for her age came in and offered her hand. "Oh, I wanted to meet you, Shelly. I've heard so much about you. I'm Doreen Hughes." Black penciled eyebrows scrunched together and her entire face puckered like she'd sucked on a lemon. "Am I to understand you're dating Sylvie's son?"

"We're just friends. And my name is Shell, not Shelly. Excuse me." Shell hurried out, managed to sidestep the straggling crowd, and fled outside to freedom.

—⁓—

Ryler jogged to catch up with her. Though Shell had a good head start, her heels slowed her progress. "Shell."

Halfway down the long drive of the B&B, she stopped. With a big sigh, she turned to face him.

"What?"

"You okay?"

"Fine."

"We're all going to lunch at the folks' house in Searcy. Want to come?"

"No, you go with your family."

"I feel kind of out of place with them."

"Trust me, you're not. You fit right in. It's in your blood."

"I was hoping you'd come with me."

"You don't need me tagging along, Ryler. Just go. Have a good time with your family. I'm going to Conway to spend the rest of the day with Chance, anyway."

"When do I get to meet him?"

"You don't." There was something final in her eyes.

"You're coming back, aren't you?"

"This place isn't finished, is it?" Sarcasm tinged her voice as she gestured toward the mess in the front yard. "I think I'll spend the night, though, and come back early in the morning."

"Are we okay?"

"We, as in. . . ?"

"We, as in us. I'm trying to build a relationship with you, Shell."

"We've got a lot going on right now." Her eyes were too shiny. "You're getting to know a whole new family. And I—I just want to get home to Chance. Besides, I've got a grand opening bash to plan.

"In two weeks this job will be done. Until then, I can't think about much else. Let's see how it goes then. Maybe absence won't make the heart grow fonder."

"So you're basically saying you don't want to see me."

She rolled her eyes. "I'm saying, you need to spend time with your new-found family and I need to spend time with my son and party planning. That doesn't leave much time for anything else."

"I'll make time."

"Not now, Ryler. Let's concentrate on getting this job finished." She turned away and ran toward her apartment.

Finish the job so she could walk out of his life again. He couldn't let her do it.

—⁂—

Ryler mentally patted himself on the back for giving his helper the day off with only a week left before the grand opening. He snuck a glance at Shell crawling around on her hands and knees, with dirt on her nose, looking way too cute.

With a grin, he flipped a trowel of dirt on her back.

Shell stiffened then turned and flung a fistful in his face.

Retaliation came as he smeared another handful down her shoulder.

Her world-weary sigh grated on his nerves.

"Ryler, please. We've got work to do."

He tackled her and rolled her over, poised with a handful over her mouth. Blue eyes pleaded. "We need to finish this job."

He dropped the dirt on the ground. "You've got something on your nose." As he wiped the smear away, more than anything, he wanted to kiss her. His gaze locked on her lips.

# Chapter 9

Good thing the workers are all inside." Pushing away from him, she hurried to put some distance between them. "Truce."

Her rejection sliced through him.

"Except this nice, plump earthworm would look great in your hair."

She screamed, jumped up, and ran.

"I was kidding."

"Well, it's not funny."

"You're afraid of earthworms."

"Not really afraid of them. They're just so"—she shivered—"so yucky."

He laughed and shoved the worm in her direction again.

Though she was ten feet away from him, she did a heebie-jeebie dance. "Stop it."

"Ryler, really." Sylvie's tone reprimanded. "Stop torturing the poor girl."

His mother stood with Helen Fenwick.

What to call her? Mother? Mom? "Afternoon, Sylvie."

Shell's eyes widened.

"I'm sure you remember Helen. Helen, my son Ryler."

"Nice to meet you, ma'am. I'd offer a handshake, but. . ." Ryler swiped his hands together.

"I was at the floral shop, where Helen works part-time, this morning. Adrea sent her over to discuss the arrangements for the grand opening and I thought I'd join her to see how things were coming here." Sylvie looked as if she might pounce on him with a hug, despite the grime.

"I can't." Shell rubbed shaky hands down her thighs. "Ryler's helper isn't here today, so I have to help him. And besides, I'm a mess."

"Heavens, Ryler, what did you do, roll her in the dirt?"

He winked at Shell. "I can spare you for a bit." But not for long. Too long and he'd miss her. But he knew she needed to make peace with Helen.

With a hard swallow, Shell clapped her hands together. "Maybe, if Helen can excuse my appearance, I could spare an hour or so."

"Oh, it won't take nearly that long, dear, and a little dirt never hurt anything. Adrea wanted me to check each room's size, so we can scale the arrangements to fit."

—⁓—

Tough choice. Shell ground her back teeth together. Deal with Ryler or Wade's mother?

"I'll stay here and keep Ryler company." Sylvie perched on a white iron bench, well away from the dirt.

Great. Alone with Wade's mother. Shell wasn't sure she'd made the right decision as she led Helen to the house.

"There are a lot of stairs." Shell slowed her pace to match Helen's. "Are you sure you'll be all right?"

"I'm fine." Helen leaned into her cane with each step. "The exercise will be good for me. You know, I never had a bit of trouble with arthritis until I broke this hip."

Did Helen know she'd gotten pregnant? Did she think there had been an abortion? A miscarriage? Whatever Helen thought, Chance's grandmother was oblivious to his existence.

"Thank you for coming to the funeral."

Shell's breath caught. "You seem okay."

"I lean on Jesus and I have peace about where Wade is." Helen grasped Shell's arm as they stepped inside the house.

"When did Wade become a Christian?"

"About the time he went into rehab and then had that long stretch of sobriety."

They stopped in the living room. "Oh my, Shell, you've done wonders with this place. It's lovely."

"Thank you." A sense of accomplishment put a real smile on her face.

"I know what you're thinking."

"You do?"

"You're wondering how I can believe Wade is in heaven after all the bad things he did."

"Well—"

"God says, 'I will never leave thee, nor forsake thee.' That's in Hebrews 13:5. We might turn our backs on Him, but He's faithful. And besides, in the end, Wade made peace with God. I can't tell you how I've clung to that. He was drunk and not in his right mind when he. . ."

"I'm glad you're okay. You've been through a lot."

"Sometimes, I feel alone, but God reminds me I've got Him, my church, and countless friends."

*And a grandson you don't know about.*

Helen squeezed her arm. "I'm excited about the grand opening. This project will be so much fun."

Shell's heart twisted with a mix of emotions. After the grand opening, Shell would go home. Home to Chance. Away from Ryler. For good.

—⁓—

Ryler took his ball cap off and threw it onto his truck seat. Scrubbing his hand over his curls, he tried to erase the ring of flattened hair around his head a full day of work caused. No use, he plopped the hat back on. He probably should wait and stop by the RoZark Hills Roasterie before work in the morning, but his cupboard was bare. No coffee. He couldn't go home without it. And he'd already placed his order earlier in the day.

He pulled in and parked next to a familiar dark maroon Cadillac. Darrell hadn't mentioned he'd be in town today. Climbing out of his truck, he glanced down at his dirt-and-grass-streaked jeans. His work boots were caked in mud. They might not let him in. He stomped both feet and tried to dust some of the grime from his clothing.

Surely they'd forgive a guy suffering from coffee withdrawals for stopping in straight from work.

The bell jingled above the door as he opened it. He closed his eyes and inhaled the coffee aroma, almost tasting a savory cup in the air.

The owner was talking to someone, so Ryler went to the shelf with his favorite chocolate-covered coffee beans. Five of these babies and the top of his head buzzed. He picked his favorite, white chocolate.

"Now, our Blueberry Cobbler blend would be a nice morning coffee for your guests."

"Oh, that sounds heavenly."

Shell's voice.

Ryler stiffened.

Peering around the silver shelf loaded with fancy coffee cups and pots, he spotted her. With Darrell. Standing too close to her.

He could quietly back out the door, but the bell would ring and she'd probably already seen him.

"Once the B&B opens, Shell will have full authority to try new blends, but I'd like something more—"

"Darrell means the new manager he's going to hire *any day now* will have full authority. I won't be here."

Darrell spotted him and rolled his eyes. "Don't you think we need something more manly for the B&B? Would you want blueberry cobbler coffee?"

Ryler cleared his throat. "I'm a Columbian kind of guy, myself."

"We have your order ready. One pound of Columbian La Ladera. I'll be right with you."

"Now, that sounds like coffee." Darrell surveyed the list of flavors.

"That would be a nice evening coffee. Not too heavy, but rich flavor with a hint of caramel," the wife half of the owner team said as she grinned at Ryler. "The new B&B is going to serve our coffee."

"They won't regret it. Best coffee in the state."

"Did you know her husband set up the first Starbucks factory in New York?" Darrell touched Shell's elbow.

Ryler's breath stalled. "I'll come back. I'm kind of embarrassed coming in here looking like this anyway."

"Oh, you're fine." The owner waved a carefree hand at him.

"Here, ring him up real quick." Darrell stepped aside, linking his arm with Shell's. "No sense in you coming back."

Shell never even looked at him as Ryler handed the owner a ten and a five and grabbed his treats. "Keep the change."

"You sure? Don't you want a bag?"

"No, I'm fine. Thanks." Ryler rushed out and jumped into his truck.

So why was she with Darrell? And why wasn't Darrell's wife with him? Why did it require Shell *and* Darrell to choose coffee for the B&B?

———

Finally, the grand opening.

Standing on her haven, the balcony, Shell took deep breaths.

The orchestra played from the pristine lawn in front of the miniature Romance Waterfalls. The stringed instruments, backed by trickling water, soothed her frayed nerves.

All evening, she'd avoided Ryler. Since Darrell still hadn't hired a manager, she'd tag-teamed with Eva as they'd answered question after question, given tour after tour, and greeted guest after guest.

She'd even given tours of the apartment. Officially the honeymoon suite now, as all of her things were already packed.

The soft breeze ruffled the sheer overlay of her pale blue dress. Since many on the guest list were from Searcy, countless wide-eyed guests had stared at her, as if they didn't know she could clean up so well. As if they couldn't imagine Wade Fenwick's floozy had achieved such an accomplishment as the immaculate Rose Bud Bed & Breakfast.

"There you are." Darrell's voice came from behind her.

She turned to face him and smiled at an older, well-to-do couple beside him.

"Mr. and Mrs. Morris Vanderhaven, meet Shell Evans, the mastermind behind this renovation project."

Shell's mouth went dry. The last time she'd seen Mr. Vanderhaven, she was fifteen and he'd been in her mother's bed.

Now, he looked as if he might pass out.

"The Vanderhavens live in Searcy, and Morris is the president of Home Town Bank."

Might as well put the old philanderer's mind at ease.

Shell mustered up a smile and offered her hand. "So nice to meet you both."

"This place is absolutely gorgeous." Mrs. Vanderhaven's natural Southern belle drawl warmed Shell's heart.

Such a sweet lady didn't deserve an unfaithful husband.

"Morris, I'd love to spend our next anniversary here."

Mr. Vanderhaven cleared his throat. "Well, um, we'll see."

# ARKANSAS WEDDINGS

"I wish I could stay here, too." Shell clutched the railing. "But the renovation project is finished, so I'll be going back to the apartments I manage in Conway."

Mr. Vanderhaven visibly relaxed. "Perhaps we could make arrangements to stay here."

"The clerks are already in the lobby taking reservations."

"Oh, let's hurry." Mrs. Vanderhaven led her anxious husband through the door. "I want one of these two rooms close to the balcony."

"I'll be right there." Darrell's eyebrows drew together. "What was that about?"

"Trust me, you don't want to know."

"You okay?" He put a brotherly arm around her shoulders.

"A little worse for wear."

A series of loud pops made her jump. Fireworks of every color streaked through the sky.

"We should have put this shindig off another two weeks and scheduled it for the Fourth of July."

"I couldn't take another two weeks, and besides, it's on a Thursday this year. We couldn't have a grand opening on a Thursday."

"You made this place what I always knew it could be, and tomorrow you can go home to Chance." He gave her arm a squeeze. "I sure wish my wonderful wife didn't have to commute back and forth to run this place."

Shell sighed. "You're not guilting me into staying. All you have to do is hire someone."

"None of the applicants were right, since the perfect manager refused to apply," he said pointedly. "I better go make sure Mrs. Vanderhaven gets the exact room she wants. You coming? I still need you to help Eva work the crowd."

"In a minute." Closing her eyes, Shell inhaled the honeysuckle scent of the evening air as Darrell's footsteps faded away.

"Shell Evans." A male voice sliced through her peace.

She turned around.

Pete Callaway stood in the doorway. Pete Callaway, her first crush. The pimple-faced senior who'd taken her virginity during her sophomore year, then tossed her aside for his next conquest a few months later. The pimples were gone, but he was still gangly, all legs, and painfully thin.

"Hi, Pete." Nary a quiver in her voice. She mentally patted herself on the back.

"I couldn't believe my eyes when I looked up here and saw you standing at the railing. You look great. Really great." His gaze wandered slowly over every inch of her. "I haven't seen you since you were dating Wade."

She bit down the bitter revulsion threatening to rise up in her throat. What had she ever seen in him?

"I guess you don't live around here." She stepped back toward the railing.

362

"Everyone knew I was here within a week of my arrival."

"I'm still in Romance. My numerous rental properties keep me really busy." His chest puffed up as he spoke.

Two old houses. Guess that was numerous to him. "Well, I better get back to my guests." She tried to slip past him.

He grabbed her wrist. "Now don't run off just yet. Maybe we could have coffee. Or *something*."

Forcing herself not to cringe, she smiled. "No thank you."

"We could get reacquainted, if you know what I mean." Alcohol soured his breath, even though Grace was only serving tea and coffee.

"I know exactly what you mean." She tried to pull her wrist away, but he held fast. "And I'm not interested."

"Oh come on, Shell. The apple doesn't fall far from the tree."

Despite his painful grip, she managed to jerk her arm free.

"Keep your hands off her." Ryler's steely tone came from the doorway.

Pete whirled around. Both eyebrows rose. "Ryler Grant, isn't it? I was just welcoming Shell back to the area. Nice to see you here."

"Is it?"

"I better be getting back to the party." Pete slunk through the door.

She turned away from Ryler and worked at keeping her voice steady. "This turned into quite the bash. I was hoping for a hundred guests, but I think it's more like two. Good thing I ordered extra food."

Footsteps closed in on her. "You okay?" His voice came from just behind her. "Fine."

He joined her at the railing. Tenderly, he caught her reddened wrist and inspected the marks. "I take it you know my landlord."

She sighed, not wanting to get into it, yet knowing Ryler wouldn't let it rest. "Remember the high school boyfriend Collin tried to steal me away from?"

"Pete?" He let go of her. "A real winner."

"The place looks great, doesn't it? We did a great job."

"We make a great team." His breath stirred the hair at the crown of her head.

She shivered.

"What now?"

"You find another job. I go back to Conway."

"But we make a great team."

She shrugged. "Who knows? We might work together again someday."

Gently gripping her shoulders, Ryler turned her to face him. "That's not what I meant, Shell. I want a future with you."

The brown pinstripe suit accentuated his broad shoulders and the moss-colored shirt mirrored his eyes. The evening breeze blew his dark chocolate waves.

Determination slipping, her gaze dropped to his chest. "My future is in Conway."

"Mine could be, too. I bet there's lots of landscaping jobs there."

"No. Your future is here—with your family."

"I love you, Shell." He tipped her chin up, until her gaze met his.

Wanting to press her cheek into his palm, her throat constricted. She swallowed hard, biting back the reciprocated words that threatened to tumble out. "It can't work. We're too different."

"You're more like me than anyone I've ever known. It's what initially drew me to you. We were both broken and used. Now we're Christians, healing and changing. Let's heal and change together."

"You're blue-blooded Kroft and I'm—"

"You're the most beautiful woman I've ever known, inside and out."

"My mother prostituted herself, Ryler."

"But that has nothing to do with who you are."

"Haven't you ever heard 'the apple doesn't fall far from the tree'? Even if I could forget my past, these high-class citizens can't. I see it in their eyes every time they look at me." She scanned the crowd below: Doreen Hughes, the Vanderhavens, and even Pete Callaway. She shuddered. *Do you know who her mother is?*

"You're imagining things."

She closed her eyes. "You saw Pete. You know what he wanted—what he expected—from me. I can't stay here and get away from that."

"Shell, stop it and listen to me. I want to marry you. I want us to raise Chance. Here or in Conway, wherever you want. I want us to build a family together, maybe even have kids of our own someday."

"I'll never bring my son to this self-righteous town." *And I'll never let him down by telling him I'm his mother.*

"Shell," Darrell called.

Ryler's hands dropped to his sides.

She spotted her boss below the balcony. "I'll be right there."

"Sorry to interrupt, Ryler, but I need my right-hand gal down here."

"Maybe I was wrong about you." Ryler shook his head. "Maybe you are like your mother. Maybe you're shirking your responsibility. Maybe you're not raising your son so you can be free. Free to collect hearts you're unwilling to commit to."

"What's that supposed to mean?"

"From the moment I've known you, there's been only one constant in your life."

She shrugged, waiting for him to clue her in.

"Darrell. I saw him up here with you and whenever he beckons, you run to his side."

"I'm supposed to be working tonight." Shell bristled. "And Darrell is one of the finest men I've ever known."

"Oh yeah, then why is he cheating on his wife with you?" He turned away. "You don't care about anyone but yourself. At least my mother was forced to give me up."

Ryler stalked through the door.

On jelly legs, Shell scurried to the porch swing. Doubled over, she covered her face with both hands. Sobs shook her shoulders.

———

Ryler stormed down the stairs and pushed through the crowd.

He'd seen Darrell up there with her, his arm around her. How could he have been so stupid? Obviously, it had been Darrell all along. Shell didn't want a commitment and Darrell couldn't commit. They were perfect for each other.

Shell was a Christian now, but she didn't have a clue about right and wrong. Maybe she was one of those Grayson spoke about. Maybe she thought the rules didn't apply to her. Maybe she'd just been playing him and hadn't accepted Christ at all.

"Ryler," Pastor Grayson called. "This is Doreen Hughes. She was just asking me who did the landscaping."

His gaze rested on the multitude of roses in the garden surrounding the Romance waterfall replica, but the beauty failed to soothe the turmoil roiling within him.

"I'm sorry, I'm not feeling well." Ignoring the older woman, he headed for his SUV, jumped in, and started the engine. The car next to him had parked crooked. With a heavy sigh, he eased back and forth several times before he could safely get out of the slot. Finally free, he stomped the gas and roared down the long drive, spinning gravel as he careened onto the highway.

# Chapter 10

Shell toured the house one last time. Her eyes, still puffy from last night's sobs, felt as heavy as her heart. A small reservation desk had been situated in part of the entry. The wood floors and plank walls gleamed.

Opening the door to the restroom behind the desk, she scanned the flawless tile surrounding the antique commode and pedestal sink. The downstairs bedroom was all done in sage and cream with shimmery, satin curtains. Plenty of closet space left beside the new bathroom.

Cutting through the entry, she stepped into the living room and ran her hand over the wall. Smooth as glass. The antique camelback couch, wingback chairs, and a gold chaise lounge facing the ancient fireplace, with the soot marks gone.

Thick tapestry curtains in gold, sage, and red paisley graced each window in the room. The wainscot in the kitchen and dining room was a pristine white. Billowy, lacy white curtains provided the bay window a bit of privacy, but still let plenty of light in. New antique-look fixtures gave the kitchen a cozy feel.

The narrow staircase up to the former servants' quarters hadn't been widened, but the steps had been, making the climb a bit easier. Both rooms done in gold and red had a rich, royal feel to them. The new bathroom was nice and roomy, still leaving plenty of closet.

She descended the stairs and retraced her path to the main staircase. The paneling in the upstairs landing had been removed and the nail holes painstakingly filled. The stairway up to the attic had been widened. This bedroom was her favorite. All done in cream and gold with velvet curtains, tasseled tiebacks, and molded valances. The iron bed frame was burnished umber with streaks of gold in the metal.

The bedroom on the left of the landing was red and cream with moiré curtains and swag valances. The bedroom on the right used the same fabrics in terra cotta and cream. Each bathroom continued the soothing color combination of each distinct room decor.

Perfect. Though modern, the entire place looked as if she'd stepped back in time. She descended the stairs and stepped outside. Closing the door with a final *thud*, she turned the knob to make sure it locked.

Head held high, she strode to her car and started the engine. The waterfall painting tugged at her, but it held too many memories of Ryler. Better to leave it. Pulling out of the drive, she turned toward Conway for the final time.

Home to Chance. Away from Ryler. Tears rimmed her lashes as the miles multiplied behind her.

—∞—

Chance played at Shell's feet, surrounded by sturdy, plastic trucks, cars, and tractors. "Vroom, vroom." His chunky little fingers launched a hot rod sailing across the floor and into her foot. He giggled and did it again.

She should be happy. This is where she'd wanted to be for months. With Chance.

But at the price of Ryler.

How could he think such things of her? Her eyes stung and she blinked several times. She'd gotten saved when he had. And even before that, she'd done lots of things she wasn't proud of, but she'd never had anything to do with married men.

And the thing that bothered her most was what he'd said about Chance. Was she shirking her responsibility?

No, everything she'd done was for Chance's sake. On his hands and knees, he crawled in a rapid circle, vrooming his little car as fast as he could. Happy and healthy.

She'd done the right thing in giving him up. Hadn't she?

—∞—

Tempted to stay home, Ryler had forced himself to get ready and drive to church instead. He was getting baptized today. He should be filled with joy.

Stepping inside the sanctuary, he scanned the crowd. No Shell. He really hadn't expected her. But she was supposed to have gotten baptized, too. He swallowed the bitter disappointment rising in his throat.

The older woman from last night's party entered from the side door.

*Concentrate on work.* It was all he had. That and a new family. But work was familiar. He could lose himself in work.

He hurried to speak with the woman. "Ma'am?"

"Yes." She turned to face him.

"I'm sorry I couldn't speak with you last night." He offered his hand. "I'm Ryler Grant."

"I hope you're feeling better." The older woman smiled. "Do you have a card? I'm a friend of your mother's and I'd like to have some work done on my grounds."

Ryler dug in his pocket. "Sure. Give me a call."

"Thank you, I will." Mrs. Hughes stashed the card in her purse and moved on.

Pastor Grayson caught up with him. "You all ready to get baptized?"

"I am."

"Is Shell okay?"

His jaw clenched. "I have no clue."

"She called and said she wouldn't be getting baptized today."

Ryler closed his eyes. "I thought she might back out."

"How are things? Between you, I mean?"

"She's moving back to Conway."

"I thought y'all were working toward something permanent."

"I wanted to." Ryler's heart did a little jolt. "But obviously, she didn't. I think her old lifestyle's still got a grip on her."

"Just give her time. Some folks can't wait to start fresh when they get saved." Pastor Grayson clapped him on the back. "Some it takes a while. She'll be fine, as long as she stays in church."

Except that she'd already turned away and embraced a married man.

The harpist trilled a hymn, a hint that the morning devotion would begin soon.

A hand slid into his elbow and Sylvie's pricey perfume announced her presence. "There you are, dear."

"Son." Martin's tremors had eased. "Heard you're getting baptized this morning."

"Yes."

"I'm proud of you." Martin's watery eyes closed for a moment.

Ryler swallowed. "Right back at ya."

Linking her free arm with Martin's, Sylvie led them to the Kroft pew.

—⁓—

Shell jiggled her feet under the table as the Sunday school class began. The first she'd ever attended as an adult. Her mind strayed to Ryler. He was getting baptized today. And she was supposed to have joined him. But she wasn't worthy. Everywhere she turned, her past rose up to remind her of exactly who she was.

"Then Peter opened his mouth, and said, 'Of a truth I perceive that God is no respecter of persons.'" The women's teacher, a middle-aged woman with gray-streaked hair, looked up from her Bible. "We live in the age of grace. God's marvelous grace. He is no respecter of persons.

"That means if the murderer accepts Christ, he is no worse than the saved soul who told a little white lie. The redeemed adulterer is no worse than the Christian homeless man who stole a loaf of bread to feed his family. The woman with the alabaster jar, Mary Magdalene, and the woman at the well all had bad reputations, but Jesus accepted them all."

A lump lodged in Shell's throat. She wanted to ask who the women were, but she was probably the only one in the class who didn't know. Oh, if only she knew the Bible like everyone else seemed to. Even Ryler.

Ryler.

"Turn to John 8:1–11." Pages rustled together as class members flipped to the right chapter. At least Shell could find John in the Bible Savannah had bought her.

She followed the verses as the teacher read about the woman caught in adultery. "And Jesus said unto her, 'Neither do I condemn thee: go, and sin no more.'"

Jesus' words sank into Shell's soul.

The teacher continued. "If you accept Jesus Christ as your Savior, you are worthy. He counts you worthy. He forgives you and He can no longer see your sin. So, why do we keep looking back and holding on to it? The truth will set you free. Grab on to His truth, give Him your sins, and stop taking them back. Live the redeemed life He wants you to live."

*I will.* Starting now.

Shell bowed her head and silently prayed. *Thank You, Lord, for saving my soul. Forgive me for not believing You could make me new. Forgive me for all the things I've done and help me to forgive myself.*

*Thank You for this child You've given me, Lord. Give me courage to do what's right by him. And thank You for placing Ryler in my life this second time. Please don't let it be too late for us. Help us to build a relationship with You in the center and help us to glorify You.*

───※───

Shell slowed the rocking chair as Chance grew heavier against her shoulder. The taupe walls, safari animal border, and curtains soothed her frayed nerves.

Humming "Amazing Grace" she inhaled his scent of baby shampoo. At eighteen months, he was getting too big to rock. Already, his legs were long enough she had to prop his feet up in each side of the chair to make sure they didn't get squished.

She hated to put him down, but she needed to speak to Savannah and Jake without Chance overhearing. He didn't stir as she gently laid him in his toddler bed.

Jake relaxed in his recliner with the sports section, while Savannah curled on the couch with her hand on the bulge of her stomach, reading an inspirational novel.

"Hey, y'all."

"Chance asleep?" Savannah put her book down.

She hugged herself. "I've been thinking."

Jake lowered the newspaper, his brows drawn together. "You want him back?"

Shell paced the room. "Darrell always planned for me to manage the B&B. I'm moving to Rose Bud and I'd like to take Chance with me, on frequent visits. There's a really good day care, right next door." Her words tumbled out. "And most of the time, he could probably hang out with me." Darrell would probably let her keep some toys for him and a crib there.

"So you want him back?" Savannah's chin trembled.

"I don't want to just jerk him away from the people he's known as Mommy and Daddy." Her words tumbled out. "I want to take it slow. Over the next few weeks, I'd like us to explain who his real mommy is." *We'll talk about Daddy when he's old enough to understand.* "If these frequent trips work out and he adjusts well, then I'd like him to live with me."

"All fine and good, but do you have to move to Rose Bud?" Jake wadded the paper and stashed it by his chair, lowering his feet to the floor.

"I guess this has something to do with Ryler?" Savannah sat upright and patted the seat beside her.

Shell's stomach knotted. She sank to the couch. "I'm hoping it does. He wants to marry me and I said no because—well, it's a long story."

"Savannah and I have always expected you to reclaim Chance." Jake's voice cracked. "We've loved him and raised him, knowing we might lose him."

"I'm sorry." Her gaze dropped to the floor. They'd been so good to her and in return, she'd broken their hearts. A weight settled on her shoulders, and she couldn't bring herself to look at Savannah sniffling beside her.

"Don't be. He should be with you. We've both always agreed on that, but we wanted to make sure you were stable and devoted to him."

"I am now."

"I know." Savannah squeezed her hand. "We're so proud of you."

"But it will be hard on y'all if it works out."

"Yes, but we knew that from the beginning." Savannah patted her stomach. "This baby won't replace Chance. We'll always love him as if he were our own."

"I know and I love you both for being there for him when I didn't feel able." Her gaze scanned the many family pictures lining the taupe walls. Pictures of Jake, Savannah, and Chance. Pictures of her, Savannah, and Chance. Pictures of just her with Chance. They'd painstakingly included her in the family unit.

"Who is this Ryler?" Jake asked.

"He's a Christian. He's a stable, good man from a good family."

"That's my only concern." Jake cleared his throat. "I don't want Chance jerked around. What if it doesn't work out with Ryler? And the reality of raising a child sets in and you don't feel up to the challenge?"

"Ryler's the one who convinced me Chance should be with me. He knows I'm a package deal. He wants to marry me and raise Chance."

But did he still want her? And if he really thought those awful things about her, did she want him?

She sucked in a deep breath, blinking away tears. "But don't worry, Jake. With or without Ryler, I want Chance with me and he'll be my first priority.

"Even if things don't work out with him"—her stomach did an odd tilt—"or if the reality of an eighteen-month-old is too much for him, then Chance and I will be fine without him." The words tasted bitter. "Either way, Chance comes first. The way he should have from the beginning."

"He's always come first." Savannah squeezed her hand again. "You were convinced that us raising him was better for him. It's not like you gave him up because you didn't want him."

Tears singed Shell's eyes. "You're right, and it was the hardest thing I've ever done."

"When do you plan on leaving?" Savannah's voice wobbled.

"Saturday morning, if it's okay with y'all and Chance. I've got some things to take care of here, like moving my stuff and talking with Darrell. And I want to ease Chance into this. There's no rush."

Except her heart longed for Ryler. Could they get past his absurd accusations about Darrell? Could they look toward the future, together?

"We'll try a couple of days to start with. I want him to meet a couple of people, but if he gets homesick, I'll bring him back early. I promise. The last thing I want is for my son to be miserable."

"Then, you have our blessing." Jake strode over and squeezed between them, hugging them both.

Singsong jabber from the backseat warmed Shell's soul. Chance was a great little traveler.

Ryler's SUV was gone. Across the street, Collin's car was, too. Where could Ryler be? The trash cans that usually sat by the road were gone. With the curtains pulled shut, the house looked oddly abandoned. Surely he couldn't have cleared out in a week's time. *Lord, please don't let him have left town.*

For the next seven miles, she prayed.

Several cars were parked in the B&B lot. Business was booming.

An eighth of a mile farther, Hayden's truck sat in the drive of his and Laken's house, but her car was gone. All three siblings gone. Breakfast at the Krofts'.

Shell concentrated on the mailbox numbers. She had to introduce Chance to someone else first.

In the front yard of a neat house, Helen worked with a hoe in a flower garden. Turning, she shielded her eyes from the sun's glare and smiled as Shell got out. "Hello, what a nice surprise."

"I have someone with me I'd like you to meet." Shell ducked into the backseat and undid Chance's safety harness. His pale green short set, with dolphins swimming around the waist, was clean and adorable. Perfect for meeting his grandmother.

He giggled as she swooped him up in the air and propped him on her hip. She strode toward Helen.

"What a cutie." Helen tickled a bare foot.

Chance responded with a gurgly giggle.

"He had shoes on, but he loves taking them off."

"Let's go inside, so he can get down." Helen led the way to the house. "Goodness me, I don't have any toys. I don't usually get such young, handsome visitors."

"I have some in my bag, but maybe we'll keep some here in the future. I think Chance will be visiting often."

Helen frowned as they stepped inside. Obviously questions quivered on her lips, but manners kept her from asking.

Pictures of Wade stared at Shell from every wall and surface. She shivered, wishing she could go back and undo things. Yet, if she'd never stolen Wade from Adrea, she wouldn't have Chance. It was amazing what blessings God gave, even through horrible circumstances.

She regretted beginning Wade's tailspin, but she couldn't do anything about it. All she could do was share her blessing with Helen.

"Please sit down, Helen. I thought you might want to hold Chance, and I have wonderful news that will come as a bit of a shock."

"Okay." Helen sat in a rocker.

"Perfect, Chance loves to rock." She kissed his chubby cheek. "Remember Miss Helen I told you about? Do you want to go see her?"

With a grin, Helen reached for him.

Chance didn't shy away when Shell settled him in Helen's lap.

"What a friendly boy you are."

"He's used to being passed around at our church in Conway." Shell smoothed a curl away from his face. "Helen, I hope you won't be angry with me."

"Why would I be angry, dear?"

Shell took a deep breath and knelt beside Helen. "Because you're just now getting to hold your grandson for the first time."

A gasp escaped and Helen's lips trembled. "Wade's son?"

"I'm so sorry." Shell's vision blurred. "I should have told you long before now."

Helen hugged Chance to her.

"It's okay, Chance." Shell patted his back. "Grandma Helen loves you. I told you she'd be excited to see you. She's crying happy tears and she's not trying to put you to sleep. No nap time."

As Helen took the hint and loosed her grip on him, he settled back in her lap making a rocking motion.

With a watery laugh, Helen rocked the chair. "Grandma Helen is very happy. Happier than she's been in years."

—⁂—

Ten a.m. Shell checked each house again. Ryler and Collin still gone. She drove the seven miles to Rose Bud. Cars had cleared out of the B&B. Down the road, Laken's car still wasn't home.

She'd have to head to Searcy. Thankfully, Helen had insisted Chance stay with her for as long as Shell needed. She'd wanted to take him with her, but what if things didn't go as planned? What if Ryler was still angry? Chance didn't need to witness any scenes and this one could go past his nap time.

Plans had already been promised for a picnic in the park tomorrow. And it sounded like Helen wanted to completely stop working at the florist and be at the B&B daily. No day care needed. It felt really good to make a lonely woman's day.

A red car met her. Hayden and Laken waved.

Collin's black Lexus was next, with him and Jill waving.

Any minute Ryler would be along. Last to leave because Sylvie wouldn't let go of him. With complete understanding, Shell thought of all the times she'd relinquished Chance to Savannah. Not anymore. *Lord, please help Chance easily adjust.*

Pulling onto the side of the road, Shell waited for a glimpse of a charcoal SUV.

A dark SUV came into view. She held her breath as it drew closer then huffed it out. Wrong model, navy blue.

Another dark SUV approached with a U-Haul on the back. Her breath caught. It was him.

Ryler slowed as he neared and pulled onto the shoulder across from her. He got out and jogged over. A deep frown marred his handsome features. "Car trouble?"

"You're moving?" Her voice quivered.

"I decided not to support the kind of landlord who gets his kicks by manhandling women, so I'm staying with Sylvie and Martin until I decide what's next. I'm headed back for the last load."

She blew out another big breath. "That'll be good for all of you. Make up for lost time and get to know one another."

"Martin's going into rehab for a month and Sylvie was nervous about being alone." He splayed both palms upward. "What are you doing here?"

"I met Laken and Collin, so I figured you'd be along soon. We need to talk. The B&B or the park?"

"The B&B." He ran a hand through his hair. "What's going on?"

"I'll tell you all about it there."

With a deepening frown, he jogged back to his SUV. He waited until Shell turned around in a driveway before pulling out behind her.

Her insides turned jittery. What if he'd changed his mind? What if she'd hurt him and he didn't want her? What if he didn't believe her about Darrell? *Lord, please work things out for us.*

She turned into the drive of the B&B and he followed. Her insides lurched as she stepped out of her car.

The green lush grass spread around the house like a carpet. Not a weed in sight. Roses and blossoms of every color surrounded each fountain, with benches in the midst and stone walkways leading to the house and the driveway. The miniature Romance Waterfalls splashed and trickled.

"Why didn't you ever plant anything at your rental house?"

"I never planned to put down any roots there."

*Me neither.* All she'd wanted was to finish the job and get out of town. Now all she wanted was to stay. With Ryler. Forever.

The balcony was empty. "Let's go up there."

"Sure." Ryler slowed his pace to match hers.

He strode to the porch, opened the arched-window door, and ushered her inside.

The clerk at the desk looked up. "Hi, Shell. Eva and Darrell are so relieved you're coming to manage this place."

Ryler's eyes widened.

"I'm excited, too. Nelda? Right? We're just going to borrow the balcony for a few minutes."

"That's fine. I think all our guests are out sightseeing."

Nerve endings buzzed with his nearness as Shell climbed the wide staircase and reached the landing.

Ryler opened the door to the balcony for her. "You're staying here?"

She perched on the swing and patted the seat beside her. "I brought Chance with me."

"Where is he?" Ryler shoved his hands in his pockets and remained standing.

"At Helen's, getting acquainted with his grandmother."

Ryler gasped. "I'm glad. She needed to know about him. I'm proud of you for doing the right thing."

"Me, too. She's so happy and Chance latched on to her. But I need to get back soon."

"So that's why you came back? For Helen."

# Chapter 11

S it down." She patted the seat beside her again. "Please."

He sat and drew an imaginary line between them.

Her laugh came out watery. "Remember when you asked me why I left when you wanted me to move in with you?"

"I'm glad you didn't now."

Closing her eyes, she swallowed hard, loving him so much it hurt inside. "You're not going to make this easy, are you?"

"That's not what I—"

"You said I was only looking for Mr. Right Now, but I found more than I was looking for."

"You did?" His gaze stayed firmly on the floor.

"In my experience, men don't stick around. So, I left before you did."

"Why'd you leave this time?"

She sucked in a deep breath. "Once I found out your blood was blue, I didn't think I was worthy."

"Blue blood? Me?" His laugh echoed sarcasm. "Talk about not being worthy."

"But we both are, don't you see? I just needed to hear it from a higher source." A yellow butterfly flitted about. Once a bumpy, wormlike caterpillar. Now a new creature. "Last Sunday, God told me I was worthy. Of Him and of you. Not directly, but through a Sunday school teacher. If Mary Magdalene can become a respected member of the community and Christ's inner circle, through His love, so can I."

"I tried to tell you that."

She shrugged. "I know, but I was too beat down by my mother, jerks, and snobs to hear it."

"I need to know about Darrell. What's going on there?"

Grabbing his chin, she forced him to look at her. "Nothing. When I first moved to Conway, Darrell gave me a job cleaning apartments. His manager quit, so he trained me. Eva took me under her wing. If not for them, I'd probably be in some menial job, barely scraping by on minimum wage." Or following in her mother's footsteps.

"You crossed the line." He traced the imaginary line between them. "So Eva knows about you."

Shell bit her lip. "There's nothing to know about. Eva's an interior decorator and realized I had talent in that area. She mentored me and allowed me to design and decorate the clubhouse and condos when they bought the golf course in Searcy. And the whole time, they invited me to church and witnessed to me, but I guess I wasn't ready to hear it."

"What about that day at the roasterie? Did it really require you and Darrell, without Eva, to order coffee?"

"Eva was in the roasterie watching a demonstration." She rolled her eyes. "Do you really think that if Darrell and I were an item, we'd hang around together in public?"

Ryler's eyes squeezed shut. "So there's never been anything between you and Darrell?" A smile played over his lips and he turned them into her palm.

She shivered and her heart somersaulted. His gentle touch warmed her soul. "I spent my entire childhood watching my mother destroy marriages. A distraught wife even came to our house packing a gun and I think she'd have shot my mother if not for Savannah and me. Trust me, I would never get involved with married men. Besides, Darrell is one of the most honorable men I know and he's crazy about his wife."

"He treated you more honorably than I did." Ryler hung his head. "I'm sorry for accusing you of that. I didn't see Eva at the roasterie and when I saw you up here on our balcony with him at the grand opening, my old jealousy surfaced."

*Our balcony.* Her heart danced.

"And I'm sorry for the things I said about Chance, too. You've obviously always put his needs first. I was hurt and lashed out with angry words."

She traced his jawline with her fingertips. "Eva's been running this place, but that was never their plan. They always hoped I'd stay here. I'm planning to. As long as that's where you'll be."

"What about Chance?"

"We'll work it out. Like you said once, I bet there are lots of landscaping jobs in Conway. I'm not going anywhere without you."

He turned her hand over and kissed the back of it.

"There's another reason why I left the first time."

"What's that?"

"I thought I could get over you."

He grinned. "But it didn't work."

"I love you, Ryler."

"Oh Shell. We've wasted so much time." He leaned his forehead against hers.

"No more wasted time. I want you to meet Chance. With my sister and brother-in-law's blessing, I'm going to bring him to live with me. Slowly at first, only if he adjusts well, and I'm going to tell him who his mommy is. If it works, we'll talk about his daddy when he's old enough. I have to do what's best for him."

"I'm glad. A child should be with his mother."

She slid from the swing and knelt on one knee beside him. "Ryler Grant or Martin Rothwell Kroft Jr. or whoever you are, will you marry me?"

"I'll think about it, only if you'll drop the Martin Rothwell Kroft bit."

Think about it? Her heart crashed against her ribs as she tried to play along with his humor. "If you insist, Rothwell."

"Maybe you can call me that when I get on your nerves."

"You'll never get on my nerves."

"Even after sixty or seventy years?"

"Never. So, is that a yes?"

"There's just one little problem."

"What?"

"We don't have anywhere to live."

She certainly didn't want to live across the street from Wade's old house where so many bad memories dwelled. "We need a fresh start, anyway. Darrell's letting me stay in the apartment/honeymoon suite until I come up with something permanent."

"I could live quite happily with you in a honeymoon suite. We'll figure out something permanent together. Maybe buy land and build a house."

Her heart sank. What about all his starting over and following the Bible's principles?

"I won't live with you, Ryler." Her voice quivered. "Not until after the wedding."

"I meant after the wedding." He kissed her hand. "I'm glad you never moved in with me. I want us to build our lives together, with God's blessing. I'll marry you on our balcony on the Fourth of July."

A relieved sigh escaped, but her eyes widened. "Less than a week away?"

"It's perfect because from the moment I first kissed you, Shell Evans, I've seen fireworks."

Her vision blurred. His lips sought hers and fireworks blasted through her veins.

—⁂—

Hand in hand, Ryler walked Shell toward Helen's door. "What if he doesn't like me?"

"He'll love you and he's not shy. Savannah and Jake attend a large church, so Chance is used to being passed around by the entire congregation." Shell knocked.

Helen opened the door. The little towheaded boy Ryler had seen in Shell's framed picture clutched Helen's skirt.

Scooping him up, Shell kissed his chubby cheek.

"He was an absolute angel," Helen gushed. "The entire time. Reminds me of—" Her eyes watered. "Please, come in."

The humble little house was neat and tidy. Cozy, with pictures lining the walls. Chance favored the blond man in most of them.

Shell patted Helen's arm. "I was afraid he'd get fussy as nap time neared."

"Not a peep. Ryler, it's nice to see you."

"Thank you, ma'am." His gaze riveted on Chance.

"Chance, this is Ryler. My fiancé. That means we're getting married." Shell bounced the child up and down on her hip.

"Hi." Chance chewed on his fist.

"Hi." Ryler's vision blurred. Chance deserved a chance at a real family, at having a father who loved him. With this child, Ryler would make up for Shell's rough upbringing and the last lonely twelve years of his life. This boy would be loved by two parents.

"Congratulations." Helen hugged Shell then gestured them to the couch. "When's the happy occasion?"

"Independence Day."

Helen's eyes widened. "This Thursday?"

"Know any florists who could whip something up?" Shell smiled as Chance clambered over to Ryler's lap.

"I believe I do."

"See, he loves you," Shell whispered. "Just like his mommy does."

— ∞ —

Standing in her favorite gold and cream attic bedroom of the B&B, Shell smoothed her hands down her dress. Never had she imagined she'd wear a white wedding gown with everything it traditionally signified. But in God's eyes, she was pure. And His opinion was all that mattered.

A knock sounded on the door.

"Ryler?"

"Eva said you wanted to see me." He opened the door, wearing a navy pinstripe tuxedo. The red tie and cummerbund set off his dark coloring.

And her heart. "Hey, handsome."

"Hello, beautiful." He pulled her into his arms. "In approximately two hours, we'll be on our honeymoon. Right here in this very room."

"I can't believe Darrell ran the guests out for the entire afternoon and appeased them with an extra night free. Especially on a holiday weekend. It's like a fairy tale. But I don't understand why we had to have the entire place." She giggled. "All we need is one room and we could have stayed in the suite."

"You'll see later. Speaking of fairy tales, Sylvie wants you to wear these." He fished a long box from inside his jacket and opened it to reveal a strand of pearls. "They belonged to my great-grandmother."

Shell's hand flew to her heart. "They're lovely."

"Not as lovely as you." He stepped behind her.

Holding her hair up so he could fasten the strand, she shivered when his knuckle grazed her neck.

It seemed like as good a time as any. Maybe he wouldn't get too mad. "I saw a lawyer the other day."

"Funny. Me, too." The pearls clasped into place.

"What for?" She turned to face him.

He fished an envelope from an inside pocket. "I want to adopt Chance."

Her vision blurred. "Oh Ryler."

"He's part of you. I love him, Shell, and I want to be his father. Legally and in every sense of the word."

"I want you to be his father, too."

"Is that why you went to the lawyer?"

Shaking her head, she gulped a deep breath and grabbed the envelope from the dresser. "I had this drawn up."

Ryler unfolded the legal document and scanned it. "A prenup. You had a prenup drawn up without telling me?" His neck reddened.

She winced. "I knew you'd never agree."

"Why, Shell? I don't want this. You know I don't want this." His jaw clenched.

"I don't want anyone to think I married you for your money." *Especially not you.*

"Who cares what anyone thinks, other than God and us?" He ran a hand through his hair. "I thought you were past this unworthy business."

"I am. But I want you and everyone else to know that your money doesn't matter to me. That I love you. You know—rich or poor, in sickness or in health. Just humor me."

He sighed. "Until death do us part. But that's just it, Shell. If it's until death do us part, we don't need this."

"I do." She kissed him. "Please don't be angry. Let's go get married."

She hurried to the landing to let Darrell know she was ready. Ryler hesitated a moment at the top of the stairs.

Her heart plunged to her toes. Surely, he wasn't angry enough to leave her at the altar.

"Ryler?" Uncertainty echoed in her voice.

"Don't worry." He descended and kissed the tip of her nose. "I'm not going anywhere, my stubborn bride."

Ryler winked then strode out to the balcony.

Blowing out a big breath, Shell's hands shook as she clutched her red rose bouquet.

"Relax." Darrell offered his elbow as the wedding march began. "You're supposed to enjoy this day."

The door opened and they joined Ryler standing with his best man,

Collin. Savannah served as matron of honor. Chance fiddled with the satin pillow holding their rings and scattered crimson petals long after the music stopped. Guests stood between the house and the front garden.

Six red, white, and blue carnation bouquets lined the balcony with half-moon, gathered American flags fanning out underneath and white, silk wisteria cascaded from the railing.

Perfect. Everything was perfect. Especially the groom.

Pastor Grayson opened with prayer and read several Bible verses on marriage.

Facing one another, she and Ryler took turns reciting their vows. Tears blurred her vision as she promised her heart, trust, and future to the only man she'd ever loved.

"Do you vow to love and to cherish one another, for richer, for poorer, in sickness and in health, until death do you part?"

Gently, Ryler slid the ring on her finger. "I do."

Solid. Permanent.

She slipped the matching gold band on his finger. "I do."

"I now pronounce—"

"Wait." Ryler held up one hand then pulled the prenup from his pocket. "I can't do it, Shell," he whispered.

She gasped. Her heart took a nosedive.

Ryler turned toward their guests. "Friends and family, Shell is worried folks might think she's marrying me for the Kroft money, so she had a pre-nuptial agreement drawn up. But we're forever and this thing means we're iffy." He ripped the document in two and stuck it back in his pocket. "Now you know, as I do, that her heart is pure. Carry on, Preacher."

Grayson raised an eyebrow. "Y'all don't need to discuss this further?"

"No. Get to the husband and wife part. Let no man put asunder and all the good stuff."

Pastor Grayson looked at Shell.

She nodded, her heart welling with love. Ryler trusted her and made sure everyone else did, too.

"I now pronounce you husband and wife. What God hath joined together, let no man put asunder. Ryler, you may kiss your bride."

His heart-stopping kiss made her dizzy. Squeals and loud, rapid pops surrounded them. Shell jumped. Fireworks blazed flickering, gunpowder trails through the afternoon sky.

—∞—

Even after an hour of pictures on the balcony, in the various gardens, and around all four fountains, the guests still lingered as the reception wrapped up.

Ryler sighed. *Go home now. Please. Would love to be alone with my bride.*

"So." Ryler wrapped his arms around her waist from behind as she gazed at the miniature Romance Waterfalls in front of the house. "We've got the whole place to ourselves for two hours and the attic room for two more days."

She leaned back against him and he propped his chin on her head. "Per your request, the ringer is off, with the answering machine on, and the staff is gone, except for the cook who's available whenever we call. Eva's handling my duties once the other guests return."

"There you are." Darrell's voice came from behind them.

Ryler stiffened and turned to face him without letting Shell go.

"With the groom's permission, I'd like to hug the bride."

Ryler tightened his arms around her.

"Relax, Ryler. Shell's like a daughter to me, and I've got my own bride I'm still head over heels in love with after seventeen years."

"Sorry. Old habit." Ryler let go of her.

Darrell gave her a brotherly hug. "I'm proud of you."

"Thanks. Me, too."

"There's a clearing south of here. . ." Darrell gestured behind the honeymoon suite on the opposite side from the day care. "It's surrounded by oaks, sycamores, and wisteria vines in the spring. I thought Eva and I might build there someday, but she likes the city. So, if you both like it, we'd like to give you five acres as a wedding gift."

Like some charity case.

"We can buy it." Ryler's spine stiffened. "We planned to look for land."

"Relax." Darrell patted Ryler on the shoulder. "I know you can buy it. You're a Kroft. But Shell has always done a great job for me and she's never gotten a bonus. I like you, Ryler. You're an honorable man, and I know you'll be good to her. I'd like to give you both a gift. Or I should say, Eva and I would like to give you this gift. So, please take it."

Ryler knew Darrell was harmless. Even if he were interested in Shell, Ryler trusted her. But for almost a year, he'd considered Darrell a threat and old issues died hard.

"I don't know what to say." Ryler cleared his throat.

"Say thank you." Darrell offered his hand.

"Thank you." Ryler accepted the handshake.

"Now, don't take it if you don't love it. We've got a hundred and fifty acres here. If there's another spot you like better, let me know."

"Thank you, Darrell." Shell gave him a peck on the cheek.

Ryler didn't even flinch.

"You're welcome. Now, I'll round up my lovely bride and leave. Maybe the rest of the guests will take the hint."

—◦◦◦—

Shivers moved through Shell as Ryler inconspicuously nibbled on her ear.

"Stop it." She giggled. "That tickles."

"Do you think they'll ever go so we can get to the fun part? Why aren't they leaving?"

They'd made a point of rounding the entire house, speaking with each guest. Now back at the front waterfall, guests still milled about.

"They're probably waiting for us to go. Most brides and grooms don't honeymoon at the same place they have the wedding."

"You're right. I'll see if I can speed things along."

"Ryler! Don't." She grabbed his arm, fingers tingling at his massive bicep.

"Why not?"

"It's rude."

"It's rude for people to keep me away from my bride when I've lived like a Boy Scout for almost a year. Now we're legal and these people won't go."

"These people are our friends and family."

"Well, they're starting to smell like three-day-old fish."

He clapped his hands. "May I have your attention please? My lovely wife and I are going to say final good-byes to our families. Since we're honeymooning here, you can throw birdseed while we go inside and then feel free to go."

Laughter canvassed the crowd.

"Why didn't you just say so?" Collin hugged Ryler with a macho smack on the back.

"I think I just did."

Laken hugged Ryler, followed by Sylvie and a much steadier Martin. Each Kroft member hugged Shell, murmuring sincere welcomes into the family.

She scooped Chance up. "I love you and I'll see you in three days."

Savannah hugged her. As Jake took Chance from her, Ryler kissed her son's cheek.

"Okay, we're going inside now." He grabbed her hand, turned, and ran toward the house in a shower of birdseed. Fireworks blasted and the smell of gunpowder drifted overhead as the departing crowd cheered.

Ryler took her hand and they stepped inside.

As the door closed behind them, he clicked the lock in place and bowed. "My lady."

He scooped her up in his arms.

She laughed. "Ryler, what are you doing? We already crossed the threshold."

"I've really, really, really been looking forward to tonight." Cradling her, he growled in her ear. "For months and months on end."

She giggled. "Me, too."

"I want our first time—not our first time, but our first legal, right-in-God's-sight time—to be special." He carried her up the stairs in a flurry of white satin and lace, *Gone with the Wind* style.

Only she didn't fight him.

At the top of the stairs, he nudged the attic bedroom door open. The gold room. Her favorite. Just inside, he set her down.

Certain she'd swoon as his lips claimed hers, she clung to him and her heart raced for the only man who'd ever made her feel like a lady.